THE
LOVELY
BONES

ALICE SEBOLD

LITTLE, BROWN AND COMPANY

NEW YORK BOSTON LONDON

Copyright © 2002 by Alice Sebold
Excerpt from *The Almost Moon* copyright © 2007 by Alice Sebold
All rights reserved. Except as permitted under the U.S. Copyright Act of 1976, no part of this publication may be reproduced, distributed, or transmitted in any form or by any means, or stored in a database or retrieval system, without the prior written permission of the publisher.

Little, Brown and Company
Hachette Book Group
237 Park Avenue
New York, NY 10017
Visit our website at www.HachetteBookGroup.com

Printed in the United States of America

Originally published in hardcover by Little, Brown and Company
First Back Bay international edition, January 2003
First Little, Brown and Company mass market edition, September 2006
First Media Tie-in edition, October 2009

10 9 8 7 6 5 4 3

ATTENTION CORPORATIONS AND ORGANIZATIONS:
Most HACHETTE BOOK GROUP books are available at quantity discounts with bulk purchase for educational, business, or sales promotional use. For information, please call or write:
Special Markets Department, Hachette Book Group
237 Park Avenue, New York, NY 10017
Telephone: 1-800-222-6747 Fax: 1-800-477-5925

Always, Glen

THE

LOVELY

BONES

Inside the snow globe on my father's desk, there was a penguin wearing a red-and-white-striped scarf. When I was little my father would pull me into his lap and reach for the snow globe. He would turn it over, letting all the snow collect on the top, then quickly invert it. The two of us watched the snow fall gently around the penguin. The penguin was alone in there, I thought, and I worried for him. When I told my father this, he said, "Don't worry, Susie; he has a nice life. He's trapped in a perfect world."

O N E

—

My name was Salmon, like the fish; first name, Susie. I was fourteen when I was murdered on December 6, 1973. In newspaper photos of missing girls from the seventies, most looked like me: white girls with mousy brown hair. This was before kids of all races and genders started appearing on milk cartons or in the daily mail. It was still back when people believed things like that didn't happen.

In my junior high yearbook I had a quote from a Spanish poet my sister had turned me on to, Juan Ramón Jiménez. It went like this: "If they give you ruled paper, write the other way." I chose it both because it expressed my contempt for my structured surroundings à la the classroom and because, not being some dopey quote from a rock group, I thought it marked me as literary. I was a member of the Chess Club and Chem Club and burned everything I tried to make in Mrs. Delminico's home ec class. My favorite teacher was Mr. Botte, who taught biology and liked to animate the frogs and crawfish we had to dissect by making them dance in their waxed pans.

I wasn't killed by Mr. Botte, by the way. Don't think every person you're going to meet in here is suspect. That's the problem. You never know. Mr. Botte came to my memorial (as, may I add, did almost the entire junior high school — I was never so popular) and cried quite a bit. He had a sick kid. We all knew this, so when he laughed at his own jokes, which were rusty way before I had him, we laughed too, forcing it sometimes just to make him happy. His daughter died a year and a half after I did. She had leukemia, but I never saw her in my heaven.

My murderer was a man from our neighborhood. My mother liked his border flowers, and my father talked to him once about fertilizer. My murderer believed in old-fashioned things like eggshells and coffee grounds, which he said his own mother had used. My father came home smiling, making jokes about how the man's garden might be beautiful but it would stink to high heaven once a heat wave hit.

But on December 6, 1973, it was snowing, and I took a shortcut through the cornfield back from the junior high. It was dark out because the days were shorter in winter, and I remember how the broken cornstalks made my walk more difficult. The snow was falling lightly, like a flurry of small hands, and I was breathing through my nose until it was running so much that I had to open my mouth. Six feet from where Mr. Harvey stood, I stuck my tongue out to taste a snowflake.

"Don't let me startle you," Mr. Harvey said.

Of course, in a cornfield, in the dark, I was startled.

After I was dead I thought about how there had been the light scent of cologne in the air but that I had not been paying attention, or thought it was coming from one of the houses up ahead.

"Mr. Harvey," I said.

"You're the older Salmon girl, right?"

"Yes."

"How are your folks?"

Although the eldest in my family and good at acing a science quiz, I had never felt comfortable with adults.

"Fine," I said. I was cold, but the natural authority of his age, and the added fact that he was a neighbor and had talked to my father about fertilizer, rooted me to the spot.

"I've built something back here," he said. "Would you like to see?"

"I'm sort of cold, Mr. Harvey," I said, "and my mom likes me home before dark."

"It's after dark, Susie," he said.

I wish now that I had known this was weird. I had never told him my name. I guess I thought my father had told him one of the embarrassing anecdotes he saw merely as loving testaments to his children. My father was the kind of dad who kept a nude photo of you when you were three in the downstairs bathroom, the one that guests would use. He did this to my little sister, Lindsey, thank God. At least I was spared that indignity. But he liked to tell a story about how, once Lindsey was born, I was so jealous that one day while he was on the phone in the other room, I moved down the couch — he could see me from where he stood — and tried to pee on top of Lindsey in her carrier. This story humiliated me every time he told it, to the pastor of our church, to our neighbor Mrs. Stead, who was a therapist and whose take on it he wanted to hear, and to everyone who ever said "Susie has a lot of spunk!"

"Spunk!" my father would say. "Let me tell you about spunk," and he would launch immediately into his Susie-peed-on-Lindsey story.

But as it turned out, my father had not mentioned us to Mr. Harvey or told him the Susie-peed-on-Lindsey story.

Mr. Harvey would later say these words to my mother when he ran into her on the street: "I heard about the horrible, horrible tragedy. What was your daughter's name, again?"

"Susie," my mother said, bracing up under the weight of it, a weight that she naively hoped might lighten someday, not knowing that it would only go on to hurt in new and varied ways for the rest of her life.

Mr. Harvey told her the usual: "I hope they get the bastard. I'm sorry for your loss."

I was in my heaven by that time, fitting my limbs together, and couldn't believe his audacity. "The man has no shame," I said to Franny, my intake counselor. "Exactly," she said, and made her point as simply as that. There wasn't a lot of bullshit in my heaven.

Mr. Harvey said it would only take a minute, so I followed him a little farther into the cornfield, where fewer stalks were broken off because no one used it as a shortcut to the junior high. My mom had told my baby brother, Buckley, that the corn in the field was inedible when he asked why no one from the neighborhood ate it. "The corn is for horses, not humans," she said. "Not dogs?" Buckley asked. "No," my mother answered. "Not dinosaurs?" Buckley asked. And it went like that.

"I've made a little hiding place," said Mr. Harvey.

He stopped and turned to me.

"I don't see anything," I said. I was aware that Mr. Harvey was looking at me strangely. I'd had older men look at me that way since I'd lost my baby fat, but they usually didn't lose their marbles over me when I was wearing my royal blue parka and yellow elephant bell-bottoms. His glasses were small and round with gold frames, and his eyes looked out over them and at me.

"You should be more observant, Susie," he said.

I felt like observing my way out of there, but I didn't. Why didn't I? Franny said these questions were fruitless: "You didn't and that's that. Don't mull it over. It does no good. You're dead and you have to accept it."

"Try again," Mr. Harvey said, and he squatted down and knocked against the ground.

"What's that?" I asked.

My ears were freezing. I wouldn't wear the multicolored cap with the pompom and jingle bells that my mother had made me one Christmas. I had shoved it in the pocket of my parka instead.

I remember that I went over and stomped on the ground near him. It felt harder even than frozen earth, which was pretty hard.

"It's wood," Mr. Harvey said. "It keeps the entrance from collapsing. Other than that it's all made out of earth."

"What is it?" I asked. I was no longer cold or weirded out by the look he had given me. I was like I was in science class: I was curious.

"Come and see."

It was awkward to get into, that much he admitted

once we were both inside the hole. But I was so amazed by how he had made a chimney that would draw smoke out if he ever chose to build a fire that the awkwardness of getting in and out of the hole wasn't even on my mind. You could add to that that escape wasn't a concept I had any real experience with. The worst I'd had to escape was Artie, a strange-looking kid at school whose father was a mortician. He liked to pretend he was carrying a needle full of embalming fluid around with him. On his notebooks he would draw needles spilling dark drips.

"This is neato!" I said to Mr. Harvey. He could have been the hunchback of Notre Dame, whom we had read about in French class. I didn't care. I completely reverted. I was my brother Buckley on our day-trip to the Museum of Natural History in New York, where he'd fallen in love with the huge skeletons on display. I hadn't used the word *neato* in public since elementary school.

"Like taking candy from a baby," Franny said.

I can still see the hole like it was yesterday, and it was. Life is a perpetual yesterday for us. It was the size of a small room, the mud room in our house, say, where we kept our boots and slickers and where Mom had managed to fit a washer and dryer, one on top of the other. I could almost stand up in it, but Mr. Harvey had to stoop. He'd created a bench along the sides of it by the way he'd dug it out. He immediately sat down.

"Look around," he said.

I stared at it in amazement, the dug-out shelf above him where he had placed matches, a row of batteries, and a battery-powered fluorescent lamp that cast the only light in the room—an eerie light that would make his features hard to see when he was on top of me.

There was a mirror on the shelf, and a razor and shaving cream. I thought that was odd. Wouldn't he do that at home? But I guess I figured that a man who had a perfectly good split-level and then built an underground room only half a mile away had to be kind of loo-loo. My father had a nice way of describing people like him: "The man's a character, that's all."

So I guess I was thinking that Mr. Harvey was a character, and I liked the room, and it was warm, and I wanted to know how he had built it, what the mechanics of the thing were and where he'd learned to do something like that.

But by the time the Gilberts' dog found my elbow three days later and brought it home with a telling corn husk attached to it, Mr. Harvey had closed it up. I was in transit during this. I didn't get to see him sweat it out, remove the wood reinforcement, bag any evidence along with my body parts, except that elbow. By the time I popped up with enough wherewithal to look down at the goings-on on Earth, I was more concerned with my family than anything else.

My mother sat on a hard chair by the front door with her mouth open. Her pale face paler than I had ever seen it. Her blue eyes staring. My father was driven into motion. He wanted to know details and to comb the cornfield along with the cops. I still thank God for a small detective named Len Fenerman. He assigned two uniforms to take my dad into town and have him point out all the places I'd hung out with my friends. The uniforms kept my dad busy in one mall for the whole first day. No one had told Lindsey, who was thirteen and would have been old enough, or Buckley, who was four and would, to be honest, never fully understand.

Mr. Harvey asked me if I would like a refreshment. That was how he put it. I said I had to go home.

"Be polite and have a Coke," he said. "I'm sure the other kids would."

"What other kids?"

"I built this for the kids in the neighborhood. I thought it could be some sort of clubhouse."

I don't think I believed this even then. I thought he was lying, but I thought it was a pitiful lie. I imagined he was lonely. We had read about men like him in health class. Men who never married and ate frozen meals every night and were so afraid of rejection that they didn't even own pets. I felt sorry for him.

"Okay," I said, "I'll have a Coke."

In a little while he said, "Aren't you warm, Susie? Why don't you take off your parka."

I did.

After this he said, "You're very pretty, Susie."

"Thanks," I said, even though he gave me what my friend Clarissa and I had dubbed the skeevies.

"Do you have a boyfriend?"

"No, Mr. Harvey," I said. I swallowed the rest of my Coke, which was a lot, and said, "I got to go, Mr. Harvey. This is a cool place, but I have to go."

He stood up and did his hunchback number by the six dug-in steps that led to the world. "I don't know why you think you're leaving."

I talked so that I would not have to take in this knowledge: Mr. Harvey was no character. He made me feel skeevy and icky now that he was blocking the door.

"Mr. Harvey, I really have to get home."

"Take off your clothes."

"What?"

"Take your clothes off," Mr. Harvey said. "I want to check that you're still a virgin."

"I am, Mr. Harvey," I said.

"I want to make sure. Your parents will thank me."

"My parents?"

"They only want good girls," he said.

"Mr. Harvey," I said, "please let me leave."

"You aren't leaving, Susie. You're mine now."

Fitness was not a big thing back then; *aerobics* was barely a word. Girls were supposed to be soft, and only the girls we suspected were butch could climb the ropes at school.

I fought hard. I fought as hard as I could not to let Mr. Harvey hurt me, but my hard-as-I-could was not hard enough, not even close, and I was soon lying down on the ground, in the ground, with him on top of me panting and sweating, having lost his glasses in the struggle.

I was so alive then. I thought it was *the worst thing in the world* to be lying flat on my back with a sweating man on top of me. To be trapped inside the earth and have no one know where I was.

I thought of my mother.

My mother would be checking the dial of the clock on her oven. It was a new oven and she loved that it had a clock on it. "I can time things to the minute," she told her own mother, a mother who couldn't care less about ovens.

She would be worried, but more angry than worried, at my lateness. As my father pulled into the garage, she would rush about, fixing him a cocktail, a dry sherry, and put on an exasperated face: "You know junior high," she would say. "Maybe it's Spring Fling." "Abigail," my father would say, "how can it be Spring Fling when it's snowing?" Having failed with this, my mother might rush Buckley into the room and say, "Play with your father," while she ducked into the kitchen and took a nip of sherry for herself.

Mr. Harvey started to press his lips against mine. They were blubbery and wet and I wanted to scream but I was too afraid and too exhausted from the fight. I had been kissed once by someone I liked. His name was Ray and he was Indian. He had an accent and was dark. I wasn't supposed to like him. Clarissa called his large eyes, with their half-closed lids, "freak-a-delic," but he was nice and smart and helped me cheat on my algebra exam while pretending he hadn't. He kissed me by my locker the day before we turned in our photos for the yearbook. When the yearbook came out at the end of the summer, I saw that under his picture he had answered the standard "My heart belongs to" with "Susie Salmon." I guess he had had plans. I remember that his lips were chapped.

"Don't, Mr. Harvey," I managed, and I kept saying that one word a lot. *Don't.* And I said *please* a lot too. Franny told me that almost everyone begged "please" before dying.

"I want you, Susie," he said.

"Please," I said. "Don't," I said. Sometimes I combined them. "Please don't" or "Don't please." It was like insisting that a key works when it doesn't or yelling "I've got it, I've got it, I've got it" as a softball goes sailing over you into the stands.

"Please don't."

But he grew tired of hearing me plead. He reached into the pocket of my parka and balled up the hat my mother had made me, smashing it into my mouth. The only sound I made after that was the weak tinkling of bells.

As he kissed his wet lips down my face and neck and then began to shove his hands up under my shirt, I wept. I began to leave my body; I began to inhabit the air and the silence. I wept and struggled so I would not feel. He ripped open my pants, not having found the invisible zipper my mother had artfully sewn into their side.

"Big white panties," he said.

I felt huge and bloated. I felt like a sea in which he stood and pissed and shat. I felt the corners of my body were turning in on themselves and out, like in cat's cradle, which I played with Lindsey just to make her happy. He started working himself over me.

"Susie! Susie!" I heard my mother calling. "Dinner is ready."

He was inside me. He was grunting.

"We're having string beans and lamb."

I was the mortar, he was the pestle.

"Your brother has a new finger painting, and I made apple crumb cake."

Mr. Harvey made me lie still underneath him and listen to the beating of his heart and the beating of mine. How mine skipped like a rabbit, and how his thudded, a hammer against cloth. We lay there with our bodies touching, and, as I shook, a powerful knowledge took hold. He had done this thing to me and I had lived. That was all. I was still breathing. I heard his heart. I smelled his breath. The dark earth surrounding us smelled like what it was, moist dirt where worms and animals lived their daily lives. I could have yelled for hours.

I knew he was going to kill me. I did not realize then that I was an animal already dying.

"Why don't you get up?" Mr. Harvey said as he rolled to the side and then crouched over me.

His voice was gentle, encouraging, a lover's voice on a late morning. A suggestion, not a command.

I could not move. I could not get up.

When I would not — was it only that, only that I would not follow his suggestion? — he leaned to the side and felt, over his head, across the ledge where his razor and shaving cream sat. He brought back a knife. Unsheathed, it smiled at me, curving up in a grin.

He took the hat from my mouth.

"Tell me you love me," he said.

Gently, I did.

The end came anyway.

TWO

When I first entered heaven I thought everyone saw what I saw. That in everyone's heaven there were soccer goalposts in the distance and lumbering women throwing shot put and javelin. That all the buildings were like suburban northeast high schools built in the 1960s. Large, squat buildings spread out on dismally landscaped sandy lots, with overhangs and open spaces to make them feel modern. My favorite part was how the colored blocks were turquoise and orange, just like the blocks in Fairfax High. Sometimes, on Earth, I had made my father drive me by Fairfax High so I could imagine myself there.

Following the seventh, eighth, and ninth grades of middle school, high school would have been a fresh start. When I got to Fairfax High I would insist on being called Suzanne. I would wear my hair feathered or up in a bun. I would have a body that the boys wanted and the girls envied, but I'd be so nice on top of it all that they would feel too guilty to do anything but worship me. I liked to think of myself — having reached a sort of queenly status — as protecting misfit kids in the cafeteria. When someone taunted Clive Saunders for walking like a girl, I would deliver swift vengeance with my foot to the taunter's less-protected parts. When the boys teased Phoebe Hart for her sizable breasts, I would give a speech on why boob jokes weren't funny. I had to forget that I too had made lists in the margins of my notebook when Phoebe walked by: Winnebagos, Hoo-has, Johnny Yellows. At the end of my reveries, I sat in the back of the car as my father drove. I was beyond reproach. I would overtake high school in a matter of days, not years, or, inexplicably, earn an Oscar for Best Actress during my junior year.

These were my dreams on Earth.

After a few days in heaven, I realized that the javelin-throwers and the shot-putters and the boys who played basketball on the cracked blacktop were all in their own version of heaven. Theirs just fit with mine — didn't duplicate it precisely, but had a lot of the same things going on inside.

I met Holly, who became my roommate, on the third day. She was sitting on the swing set. (I didn't question that a high school had swing sets: that's what made it heaven. And no flat-benched swings — only bucket seats made out of hard black rubber that cradled you and that you could bounce in a bit before swinging.) Holly sat reading a book in a weird alphabet that I associated with the pork-fried rice my father brought home from Hop Fat

Kitchen, a place Buckley loved the name of, loved so much he yelled "Hop Fat!" at the top of his lungs. Now I know Vietnamese, and I know that Vietnamese is not what Herman Jade, who owned Hop Fat, was, and that Herman Jade was not Herman Jade's real name but one he adopted when he came to the U.S. from China. Holly taught me all this.

"Hi," I said. "My name is Susie."

Later she would tell me she picked her name from a movie, *Breakfast at Tiffany's*. But that day it rolled right off her tongue.

"I'm Holly," she said. Because she wanted no trace of an accent in her heaven, she had none.

I stared at her black hair. It was shiny like the promises in magazines. "How long have you been here?" I asked.

"Three days."

"Me too."

I sat down on the swing next to her and twisted my body around and around to tie up the chains. Then I let go and spun until I stopped.

"Do you like it here?" she asked.

"No."

"Me either."

So it began.

We had been given, in our heavens, our simplest dreams. There were no teachers in the school. We never had to go inside except for art class for me and jazz band for Holly. The boys did not pinch our backsides or tell us we smelled; our textbooks were *Seventeen* and *Glamour* and *Vogue*.

And our heavens expanded as our relationship grew. We wanted many of the same things.

Franny, my intake counselor, became our guide. Franny was old enough to be our mother — mid-forties — and it took Holly and me a while to figure out that this had been something we wanted: our mothers.

In Franny's heaven, she served and was rewarded by results and gratitude. On Earth she had been a social worker for the homeless and destitute. She worked out of a church named Saint Mary's that served meals to women and children only, and she did everything there from manning the phones to swatting the roaches — karate-chop style. She was shot in the face by a man looking for his wife.

Franny walked over to Holly and me on the fifth day. She handed us two Dixie Cups of lime Kool-Aid and we drank. "I'm here to help," she said.

I looked into her small blue eyes surrounded by laugh lines and told her the truth. "We're bored."

Holly was busy trying to reach her tongue out far enough to see if it had turned green.

"What do you want?" Franny asked.

"I don't know," I said.

"All you have to do is desire it, and if you desire it enough and understand why — really know — it will come."

It seemed so simple and it was. That's how Holly and I got our duplex.

I hated our split-level on Earth. I hated my parents' furniture, and how our house looked out onto another house and another house and another — an echo of sameness riding up over the hill. Our duplex looked out onto a park, and in the distance, just close enough to know we weren't alone, but not too close, we could see the lights of other houses.

Eventually I began to desire more. What I found strange was how much I desired to know what I had not known on Earth. I wanted to be allowed to grow up.

"People grow up by living," I said to Franny. "I want to live."

"That's out," she said.

"Can we at least watch the living?" asked Holly.

"You already do," she said.

"I think she means whole lives," I said, "from beginning to end, to see how they did it. To know the secrets. Then we can pretend better."

"You won't experience it," Franny clarified.

"Thank you, Brain Central," I said, but our heavens began to grow.

There was the high school still, all the Fairfax architecture, but now there were roads leading out.

"Walk the paths," Franny said, "and you'll find what you need."

So that's when Holly and I set out. Our heaven had an ice cream shop where, when you asked for peppermint stick ice cream, no one ever said, "It's seasonal"; it had a newspaper where our pictures appeared a lot and made us look important; it had real men in it and beautiful women too, because Holly and I were devoted to fashion magazines. Sometimes Holly seemed like she wasn't paying attention, and other times she was gone when I went looking for her. That was when she went to a part of heaven we didn't share. I missed her then, but it was an odd sort of missing because by then I knew the meaning of forever.

I could not have what I wanted most: Mr. Harvey dead and me living. Heaven wasn't perfect. But I came to believe that if I watched closely, and desired, I might change the lives of those I loved on Earth.

My father was the one who took the phone call on December ninth. It was the beginning of the end. He gave the police my blood type, had to describe the lightness of my skin. They asked him if I had any identifying features. He began to describe my face in detail, getting lost in it. Detective Fenerman let him go on, the next news too horrible to interrupt with. But then he said it: "Mr. Salmon, we have found only a body part."

My father stood in the kitchen and a sickening shiver overtook him. How could he tell that to Abigail?

"So you can't be certain that she's dead?" he asked.

"Nothing is ever certain," Len Fenerman said.

That was the line my father said to my mother: "Nothing is ever certain."

For three nights he hadn't known how to touch my mother or what to say. Before, they had never found themselves broken together. Usually, it was one needing the other but not both needing each other, and so there had been a way, by touching, to borrow from the stronger one's strength. And they had never understood, as they did now, what the word *horror* meant.

"Nothing is ever certain," my mother said, clinging to it as he had hoped she might.

My mother had been the one who knew the meaning of each charm on my bracelet — where we had gotten it and why I liked it. She made a meticulous list of what I'd carried and worn. If found miles away and in isolation along a road, these clues might lead a policeman there to link it to my death.

In my mind I had wavered between the bittersweet joy of seeing my mother name all the things I carried and loved and her futile hope that these things mattered. That a stranger who found a cartoon character eraser or a rock star button would report it to the police.

After Len's phone call, my father reached out his hand and the two of them sat in the bed together, staring straight in front of them. My mother numbly clinging to this list of things, my father feeling as if he were entering a dark tunnel. At some point, it began to rain. I could feel them both thinking the same thing then, but neither of them said it. That I was out there somewhere, in the rain. That they hoped I was safe. That I was dry somewhere, and warm.

Neither of them knew who fell asleep first; their bones aching with exhaustion, they drifted off and woke guiltily at the same time. The rain, which had changed several times as the temperature dropped, was now hail, and the sound of it, of small stones of ice hitting the roof above them, woke them together.

They did not speak. They looked at each other in the small light cast from the lamp left on across the room. My mother began to cry, and my father held her, wiped her tears with the pad of his thumbs as they crested her cheekbones, and kissed her very gently on the eyes.

I looked away from them then, as they touched. I moved my eyes into the cornfield, seeing if there was anything that in the morning the police might find. The hail bent the stalks and drove all the animals into their holes. Not so deep beneath the earth were the warrens of the wild rabbits I loved, the bunnies that ate the vegetables and flowers in the neighborhood nearby and that sometimes, unwittingly, brought poison home to their dens. Then, inside the earth and so far away from the man or woman who had laced a garden with toxic bait, an entire family of rabbits would curl into themselves and die.

On the morning of the tenth, my father poured the Scotch down the kitchen sink. Lindsey asked him why.

"I'm afraid I might drink it," he said.

"What was the phone call?" my sister asked.

"What phone call?"

"I heard you say that thing you always say about Susie's smile. About stars exploding."

"Did I say that?"

"You got kind of goofy. It was a cop, wasn't it?"

"No lies?"

"No lies," Lindsey agreed.

"They found a body part. It might be Susie's."

It was a hard sock in the stomach. "What?"

"Nothing is ever certain," my father tried.

Lindsey sat down at the kitchen table. "I'm going to be sick," she said.

"Honey?"

"Dad, I want you to tell me what it was. Which body part, and then I'm going to need to throw up."

My father got down a large metal mixing bowl. He brought it to the table and placed it near Lindsey before sitting down.

"Okay," she said. "Tell me."

"It was an elbow. The Gilberts' dog found it."

He held her hand and then she threw up, as she had promised, into the shiny silver bowl.

Later that morning the weather cleared, and not too far from my house the police roped off the cornfield and began their search. The rain, sleet, snow, and hail melting and mixing had left the ground sodden; still, there was an obvious area where the earth had been freshly manipulated. They began there and dug.

In places, the lab later found, there was a dense concentration of my blood mixed with the dirt, but at the time, the police grew more and more frustrated, plying the cold wet ground and looking for girl.

Along the border of the soccer field, a few of my neighbors kept a respectful distance from the police tape, wondering at the men dressed in heavy blue parkas wielding shovels and rakes like medical tools.

My father and mother remained at home. Lindsey stayed in her room. Buckley was nearby at his friend Nate's house, where he spent a lot of time these days. They had told him I was on an extended sleepover at Clarissa's.

I knew where my body was but I could not tell them. I watched and waited to see what they would see. And then, like a thunderbolt, late in the afternoon, a policeman held up his earth-caked fist and shouted.

"Over here!" he said, and the other officers ran to surround him.

The neighbors had gone home except for Mrs. Stead. After conferring around the discovering policeman, Detective Fenerman broke their dark huddle and approached her.

"Mrs. Stead?" he said over the tape that separated them.

"Yes."

"You have a child in the school?"

"Yes."

"Could you come with me, please?"

A young officer led Mrs. Stead under the police tape and over the bumpy, churned-up cornfield to where the rest of the men stood.

"Mrs. Stead," Len Fenerman said, "does this look familiar?" He held up a paperback copy of *To Kill a Mockingbird.* "Do they read this at the school?"

"Yes," she said, her face draining of color as she said the small word.

"Do you mind if I ask you . . ." he began.

"Ninth grade," she said, looking into Len Fenerman's slate blue eyes. "Susie's grade." She was a therapist and relied on her ability to hear bad news and discuss rationally the difficult details of her patients' lives, but she found herself leaning into the young policeman who had led her over. I could feel her wishing that she had gone home when the other neighbors had left, wishing that she was in the living room with her husband, or out in the backyard with her son.

"Who teaches the class?"

"Mrs. Dewitt," Mrs. Stead said. "The kids find it a real relief after *Othello.*"

"*Othello?*"

"Yes," she said, her knowledge of the school suddenly very important right now — all the policemen listening. "Mrs. Dewitt likes to modulate her reading list, and she does a big push right before Christmas with Shakespeare.

Then she passes out Harper Lee as a reward. If Susie was carrying around *To Kill a Mockingbird* it means she must have turned in her paper on *Othello* already."

All of this checked out.

The police made calls. I watched the circle widen. Mrs. Dewitt had my paper. Eventually, she sent it back to my parents, unmarked, through the mail. "Thought you would want to have this," Mrs. Dewitt had written on a note attached to it. "I'm so very very sorry." Lindsey inherited the paper because it was too painful for my mother to read. "The Ostracized: One Man Alone," I had called it. Lindsey had suggested "The Ostracized," and I made up the other half. My sister punched three holes down the side of it and fastened each carefully handwritten page into an empty notebook. She put it in her closet under her Barbie case and the box that held her perfect-condition Raggedy Ann and Andy that I'd envied.

Detective Fenerman called my parents. They had found a schoolbook, they believed, that might have been given to me that last day.

"But it could be anyone's," my father said to my mother as they began another restless vigil. "Or she could have dropped it along the way."

Evidence was mounting, but they refused to believe.

Two days later, on December twelfth, the police found my notes from Mr. Botte's class. Animals had carried off the notebook from its original burial site — the dirt did not match the surrounding samples, but the graph paper, with its scribbled theories that I could never understand but still dutifully recorded, had been found when a cat knocked down a crow's nest. Shreds of the paper were laced among the leaves and twigs. The police unbraided the graph paper, along with strips of another kind of paper, thinner and brittle, that had no lines.

The girl who lived in the house where the tree stood recognized some of the handwriting. It was not my writing, but the writing of the boy who had a crush on me: Ray Singh. On his mother's special rice paper Ray had written me a love note, which I never read. He had tucked it into my notebook during our Wednesday lab. His hand was distinct. When the officers came they had to piece together the scraps of my biology notebook and of Ray Singh's love note.

"Ray is not feeling well," his mother said when a detective called his house and asked to speak to him. But they found out what they needed from her. Ray nodded to her as she repeated the policeman's questions to her son. Yes, he had written Susie Salmon a love note. Yes, he had put it in her notebook after Mr. Botte had asked her to collect the pop quiz. Yes, he had called himself the Moor.

Ray Singh became the first suspect.

"That sweet boy?" my mother said to my father.

"Ray Singh is nice," my sister said in a monotone at dinner that night.

I watched my family and knew they knew. It was not Ray Singh.

The police descended on his house, leaning heavily on him, insinuating things. They were fueled by the guilt they read into Ray's dark skin, by the rage they felt at his manner, and by his beautiful yet too exotic and unavailable mother. But Ray had an alibi. A whole host of nations could be called to testify on his behalf. His father, who taught postcolonial history at Penn, had urged his son to represent the teenage experience at a lecture he gave at the International House on the day I died.

At first Ray's absence from school had been seen as evidence of his guilt, but once the police were presented with a list of forty-five attendees who had seen Ray speak at "Suburbia: The American Experience," they had to concede his innocence. The police stood outside the Singh house and snapped small twigs from the hedges. It would have been so easy, so magical, their answer literally falling out of the sky from a tree. But rumors spread and, in school, what little headway Ray had made socially was reversed. He began to go home immediately after school.

All this made me crazy. Watching but not being able to steer the police toward the green house so close to my parents, where Mr. Harvey sat carving finials for a gothic dollhouse he was building. He watched the news and scanned the papers, but he wore his own innocence like a comfortable old coat. There had been a riot inside him and now there was calm.

I tried to take solace in Holiday, our dog. I missed him in a way I hadn't yet let myself miss my mother and father, my sister and brother. That way of missing would mean that I had accepted that I would never be with them again; it might sound silly but I didn't believe it, would not believe it. Holiday stayed with Lindsey at night, stood by my father each time he answered the door to a new unknown. Gladly partook of any clandestine eating on the part of my mother. Let Buckley pull his tail and ears inside the house of locked doors.

There was too much blood in the earth.

On December fifteenth, among the knocks on the door that signaled to my family that they must numb themselves

further before opening their house to strangers — the kind
but awkward neighbors, the bumbling but cruel reporters —
came the one that made my father finally believe.

It was Len Fenerman, who had been so kind to him,
and a uniform.

They came inside, by now familiar enough with the
house to know that my mother preferred them to come in
and say what they had to say in the living room so that
my sister and brother would not overhear.

"We've found a personal item that we believe to be
Susie's," Len said. Len was careful. I could see him calculating his words. He made sure to specify so that my
parents would be relieved of their first thought — that the
police had found my body, that I was, for certain, dead.

"What?" my mother said impatiently. She crossed her
arms and braced for another inconsequential detail in
which others invested meaning. She was a wall.
Notebooks and novels were nothing to her. Her daughter
might survive without an arm. A lot of blood was a lot of
blood. It was not a body. Jack had said it and she believed: Nothing is ever certain.

But when they held up the evidence bag with my hat inside, something broke in her. The fine wall of leaden crystal
that had protected her heart — somehow numbed her into
disbelief — shattered.

"The pompom," Lindsey said. She had crept into the
living room from the kitchen. No one had seen her come
in but me.

My mother made a sound and reached out her hand.
The sound was a metallic squeak, a human-as-machine
breaking down, uttering last sounds before the whole engine locks.

"We've tested the fibers," Len said. "It appears who-ever accosted Susie used this during the crime."

"What?" my father asked. He was powerless. He was being told something he could not comprehend.

"As a way to keep her quiet."

"What?"

"It is covered with her saliva," the uniformed officer, who had been silent until now, volunteered. "He gagged her with it."

My mother grabbed it out of Len Fenerman's hands, and the bells she had sewn into the pompom sounded as she landed on her knees. She bent over the hat she had made me.

I saw Lindsey stiffen at the door. Our parents were un-recognizable to her; everything was unrecognizable.

My father led the well-meaning Len Fenerman and the uniformed officer to the front door.

"Mr. Salmon," Len Fenerman said, "with the amount of blood we've found, and the violence I'm afraid it im-plies, as well as other material evidence we've discussed, we must work with the assumption that your daughter has been killed."

Lindsey overheard what she already knew, had known since five days before, when my father told her about my elbow. My mother began to wail.

"We'll be working with this as a murder investigation from this point out," Fenerman said.

"But there is no body," my father tried.

"All evidence points to your daughter's death. I'm very sorry."

The uniformed officer had been staring to the right of my father's pleading eyes. I wondered if that was something they'd taught him in school. But Len Fenerman met my father's gaze. "I'll call to check in on you later today," he said.

By the time my father turned back to the living room, he was too devastated to reach out to my mother sitting on the carpet or my sister's hardened form nearby. He could not let them see him. He mounted the stairs, thinking of Holiday on the rug in the study. He had last seen him there. Into the deep ruff of fur surrounding the dog's neck, my father would let himself cry.

That afternoon the three of them crept forward in silence, as if the sound of footsteps might confirm the news. Nate's mother knocked on the door to return Buckley. No one answered. She stepped away, knowing something had changed inside the house, which looked exactly like the ones on either side of it. She made herself my brother's co-conspirator, telling him they would go out for ice cream and ruin his appetite.

At four, my mother and father ended up standing in the same room downstairs. They had come in from opposite doorways.

My mother looked at my father: "Mother," she said, and he nodded his head. He made the phone call to my only living grandparent, my mother's mother, Grandma Lynn.

I worried that my sister, left alone, would do something rash. She sat in her room on the old couch my parents had given up on and worked on hardening herself. *Take deep*

*breaths and hold them. Try to stay still for longer and
longer periods of time. Make yourself small and like a
stone. Curl the edges of yourself up and fold them under
where no one can see.*

My mother told her it was her choice whether she
wanted to return to school before Christmas — there was
only one week left — but Lindsey chose to go.

On Monday, in homeroom, everyone stared at her as
she approached the front of the classroom.

"The principal would like to see you, dear," Mrs.
Dewitt confided in a hush.

My sister did not look at Mrs. Dewitt when she was
speaking. She was perfecting the art of talking to someone while looking through them. That was my first clue
that something would have to give. Mrs. Dewitt was also
the English teacher, but more importantly she was married to Mr. Dewitt, who coached boys' soccer and had encouraged Lindsey to try out for his team. My sister liked
the Dewitts, but that morning she began looking into the
eyes of only those people she could fight against.

As she gathered her things, she heard whispers
everywhere. She was certain that right before she left
the room Danny Clarke had whispered something to
Sylvia Henley. Someone had dropped something near
the back of the classroom. They did this, she believed,
so that on their way to pick it up and back again, they
could say a word or two to their neighbor about the dead
girl's sister.

Lindsey walked through the hallways and in and out of
the rows of lockers — dodging anyone who might be
near. I wished I could walk with her, mimic the principal
and the way he always started out a meeting in the audi-

torium: "Your principal is your pal with principles!" I would whine in her ear, cracking her up.

But while she was blessed with empty halls, when she reached the main office she was cursed with the drippy looks of consoling secretaries. No matter. She had prepared herself at home in her bedroom. She was armed to the teeth for any onslaught of sympathy.

"Lindsey," Principal Caden said, "I received a call from the police this morning. I'm sorry to hear of your loss."

She looked right at him. It was not so much a look as a laser. "What exactly is my loss?"

Mr. Caden felt he needed to address issues of children's crises directly. He walked out from behind his desk and ushered Lindsey onto what was commonly referred to by the students as The Sofa. Eventually he would replace The Sofa with two chairs, when politics swept through the school district and told him, *It is not good to have a sofa here — chairs are better. Sofas send the wrong message.*

Mr. Caden sat on The Sofa and so did my sister. I like to think she was a little thrilled, in that moment, no matter how upset, to be on The Sofa itself. I like to think I hadn't robbed her of everything.

"We're here to help in any way we can," Mr. Caden said. He was doing his best.

"I'm fine," she said.

"Would you like to talk about it?"

"What?" Lindsey asked. She was being what my father called "petulant," as in, "Susie, don't speak to me in that petulant tone."

"Your loss," he said. He reached out to touch my sister's knee. His hand was like a brand burning into her.

"I wasn't aware I had lost anything," she said, and in a Herculean effort she made the motions of patting her shirt and checking her pockets.

Mr. Caden didn't know what to say. He had had Vicki Kurtz fall apart in his arms the year before. It had been difficult, yes, but now, in hindsight, Vicki Kurtz and her dead mother seemed an artfully handled crisis. He had led Vicki Kurtz to the couch — no, no, Vicki had just gone right over and sat down on it — he had said, "I'm sorry for your loss," and Vicki Kurtz had burst like an overinflated balloon. He held her in his arms as she sobbed, and sobbed, and that night he brought his suit to the dry cleaner's.

But Lindsey Salmon was another thing altogether. She was gifted, one of the twenty students from his school who had been selected for the statewide Gifted Symposium. The only trouble in her file was a slight altercation early in the year when a teacher reprimanded her for bringing obscene literature — *Fear of Flying* — into the classroom.

"Make her laugh," I wanted to say to him. "Bring her to a Marx Brothers movie, sit on a fart cushion, show her the boxers you have on with the little devils eating hot dogs on them!" All I could do was talk, but no one on Earth could hear me.

The school district made everyone take tests and then decided who was gifted and who was not. I liked to suggest to Lindsey that I was much more pissed off by her hair than by my dumbo status. We had both been born with masses of blond hair, but mine quickly fell out and was replaced with a grudging growth of mousy brown. Lindsey's stayed and acquired a sort of mythical place. She was the only true blonde in our family.

But once called gifted, it had spurred her on to live up to the name. She locked herself in her bedroom and read big books. When I read *Are You There God? It's Me, Margaret,* she read Camus's *Resistance, Rebellion, and Death.* She might not have gotten most of it, but she carried it around, and that made people — including teachers — begin to leave her alone.

"What I'm saying, Lindsey, is that we all miss Susie," Mr. Caden said.

She did not respond.

"She was very bright," he tried.

She stared blankly back at him.

"It's on your shoulders now." He had no idea what he was saying, but he thought the silence might mean he was getting somewhere. "You're the only Salmon girl now."

Nothing.

"You know who came in to see me this morning?" Mr. Caden had held back his big finish, the one he was sure would work. "Mr. Dewitt. He's considering coaching a girls' team," Mr. Caden said. "The idea is all centered around you. He's watched how good you are, as competitive as his boys, and he thinks other girls would come out if you led the charge. What do you say?"

Inside, my sister's heart closed like a fist. "I'd say it would be pretty hard to play soccer on the soccer field when it's approximately twenty feet from where my sister was supposedly murdered."

Score!

Mr. Caden's mouth opened and he stared at her.

"Anything else?" Lindsey asked.

"No, I . . ." Mr. Caden reached out his hand again. There was a thread still — a desire to understand. "I want you to know how sorry we are," he said.

"I'm late for first period," she said.

In that moment she reminded me of a character in the Westerns my father loved, the ones we watched together on late-night TV. There was always a man who, after he shot his gun, raised the pistol to his lips and blew air across the opening.

Lindsey got up and took the walk out of Principal Caden's office slow. The walks away were her only rest time. Secretaries were on the other side of the door, teachers were at the front of the class, students in every desk, our parents at home, police coming by. She would not break. I watched her, felt the lines she repeated over and over again in her head. *Fine. All of it is fine.* I was dead, but that was something that happened all the time — people died. As she left the outer office that day, she appeared to be looking into the eyes of the secretaries, but she was focusing on their misapplied lipstick or two-piece paisley crepe de chine instead.

At home that night she lay on the floor of her room and braced her feet under her bureau. She did ten sets of sit-ups. Then she got into push-up position. Not the girl's kind. Mr. Dewitt had told her about the kind he had done in the Marines, head-up, or one-handed, clapping between. After she did ten push-ups, she went to her shelf and chose the two heaviest books — her dictionary and a world almanac. She did biceps curls until her arms ached. She focused only on her breathing. The in. The out.

* * *

I sat in the gazebo in the main square of my heaven (our neighbors, the O'Dwyers, had had a gazebo; I had grown up jealous for one), and watched my sister rage.

Hours before I died, my mother hung on the refrigerator a picture that Buckley had drawn. In the drawing a thick blue line separated the air and ground. In the days that followed I watched my family walk back and forth past that drawing and I became convinced that that thick blue line was a real place — an Inbetween, where heaven's horizon met Earth's. I wanted to go there into the cornflower blue of Crayola, the royal, the turquoise, the sky.

Often I found myself desiring simple things and I would get them. Riches in furry packages. Dogs.

Every day in my heaven tiny dogs and big dogs, dogs of every kind, ran through the park outside my room. When I opened the door I saw them fat and happy, skinny and hairy, lean and hairless even. Pitbulls rolled on their backs, the nipples of the females distended and dark, begging for their pups to come and suckle them, happy in the sun. Bassets tripped over their ears, ambling forward, nudging the rumps of dachshunds, the ankles of greyhounds, and the heads of the Pekingese. And when Holly took her tenor sax, set herself up outside the door that looked onto the park, and played the blues, the hounds all ran to form her chorus. On their haunches they sat wailing. Other doors opened then, and women stepped out from where they lived alone or with roommates. I would step outside, Holly would go into an endless encore, the sun going down, and we would dance with the dogs — all of us together. We chased them, they chased us. We circled tail to tail. We wore spotted gowns, flowered gowns, striped gowns, plain. When the moon was high the music would stop. The dancing stopped. We froze.

Mrs. Bethel Utemeyer, the oldest resident of my heaven, would bring out her violin. Holly trod lightly on her horn. They would do a duet. One woman old and silent, one woman not past girl yet. Back and forth, a crazy schizoid solace they'd create.

All the dancers would slowly go inside. The song reverberated until Holly, for a final time, passed the tune over, and Mrs. Utemeyer, quiet, upright, historical, finished with a jig.

The house asleep by then; this was my Evensong.

THREE

The odd thing about Earth was what we saw when we looked down. Besides the initial view that you might suspect, the old ants-from-the-skyscraper phenomenon, there were souls leaving bodies all over the world.

Holly and I could be scanning Earth, alighting on one scene or another for a second or two, looking for the unexpected in the most mundane moment. And a soul would run by a living being, touch them softly on the shoulder or cheek, and continue on its way to heaven. The dead are never exactly seen by the living, but many people seem acutely aware of something changed around them. They speak of a chill in the air. The mates of the deceased wake from dreams and see a figure standing at the end of their bed, or in a doorway, or boarding, phantom-like, a city bus.

On my way out of Earth, I touched a girl named Ruth. She went to my school but we'd never been close. She was standing in my path that night when my soul shrieked out of Earth. I could not help but graze her. Once released from life, having lost it in such violence, I couldn't calculate my steps. I didn't have time for contemplation. In violence, it is the getting away that you concentrate on. When you begin to go over the edge, life receding from you as a boat recedes inevitably from shore, you hold on to death tightly, like a rope that will transport you, and you swing out on it, hoping only to land away from where you are.

Like a phone call from the jail cell, I brushed by Ruth Connors — wrong number, accidental call. I saw her standing there near Mr. Botte's red and rusted Fiat. When I streaked by her, my hand leapt out to touch her, touch the last face, feel the last connection to Earth in this not-so-standard-issue teenage girl.

On the morning of December seventh, Ruth complained to her mother about having had a dream that seemed too real to be a dream. When her mother asked her what she meant, Ruth said, "I was crossing through the faculty parking lot, and suddenly, down out of the soccer field, I saw a pale running ghost coming toward me."

Mrs. Connors stirred the hardening oatmeal in its pot. She watched her daughter gesticulating with the long thin fingers of her hands — hands she had inherited from her father.

"It was female, I could sense that," Ruth said. "It flew up out of the field. Its eyes were hollow. It had a thin white veil over its body, as light as cheesecloth. I could see its face through it, the features coming up through it, the nose, the eyes, the face, the hair."

Her mother took the oatmeal off the stove and lowered the flame. "Ruth," she said, "you're letting your imagination get the best of you."

Ruth took the cue to shut up. She did not mention the dream that was not a dream again, even ten days later, when the story of my death began to travel through the halls of the school, receiving add-on nuances as all good horror stories do. They were hard-pressed, my peers, to make the horror any more horrible than it was. But the details were still missing — the what and when and who became hollow bowls to fill with their conjectures. Devil Worship. Midnight. Ray Singh.

Try as I might, I could not point Ruth strongly enough to what no one had found: my silver charm bracelet. I thought it might help her. It lay exposed, waiting for a hand to reach out, a hand that would recognize it and think, *Clue*. But it was no longer in the cornfield.

Ruth began writing poetry. If her mother or her more approachable teachers did not want to hear the darker reality she had experienced, she would cloak this reality in poetry.

How I wished Ruth could have gone to my family and talked to them. In all likelihood, no one but my sister would have even known her name. Ruth was the girl who got chosen next to last in gym. She was the girl who, when a volleyball sailed in her direction, cowered where she stood while the ball hit the gymnasium floor beside her, and her teammates and the gym teacher tried hard not to groan.

As my mother sat in the straight-backed chair in our hallway, watching my father run in and out on his various errands of responsibility — he would now be hyperaware of the movements and the whereabouts of his young son, of his wife, and of his remaining daughter — Ruth took our accidental meeting in the school parking lot and went underground.

She went through old yearbooks and found my class photos, as well as any activities photos like Chem Club, and cut them out with her mother's swan-shaped embroidery scissors. Even as her obsession grew I remained wary of her, until that last week before Christmas when she saw something in the hallway of our school.

It was my friend Clarissa and Brian Nelson. I'd dubbed Brian "the scarecrow" because even though he had incredible shoulders that all the girls mooned over, his face reminded me of a burlap sack stuffed with straw. He wore a floppy leather hippie hat and smoked hand-rolled cigarettes in the student smoking lounge. According to my mother, Clarissa's penchant for baby blue eye shadow was an early warning sign, but I'd always liked her for just this reason. She did things I wasn't allowed to do: she lightened her long hair, she wore platform shoes, she smoked cigarettes after school.

Ruth came upon the two of them, but they didn't see her. She had a pile of huge books she had borrowed from Mrs. Kaplan, the social science teacher. They were all early feminist texts, and she held them with their spines resting against her stomach so that no one could see what they were. Her father, a building contractor, had made her a gift of two super-strong elastic book bands. Ruth had placed two of them around the volumes she planned to read over vacation.

Clarissa and Brian were giggling. His hand was inside her shirt. As he inched it up, her giggling increased, but she thwarted his advances each time by twisting or moving an inch or two away. Ruth stood apart from this, as she did most things. She would have passed it in her usual manner, head down/eyes averted, but everyone knew Clarissa had been my friend. So she watched.

"Come on, honey," Brian said, "just a little mound of love. Just one."

I noticed Ruth's lip curl in disgust. Mine was curling up in heaven.

"Brian, I can't. Not here."

"How 'bout out in the cornfield?" he whispered.

Clarissa giggled nervously but nuzzled the space between his neck and shoulder. For now, she would deny him.

After that, Clarissa's locker was burgled.

Gone were her scrapbook, random photos stuck to the inside of her locker, and Brian's stash of marijuana, which he had hidden there without Clarissa's knowledge.

Ruth, who had never been high, spent that night emptying out the tobacco from her mother's long brown More 100s and stuffing them with pot. She sat in the toolshed with a flashlight, looking at photos of me and smoking more grass than even the potheads at school could suck down.

Mrs. Connors, standing at the kitchen window doing dishes, caught a whiff of the scent coming from the toolshed.

"I think Ruth is making friends at school," she said to her husband, who sat over his copy of the *Evening Bulletin* with a cup of coffee. At the end of his workday he was too tired even to speculate.

"Good," he said.

"Maybe there's hope for her yet."

"Always," he said.

When Ruth tottered in later that night, her eyes bleary from using the flashlight and from the eight More cigarettes she'd smoked, her mother greeted her with a smile and told her there was blueberry pie in the kitchen. It took a few days and some non-Susie-Salmon-focused research, but Ruth discovered why she had eaten the entire pie in one sitting.

The air in my heaven often smelled like skunk — just a hint of it. It was a smell that I had always loved on Earth. When I breathed it in, I could feel the scent as well as smell it. It was the animal's fear and power mixed together to form a pungent, lingering musk. In Franny's heaven it smelled like pure, grade-A tobacco. In Holly's it smelled like kumquats.

I would sit whole days and nights in the gazebo and watch. See Clarissa spin away from me, toward the comfort of Brian. See Ruth staring at her from behind a corner near the home ec room or outside the cafeteria near the nurse's station. At the start, the freedom I had to see the whole school was intoxicating. I would watch the assistant football coach leave anonymous chocolates for the married science teacher, or the head of the cheerleading squad trying to capture the attention of the kid who had been expelled so many times, from so many schools, even he had lost count. I watched the art teacher make love to his girlfriend in the kiln room and the principal moon over the assistant football coach. I concluded that this assistant football coach was a stud in the world of Kennet Junior High, even if his square jaw left me cold.

On the way back to the duplex each night I would pass under old-time street lamps that I had seen once in a play of *Our Town*. The globes of light hung down in an arc from an iron post. I had remembered them because when I saw the play with my family, I thought of them as giant, heavy berries full of light. I made a game in heaven of positioning myself so that my shadow plucked the berries as I made my way home.

After watching Ruth one night I met Franny in the midst of this. The square was deserted, and leaves began to swirl around in an eddy up ahead. I stood and looked at her — at the laugh lines that were clustered near her eyes and mouth.

"Why are you shivering?" Franny asked.

And though the air was damp and chilly I could not say that that was why.

"I can't help thinking of my mother," I said.

Franny took my left hand in both of hers and smiled.

I wanted to kiss her lightly on the cheek or have her hold me, but instead I watched her walk off in front of me, saw her blue dress trail away. I knew that she was not my mother; I could not play pretend.

I turned around and went back to the gazebo. I felt the moist air lace its way up along my legs and arms, lifting, ever so slightly, the ends of my hair. I thought of spider webs in the morning, how they held small jewels of dew, how, with a light movement of the wrist, I used to destroy them without thinking.

On the morning of my eleventh birthday I had woken up very early. No one else was up, or so I thought. I crept downstairs and looked into the dining room, where I assumed my presents would be. But there was nothing there. Same table as yesterday. But as I turned around I saw it lying on my mother's desk in the living room. The fancy desk with an always-clean surface. "The bill-paying desk" was what they called it. Swaddled in tissue paper but not yet wrapped was a camera — what I had asked for with a tinge of whining in my voice, so sure they would not get it for me. I went over to it and stared down. It was an Instamatic, and lying beside it were three cartridges of film and a box of four square flashbulbs. It was my first machine, my starter kit to becoming what I wanted to be. A wildlife photographer.

I looked around. No one. I saw through the front blinds, which my mother always kept at a half-slant — "inviting but discreet" — that Grace Tarking, who lived down the street and went to a private school, was walking with ankle weights strapped to her feet. Hurriedly I loaded the camera and I began to stalk Grace Tarking as I would, I imagined, when I grew older, stalk wild elephants and rhinos. Here I hid behind blinds and windows, there it would be high reeds. I was quiet, what I thought of as stealthy, gathering the long hem of my flannel nightgown up in my free hand. I traced her movements past our living room, front hall, into the den on the other side. As I watched her receding form I had a brainstorm — I would run into the backyard, where I could see her with no barriers.

So I ran on tiptoe into the back of the house, only to find the door to the porch wide open.

When I saw my mother, I forgot all about Grace Tarking. I wish I could explain it better than this, but I had never seen her sitting so still, so *not there* somehow. Outside the screened-in porch she was sitting on an aluminum fold-out chair that was facing the backyard. In her hand she held a saucer and in the saucer was her customary cup of coffee. That morning there were no lipstick marks because there was no lipstick until she put it on for . . . who? I had never thought to ask the question. My father? Us?

Holiday was sitting near the birdbath, panting happily, but he did not notice me. He was watching my mother. She had a stare that stretched to infinity. She was, in that moment, not my mother but something separate from me. I looked at what I had never seen as anything but Mom and saw the soft powdery skin of her face — powdery without makeup — soft without help. Her eyebrows and eyes were a set-piece together. "Ocean Eyes," my father called her when he wanted one of her chocolate-covered cherries, which she kept hidden in the liquor cabinet as her private treat. And now I understood the name. I had thought it was because they were blue, but now I saw it was because they were bottomless in a way that I found frightening. I had an instinct then, not a developed thought, and it was that, before Holiday saw and smelled me, before the dewy mist hovering over the grass evaporated and the mother inside her woke as it did every morning, I should take a photograph with my new camera.

When the roll came back from the Kodak plant in a special heavy envelope, I could see the difference immediately. There was only one picture in which my mother was Abigail. It was that first one, the one taken of her unawares, the one captured before the click startled her into the mother of the birthday girl, owner of the happy dog, wife to the loving man, and mother again to another girl and a cherished boy. Homemaker. Gardener. Sunny neighbor. My mother's eyes were oceans, and inside them there was loss. I thought I had my whole life to understand them, but that was the only day I had. Once upon Earth I saw her as Abigail, and then I let it slip effortlessly back — my fascination held in check by wanting her to be that mother and envelop me as that mother.

I was in the gazebo thinking of the photo, thinking of my mother, when Lindsey got up in the middle of the night and crept across the hall. I watched her as I would a burglar circling a house in a movie. I knew when she turned the knob to my room it would give. I knew she would get in, but what would she do in there? Already my private territory had become a no man's land in the middle of our house. My mother had not touched it. My bed was still unmade from the hurried morning of my death. My flowered hippo lay among the sheets and pillows, and so did an outfit I'd discarded before I chose the yellow bell-bottoms.

Lindsey walked across the soft rug and touched the navy skirt and red and blue crocheted vest that were two separate, heatedly despised balls. She had an orange and green vest made from the same pattern. She took the vest and spread it out flat on the bed, smoothing it. It was ugly and precious all at once. I could see that. She petted it.

Lindsey traced the outline of the gold tray I kept on my dresser, filled with pins from elections and school. My favorite was a pink pin that said "Hippy-Dippy Says Love," which I'd found in the school parking lot but had had to promise my mother I wouldn't wear. I kept a lot of pins on that tray and pinned to a giant felt banner from Indiana University, where my father had gone to school.

I thought she would steal them — take one or two to wear — but she didn't. She didn't even pick them up. She just swept her fingertips over everything on the tray. Then she saw it, a tiny white corner sticking out from underneath. She pulled.

It was the picture.

A deep breath rushed out of her, and she sat down on the floor, her mouth still open and her hand still holding the picture. The tethers were rushing and whipping around her, like a canvas tent come loose from its stakes. She too, like me until the morning of that photograph, had never seen the mother-stranger. She had seen the photos right after. My mother looking tired but smiling. My mother and Holiday standing in front of the dogwood tree as the sun shot through her robe and gown. But I had wanted to be the only one in the house that knew my mother was also someone else — someone mysterious and unknown to us.

The first time I broke through, it was an accident. It was December 23, 1973.

Buckley was sleeping. My mother had taken Lindsey to the dentist. That week they had agreed that each day, as a family, they would spend time trying to move forward. My father had assigned himself the task of cleaning the upstairs guest room, which long ago had become his den.

His own father had taught him how to build ships in bottles. They were something my mother, sister, and brother couldn't care less about. It was something I adored. The den was full of them.

All day at work he counted numbers — due diligence for a Chadds Ford insurance firm — and at night he built the ships or read Civil War books to unwind. He would call me in whenever he was ready to raise the sail. By then the ship would have been glued fast to the bottom of the bottle. I would come in and my father would ask me to shut the door. Often, it seemed, the dinner bell rang immediately, as if my mother had a sixth sense for things that didn't include her. But when this sense failed her, my job was to hold the bottle for him.

"Stay steady," he'd say. "You're my first mate."

Gently he would draw the one string that still reached out of the bottle's neck, and, voilà, the sails all rose, from simple mast to clipper ship. We had our boat. I couldn't clap because I held the bottle, but I always wanted to. My father worked quickly then, burning the end of the string off inside the bottle with a coat hanger he'd heated over a candle. If he did it improperly, the ship would be ruined, or, worse still, the tiny paper sails would catch on fire and suddenly, in a giant whoosh, I would be holding a bottle of flames in my hands.

Eventually my father built a balsa wood stand to replace me. Lindsey and Buckley didn't share my fascination. After trying to create enough enthusiasm for all three of them, he gave up and retreated to his den. One ship in a bottle was equal to any other as far as the rest of my family was concerned.

But as he cleaned that day he talked to me.

"Susie, my baby, my little sailor girl," he said, "you always liked these smaller ones."

I watched him as he lined up the ships in bottles on his desk, bringing them over from the shelves where they usually sat. He used an old shirt of my mother's that had been ripped into rags and began dusting the shelves. Under his desk there were empty bottles — rows and rows of them we had collected for our future ship-building. In the closet were more ships — the ships he had built with his own father, ships he had built alone, and then those we had made together. Some were perfect, but their sails browned; some had sagged or toppled over after years. Then there was the one that had burst into flames in the week before my death.

He smashed that one first.

My heart seized up. He turned and saw all the others, all the years they marked and the hands that had held them. His dead father's, his dead child's. I watched him as he smashed the rest. He christened the walls and wooden chair with the news of my death, and afterward he stood in the guest room/den surrounded by green glass. The bottles, all of them, lay broken on the floor, the sails and boat bodies strewn among them. He stood in the wreckage. It was then that, without knowing how, I revealed myself. In every piece of glass, in every shard and sliver, I cast my face. My father glanced down and around him, his eyes roving across the room. Wild. It was just for a second, and then I was gone. He was quiet for a moment, and then he laughed — a howl coming up from the bottom of his stomach. He laughed so loud and deep, I shook with it in my heaven.

He left the room and went down the two doors to my bedroom. The hallway was tiny, my door like all the others, hollow enough to easily punch a fist through. He was about to smash the mirror over my dresser, rip the wallpaper down with his nails, but instead he fell against my bed, sobbing, and balled the lavender sheets up in his hands.

"Daddy?" Buckley said. My brother held the door-knob with his hand.

My father turned but was unable to stop his tears. He slid to the floor with the sheets still in his fists, and then he opened up his arms. He had to ask my brother twice, which he had never had to do before, but Buckley came to him.

My father wrapped my brother inside the sheets that smelled of me. He remembered the day I'd begged him to paint and paper my room purple. Remembered moving in the old *National Geographic*s to the bottom shelves of my bookcases. (I had wanted to steep myself in wildlife photography.) Remembered when there was just one child in the house for the briefest of time until Lindsey arrived.

"You are so special to me, little man," my father said, clinging to him.

Buckley drew back and stared at my father's creased face, the fine bright spots of tears at the corners of his eyes. He nodded seriously and kissed my father's cheek. Something so divine that no one up in heaven could have made it up; the care a child took with an adult.

My father draped the sheets around Buckley's shoulders and remembered how I would fall out of the tall four-poster bed and onto the rug, never waking up. Sitting in his study in his green chair and reading a book, he would be startled by the sound of my body landing. He would get up and walk the short distance to my bedroom. He liked to watch me sleeping soundly, unchecked by nightmare or even hardwood floor. He swore in those moments that his children would be kings or rulers or artists or doctors or wildlife photographers. Anything they dreamed they could be.

A few months before I died, he had found me like this, but tucked inside my sheets with me was Buckley, in his pajamas, with his bear, curled up against my back, sucking sleepily on his thumb. My father had felt in that moment the first flicker of the strange sad mortality of being a father. His life had given birth to three children, so the number calmed him. No matter what happened to Abigail or to him, the three would have one another. In that way the line he had begun seemed immortal to him, like a strong steel filament threading into the future, continuing past him no matter where he might fall off. Even in deep snowy old age.

He would find his Susie now inside his young son. Give that love to the living. He told himself this — spoke it aloud inside his brain — but my presence was like a tug on him, it dragged him back back back. He stared at the small boy he held in his arms. *"Who are you?"* he found himself asking. *"Where did you come from?"*

I watched my brother and my father. The truth was very different from what we learned in school. The truth was that the line between the living and the dead could be, it seemed, murky and blurred.

FOUR

In the hours after I was murdered, as my mother made phone calls and my father began going door to door in the neighborhood looking for me, Mr. Harvey had collapsed the hole in the cornfield and carried away a sack filled with my body parts. He passed within two houses of where my father stood talking to Mr. and Mrs. Tarking. He kept to the property line in between two rows of warring hedge — the O'Dwyers' boxwood and the Steads' goldenrod. His body brushed past the sturdy green leaves, leaving traces of me behind him, smells the Gilberts' dog would pick up and follow to find my elbow, smells the sleet and rain of the next three days would wash away before police dogs could even be thought of. He carried me back to his house, where, while he went inside to wash up, I waited for him.

After the house changed hands, the new owners tsk-tsked at the dark spot on the floor of their garage. As she brought prospective buyers through, the realtor said it was an oil stain, but it was me, seeping out of the bag Mr. Harvey carried and spilling onto the concrete. The beginning of my secret signals to the world.

It would be some time before I realized what you've undoubtedly already assumed, that I wasn't the first girl he'd killed. He knew to remove my body from the field. He knew to watch the weather and to kill during an arc of light-to-heavy precipitation because that would rob the police of evidence. But he was not as fastidious as the police liked to think. He forgot my elbow, he used a cloth sack for a bloody body, and if someone, anyone, had been watching, maybe they would have thought it strange to see their neighbor walk a property line that was a tight fit, even for children who liked to pretend the warring hedges were a hideout.

As he scoured his body in the hot water of his suburban bathroom — one with the identical layout to the one Lindsey, Buckley, and I shared — his movements were slow, not anxious. He felt a calm flood him. He kept the lights out in the bathroom and felt the warm water wash me away and he felt thoughts of me then. My muffled scream in his ear. My delicious death moan. The glorious white flesh that had never seen the sun, like an infant's, and then split, so perfectly, with the blade of his knife. He shivered under the heat, a prickling pleasure creating goose bumps up and down his arms and legs. He had put me in the waxy cloth sack and thrown in the shaving cream and razor from the mud ledge, his book of sonnets, and finally the bloody knife. They were tumbled together with my knees, fingers, and toes, but he made a note to extract them before my blood grew too sticky later that night. The sonnets and the knife, at least, he saved.

* * *

At Evensong, there were all sorts of dogs. And some of them, the ones I liked best, would lift their heads when they smelled an interesting scent in the air. If it was vivid enough, if they couldn't identify it immediately, or if, as the case may be, they knew exactly what it was — their brains going, "Um steak tartare" — they'd track it until they came to the object itself. In the face of the real article, the true story, they decided then what to do. That's how they operated. They didn't shut down their desire to know just because the smell was bad or the object was dangerous. They hunted. So did I.

Mr. Harvey took the waxy orange sack of my remains to a sinkhole eight miles from our neighborhood, an area that until recently had been desolate save for the railroad tracks and a nearby motorcycle repair shop. In his car he played a radio station that looped Christmas carols during the month of December. He whistled inside his huge station wagon and congratulated himself, felt full-up. Apple pie, cheeseburger, ice cream, coffee. Full. Better and better he was getting now, never using an old pattern that would bore him but making each kill a surprise to himself, a gift to himself.

The air inside the station wagon was cold and fragile. I could see the moist air when he exhaled, and this made me want to palpate my own stony lungs.

He drove the reed-thin road that cut between two new industrial lots. The wagon fishtailed coming up out of a particularly deep pothole, and the safe that held the sack that held my body smashed against the inside hub of the wagon's back wheel, cracking the plastic. "Damn," Mr.

Harvey said. But he picked up his whistling again without pause.

I had a memory of going down this road with my father at the wheel and Buckley sitting nestled against me — one seat belt serving the two of us — in an illegal joyride away from the house.

My father had asked if any of us kids wanted to watch a refrigerator disappear.

"The earth will swallow it!" he said. He put on his hat and the dark cordovan gloves I coveted. I knew gloves meant you were an adult and mittens meant you weren't. (For Christmas 1973, my mother had bought me a pair of gloves. Lindsey ended up with them, but she knew they were mine. She left them at the edge of the cornfield one day on her way home from school. She was always doing that — bringing me things.)

"The earth has a mouth?" Buckley asked.

"A big round mouth but with no lips," my father said.

"Jack," my mother said, laughing, "stop it. Do you know I caught him outside growling at the snapdragons?"

"I'll go," I said. My father had told me that there was an abandoned underground mine and it had collapsed to create a sinkhole. I didn't care; I liked to see the earth swallow something as much as the next kid.

So when I watched Mr. Harvey take me out to the sinkhole, I couldn't help but think how smart he was. How he put the bag in a metal safe, placing me in the middle of all that weight.

It was late when he got there, and he left the safe in his Wagoneer while he approached the house of the Flanagans, who lived on the property where the sinkhole was. The Flanagans made their living by charging people to dump their appliances.

Mr. Harvey knocked on the door of the small white house and a woman came to answer it. The scent of rosemary and lamb filled my heaven and hit Mr. Harvey's nose as it trailed out from the back of the house. He could see a man in the kitchen.

"Good evening, sir," Mrs. Flanagan said. "Got an item?"

"Back of my wagon," Mr. Harvey said. He was ready with a twenty-dollar bill.

"What you got in there, a dead body?" she joked.

It was the last thing on her mind. She lived in a warm if small house. She had a husband who was always home to fix things and to be sweet on her because he never had to work, and she had a son who was still young enough to think his mother was the only thing in the world.

Mr. Harvey smiled, and, as I watched his smile break across his face, I would not look away.

"Old safe of my father's, finally got it out here," he said. "Been meaning to do it for years. No one remembers the combination."

"Anything in it?" she asked.

"Stale air."

"Back her up then. You need any help?"

"That would be lovely," he said.

The Flanagans never suspected for a moment that the girl they read about in the papers over the next few years — MISSING, FOUL PLAY SUSPECTED; ELBOW FOUND BY NEIGHBORING DOG; GIRL, 14, BELIEVED KILLED IN STOLFUZ CORNFIELD; WARNINGS TO OTHER YOUNG WOMEN; TOWNSHIP TO REZONE ADJOINING LOTS TO HIGH SCHOOL; LINDSEY SALMON, SISTER OF DEAD GIRL, GIVES VALEDICTORIAN

SPEECH — could have been in the gray metal safe that a lonely man brought over one night and paid them twenty dollars to sink.

On the way back to the wagon Mr. Harvey put his hands in his pockets. There was my silver charm bracelet. He couldn't remember taking it off my wrist. Had no memory of thrusting it into the pocket of his clean pants. He fingered it, the fleshy pad of his index finger finding the smooth gold metal of the Pennsylvania keystone, the back of the ballet slipper, the tiny hole of the minuscule thimble, and the spokes of the bicycle with wheels that worked. Down Route 202, he pulled over on the shoulder, ate a liverwurst sandwich he'd prepared earlier that day, then drove to an industrial park they were building south of Downingtown. No one was on the construction lot. In those days there was no security in the suburbs. He parked his car near a Port-o-John. His excuse was prepared in the unlikely event that he needed one.

It was this part of the aftermath that I thought of when I thought of Mr. Harvey — how he wandered the muddy excavations and got lost among the dormant bulldozers, their monstrous bulk frightening in the dark. The sky of the earth was dark blue on the night following my death, and out in this open area Mr. Harvey could see for miles. I chose to stand with him, to see those miles ahead as he saw them. I wanted to go where he would go. The snow had stopped. There was wind. He walked into what his builder's instincts told him would soon be a false pond, and he stood there and fingered the charms one last time. He liked the Pennsylvania keystone, which my father had had engraved with my initials — my favorite was the tiny bike — and he pulled it off and placed it in his pocket. He threw the bracelet, with its remaining charms, into the soon-to-be man-made lake.

Two days before Christmas, I watched Mr. Harvey read a book on the Dogon and Bambara of Mali. I saw the bright spark of an idea when he was reading of the cloth and ropes they used to build shelters. He decided he wanted to build again, to experiment as he had with the hole, and he settled on a ceremonial tent like the ones described in his reading. He would gather the simple materials and raise it in a few hours in his backyard.

After smashing all the ships in bottles, my father found him there.

It was cold out, but Mr. Harvey wore only a thin cotton shirt. He had turned thirty-six that year and was experimenting with hard contacts. They made his eyes perpetually bloodshot, and many people, my father among them, believed he had taken to drink.

"What's this?" my father asked.

Despite the Salmon men's heart disease, my father was hardy. He was a bigger man than Mr. Harvey, so when he walked around the front of the green shingled house and into the backyard, where he saw Harvey erecting things that looked like goalposts, he seemed bluff and able. He was buzzing from having seen me in the shattered glass. I watched him cut through the lawn, ambling as school kids did on their way toward the high school. He stopped just short of brushing Mr. Harvey's elderberry hedge with his palm.

"What's this?" he asked again.

Mr. Harvey stopped long enough to look at him and then turned back to his work.

"A mat tent."

"What's that?"

"Mr. Salmon," he said, "I'm sorry for your loss."

Drawing himself up, my father gave back what the ritual demanded.

"Thank you." It was like a rock perched in his throat.

There was a moment of quiet, and then Mr. Harvey, sensing my father had no intention of leaving, asked him if he wanted to help.

So it was that, from heaven, I watched my father build a tent with the man who'd killed me.

My father did not learn much. He learned how to lash arch pieces onto pronged posts and to weave more slender rods through these pieces to form semiarches in the other direction. He learned to gather the ends of these rods and lash them to the crossbars. He learned he was doing this because Mr. Harvey had been reading about the Imezzureg tribe and had wanted to replicate their tents. He stood, confirmed in the neighborhood opinion that the man was odd. So far, that was all.

But when the basic structure was done — a one-hour job — Mr. Harvey went toward the house without giving a reason. My father assumed it was breaktime. That Mr. Harvey had gone in to get coffee or brew a pot of tea.

He was wrong. Mr. Harvey went into the house and up the stairs to check on the carving knife that he had put in his bedroom. It was still in the nightstand, on top of which he kept his sketch pad where, often, in the middle of the night, he drew the designs in his dreams. He looked inside a crumpled paper grocery sack. My blood on the blade had turned black. Remembering it, remembering his act in the hole, made him remember what he had read about a particular tribe in southern Ayr. How, when a tent was made for a newly married couple, the women of the tribe made the sheet that would cover it as beautiful as they could.

It had begun to snow outside. It was the first snow since my death, and this was not lost on my father.

"I can hear you, honey," he said to me, even though I wasn't talking. "What is it?"

I focused very hard on the dead geranium in his line of vision. I thought if I could make it bloom he would have his answer. In my heaven it bloomed. In my heaven geranium petals swirled in eddies up to my waist. On Earth nothing happened.

But through the snow I noticed this: my father was looking toward the green house in a new way. He had begun to wonder.

Inside, Mr. Harvey had donned a heavy flannel shirt, but what my father noticed first was what he carried in his arms: a stack of white cotton sheets.

"What are those for?" my father asked. Suddenly he could not stop seeing my face.

"Tarps," said Mr. Harvey. When he handed a stack to my father, the back of his hand touched my father's fingers. It was like an electric shock.

"You know something," my father said.

He met my father's eyes, held them, but did not speak.

They worked together, the snow falling, almost wafting, down. And as my father moved, his adrenaline raced. He checked what he knew. Had anyone asked this man where he was the day I disappeared? Had anyone seen this man in the cornfield? He knew his neighbors had been questioned. Methodically, the police had gone from door to door.

My father and Mr. Harvey spread the sheets over the domed arch, anchoring them along the square formed by the crossbars that linked the forked posts. Then they hung the remaining sheets straight down from these crossbars so that the bottoms of the sheets brushed the ground.

By the time they had finished, the snow sat gingerly on the covered arches. It filled in the hollows of my father's shirt and lay in a line across the top of his belt. I ached. I realized I would never rush out into the snow with Holiday again, would never push Lindsey on a sled, would never teach, against my better judgment, my little brother how to compact snow by shaping it against the base of his palm. I stood alone in a sea of bright petals. On Earth the snowflakes fell soft and blameless, a curtain descending.

Standing inside the tent, Mr. Harvey thought of how the virgin bride would be brought to a member of the Imezzureg on a camel. When my father made a move toward him, Mr. Harvey put his palm up.

"That's enough now," he said. "Why don't you go on home?"

The time had come for my father to think of something to say. But all he could think of was this: "Susie," he whispered, the second syllable whipped like a snake.

"We've just built a tent," Mr. Harvey said. "The neighbors saw us. We're friends now."

"You know something," my father said.

"Go home. I can't help you."

Mr. Harvey did not smile or step forward. He retreated into the bridal tent and let the final monogrammed white cotton sheet fall down.

FIVE

Part of me wished swift vengeance, wanted my father to turn into the man he could never have been — a man violent in rage. That's what you see in movies, that's what happens in the books people read. An everyman takes a gun or a knife and stalks the murderer of his family; he does a Bronson on them and everyone cheers.

What it *was* like:

Every day he got up. Before sleep wore off, he was who he used to be. Then, as his consciousness woke, it was as if poison seeped in. At first he couldn't even get up. He lay there under a heavy weight. But then only movement could save him, and he moved and he moved and he moved, no movement being enough to make up for it. The guilt on him, the hand of God pressing down on him, saying, *You were not there when your daughter needed you.*

* * *

Before my father left for Mr. Harvey's, my mother had been sitting in the front hall next to the statue they'd bought of St. Francis. She was gone when he came back. He'd called for her, said her name three times, said it like a wish that she would not appear, and then he ascended the steps to his den to jot things down in a small spiral notebook: "A drinker? Get him drunk. Maybe he's a talker." He wrote this next: "I think Susie watches me." I was ecstatic in heaven. I hugged Holly, I hugged Franny. My father knew, I thought.

Then Lindsey slammed the front door more loudly than usual, and my father was glad for the noise. He was afraid of going further in his notes, of writing the words down. The slamming door echoed down the strange afternoon he'd spent and brought him into the present, into activity, where he needed to be so he would not drown. I understood this — I'm not saying I didn't resent it, that it didn't remind me of sitting at the dinner table and having to listen to Lindsey tell my parents about the test she'd done so well on, or about how the history teacher was going to recommend her for the district honors council, but Lindsey was living, and the living deserved attention too.

She stomped up the stairs. Her clogs slammed against the pine boards of the staircase and shook the house.

I may have begrudged her my father's attention, but I respected her way of handling things. Of everyone in the family, it was Lindsey who had to deal with what Holly called the Walking Dead Syndrome — when other people see the dead person and don't see you.

When people looked at Lindsey, even my father and mother, they saw me. Even Lindsey was not immune. She avoided mirrors. She now took her showers in the dark.

She would leave the dark shower and feel her way over to the towel rack. She would be safe in the dark — the moist steam from the shower still rising off the tiles encased her. If the house was quiet or if she heard murmurs below her, she knew she would be undisturbed. This was when she could think of me and she did so in two ways: she either thought *Susie,* just that one word, and cried there, letting her tears roll down her already damp cheeks, knowing no one would see her, no one would quantify this dangerous substance as grief, or she would imagine me running, imagine me getting away, imagine herself being taken instead, fighting until she was free. She fought back the constant question, *Where is Susie now?*

My father listened to Lindsey in her room. Bang, the door was slammed shut. Thump, her books were thrown down. Squeak, she fell onto her bed. Her clogs, boom, boom, were kicked off onto the floor. A few minutes later he stood outside her door.

"Lindsey," he said upon knocking.

There was no answer.

"Lindsey, can I come in?"

"Go away," came her resolute answer.

"Come on now, honey," he pleaded.

"Go away!"

"Lindsey," my father said, sucking in his breath, "why can't you let me in?" He placed his forehead gently against the bedroom door. The wood felt cool and, for a second, he forgot the pounding of his temples, the suspicion he now held that kept repeating itself. *Harvey, Harvey, Harvey.*

In sock feet, Lindsey came silently to the door. She un-

locked it as my father drew back and prepared a face that
he hoped said "Don't run."

"What?" she said. Her face was rigid, an affront.
"What is it?"

"I want to know how you are," he said. He thought of the
curtain falling between him and Mr. Harvey, how a certain
capture, a lovely blame, was lost to him. He had his family
walking through the streets, going to school, passing, on
their way, Mr. Harvey's green-shingled house. To get the
blood back in his heart he needed his child.

"I want to be alone," Lindsey said. "Isn't that obvious?"

"I'm here if you need me," he said.

"Look, Dad," my sister said, making her one concession for him, "I'm handling this alone."

What could he do with that? He could have broken the
code and said, "I'm not, I can't, don't make me," but he
stood there for a second and then retreated. "I understand," he said first, although he didn't.

I wanted to lift him up, like statues I'd seen in art history books. A woman lifting up a man. The rescue in reverse. Daughter to father saying, "It's okay. You're okay.
Now I won't let anything hurt."

Instead, I watched him as he went to place a call to
Len Fenerman.

The police in those first weeks were almost reverent.
Missing dead girls were not a common occurrence in the
suburbs. But with no leads coming in on where my body
was or who had killed me, the police were getting nervous. There was a window of time during which physical
evidence was usually found; that window grew smaller
every day.

"I don't want to sound irrational, Detective Fenerman," my father said.

"Len, please." Tucked in the corner of his desk blotter was the school picture Len Fenerman had taken from my mother. He had known, before anyone said the words, that I was already dead.

"I'm certain there's a man in the neighborhood who knows something," my father said. He was staring out the window of his upstairs den, toward the cornfield. The man who owned it had told the press he was going to let it sit fallow for now.

"Who is it, and what led you to believe this?" Len Fenerman asked. He chose a stubby, chewed pencil from the front metal lip of his desk drawer.

My father told him about the tent, about how Mr. Harvey had told him to go home, about saying my name, about how weird the neighborhood thought Mr. Harvey was with no regular job and no kids.

"I'll check it out," Len Fenerman said, because he had to. That was the role he played in the dance. But what my father had given him offered him little or nothing to work with. "Don't talk to anyone and don't approach him again," Len warned.

When my father hung up the phone he felt strangely empty. Drained, he opened the door to his den and closed it quietly behind him. In the hallway, for the second time, he called my mother's name: "Abigail."

She was in the downstairs bathroom, sneaking bites from the macaroons my father's firm always sent us for Christmas. She ate them greedily; they were like suns bursting open in her mouth. The summer she was pregnant with me, she wore one gingham maternity dress over and over, refusing to spend money on another, and ate all she wanted, rubbing her belly and saying, "Thank you, baby," as she dribbled chocolate on her breasts.

There was a knock down low on the door.

"Momma?" She stuffed the macaroons back in the medicine cabinet, swallowing what was already in her mouth.

"Momma?" Buckley repeated. His voice was sleepy.

"Mommmmm-maaa!"

She despised the word.

When my mother opened the door, my little brother held on to her knees. Buckley pressed his face into the flesh above them.

Hearing movement, my father went to meet my mother in the kitchen. Together they took solace in attending to Buckley.

"Where's Susie?" Buckley asked as my father spread Fluffernutter on wheat bread. He made three. One for himself, one for my mother, and one for his four-year-old son.

"Did you put away your game?" my father asked Buckley, wondering why he persisted in avoiding the topic with the one person who approached it head-on.

"What's wrong with Mommy?" Buckley asked. Together they watched my mother, who was staring into the dry basin of the sink.

"How would you like to go to the zoo this week?" my father asked. He hated himself for it. Hated the bribe and the tease — the deceit. But how could he tell his son that, somewhere, his big sister might lie in pieces?

But Buckley heard the word *zoo* and all that it meant—which to him was largely *Monkeys!*—and he began on the rippling path to forgetting for one more day. The shadow of years was not as big on his small body. He knew I was away, but when people left they always came back.

When Len Fenerman had gone door to door in the neighborhood he had found nothing remarkable at George Harvey's. Mr. Harvey was a single man who, it was said, had meant to move in with his wife. She had died sometime before this. He built dollhouses for specialty stores and kept to himself. That was all anyone knew. Though friendships had not exactly blossomed around him, the sympathy of the neighborhood had always been with him. Each split-level contained a narrative. To Len Fenerman especially, George Harvey's seemed a compelling one.

No, Harvey said, he didn't know the Salmons well. Had seen the children. Everyone knew who had children and who didn't, he noted, his head hanging down and to the left a bit. "You can see the toys in the yard. The houses are always more lively," he noted, his voice halting.

"I understand you had a conversation with Mr. Salmon recently," Len said on his second trip to the dark green house.

"Yes, is there something wrong?" Mr. Harvey asked. He squinted at Len but then had to pause. "Let me get my glasses," he said. "I was doing some close work on a Second Empire."

"Second Empire?" Len asked.

"Now that my Christmas orders are done, I can experiment," Mr. Harvey said. Len followed him into the back, where a dining table was pushed against a wall. Dozens of small lengths of what looked like miniature wainscoting were lined up on top of it.

A little strange, Fenerman thought, *but it doesn't make the man a murderer.*

Mr. Harvey got his glasses and immediately opened up. "Yes, Mr. Salmon was on one of his walks and he helped me build the bridal tent."

"The bridal tent?"

"Each year it's something I do for Leah," he said. "My wife. I'm a widower."

Len felt he was intruding on this man's private rituals. "So I understand," he said.

"I feel terrible about what happened to that girl," Mr. Harvey said. "I tried to express that to Mr. Salmon. But I know from experience that nothing makes sense at a time like this."

"So you erect this tent every year?" Len Fenerman asked. This was something he could get confirmation on from neighbors.

"In the past, I've done it inside, but I tried to do it outside this year. We were married in the winter. Until the snow picked up, I thought it would work."

"Where inside?"

"The basement. I can show you if you want. I have all of Leah's things down there still."

But Len did not go further.

"I've intruded enough," he said. "I just wanted to sweep the neighborhood a second time."

"How's your investigation coming?" Mr. Harvey asked. "Are you finding anything?"

Len never liked questions like this, though he supposed they were the right of the people whose lives he was invading.

"Sometimes I think clues find their way in good time," he said. "If they want to be found, that is." It was cryptic, sort of a Confucius-says answer, but it worked on almost every civilian.

"Have you talked to the Ellis boy?" Mr. Harvey asked.

"We talked to the family."

"He's hurt some animals in the neighborhood, I hear."

"He sounds like a bad kid, I grant you," said Len, "but he was working in the mall at the time."

"Witnesses?"

"Yes."

"That's my only idea," Mr. Harvey said. "I wish I could do more."

Len felt him to be sincere.

"He's certainly a bit tweaked at an angle," Len said when he called my father, "but I have nothing on him."

"What did he say about the tent?"

"That he built it for Leah, his wife."

"I remember Mrs. Stead told Abigail his wife's name was Sophie," my father said.

Len checked his notes. "No, Leah. I wrote it down."

My father doubted himself. Where had he gotten the name Sophie? He was sure he had heard it too, but that was years ago, at a block party, where the names of children and wives flew about like confetti between the stories people told to be neighborly and the introductions to infants and strangers too vague to remember the following day.

He did remember that Mr. Harvey had not come to the block party. He had never come to any of them. This went to his strangeness by the standards of many in the neighborhood but not by my father's own standards. He had never felt completely comfortable at these forced efforts of conviviality himself.

My father wrote "Leah?" in his book. Then he wrote, "Sophie?" Though unaware of it, he had begun a list of the dead.

On Christmas Day, my family would have been more comfortable in heaven. Christmas was largely ignored in my heaven. Some people dressed all in white and pretended they were snowflakes, but other than that, nothing.

That Christmas, Samuel Heckler came to our house on an unexpected visit. He was not dressed like a snowflake. He wore his older brother's leather jacket and a pair of ill-fitting army fatigues.

My brother was in the front room with his toys. My mother blessed the fact that she had gone early to buy his gifts. Lindsey got gloves and cherry-flavored lip gloss. My father got five white handkerchiefs that she'd ordered months ago in the mail. Save Buckley, no one wanted anything anyway. In the days before Christmas the lights on the tree were not plugged in. Only the candle that my father kept in the window of his den burned. He lit it after dark, but my mother, sister, and brother had stopped leaving the house after four o'clock. Only I saw it.

"There's a man outside!" my brother shouted. He'd been playing Skyscraper and it had yet to collapse. "He's got a suitcase."

My mother left her eggnog in the kitchen and came to the front of the house. Lindsey was suffering the mandatory presence in the family room that all holidays required. She and my father played Monopoly, ignoring the more brutal squares for each other's sake. There was no Luxury Tax, and a bad Chance wasn't recognized.

In the front hall my mother pressed her hands down along her skirt. She placed Buckley in front of her and put her arms on his shoulders.

"Wait for the man to knock," she said.

"Maybe it's Reverend Strick," my father said to Lindsey, collecting his fifteen dollars for winning second prize in a beauty contest.

"For Susie's sake, I hope not," Lindsey ventured.

My father held on to it, on to my sister saying my name. She rolled doubles and moved to Marvin Gardens.

"That's twenty-four dollars," my father said, "but I'll take ten."

"Lindsey," my mother called. "It's a visitor for you."

My father watched my sister get up and leave the room. We both did. I sat with my father then. I was the ghost on the board. He stared at the old shoe lying on its side in the box. If only I could have lifted it up, made it hop from Boardwalk to Baltic, where I always claimed the better people lived. "That's because you're a purple freak," Lindsey would say. My father would say, "I'm proud I didn't raise a snob."

"Railroads, Susie," he said. "You always liked owning those railroads."

To accentuate his widow's peak and tame his cowlick, Samuel Heckler insisted on combing his hair straight back. This made him look, at thirteen and dressed in black leather, like an adolescent vampire.

"Merry Christmas, Lindsey," he said to my sister, and held out a small box wrapped in blue paper.

I could see it happen: Lindsey's body began to knot. She was working hard keeping everyone out, everyone, but she found Samuel Heckler cute. Her heart, like an ingredient in a recipe, was reduced, and regardless of my death she was thirteen, he was cute, and he had visited her on Christmas Day.

"I heard you made gifted," he said to her, because no one was talking. "Me too."

My mother remembered then, and she switched on her autopilot hostess. "Would you like to come sit?" she managed. "I have some eggnog in the kitchen."

"That would be wonderful," Samuel Heckler said and, to Lindsey's amazement and mine, offered my sister his arm.

"What's that?" asked Buckley, trailing behind and pointing to what he thought was a suitcase.

"An alto," Samuel Heckler said.

"What?" asked Buckley.

Lindsey spoke then. "Samuel plays the alto saxophone."

"Barely," Samuel said.

My brother did not ask what a saxophone was. He knew what Lindsey was being. She was being what I called snooty-wooty, as in "Buckley, don't worry, Lindsey's being snooty-wooty." Usually I'd tickle him as I said the word, sometimes burrowing into his stomach with my head, butting him and saying "snooty-wooty" over and over until his trills of laughter flowed down over me.

Buckley followed the three of them into the kitchen and asked, as he had at least once a day, "Where's Susie?"

They were silent. Samuel looked at Lindsey.

"Buckley," my father called from the adjoining room, "come play Monopoly with me."

My brother had never been invited to play Monopoly. Everyone said he was too young, but this was the magic of Christmas. He rushed into the family room, and my father picked him up and sat him on his lap.

"See this shoe?" my father said.

Buckley nodded his head.

"I want you to listen to everything I say about it, okay?"

"Susie?" my brother asked, somehow connecting the two.

"Yes, I'm going to tell you where Susie is."

I began to cry up in heaven. What else was there for me to do?

"This shoe was the piece Susie played Monopoly with," he said. "I play with the car or sometimes the wheelbarrow. Lindsey plays with the iron, and when your mother plays, she likes the cannon."

"Is that a dog?"

"Yes, that's a Scottie."

"Mine!"

"Okay," my father said. He was patient. He had found a way to explain it. He held his son in his lap, and as he spoke, he felt Buckley's small body on his knee — the very human, very warm, very alive weight of it. It comforted him. "The Scottie will be your piece from now on. Which piece is Susie's again?"

"The shoe," Buckley said.

"Right, and I'm the car, your sister's the iron, and your mother is the cannon."

My brother concentrated very hard.

"Now let's put all the pieces on the board, okay? You go ahead and do it for me."

Buckley grabbed a fist of pieces and then another, until all the pieces lay between the Chance and Community Chest cards.

"Let's say the other pieces are our friends."

"Like Nate?"

"Right, we'll make your friend Nate the hat. And the board is the world. Now if I were to tell you that when I rolled the dice, one of the pieces would be taken away, what would that mean?"

"They can't play anymore?"

"Right."

"Why?" Buckley asked.

He looked up at my father; my father flinched.

"Why?" my brother asked again.

My father did not want to say "because life is unfair" or "because that's how it is." He wanted something neat, something that could explain death to a four-year-old. He placed his hand on the small of Buckley's back.

"Susie is dead," he said now, unable to make it fit in the rules of any game. "Do you know what that means?"

Buckley reached over with his hand and covered the shoe. He looked up to see if his answer was right.

My father nodded. "You won't see Susie anymore, honey. None of us will." My father cried. Buckley looked up into the eyes of our father and did not fully understand.

Buckley kept the shoe on his dresser, until one day it wasn't there anymore and no amount of looking for it could turn it up.

In the kitchen my mother finished her eggnog and excused herself. She went into the dining room and counted silverware, methodically laying out the three kinds of forks, the knives, and the spoons, making them "climb the stairs" as she'd been taught when she worked in Wanamaker's bridal shop before I was born. She wanted a cigarette and for her children who were living to disappear for a little while.

"Are you going to open your gift?" Samuel Heckler asked my sister.

They stood at the counter, leaning against the dishwasher and the drawers that held napkins and towels. In the room to their right sat my father and brother; on the other side of the kitchen, my mother was thinking Wedgwood Florentine, Cobalt Blue; Royal Worcester, Mountbatten; Lenox, Eternal.

Lindsey smiled and pulled at the white ribbon on top of the box.

"My mom did the ribbon for me," Samuel Heckler said.

She tore the blue paper away from the black velvet box. Carefully she held it in her palm once the paper was off. In heaven I was excited. When Lindsey and I played Barbies, Barbie and Ken got married at sixteen. To us there was only one true love in everyone's life; we had no concept of compromise, or retries.

"Open it," Samuel Heckler said.

"I'm scared."

"Don't be."

He put his hand on her forearm and—Wow!—what I felt when he did that. Lindsey had a cute boy in the kitchen, vampire or no! This was news, this was a bulletin—I was suddenly privy to everything. She never would have told me any of this stuff.

What the box held was typical or disappointing or miraculous depending on the eye. It was typical because he was a thirteen-year-old boy, or it was disappointing because it was not a wedding ring, or it was miraculous. He'd given her a half a heart. It was gold and from inside his Hukapoo shirt, he pulled out the other side. It hung around his neck on a rawhide cord.

Lindsey's face flushed; mine flushed up in heaven.

I forgot my father in the family room and my mother counting silver. I saw Lindsey move toward Samuel Heckler. She kissed him; it was glorious. I was almost alive again.

SIX

Two weeks before my death, I left the house later than usual, and by the time I reached the school, the blacktop circle where the school buses usually hovered was empty.

A hall monitor from the discipline office would write down your name if you tried to get in the front doors after the first bell rang, and I didn't want to be paged during class to come and sit on the hard bench outside Mr. Peterford's room, where, it was widely known, he would bend you over and paddle your behind with a board. He'd asked the shop teacher to drill holes into it for less wind resistance on the downstroke and more pain when it landed against your jeans.

I had never been late enough or done anything bad enough to meet the board, but in my mind as in every other kid's I could visualize it so well my butt would sting. Clarissa had told me that the baby stoners, as they were called in junior high, used the back door to the stage, which was always left open by Cleo, the janitor, who had dropped out of high school as a full-blown stoner.

So that day I crept into the backstage area, watching my step, careful not to trip over the various cords and wires. I paused near some scaffolding and put down my book bag to brush my hair. I'd taken to leaving the house in the jingle-bell cap and then switching, as soon as I gained cover behind the O'Dwyers' house, to an old black watch cap of my father's. All this left my hair full of static electricity, and my first stop was usually the girls' room, where I would brush it flat.

"You are beautiful, Susie Salmon."

I heard the voice but could not place it immediately. I looked around me.

"Here," the voice said.

I looked up and saw the head and torso of Ray Singh leaning out over the top of the scaffold above me.

"Hello," he said.

I knew Ray Singh had a crush on me. He had moved from England the year before but Clarissa said he was born in India. That someone could have the face of one country and the voice of another and then move to a third was too incredible for me to fathom. It made him immediately cool. Plus, he seemed eight hundred times smarter than the rest of us, and he had a crush on me. What I finally realized were affectations — the smoking jacket that he sometimes wore to school and his foreign cigarettes, which were actually his mother's — I thought were evidence of his higher breeding. He knew and saw things that the rest of us didn't see. That morning when he spoke to me from above, my heart plunged to the floor.

"Hasn't the first bell rung?" I asked.

"I have Mr. Morton for homeroom," he said. This explained everything. Mr. Morton had a perpetual hangover, which was at its peak during homeroom. He never called roll.

"What are you doing up there?"

"Climb up and see," he said, removing his head and shoulders from my view.

I hesitated.

"Come on, Susie."

It was my one day in life of being a bad kid — of at least feigning the moves. I placed my foot on the bottom rung of the scaffold and reached my arms up to the first crossbar.

"Bring your stuff," Ray advised.

I went back for my book bag and then climbed unsteadily up.

"Let me help you," he said and put his hands under my armpits, which, even though covered by my winter parka, I was self-conscious about. I sat for a moment with my feet dangling over the side.

"Tuck them in," he said. "That way no one will see us."

I did what he told me, and then I stared at him for a moment. I felt suddenly stupid — unsure of why I was there.

"Will you stay up here all day?" I asked.

"Just until English class is over."

"You're cutting English!" It was as if he said he'd robbed a bank.

"I've seen every Shakespeare play put on by the Royal

Shakespeare Company," Ray said. "That bitch has nothing to teach me."

I felt sorry for Mrs. Dewitt then. If part of being bad was calling Mrs. Dewitt a bitch, I wasn't into it.

"I like *Othello*," I ventured.

"It's condescending twaddle the way she teaches it. A sort of *Black Like Me* version of the Moor."

Ray was smart. This combined with being an Indian from England had made him a Martian in Norristown.

"That guy in the movie looked pretty stupid with black makeup on," I said.

"You mean Sir Laurence Olivier."

Ray and I were quiet. Quiet enough to hear the bell for the end of homeroom ring and then, five minutes later, the bell that meant we should be on the first floor in Mrs. Dewitt's class. As each second passed after that bell, I could feel my skin heat up and Ray's look lengthen out over my body, taking in my royal blue parka and my kelly green miniskirt with my matching Danskin tights. My real shoes sat beside me inside my bag. On my feet I had a pair of fake sheepskin boots with dirty synthetic shearing spilling out like animal innards around the tops and seams. If I had known this was to be the sex scene of my life, I might have prepared a bit, reapplied my Strawberry-Banana Kissing Potion as I came in the door.

I could feel Ray's body leaning toward me, the scaffolding underneath us squeaking from his movement. *He is from England,* I was thinking. His lips moved closer, the scaffold listed. I was dizzy — about to go under the wave of my first kiss, when we both heard something. We froze.

Ray and I lay down side by side and stared at the lights

and wires overhead. A moment later, the stage door opened and in walked Mr. Peterford and the art teacher, Miss Ryan, who we recognized by their voices. There was a third person with them.

"We are not taking disciplinary action at this time, but we will if you persist," Mr. Peterford was saying. "Miss Ryan, did you bring the materials?"

"Yes." Miss Ryan had come to Kennet from a Catholic school and taken over the art department from two ex-hippies who had been fired when the kiln exploded. Our art classes had gone from wild experiments with molten metals and throwing clay to day after day of drawing profiles of wooden figures she placed in stiff positions at the beginning of each class.

"I'm only doing the assignments." It was Ruth Connors. I recognized the voice and so did Ray. We all had Mrs. Dewitt's English class first period.

"This," Mr. Peterford said, "was not the assignment."

Ray reached for my hand and squeezed. We knew what they were talking about. A xeroxed copy of one of Ruth's drawings had been passed around in the library until it had reached a boy at the card catalog who was overtaken by the librarian.

"If I'm not mistaken," said Miss Ryan, "there are no breasts on our anatomy model."

The drawing had been of a woman reclining with her legs crossed. And it was no wooden figure with eyehooks connecting the limbs. It was a real woman, and the charcoal smudges of her eyes — whether by accident or intent — had given her a leering look that made every kid who saw it either highly uncomfortable or quite happy, thank you.

"There isn't a nose or mouth on that wooden model either," Ruth said, "but you encouraged us to draw in faces."

Again Ray squeezed my hand.

"That's enough, young lady," Mr. Peterford said. "It is the attitude of repose in this particular drawing that clearly made it something the Nelson boy would xerox."

"Is that my fault?"

"Without the drawing there would be no problem."

"So it's my fault?"

"I invite you to realize the position this puts the school in and to assist us by drawing what Miss Ryan instructs the class to draw without making unnecessary additions."

"Leonardo da Vinci drew cadavers," Ruth said softly.

"Understood?"

"Yes," said Ruth.

The stage doors opened and shut, and a moment later Ray and I could hear Ruth Connors crying. Ray mouthed the word *go,* and I moved to the end of the scaffold, dangling my foot over the side to find a hold.

That week Ray would kiss me by my locker. It didn't happen up on the scaffold when he'd wanted it to. Our only kiss was like an accident — a beautiful gasoline rainbow.

I climbed down off the scaffold with my back to her. She didn't move or hide, just looked at me when I turned around. She was sitting on a wooden crate near the back of the stage. A pair of old curtains hung to her left. She watched me walk toward her but didn't wipe her eyes.

"Susie Salmon," she said, just to confirm it. The possibility of my cutting first period and hiding backstage in the auditorium was, until that day, as remote as the smartest girl in our class being bawled out by the discipline officer.

I stood in front of her, hat in hand.

"That's a stupid hat," she said.

I lifted the jingle-bell cap and looked at it. "I know. My mom made it."

"So you heard?"

"Can I see?"

Ruth unfolded the much-handled xerox and I stared.

Using a blue ballpoint pen, Brian Nelson had made an obscene hole where her legs were crossed. I recoiled and she watched me. I could see something flicker in her eyes, a private wondering, and then she leaned over and brought out a black leather sketchbook from her knapsack.

Inside, it was beautiful. Drawings of women mostly, but of animals and men too. I'd never seen anything like it before. Each page was covered in her drawings. I realized how subversive Ruth was then, not because she drew pictures of nude women that got misused by her peers, but because she was more talented than her teachers. She was the quietest kind of rebel. Helpless, really.

"You're really good, Ruth," I said.

"Thank you," she said, and I kept looking through the pages of her book and drinking it in. I was both frightened and excited by what existed underneath the black line of the navel in those drawings — what my mother called the "baby-making machinery."

I told Lindsey I'd never have one, and when I was ten I'd spent the better part of six months telling any adult who would listen that I intended on getting my tubes tied. I didn't know what this meant, exactly, but I knew it was drastic, required surgery, and it made my father laugh out loud.

Ruth went from weird to special for me then. The drawings were so good that in that moment I forgot the rules of school, all the bells and whistles, which as kids we were supposed to respond to.

After the cornfield was roped off, searched, then abandoned, Ruth went walking there. She would wrap a large wool shawl of her grandmother's around her under the ratty old peacoat of her father's. Soon she noted that teachers in subjects besides gym didn't report her if she cut. They were happy not to have her there: her intelligence made her a problem. It demanded attention and rushed their lesson plans forward.

And she began to take rides from her father in the mornings to avoid the bus. He left very early and brought his red metal, sloped-top lunchbox, which he had allowed her to pretend was a barn for her Barbies when she was little, and in which he now tucked bourbon. Before he let her out in the empty parking lot, he would stop his truck but keep the heater running.

"Going to be okay today?" he always asked.

Ruth nodded.

"One for the road?"

And without nodding this time she handed him the lunchbox. He opened it, unscrewed the bourbon, took a deep swallow, and then passed it to her. She threw her head back dramatically and either placed her tongue against the glass so very little would make it to her mouth, or took a small, wincing gulp if he was watching her.

She slid out of the high cab. It was cold, bitterly cold, before the sun rose. Then she remembered a fact from one of our classes: people moving are warmer than people at rest. So she began to walk directly to the cornfield, keeping a good pace. She talked to herself, and sometimes she thought about me. Often she would rest a moment against the chain-link fence that separated the soccer field from the track, while she watched the world come alive around her.

So we met each morning in those first few months. The sun would come up over the cornfield and Holiday, let loose by my father, would come to chase rabbits in and out of the tall dry stalks of dead corn. The rabbits loved the trimmed lawns of the athletic fields, and as Ruth approached she'd see their dark forms line up along the white chalk of the farthest boundaries like some sort of tiny sports team. She liked the idea of this and I did too. She believed stuffed animals moved at night when humans went to sleep. She still thought in her father's lunchbox there might be minute cows and sheep that found time to graze on the bourbon and baloney.

When Lindsey left the gloves from Christmas for me, in between the farthest boundary of the soccer field and the cornfield, I looked down one morning to see the rabbits investigate: sniff at the corners of the gloves lined with their own kin. Then I saw Ruth pick them up before Holiday grabbed them. She turned the bottom of one glove so the fur faced out and held it up to her cheek. She looked up to the sky and said, "Thank you." I liked to think she was talking to me.

I grew to love Ruth on those mornings, feeling that in some way we could never explain on our opposite sides of the Inbetween, we were born to keep each other company. Odd girls who had found each other in the strangest way — in the shiver she had felt when I passed.

Ray was a walker, like me, living at the far end of our development, which surrounded the school. He had seen Ruth Connors walking alone out on the soccer fields. Since Christmas he had come and gone to school as quickly as he could, never lingering. He wanted my killer to be caught almost as much as my parents did. Until he was, Ray could not wipe the traces of suspicion off himself, despite his alibi.

He chose a morning when his father was not going to work at the university and filled his father's thermos with his mother's sweet tea. He left early to wait for Ruth and made a little camp of the cement shot-put circle, sitting on the metal curve against which the shot-putters braced their feet.

When he saw her walking on the other side of the chain-link fence that separated the school from the soccer field and inside which was the most revered of the sports fields — the football one — he rubbed his hands together and prepared what he wanted to say. His bravery this time came not from having kissed me — a goal he'd set himself a full year before its completion — but from being, at fourteen, intensely lonely.

I watched Ruth approach the soccer field, thinking she was alone. In an old home her father had gone to scavenge, he had found her a treat to go along with her new hobby — an anthology of poems. She held them close.

She saw Ray stand up when she was still some distance away.

"Hello, Ruth Connors!" he called and waved his arms.

Ruth looked over, and his name came into her head: Ray Singh. But she didn't know much more than that. She had heard the rumors about the police being over at his house, but she believed what her father had said — "No kid did that" — and so she walked over to him.

"I prepared tea and have it in my thermos here," Ray said. I blushed for him up in heaven. He was smart when it came to *Othello,* but now he was acting like a geek.

"No thank you," Ruth said. She stood near him but with a definite few feet more than usual still in between. Her fingernails were pressed into the worn cover of the poetry anthology.

"I was there that day, when you and Susie talked backstage," Ray said. He held the thermos out to her. She made no move closer and didn't respond.

"Susie Salmon," he clarified.

"I know who you mean," she said.

"Are you going to the memorial service?"

"I didn't know there was one," she said.

"I don't think I'm going."

I was staring hard at his lips. They were redder than usual from the cold. Ruth took a step forward.

"Do you want some lip balm?" Ruth asked.

Ray lifted his wool gloves up to his lips, where they snagged briefly on the chapped surface that I had kissed. Ruth dug her hands in the peacoat pocket and pulled out her Chap Stick. "Here," she said, "I have tons of them. You can keep it."

"That's so nice," he said. "Will you at least sit with me until the buses come?"

They sat together on the shot-putters' cement platform. Again I was seeing something I never would have seen: the two of them together. It made Ray more attractive to me than he had ever been. His eyes were the darkest gray. When I watched him from heaven I did not hesitate to fall inside of them.

It became a ritual for the two of them. On the days that his father taught, Ruth brought him a little bourbon in her father's flask; otherwise they had sweet tea. They were cold as hell, but that didn't seem to matter to them.

They talked about what it was like to be a foreigner in Norristown. They read poems aloud from Ruth's anthology. They talked about how to become what they wanted to be. A doctor for Ray. A painter/poet for Ruth. They made a secret club of the other oddballs they could point out in our class. There were the obvious ones like Mike Bayles, who had taken so much acid no one understood how he was still in school, or Jeremiah, who was from Louisiana and so just as much a foreigner as Ray. Then there were the quiet ones. Artie, who talked excitedly to anyone about the effects of formaldehyde. Harry Orland, who was so painfully shy he wore his gym shorts over his jeans. And Vicki Kurtz, who everyone thought was okay after the death of her mother, but whom Ruth had seen sleeping in a bed of pine needles behind the junior high's regulating plant. And, sometimes, they would talk about me.

"It's so strange," Ruth said. "I mean, it's like we were in the same class since kindergarten but that day backstage in the auditorium was the first time we ever looked at each other."

"She was great," Ray said. He thought of our lips

brushing past one another as we stood alone in a column of lockers. How I had smiled with my eyes closed and then almost run away. "Do you think they'll find him?"

"I guess so. You know, we're only like one hundred yards away from where it happened."

"I know," he said.

They both sat on the thin metal rim of the shot-putters' brace, holding tea in their gloved hands. The cornfield had become a place no one went. When a ball strayed from the soccer field, a boy took a dare to go in and get it. That morning the sun was slicing right through the dead stalks as it rose, but there was no heat from it.

"I found these here," she said, indicating the leather gloves.

"Do you ever think about her?" he asked.

They were quiet again.

"All the time," Ruth said. A chill ran down my spine. "Sometimes I think she's lucky, you know. I hate this place."

"Me too," Ray said. "But I've lived other places. This is just a temporary hell, not a permanent one."

"You're not implying . . ."

"She's in heaven, if you believe in that stuff."

"You don't?"

"I don't think so, no."

"I do," Ruth said. "I don't mean la-la angel-wing crap, but I do think there's a heaven."

"Is she happy?"

"It *is* heaven, right?"

"But what does that mean?"

The tea was stone-cold and the first bell had already

rung. Ruth smiled into her cup. "Well, as my dad would say, it means she's out of this shithole."

When my father knocked on the door of Ray Singh's house, he was struck dumb by Ray's mother, Ruana. It was not that she was immediately welcoming, and she was far from sunny, but something about her dark hair, and her gray eyes, and even the strange way she seemed to step back from the door once she opened it, all of these things overwhelmed him.

He had heard the offhand comments the police made about her. To their mind she was cold and snobbish, condescending, odd. And so that was what he imagined he would find.

"Come in and sit," she'd said to him when he pronounced his name. Her eyes, on the word *Salmon*, had gone from closed to open doorways — dark rooms where he wanted to travel firsthand.

He almost lost his balance as she led him into the small cramped front room of their house. There were books on the floor with their spines facing up. They came out three rows deep from the wall. She was wearing a yellow sari and what looked like gold lamé capri pants underneath. Her feet were bare. She padded across the wall-to-wall and stopped at the couch. "Something to drink?" she asked, and he nodded his head.

"Hot or cold?"

"Hot."

As she turned the corner into a room he couldn't see, he sat down on the brown plaid couch. The windows across from him under which the books were lined were draped with long muslin curtains, which the harsh day-light outside had to fight to filter through. He felt suddenly very warm, almost close to forgetting why that morning he had double-checked the Singhs' address.

A little while later, as my father was thinking of how tired he was and how he had promised my mother to pick up some long-held dry cleaning, Mrs. Singh returned with tea on a tray and put it down on the carpet in front of him.

"We don't have much furniture, I'm afraid. Dr. Singh is still looking for tenure."

She went into an adjoining room and brought back a purple floor pillow for herself, which she placed on the floor to face him.

"Dr. Singh is a professor?" my father asked, though he knew this already, knew more than he was comfortable with about this beautiful woman and her sparsely furnished home.

"Yes," she said, and poured the tea. It was quiet. She held out a cup to him, and as he took it she said, "Ray was with him the day your daughter was killed."

He wanted to fall over into her.

"That must be why you've come," she continued.

"Yes," he said, "I want to talk to him."

"He's at school right now," she said. "You know that." Her legs in the gold pants were tucked to her side. The nails on her toes were long and unpolished, their surface gnarled from years of dancing.

"I wanted to come by and assure you I mean him no harm," my father said. I watched him. I had never seen him like this before. The words fell out of him like burdens he was delivering, backlogged verbs and nouns, but he was watching her feet curl against the dun-colored rug and the way the small pool of numbed light from the curtains touched her right cheek.

"He did nothing wrong and loved your little girl. A schoolboy crush, but still."

Schoolboy crushes happened all the time to Ray's mother. The teenager who delivered the paper would pause on his bike, hoping that she would be near the door when she heard the thump of the *Philadelphia Inquirer* hit the porch. That she would come out and, if she did, that she would wave. She didn't even have to smile, and she rarely did outside her house — it was the eyes, her dancer's carriage, the way she seemed to deliberate over the smallest movement of her body.

When the police had come they had stumbled into the dark front hall in search of a killer, but before Ray even reached the top of the stairs, Ruana had so confused them that they were agreeing to tea and sitting on silk pillows. They had expected her to fall into the grooves of the patter they relied on with all attractive women, but she only grew more erect in posture as they tried harder and harder to ingratiate themselves, and she stood upright by the windows while they questioned her son.

"I'm glad Susie had a nice boy like her," my father said. "I'll thank your son for that."

She smiled, not showing teeth.

"He wrote her a love note," he said.

"Yes."

"I wish I had known enough to do the same," he said. "Tell her I loved her on that last day."

"Yes."

"But your son did."

"Yes."

They stared at each other for a moment.

"You must have driven the policemen nuts," he said and smiled more to himself than to her.

"They came to accuse Ray," she said. "I wasn't concerned with how they felt about me."

"I imagine it's been hard for him," my father said.

"No, I won't allow that," she said sternly and placed her cup back on the tray. "You cannot have sympathy for Ray or for us."

My father tried to stutter out a protest.

She placed her hand in the air. "You have lost a daughter and come here for some purpose. I will allow you that and that only, but trying to understand our lives, no."

"I didn't mean to offend," he said. "I only . . ."

Again, the hand up.

"Ray will be home in twenty minutes. I will talk to him first and prepare him, then you may talk to my son about your daughter."

"What did I say?"

"I like that we don't have much furniture. It allows me to think that someday we might pack up and leave."

"I hope you'll stay," my father said. He said it because he had been trained to be polite from an early age, a training he passed on to me, but he also said it because part of him wanted more of her, this cold woman who was not exactly cold, this rock who was not stone.

"With all gentleness," she said, "you don't even know me. We'll wait together for Ray."

My father had left our house in the midst of a fight between Lindsey and my mother. My mother was trying to get Lindsey to go with her to the Y to swim. Without thinking, Lindsey had blared, "I'd rather die!" at the top of her lungs. My father watched as my mother froze, then burst, fleeing to their bedroom to wail behind the door. He quietly tucked his notebook in his jacket pocket, took the car keys off the hook by the back door, and snuck out.

In those first two months my mother and father moved in opposite directions from each other. One stayed in, the other went out. My father fell asleep in his den in the green chair, and when he woke he crept carefully into the bedroom and slid into bed. If my mother had most of the sheets he would lie without them, his body curled up tight, ready to spring at a moment's notice, ready for anything.

"I know who killed her," he heard himself say to Ruana Singh.

"Have you told the police?"

"Yes."

"What do they say?"

"They say that for now there is nothing but my suspicion to link him to the crime."

"A father's suspicion . . ." she began.

"Is as powerful as a mother's intuition."

This time there were teeth in her smile.

"He lives in the neighborhood."

"What are you doing?"

"I'm investigating all leads," my father said, knowing how it sounded as he said it.

"And my son . . ."

"Is a lead."

"Perhaps the other man frightens you too much."

"But I have to do something," he protested.

"Here we are again, Mr. Salmon," she said. "You misinterpret me. I am not saying you are doing the wrong thing by coming here. It is the right thing in its way. You want to find something soft, something warm in all this. Your searching led you here. That's a good thing. I am only concerned that it be good, too, for my son."

"I mean no harm."

"What is the man's name?"

"George Harvey." It was the first time he'd said it aloud to anyone but Len Fenerman.

She paused and stood. Turning her back to him, she walked over to first one window and then the other and drew the curtains back. It was the after-school light that she loved. She watched for Ray as he walked up the road.

"Ray will come now. I will go to meet him. If you'll excuse me I need to put on my coat and boots." She paused. "Mr. Salmon," she said, "I would do exactly what you are doing: I would talk to everyone I needed to, I would not tell too many people his name. When I was sure," she said, "I would find a quiet way, and I would kill him."

He could hear her in the hallway, the metal clank of hangers as she got her coat. A few minutes later the door was opened and closed. A cold breeze came in from the outside and then out on the road he could see a mother greet her son. Neither of them smiled. Their heads bent low. Their mouths moved. Ray took in the fact that my father was waiting for him inside his home.

At first my mother and I thought it was just the obvious that marked Len Fenerman as different from the rest of the force. He was smaller than the hulking uniforms who frequently accompanied him. Then there were the less obvious traits too — the way he often seemed to be thinking to himself, how he wasn't much for joking or trying to be anything but serious when he talked about me and the circumstances of the case. But, talking with my mother, Len Fenerman had shown himself for what he was: an optimist. He believed my killer would be caught.

"Maybe not today or tomorrow," he said to my mother, "but someday he'll do something uncontrollable. They are too uncontrolled in their habits not to."

My mother was left to entertain Len Fenerman until my father arrived home from the Singhs'. On the table in the family room Buckley's crayons were scattered across the butcher paper my mother had laid down. Buckley and Nate had drawn until their heads began to nod like heavy flowers, and my mother had plucked them up in her arms, first one and then the other, and brought them over to the couch. They slept there end to end with their feet almost touching in the center.

Len Fenerman knew enough to talk in hushed whispers, but he wasn't, my mother noted, a worshiper of children. He watched her carry the two boys but did not stand to help or comment on them the way the other policemen always did, defining her by her children, both living and dead.

"Jack wants to talk to you," my mother said. "But I'm sure you're too busy to wait."

"Not too busy."

I saw a black strand of her hair fall from where she had tucked it behind her ear. It softened her face. I saw Len see it too.

"He went over to that poor Ray Singh's house," she said and tucked the fallen hair back in its proper place.

"I'm sorry we had to question him," Len said.

"Yes," she said. "No young boy is capable of . . ." She couldn't say it, and he didn't make her.

"His alibi was airtight."

My mother took up a crayon from the butcher paper.

Len Fenerman watched my mother draw stick figures and stick dogs. Buckley and Nate made quiet sounds of sleep on the couch. My brother curled up into a fetal position and a moment later placed his thumb in his mouth to suck. It was a habit my mother had told us all we must help him break. Now she envied such easy peace.

"You remind me of my wife," Len said after a long silence, during which my mother had drawn an orange poodle and what looked like a blue horse undergoing electroshock treatment.

"She can't draw either?"

"She wasn't much of a talker when there was nothing to say."

A few more minutes passed. A yellow ball of sun. A brown house with flowers outside the door — pink, blue, purple.

"You used the past tense."

They both heard the garage door. "She died soon after we were married," he said.

"Daddy!" Buckley yelled, and leapt up, forgetting Nate and everyone else.

"I'm sorry," she said to Len.

"I am too," he said, "about Susie. Really."

In the back hall my father greeted Buckley and Nate with high cheers and calls for "Oxygen!" as he always did when we besieged him after a long day. Even if it felt false, elevating his mood for my brother was often the favorite part of his day.

My mother stared at Len Fenerman while my father walked toward the family room from the back. *Rush to the sink,* I felt like saying to her, stare down the hole and look into the earth. I'm down there waiting; I'm up here watching.

Len Fenerman had been the one that first asked my mother for my school picture when the police thought I might be found alive. In his wallet, my photo sat in a stack. Among these dead children and strangers was a picture of his wife. If a case had been solved he had written the date of its resolution on the back of the photo. If the case was still open — in his mind if not in the official files of the police — it was blank. There was nothing on the back of mine. There was nothing on his wife's.

"Len, how are you?" my father asked. Holiday up and wiggling back and forth for my father to pet him.

"I hear you went to see Ray Singh," Len said.

"Boys, why don't you go play up in Buckley's room?" my mother suggested. "Detective Fenerman and Daddy need to talk."

SEVEN

D o you see her?" Buckley asked Nate as they climbed the stairs, Holiday in tow. "That's my sister."

"No," Nate said.

"She was gone for a while, but now she's back. Race!"

And the three of them — two boys and a dog — raced the rest of the way up the long curve of the staircase.

I had never even let myself yearn for Buckley, afraid he might see my image in a mirror or a bottle cap. Like everyone else I was trying to protect him. "Too young," I said to Franny. "Where do you think imaginary friends come from?" she said.

For a few minutes the two boys sat under the framed grave rubbing outside my parents' room. It was from a tomb in a London graveyard. My mother had told Lindsey and me the story of how my father and she had wanted things to hang on their walls and an old woman they met on their honeymoon had taught them how to do grave rubbings. By the time I was in double digits most of the grave rubbings had been put down in the basement for storage, the spots on our suburban walls replaced with bright graphic prints meant to stimulate children. But Lindsey and I loved the grave rubbings, particularly the one under which Nate and Buckley sat that afternoon.

Lindsey and I would lie down on the floor underneath it. I would pretend to be the knight that was pictured, and Holiday was the faithful dog curled up at his feet. Lindsey would be the wife he'd left behind. It always dissolved into giggles no matter how solemn the start. Lindsey would tell the dead knight that a wife had to move on, that she couldn't be trapped for the rest of her life by a man who was frozen in time. I would act stormy and mad, but it never lasted. Eventually she would describe her new lover: the fat butcher who gave her prime cuts of meat, the agile blacksmith who made her hooks. "You are dead, knight," she would say. "Time to move on."

"Last night she came in and kissed me on the cheek," Buckley said.

"Did not."

"Did too."

"Really?"

"Yeah."

"Have you told your mom?"

"It's a secret," Buckley said. "Susie told me she isn't ready to talk to them yet. Do you want to see something else?"

"Sure," said Nate.

The two of them stood up to go to the children's side of the house, leaving Holiday asleep under the grave rubbing.

"Come look," Buckley said.

They were in my room. The picture of my mother had been taken by Lindsey. After reconsideration, she had come back for the "Hippy-Dippy Says Love" button too.

"Susie's room," Nate said.

Buckley put his fingers to his lips. He'd seen my mother do this when she wanted us to be quiet, and now he wanted that from Nate. He got down on his belly and gestured for Nate to follow, and they wriggled like Holiday as they made their way beneath the dust ruffle of my bed into my secret storage space.

In the material that was stretched on the underside of the box spring, there was a hole, and stuffed up inside were things I didn't want anyone else to see. I had to guard it from Holiday or he would scratch at it to try and pry the objects loose. This had been exactly what happened twenty-four hours after I went missing. My parents had searched my room hoping to find a note of explanation and then left the door open. Holiday had carried off the licorice I kept there. Strewn beneath my bed were the objects I'd kept hidden, and one of them only Buckley and Nate would recognize. Buckley unwrapped an old handkerchief of my father's and there it was, the stained and bloody twig.

The year before, a three-year-old Buckley had swallowed it. Nate and he had been shoving rocks up their noses in our backyard, and Buckley had found a small twig under the oak tree where my mother strung one end of the clothesline. He put the stick in his mouth like a cigarette. I watched him from the roof outside my bedroom window, where I was sitting painting my toenails with Clarissa's Magenta Glitter and reading *Seventeen*.

I was perpetually assigned the job of watching out for little brother. Lindsey was not thought to be old enough. Besides, she was a burgeoning brain, which meant she got to be free to do things like spend that summer afternoon drawing detailed pictures of a fly's eye on graph paper with her 130-pack of Prisma Colors.

It was not too hot out and it was summer, and I was going to spend my internment at home beautifying. I had begun the morning by showering, shampooing, and steaming myself. On the roof I air-dried and applied lacquer.

I had on two coats of Magenta Glitter when a fly landed on the bottle's applicator. I heard Nate making dare and threat sounds, and I squinted at the fly to try to make out all the quadrants of his eyes that Lindsey was coloring inside the house. A breeze came up, blowing the fringe on my cutoffs against my thighs.

"Susie, Susie!" Nate was yelling.

I looked down to see Buckley on the ground.

It was this day that I always told Holly about when we talked about rescue. I believed it was possible; she did not.

I swung my legs around and scrambled through my open window, one foot landing on the sewing stool and the other immediately in front of that one and on the braided rug and then down on my knees and out of the blocks like an athlete. I ran down the hall and slid down the banister as we'd been forbidden to do. I called Lindsey's name and then forgot her, ran out to the backyard through the screened-in porch, and jumped over the dog fence to the oak tree.

Buckley was choking, his body bucking, and I carried

him with Nate trailing into the garage, where my father's precious Mustang sat. I had watched my parents drive, and my mother had shown me how a car went from park to reverse. I put Buckley in the back and grabbed the keys from the unused terra-cotta pots where my father hid them. I sped all the way to the hospital. I burned out the emergency brake, but no one seemed to care.

"If she hadn't been there," the doctor later told my mother, "you would have lost your little boy."

Grandma Lynn predicted I'd have a long life because I had saved my brother's. As usual, Grandma Lynn was wrong.

"Wow," Nate said, holding the twig and marveling at how over time red blood turned black.

"Yeah," said Buckley. His stomach felt queasy with the memory of it. How much pain he had been in, how the faces of the adults changed as they surrounded him in the huge hospital bed. He had seen them that serious only one other time. But whereas in the hospital, their eyes had been worried and then later not, shot through with so much light and relief that they'd enveloped him, now our parents' eyes had gone flat and not returned.

I felt faint in heaven that day. I reeled back in the gazebo, and my eyes snapped open. It was dark, and across from me stood a large building that I had never been in.

I had read *James and the Giant Peach* when I was little. The building looked like the house of his aunts. Huge and dark and Victorian. It had a widow's walk. For a moment, as I readjusted to the darkness, I thought I saw a long row of women standing on the widow's walk and pointing my way. But a moment later, I saw differently. Crows were lined up, their beaks holding crooked twigs. As I stood to go back to the duplex, they took wing and followed me. Had my brother really seen me somehow, or was he merely a little boy telling beautiful lies?

EIGHT

For three months Mr. Harvey dreamed of buildings. He saw a slice of Yugoslavia where thatched-roofed dwellings on stilts gave way to rushing torrents of water from below. There were blue skies overhead. Along the fjords and in the hidden valleys of Norway, he saw wooden stave churches, the timbers of which had been carved by Viking boat-builders. Dragons and local heroes made from wood. But there was one building, from the Vologda, that he dreamed about most: the Church of the Transfiguration. And it was this dream — his favorite — that he had on the night of my murder and on the nights following until the others came back. The *not still* dreams — the ones of women and children.

I could see all the way back to Mr. Harvey in his mother's arms, staring out over a table covered with pieces of colored glass. His father sorted them into piles by shape and size, depth and weight. His father's jeweler's eyes looked deeply into each specimen for cracks and flaws. And George Harvey would turn his attention to the single jewel that hung from his mother's neck, a large oval piece of amber framed by silver, inside of which sat a whole and perfect fly.

"A builder" was all Mr. Harvey said when he was young. Then he stopped answering the question of what his father did. How could he say he worked in the desert, and that he built shacks of broken glass and old wood? He lectured George Harvey on what made a good building, on how to make sure you were constructing things to last.

So it was his father's old sketchbooks that Mr. Harvey looked at when the *not still* dreams came back. He would steep himself in the images of other places and other worlds, trying to love what he did not. And then he would begin to dream dreams of his mother the last time he had seen her, running through a field on the side of the road. She had been dressed in white. White capri pants and a tight white boat-neck shirt, and his father and she had fought for the last time in the hot car outside of Truth or Consequences, New Mexico. He had forced her out of the car. George Harvey sat still as stone in the back seat — eyes wide, no more afraid than a stone, watching it all as he did everything by then — in slow-mo. She had run without stopping, her white body thin and fragile and disappearing, while her son clung on to the amber necklace she had torn from her neck to hand him. His father had watched the road. "She's gone now, son," he said. "She won't be coming back."

NINE

My grandmother arrived on the evening before my memorial in her usual style. She liked to hire limousines and drive in from the airport sipping champagne while wearing what she called her "thick and fabulous animal" — a mink she had gotten secondhand at the church bazaar. My parents had not so much invited her as included her if she wanted to be there. In late January, Principal Caden had initiated the idea. "It will be good for your children and all the students at school," he had said. He took it upon himself to organize the event at our church. My parents were like sleepwalkers saying yes to his questions, nodding their heads to flowers or speakers. When my mother mentioned it on the phone to her mother, she was surprised to hear the words "I'm coming."

"But you don't have to, Mother."

There was a silence on my grandmother's end. "Abigail," she said, "this is Susan's funeral."

Grandma Lynn embarrassed my mother by insisting on wearing her used furs on walks around the block and by once attending a block party in high makeup. She would ask my mother questions until she knew who everyone was, whether or not my mother had seen the inside of their house, what the husband did for a living, what cars they drove. She made a solid catalog of the neighbors. It was a way, I now realized, to try to understand her daughter better. A miscalculated circling, a sad, partnerless dance.

"Jack-y," my grandmother said as she approached my parents on the front porch, "we need some stiff drinks!" She saw Lindsey then, trying to sneak up the stairs and gain a few more minutes before the required visitation. "Kid hates me," Grandma Lynn said. Her smile was frozen, her teeth perfect and white.

"Mother," my mother said. And I wanted to rush into those ocean eyes of loss. "I'm sure Lindsey is just going to make herself presentable."

"An impossibility in this house!" said my grandmother.

"Lynn," said my father, "this is a different house than last time you were here. I'll get you a drink, but I ask you to respect that."

"Still handsome as hell, Jack," my grandmother said.

My mother took my grandmother's coat. Holiday had been closed up in my father's den as soon as Buckley had yelled from his post at the upstairs window — "It's

Grandma!" My brother bragged to Nate or anyone who would listen that his grandmother had the biggest cars in the whole wide world.

"You look lovely, Mother," my mother said.

"Hmmmm." While my father was out of earshot, my grandmother said, "How is he?"

"We're all coping, but it's hard."

"Is he still muttering about that man having done it?"

"He still thinks so, yes."

"You'll be sued, you know," she said.

"He hasn't told anyone but the police."

What they couldn't see was that my sister was sitting above them on the top step.

"And he shouldn't. I realize he has to blame someone, but . . ."

"Lynn, 7 & 7 or a martini?" my father said, coming back out into the hallway.

"What are you having?"

"I'm not drinking these days, actually," my father said.

"Now there's your problem. I'll lead the way. No one has to tell me where the liquor is!"

Without her thick and fabulous animal, my grandmother was rail thin. "Starved down" was how she put it when she'd counseled me at age eleven. "You need to get yourself starved down, honey, before you keep fat on for too long. Baby fat is just another way to say ugly." She and my mother had fought about whether I was old enough for benzedrine — her own personal savior, she called it, as in, "I am offering your daughter my own personal savior and you deny her?"

When I was alive, everything my grandmother did was bad. But an odd thing happened when she arrived in her rented limo that day, opened up our house, and barged in. She was, in all her obnoxious finery, dragging the light back in.

"You need help, Abigail," my grandmother said after having eaten the first real meal my mother had cooked since my disappearance. My mother was stunned. She had donned her blue dishwashing gloves, filled the sink with sudsy water, and was preparing to do every dish. Lindsey would dry. Her mother, she assumed, would call upon Jack to pour her an after-dinner drink.

"Mother, that is so nice of you."

"Don't mention it," she said. "I'll just run out to the front hall and get my bag o' magic."

"Oh no," I heard my mother say under her breath.

"Ah, yes, the bag o' magic," said Lindsey, who had not spoken the whole meal.

"Please, Mother!" my mother protested when Grandma Lynn came back.

"Okay, kids, clear off the table and get your mother over here. I'm doing a makeover."

"Mother, that's crazy. I have all these dishes to do."

"Abigail," my father said.

"Oh no. She may get you to drink, but she's not getting those instruments of torture near me."

"I'm not drunk," he said.

"You're smiling," my mother said.

"So sue him," Grandma Lynn said. "Buckley, grab your mother's hand and drag her over here." My brother obliged. It was fun to see his mother be bossed and prodded.

"Grandma Lynn?" Lindsey asked shyly.

My mother was being led by Buckley to a kitchen chair my grandmother had turned to face her.

"What?"

"Could you teach me about makeup?"

"My God in heaven, praise the Lord, yes!"

My mother sat down and Buckley climbed up into her lap. "What's wrong, Mommy?"

"Are you laughing, Abbie?" My father smiled.

And she was. She was laughing and she was crying too.

"Susie was a good girl, honey," Grandma Lynn said. "Just like you." There was no pause. "Now lift up your chin and let me have a look at those bags under your eyes."

Buckley got down and moved onto a chair. "This is an eyelash curler, Lindsey," my grandmother instructed. "I taught your mother all of these things."

"Clarissa uses those," Lindsey said.

My grandmother set the rubber curler pads on either side of my mother's eyelashes, and my mother, knowing the ropes, looked upward.

"Have you talked to Clarissa?" my father asked.

"Not really," said Lindsey. "She's hanging out a lot with Brian Nelson. They cut class enough times to get a three-day suspension."

"I don't expect that of Clarissa," my father said. "She may not have been the brightest apple in the bunch, but she was never a troublemaker."

"When I ran into her she reeked of pot."

"I hope you're not getting into that," Grandma Lynn said. She finished the last of her 7 & 7 and slammed the highball glass down on the table. "Now, see this, Lindsey, see how when the lashes are curled it opens up your mother's eyes?"

Lindsey tried to imagine her own eyelashes, but instead saw the star-clumped lashes of Samuel Heckler as his face neared hers for a kiss. Her pupils dilated, pulsing in and out like small, ferocious olives.

"I stand amazed," Grandma Lynn said, and put her hands, one still twisted into the awkward handles of the eyelash curler, on her hips.

"What?"

"Lindsey Salmon, you have a boyfriend," my grandmother announced to the room.

My father smiled. He was liking Grandma Lynn suddenly. I was too.

"Do not," Lindsey said.

My grandmother was about to speak when my mother whispered, "Do too."

"Bless you, honey," my grandmother said, "you should have a boyfriend. As soon as I'm done with your mother, I'm giving you the grand Grandma Lynn treatment. Jack, make me an apéritif."

"An apéritif is something you . . ." my mother began.

"Don't correct me, Abigail."

My grandmother got sloshed. She made Lindsey look like a clown or, as Grandma Lynn said herself, "a grade-A 'tute." My father got what she called "finely drunkened." The most amazing thing was that my mother went to bed and left the dirty dishes in the sink.

While everyone else slept, Lindsey stood at the mirror in the bathroom, looking at herself. She wiped off some of the blush, blotted her lips, and ran her fingers over the swollen, freshly plucked parts of her formerly bushy eyebrows. In the mirror she saw something different and so did I: an adult who could take care of herself. Under the makeup was the face she'd always known as her own, until very recently, when it had become the face that reminded people of me. With lip pencil and eyeliner, she now saw, the edges of her features were delineated, and they sat on her face like gems imported from some far-off place where the colors were richer than the colors in our house had ever been. It was true what our grandmother said — the makeup brought out the blue of her eyes. The plucking of the eyebrows changed the shape of her face. The blush highlighted the hollows beneath her cheekbones ("The hollows that could stand some more hollowing," our grandmother pointed out). And her lips — she practiced her facial expressions. She pouted, she kissed, she smiled wide as if she too had had a cocktail, she looked down and pretended to pray like a good girl but cocked one eye up to see how she looked being good. She went to bed and slept on her back so as not to mess up her new face.

Mrs. Bethel Utemeyer was the only dead person my sister and I ever saw. She moved in with her son to our development when I was six and Lindsey five.

My mother said that she had lost part of her brain and that sometimes she left her son's house and didn't know where she was. She would often end up in our front yard, standing under the dogwood tree and looking out at the street as if waiting for a bus. My mother would sit her down in the kitchen and make tea for the two of them, and after she calmed her she would call her son's house to tell them where she was. Sometimes no one was home and Mrs. Utemeyer would sit at our kitchen table and stare into the centerpiece for hours. She would be there when we came home from school. Sitting. She smiled at us. Often she called Lindsey "Natalie" and reached out to touch her hair.

When she died, her son encouraged my mother to bring Lindsey and me to the funeral. "My mother seemed to have a special fondness for your children," he wrote.

"She didn't even know my name, Mom," Lindsey whined, as our mother buttoned up the infinite number of round buttons on Lindsey's dress coat. *Another impractical gift from Grandma Lynn,* my mother thought.

"At least she *called* you a name," I said.

It was after Easter, and a spring heat wave had set in that week. All but the most stubborn of that winter's snow had seeped into the earth, and in the graveyard of the Utemeyers' church snow clung to the base of the head-stones, while, nearby, buttercup shoots were making their way up.

The Utemeyers' church was fancy. "High Catholic," my father had said in the car. Lindsey and I thought this was very funny. My father hadn't wanted to come but my mother was so pregnant that she couldn't drive. For the last few months of her pregnancy with Buckley she was unable to fit behind the wheel. She was so uncomfortable most of the time that we avoided being near her for fear we'd be thrown into servitude.

But her pregnancy allowed her to get out of what Lindsey and I couldn't stop talking about for weeks and what I kept dreaming about for long after that: viewing the body. I could tell my father and mother didn't want this to happen, but Mr. Utemeyer made a beeline for the two of us when it was time to file past the casket. "Which one of you is the one she called Natalie?" he asked. We stared at him. I pointed to Lindsey.

"I'd like you to come say goodbye," he said. He smelled of a perfume sweeter than what my mother sometimes wore, and the sting of it in my nose, and my sense of exclusion, made me want to cry. "You can come too," he said to me, extending his hands so we would flank him in the aisle.

It wasn't Mrs. Utemeyer. It was something else. But it *was* Mrs. Utemeyer too. I tried to keep my eyes focused on the gleaming gold rings on her fingers.

"Mother," Mr. Utemeyer said, "I brought the little girl you called Natalie."

Lindsey and I both admitted later that we expected Mrs. Utemeyer to speak and that we had decided, individually, that if she did we were going to grab the other one and run like hell.

An excruciating second or two and it was over and we were released back to our mother and father.

I wasn't very surprised when I first saw Mrs. Bethel Utemeyer in my heaven, nor was I shocked when Holly and I found her walking hand in hand with a small blond girl she introduced as her daughter, Natalie.

The morning of my memorial Lindsey stayed in her room for as long as she could. She didn't want my mother to see the still-applied makeup until it would be too late to make her wash it off. She had also told herself it would be okay to take a dress from my closet. That I wouldn't mind.

But it was weird to watch.

She opened the door to my room, a vault that by February was being disturbed more and more, though no one, not my mother or father, nor Buckley or Lindsey, confessed to entering, nor to taking things that they didn't plan on returning. They were blind to the clues that each of them came and visited me there. Any disturbance, even if it could not possibly be blamed on Holiday, was blamed on him.

Lindsey wanted to look nice for Samuel. She opened the double doors to my closet and reviewed the mess. I hadn't been exactly orderly, so every time my mother told us to clean up, I'd shoved whatever was on the floor or bed into my closet.

Lindsey had always wanted the clothes I owned first-run but had gotten them all as hand-me-downs.

"Gosh," she said, whispering into the darkness of my closet. She realized with guilt and glee that everything she saw before her was hers now.

"Hello? Knock-knock," said Grandma Lynn.

Lindsey jumped.

"Sorry to disturb you, hon," she said. "I thought I heard you in here."

My grandmother stood in what my mother called one of her Jackie Kennedy dresses. She had never understood why unlike the rest of us her mother had no hips — she could slide into a straight-cut dress and fill it out just enough, even at sixty-two, to look perfect in it.

"What are you doing in here?" Lindsey asked.

"I need help with this zipper." Grandma Lynn turned, and Lindsey could see what she had never seen on our own mother. The back of Grandma Lynn's black bra, the top of her half-slip. She walked the step or two over to our grandmother and, trying not to touch anything but the zipper tab, zipped her up.

"How about that hook and eye up there," said Grandma Lynn. "Can you get that?"

There were powdery smells and Chanel No. 5 sprinkled all around our grandmother's neck.

"It's one of the reasons for a man — you can't do this stuff yourself."

Lindsey was as tall as our grandmother and still growing. As she took the hook and eye in either hand, she saw the fine wisps of dyed blond hair at the base of my grandmother's skull. She saw the downy gray hair trailing along her back and neck. She hooked the dress and then stood there.

"I've forgotten what she looked like," Lindsey said.

"What?" Grandma Lynn turned.

"I can't remember," Lindsey said. "I mean her neck, you know, did I ever look at it?"

"Oh honey," Grandma Lynn said, "come here." She opened up her arms, but Lindsey turned into the closet.

"I need to look pretty," she said.

"You are pretty," Grandma Lynn said.

Lindsey couldn't get her breath. One thing Grandma Lynn never did was dole out compliments. When they came, they were unexpected gold.

"We'll find you a nice outfit in here," Grandma Lynn said and strode toward my clothes. No one could shop a rack like Grandma Lynn. On the rare occasions that she visited near the start of the school year she would take the two of us out. We marveled at her as we watched her nimble fingers play the hangers like so many keys. Suddenly, hesitating only for a moment, she would pull out a dress or shirt and hold it up to us. "What do you think?" she'd ask. It was always perfect.

As she considered my separates, plucked and posed them against my sister's torso, she talked:

"Your mother's a wreck, Lindsey. I've never seen her like this before."

"Grandma."

"Hush, I'm thinking." She held up my favorite church dress. It was blackwatch wool with a Peter Pan collar. I liked it mostly because the skirt was so big I could sit in the pew cross-legged and flounce the hem down to the ground. "Where did she get *this* sack?" my grandmother asked. "Your dad, he's a mess too, but he's mad about it."

"Who was that man you asked Mom about?"

She stiffened on the question. "What man?"

"You asked Mom if Dad still was saying that *that* man did it. What man?"

"Voilà!" Grandma Lynn held up a dark blue minidress that my sister had never seen. It was Clarissa's.

"It's so short," Lindsey said.

"I'm shocked at your mother," Grandma Lynn said. "She let the kid get something stylish!"

My father called up from the hallway that he expected everyone downstairs in ten minutes.

Grandma Lynn went into preparation overdrive. She helped Lindsey get the dark blue dress over her head, and then they ran back to Lindsey's room for shoes, and then, finally, in the hallway, under the overhead light, she fixed the smudged eyeliner and mascara on my sister's face. She finished her off with firmly pressed powder, whisking the cotton pad lightly in an upward direction along either side of Lindsey's face. It wasn't until my grandmother came downstairs and my mother commented on the shortness of Lindsey's dress while looking suspiciously at Grandma Lynn that my sister and I realized Grandma Lynn didn't have a spot of makeup on her own face. Buckley rode between them in the back seat, and as they neared the church he looked at Grandma Lynn and asked what she was doing.

"When you don't have time for rouge, this puts a little life into them," she said, and so Buckley copied her and pinched his cheeks.

Samuel Heckler was standing by the stone posts that marked the path to the church door. He was dressed all in black, and beside him his older brother, Hal, stood wearing the beat-up leather jacket Samuel had worn on Christmas Day.

His brother was like a darker print of Samuel. He was tanned, and his face was weathered from riding his motorcycle full-tilt down country roads. As my family approached, Hal turned quickly and walked away.

"This must be Samuel," my grandmother said. "I'm the evil grandma."

"Shall we go in?" my father said. "It's nice to see you, Samuel."

Lindsey and Samuel led the way, while my grandmother dropped back and walked on the other side of my mother. A united front.

Detective Fenerman was standing by the doorway in an itchy-looking suit. He nodded at my parents and seemed to linger on my mother. "Will you join us?" my father asked.

"Thank you," he said, "but I just want to be in the vicinity."

"We appreciate that."

They walked into the cramped vestibule of our church. I wanted to snake up my father's back, circle his neck, whisper in his ear. But I was already there in his every pore and crevice.

He had woken up with a hangover and turned over on his side to watch my mother's shallow breathing against the pillow. His lovely wife, his lovely girl. He wanted to place his hand on her cheek, smooth her hair back from her face, kiss her — but sleeping, she was at peace. He hadn't woken a day since my death when the day wasn't something to get through. But the truth was, the memorial service day was not the worst kind. At least it was honest. At least it was a day shaped around what they were so preoccupied by: my absence. Today he would not have to pretend he was getting back to normal — whatever normal was. Today he could walk tall with grief and so could Abigail. But he knew that as soon as she woke up he would not really look at her for the rest of the day, not really look into her and see the woman he had known her to be before the day they had taken in the news of my death. At nearly two months, the idea of it as news was fading away in the hearts of all but my family — and Ruth.

She came with her father. They were standing in the corner near the glass case that held a chalice used during the Revolutionary War, when the church had been a hospital. Mr. and Mrs. Dewitt were making small talk with them. At home on her desk, Mrs. Dewitt had a poem of Ruth's. On Monday she was going to the guidance counselor with it. It was a poem about me.

"My wife seems to agree with Principal Caden," Ruth's father was saying, "that the memorial will help allow the kids to accept it."

"What do you think?" Mr. Dewitt asked.

"I think let bygones be bygones and leave the family to their own. But Ruthie wanted to come."

Ruth watched my family greet people and noted in horror my sister's new look. Ruth did not believe in makeup. She thought it demeaned women. Samuel Heckler was holding Lindsey's hand. A word from her readings popped into her head: *subjugation.* But then I saw her notice Hal Heckler through the window. He was standing out by the oldest graves in the front and pulling on a cigarette butt.

"Ruthie," her father asked, "what is it?"

She focused again and looked at him. "What's what?"

"You were staring off into space just now," he said.

"I like the way the graveyard looks."

"Ah kid, you're my angel," he said. "Let's grab a seat before the good ones get taken."

Clarissa was there, with a sheepish-looking Brian Nelson, who was wearing a suit of his father's. She made her way up to my family, and when Principal Caden and Mr. Botte saw her they fell away and let her approach.

She shook hands with my father first.

"Hello, Clarissa," he said. "How are you?"

"Okay," she said. "How are you and Mrs. Salmon?"

"We're fine, Clarissa," he said. *What an odd lie,* I thought. "Would you like to join us in the family pew?"

"Um" — she looked down at her hands — "I'm with my boyfriend."

My mother had entered some trancelike state and was

staring hard at Clarissa's face. Clarissa was alive and I was dead. Clarissa began to feel it, the eyes boring into her, and she wanted to get away. Then Clarissa saw the dress.

"Hey," she said, reaching out toward my sister.

"What is it, Clarissa?" my mother snapped.

"Um, nothing," she said. She looked at the dress again, knew she could never ask for it back now.

"Abigail?" my father said. He was attuned to her voice, her anger. Something was off.

Grandma Lynn, who stood just a bit behind my mother, winked at Clarissa.

"I was just noticing how good Lindsey looked," Clarissa said.

My sister blushed.

The people in the vestibule began to stir and part. It was the Reverend Strick, walking in his vestments toward my parents.

Clarissa faded back to look for Brian Nelson. When she found him, she joined him out among the graves.

Ray Singh stayed away. He said goodbye to me in his own way: by looking at a picture — my studio portrait — that I had given him that fall.

He looked into the eyes of that photograph and saw right through them to the backdrop of marbleized suede every kid had to sit in front of under a hot light. What did dead mean, Ray wondered. It meant lost, it meant frozen, it meant gone. He knew that no one ever really looked the way they did in photos. He knew he didn't look as wild or as frightened as he did in his own. He came to realize something as he stared at my photo — that it was not me.

I was in the air around him, I was in the cold mornings he had now with Ruth, I was in the quiet time he spent alone between studying. I was the girl he had chosen to kiss. He wanted, somehow, to set me free. He didn't want to burn my photo or toss it away, but he didn't want to look at me anymore, either. I watched him as he placed the photograph in one of the giant volumes of Indian poetry in which he and his mother had pressed dozens of fragile flowers that were slowly turning to dust.

At the service they said nice things about me. Reverend Strick. Principal Caden. Mrs. Dewitt. But my father and mother sat through it numbed. Samuel kept squeezing Lindsey's hand, but she didn't seem to notice him. She barely blinked. Buckley sat in a small suit borrowed for the occasion from Nate, who had attended a wedding that year. He fidgeted and watched my father. It was Grandma Lynn who did the most important thing that day.

During the final hymn, as my family stood, she leaned over to Lindsey and whispered, "By the door, that's him."

Lindsey looked over.

Standing just behind Len Fenerman, who was now inside the doorway and singing along, stood a man from the neighborhood. He was dressed more casually than anyone else, wearing flannel-lined khaki trousers and a heavy flannel shirt. For a moment Lindsey thought she recognized him. Their eyes locked. Then she passed out.

In all the commotion of attending to her, George Harvey slipped between the Revolutionary War gravestones behind the church and walked away without being noticed.

TEN

——

At the statewide Gifted Symposium each summer, the gifted kids from seventh to ninth grade would get together for a four-week retreat to, as I always thought of it, hang out in the trees and pick one another's brains. Around the campfire they sang oratorios instead of folk songs. In the girls' showers they would swoon over the physique of Jacques d'Amboise or the frontal lobe of John Kenneth Galbraith.

But even the gifted had their cliques. There were the Science Nerds and the Math Brains. They formed the superior, if somewhat socially crippled, highest rung of the gifted ladder. Then came the History Heads, who knew the birth and death dates of every historical figure anyone had ever heard of. They would pass by the other campers voicing cryptic, seemingly meaningless life spans: "1769 to 1821," "1770 to 1831." When Lindsey passed the

History Heads she would think the answers to herself. "Napoleon." "Hegel."

There were also the Masters of Arcane Knowledge. Everyone begrudged their presence among the gifteds. These were the kids that could break down an engine and build it back again — no diagrams or instructions needed. They understood things in a real, not theoretical, way. They seemed not to care about their grades.

Samuel was a Master. His heroes were Richard Feynman and his brother, Hal. Hal had dropped out of high school and now ran the bike shop near the sinkhole, where he serviced everyone from Hell's Angels to the elderly who rode motorized scooters around the parking lots of their retirement homes. Hal smoked, lived at home over the Hecklers' garage, and conducted a variety of romances in the back of his shop.

When people asked Hal when he was going to grow up, he said, "Never." Inspired by this, when the teachers asked Samuel what he wanted to be, he would say: "I don't know. I just turned fourteen."

Almost fifteen now, Ruth Connors knew. Out in the aluminum toolshed behind her house, surrounded by the doorknobs and hardware her father had found in old houses slated for demolition, Ruth sat in the darkness and concentrated until she came away with a headache. She would run into the house, past the living room, where her father sat reading, and up to her room, where in fits and bursts she would write her poetry. "Being Susie," "After Death," "In Pieces," "Beside Her Now," and her favorite — the one she was most proud of and carried with her to the symposium folded and refolded so often that the creases were close to cuts — "The Lip of the Grave."

Ruth had to be driven to the symposium because that morning, when the bus was leaving, she was still at home with an acute attack of gastritis. She was trying weird all-vegetable regimes and the night before had eaten a whole head of cabbage for dinner. Her mother refused to kow-tow to the vegetarianism Ruth had taken up after my death.

"This is not Susie, for Chrissakes!" her mother would say, plunking down an inch-thick sirloin in front of her daughter.

Her father drove her first to the hospital at three A.M. and then to the symposium, stopping home on the way to pick up the bag her mother had packed and left at the end of their driveway.

As the car pulled up into the camp, Ruth scanned the crowd of kids lining up for nametags. She spotted my sister among an all-male group of Masters. Lindsey had avoided putting her last name on her nametag, choosing to draw a fish instead. She wasn't exactly lying that way, but she hoped to meet a few kids from the surrounding schools who didn't know the story of my death or at least wouldn't connect her to it.

All spring she'd worn the half-a-heart pendant while Samuel wore the other half. They were shy about their af-fection for each other. They did not hold hands in the hallways at school, and they did not pass notes. They sat together at lunch; Samuel walked her home. On her four-teenth birthday he brought her a cupcake with a candle in it. Other than that, they melted into the gender-subdivided world of their peers.

* * *

The following morning Ruth was up early. Like Lindsey, Ruth was a floater at gifted camp. She didn't belong to any one group. She had gone on a nature walk and collected plants and flowers she needed help naming. When she didn't like the answers one of the Science Nerds provided, she decided to start naming the plants and flowers herself. She drew a picture of the leaf or blossom in her journal, and then what sex she thought it was, and then gave it a name like "Jim" for a simple-leaved plant and "Pasha" for a more downy flower.

By the time Lindsey stumbled into the dining hall, Ruth was in line for a second helping of eggs and sausage. She had made a big stink about no meat at home and she had to hold to it, but no one at the symposium knew of the oath she'd sworn.

Ruth hadn't talked to my sister since before my death, and then it was only to excuse herself in the hallway at school. But she'd seen Lindsey walking home with Samuel and seen her smile with him. She watched as my sister said yes to pancakes and no to everything else. She had tried to imagine herself being my sister as she had spent time imagining being me.

As Lindsey walked blindly to the next open spot in line, Ruth interceded. "What's the fish for?" Ruth asked, nodding her head toward my sister's nametag. "Are you religious?"

"Notice the direction of the fish," Lindsey said, wishing simultaneously that they had vanilla puddings at breakfast. They would go great with her pancakes.

"Ruth Connors, poet," Ruth said, by way of introduction.

"Lindsey," Lindsey said.

"Salmon, right?"

"Please don't," Lindsey said, and for a second Ruth

could feel the feeling a little more vividly—what it was like to claim me. How people looked at Lindsey and imagined a girl covered in blood.

Even among the gifteds, who distinguished themselves by doing things differently, people paired off within the first few days. It was mostly pairs of boys or pairs of girls—few serious relationships had begun by fourteen—but there was one exception that year. Lindsey and Samuel.

"K-I-S-S-I-N-G!" greeted them wherever they went. Unchaperoned, and with the heat of the summer, something grew in them like weeds. It was lust. I'd never felt it so purely or seen it move so hotly into someone I knew. Someone whose gene pool I shared.

They were careful and followed the rules. No counselor could say he had flashed a light under the denser shrubbery by the boys' dorm and found Salmon and Heckler going at it. They set up little meetings outside in back of the cafeteria or by a certain tree that they'd marked up high with their initials. They kissed. They wanted to do more but couldn't. Samuel wanted it to be special. He was aware that it should be perfect. Lindsey just wanted to get it over with. Have it behind her so she could achieve adulthood—transcend the place and the time. She thought of sex as the *Star Trek* transport. You vaporized and found yourself navigating another planet within the second or two it took to realign.

"They're going to do it," Ruth wrote in her journal. I had pinned hopes on Ruth's writing everything down. She told her journal about me passing by her in the parking lot, about how on that night I had touched her—

literally, she felt, reached out. What I had looked like then. How she dreamed about me. How she had fashioned the idea that a spirit could be a sort of second skin for someone, a protective layer somehow. How maybe if she was assiduous she could free us both. I would read over her shoulder as she wrote down her thoughts and wonder if anyone might believe her one day.

When she was imagining me, she felt better, less alone, more connected to something out there. To someone out there. She saw the cornfield in her dreams, and a new world opening, a world where maybe she could find a foothold too.

"You're a really good poet, Ruth," she imagined me saying, and her journal would release her into a daydream of being such a good poet that her words had the power to resurrect me.

I could see back to an afternoon when Ruth watched her teenage cousin undress to take a bath while Ruth sat on the bathroom rug, locked in the bathroom so her cousin could babysit her as she'd been told. Ruth had longed to touch her cousin's skin and hair, longed to be held. I wondered if this longing in a three-year-old had sparked what came at eight. That fuzzy feeling of difference, that her crushes on female teachers or her cousin were more real than the other girls' crushes. Hers contained a desire beyond sweetness and attention, it fed a longing, beginning to flower green and yellow into a crocuslike lust, the soft petals opening into her awkward adolescence. It was not so much, she would write in her journal, that she wanted to have sex with women, but that she wanted to disappear inside of them forever. To hide.

* * *

The last week of the symposium was always spent developing a final project, which the various schools would present in competition on the night before the parents returned to pick the students up. The competition wasn't announced until the Saturday breakfast of that final week, but the kids had already begun planning for it anyway. It was always a better-mousetrap competition, and so the stakes were raised year after year. No one wanted to repeat a mousetrap that had already been built.

Samuel went in search of the kids with braces. He needed the tiny rubber bands orthodontists doled out. They would work to keep the tension tight on the guiding arm of his mousetrap. Lindsey begged clean tinfoil from the retired army cook. Their trap involved reflecting light in order to confuse the mice.

"What happens if they like the way they look?" Lindsey asked Samuel.

"They can't see that clearly," Samuel said. He was stripping the paper off the wire twists from the camp garbage bag supply. If a kid looked strangely at ordinary objects around the camp, he or she was most likely thinking of how it would serve the ultimate mousetrap.

"They're pretty cute," Lindsey said one afternoon.

Lindsey had spent the better part of the night before gathering field mice with string lures and putting them under the wire mesh of an empty rabbit hutch.

Samuel watched them intently. "I could be a vet, I guess," he said, "but I don't think I'd like cutting them open."

"Do we have to kill them?" Lindsey asked. "It's a better mouse*trap,* not a better mouse death camp."

"Artie's contributing little coffins made out of balsa wood," Samuel said, laughing.

"That's sick."

"That's Artie."

"He supposedly had a crush on Susie," Lindsey said.

"I know."

"Does he talk about her?" Lindsey took a long thin stick and poked it through the mesh.

"He's asked about you, actually," Samuel said.

"What did you tell him?"

"That you're okay, that you'll be okay."

The mice kept running from the stick into the corner, where they crawled on top of one another in a useless effort to flee. "Let's build a mousetrap with a little purple velvet couch in it and we can rig up a latch so that when they sit on the couch, a door drops and little balls of cheese fall down. We can call it Wild Rodent Kingdom."

Samuel didn't press my sister like the adults did. He would talk in detail about mouse couch upholstery instead.

By that summer I had begun to spend less time watching from the gazebo because I could still see Earth as I walked the fields of heaven. The night would come and the javelin-throwers and shot-putters would leave for other heavens. Heavens where a girl like me didn't fit in. Were they horrific, these other heavens? Worse than feeling so solitary among one's living, growing peers? Or were they the stuff I dreamed about? Where you could be caught in a Norman Rockwell world forever. Turkey constantly being brought to a table full of family. A wry and twinkling relative carving up the bird.

If I walked too far and wondered loud enough the fields would change. I could look down and see horse corn and I could hear it then — singing — a kind of low humming and moaning warning me back from the edge. My head would throb and the sky would darken and it would be that night again, that perpetual yesterday lived again. My soul solidifying, growing heavy. I came up to the lip of my grave this way many times but had yet to stare in.

I did begin to wonder what the word *heaven* meant. I thought, if this were heaven, truly heaven, it would be where my grandparents lived. Where my father's father, my favorite of them all, would lift me up and dance with me. I would feel only joy and have no memory, no cornfield and no grave.

"You can have that," Franny said to me. "Plenty of people do."

"How do you make the switch?" I asked.

"It's not as easy as you might think," she said. "You have to stop desiring certain answers."

"I don't get it."

"If you stop asking why you were killed instead of someone else, stop investigating the vacuum left by your loss, stop wondering what everyone left on Earth is feeling," she said, "you can be free. Simply put, you have to give up on Earth."

This seemed impossible to me.

Ruth crept into Lindsey's dorm that night.

"I had a dream about her," she whispered to my sister.

Lindsey blinked sleepily at her. "Susie?" she asked.

"I'm sorry about the incident in the dining hall," Ruth said.

Lindsey was on the bottom of a three-tiered aluminum bunk bed. Her neighbor directly above her stirred.

"Can I get into bed with you?" Ruth asked.

Lindsey nodded.

Ruth crawled in next to Lindsey in the narrow sliver of the bed.

"What happened in your dream?" Lindsey whispered.

Ruth told her, turning her face so that Lindsey's eyes could make out the silhouette of Ruth's nose and lips and forehead. "I was inside the earth," Ruth said, "and Susie walked over me in the cornfield. I could feel her walking over me. I called out to her but my mouth filled with dirt. She couldn't hear me no matter how much I tried to yell. Then I woke up."

"I don't dream about her," Lindsey said. "I have nightmares about rats nibbling at the ends of my hair."

Ruth liked the comfort she felt next to my sister — the heat their bodies created.

"Are you in love with Samuel?"

"Yes."

"Do you miss Susie?"

Because it was dark, because Ruth was facing away from her, because Ruth was almost a stranger, Lindsey said what she felt. "More than anyone will ever know."

The principal of Devon Junior High was called away on a family matter, and it was left up to the newly appointed assistant principal of Chester Springs School to create, overnight, that year's challenge. She wanted to do something different from mousetraps.

CAN YOU GET AWAY WITH CRIME? HOW TO COMMIT THE PERFECT MURDER, announced her hurriedly drawn-up flier.

The kids loved it. The musicians and poets, the History Heads and artists, were teeming and bubbling about how to begin. They shoveled down their bacon and eggs at breakfast and compared the great unsolved murders of the past or thought of ordinary objects that could be used for fatal wounds. They began to think of whom they could plot to kill. It was all in good fun until 7:15, when my sister walked in.

Artie watched her get in line. She was still unaware, just picking up on the excitement in the air — figuring the mousetrap competition had been announced.

He kept his eye on Lindsey and saw the closest flier was posted at the end of the food line over the utensils tray. He was listening to a story about Jack the Ripper that someone at the table was relaying. He stood to return his tray.

When he reached my sister, he cleared his throat. All my hopes were pinned on this wobbly boy. "Catch her," I said. A prayer going down to Earth.

"Lindsey," Artie said.

Lindsey looked at him. "Yes?"

Behind the counter the army cook held out a spoon full of scrambled eggs to plop on her tray.

"I'm Artie, from your sister's grade."

"I don't need any coffins," Lindsey said, moving her tray down the metalwork to where there was orange juice and apple juice in big plastic pitchers.

"What?"

"Samuel told me you were building balsa wood coffins for the mice this year. I don't want any."

"They changed the competition," he said.

That morning Lindsey had decided she would take the bottom off of Clarissa's dress. It would be perfect for the mouse couch.

"To what?"

"Do you want to go outside?" Artie used his body to shadow her and block her passage to the utensils. "Lindsey," he blurted. "The competition is about murder."

She stared at him.

Lindsey held on to her tray. She kept her eyes locked on Artie.

"I wanted to tell you before you read the flier," he said.

Samuel rushed into the tent.

"What's going on?" Lindsey looked helplessly at Samuel.

"This year's competition is how to commit the perfect murder," Samuel said.

Samuel and I saw the tremor. The inside shakeoff of her heart. She was getting so good the cracks and fissures were smaller and smaller. Soon, like a sleight-of-hand trick perfected, no one would see her do it. She could shut out the whole world, including herself.

"I'm fine," she said.

But Samuel knew she wasn't.

He and Artie watched her back as she departed.

"I was trying to warn her," Artie said weakly.

Artie returned to his table. He drew hypodermics, one after another. His pen pressed harder and harder as he colored in the embalming fluid inside, as he perfected the trajectory of the three drops squirting out.

Lonely, I thought, *on Earth as it is in heaven.*

"You kill people by stabbing and cutting and shooting," Ruth said. "It's sick."

"Agreed," Artie said.

Samuel had taken my sister away to talk. Artie had seen Ruth at one of the outside picnic tables with her big blank book.

"But there are good reasons to kill," Ruth said.

"Who do you think did it?" Artie asked. He sat on the bench and braced his feet up under the table on the cross-bar.

Ruth sat almost motionless, right leg crossed over left, but her foot jiggled ceaselessly.

"How did you hear?" she asked.

"My father told us," Artie said. "He called my sister and me into the family room and made us sit down."

"Shit, what did he say?"

"First he said that horrible things happened in the world and my sister said, 'Vietnam,' and he was quiet because they always fight about that whenever it comes up. So he said, 'No, honey, horrible things happen close to home, to people we know.' She thought it was one of her friends."

Ruth felt a raindrop.

"Then my dad broke down and said a little girl had been killed. I was the one who asked who. I mean, when he said 'little girl,' I pictured *little,* you know. Not us."

It was a definite drop, and they began to land on the redwood tabletop.

"Do you want to go in?" Artie asked.

"Everyone else will be inside," Ruth said.

"I know."

"Let's get wet."

They sat still for a while and watched the drops fall around them, heard the sound against the leaves of the tree above.

"I knew she was dead. I sensed it," Ruth said, "but then I saw a mention of it in my dad's paper and I was sure. They didn't use her name at first. Just 'Girl, fourteen.' I asked my dad for the page but he wouldn't give it to me. I mean, who else and her sister hadn't been in school all week?"

"I wonder who told Lindsey?" Artie said. The rain picked up. Artie slipped underneath the table. "We're going to get soaked," he yelled up.

And then as quickly as the rain had started, it ceased. Sun came through the branches of the tree above her, and Ruth looked up past them. "I think she listens," she said, too softly to be heard.

It became common knowledge at the symposium who my sister was and how I had died.

"Imagine being stabbed," someone said.

"No thanks."

"I think it's cool."

"Think of it — she's famous."

"Some way to get famous. I'd rather win the Nobel Prize."

"Does anyone know what she wanted to be?"

"I dare you to ask Lindsey."

And they listed the dead they knew.

Grandmother, grandfather, uncle, aunt, some had a parent, rarer was a sister or brother lost young to an illness — a heart irregularity — leukemia — an unpronounceable disease. No one knew anyone who had been murdered. But now they knew me.

Under a rowboat that was too old and worn to float, Lindsey lay down on the earth with Samuel Heckler, and he held her.

"You know I'm okay," she said, her eyes dry. "I think Artie was trying to help me," she offered.

"You can stop now, Lindsey," he said. "We'll just lie here and wait until things quiet down."

Samuel's back was flush against the ground, and he brought my sister close in to his body to protect her from the dampness of the quick summer rain. Their breath began to heat the small space beneath the boat, and he could not stop it — his penis stiffened inside his jeans.

Lindsey reached her hand over.

"I'm sorry . . ." He began.

"I'm ready," my sister said.

At fourteen, my sister sailed away from me into a place I'd never been. In the walls of my sex there was horror and blood, in the walls of hers there were windows.

"How to Commit the Perfect Murder" was an old game in heaven. I always chose the icicle: the weapon melts away.

E L E V E N

When my father woke up at four A.M., the house was quiet. My mother lay beside him, lightly snoring. My brother, the only child, what with my sister attending the symposium, was like a rock with a sheet pulled up over him. My father marveled at what a sound sleeper he was — just like me. While I was still alive, Lindsey and I had had fun with that, clapping, dropping books, and even banging pot lids to see if Buckley would wake up.

Before leaving the house, my father checked on Buckley — to make sure, to feel the warm breath against his palm. Then he suited up in his thin-soled sneakers and light jogging outfit. His last task was to put Holiday's collar on.

It was still early enough that he could almost see his breath. He could pretend at that early hour that it was still winter. That the seasons had not advanced.

The morning dog walk gave him an excuse to pass by Mr. Harvey's house. He slowed only slightly — no one would have noticed save me or, if he had been awake, Mr. Harvey. My father was sure that if he just stared hard enough, just looked long enough, he would find the clues he needed in the casements of the windows, in the green paint coating the shingles, or along the driveway, where two large stones sat, painted white.

By late summer 1974, there had been no movement on my case. No body. No killer. Nothing.

My father thought of Ruana Singh: "When I was sure, I would find a quiet way, and I would kill him." He had not told this to Abigail because the advice made a sort of baseline sense that would frighten her into telling someone, and he suspected that someone might be Len.

Ever since the day he'd seen Ruana Singh and then had come home to find Len waiting for him, he'd felt my mother leaning heavily on the police. If my father said something that contradicted the police theories — or, as he saw them, the lack of them — my mother would immediately rush to fill the hole left open by my father's idea. "Len says that doesn't mean anything," or, "I trust the police to find out what happened."

Why, my father wondered, did people trust the police so much? Why not trust instinct? It was Mr. Harvey and he knew it. But what Ruana had said was *when I was sure*. Knowing, the deep-soul knowing that my father had, was not, in the law's more literal mind, incontrovertible proof.

* * *

The house that I grew up in was the same house where I was born. Like Mr. Harvey's, it was a box, and because of this I nurtured useless envies whenever I visited other people's homes. I dreamed about bay windows and cupolas, balconies, and slanted attic ceilings in a bedroom. I loved the idea that there could be trees in a yard taller and stronger than people, slanted spaces under stairs, thick hedges grown so large that inside there were hollows of dead branches where you could crawl and sit. In my heaven there were verandas and circular staircases, window ledges with iron rails, and a campanile housing a bell that tolled the hour.

I knew the floor plan of Mr. Harvey's by heart. I had made a warm spot on the floor of the garage until I cooled. He had brought my blood into the house with him on his clothes and skin. I knew the bathroom. Knew how in my house my mother had tried to decorate it to accommodate Buckley's late arrival by stenciling battleships along the top of the pink walls. In Mr. Harvey's house the bathroom and kitchen were spotless. The porcelain was yellow and the tile on the floor was green. He kept it cold. Upstairs, where Buckley, Lindsey, and I had our rooms, he had almost nothing. He had a straight chair where he would go to sit sometimes and stare out the window over at the high school, listen for the sound of band practice wafting over from the field, but mostly he spent his hours in the back on the first floor, in the kitchen building dollhouses, in the living room listening to the radio or, as his lust set in, sketching blueprints for follies like the hole or the tent.

No one had bothered him about me for several months. By that summer he only occasionally saw a squad car slow in front of his house. He was smart enough not to alter his pattern. If he was walking out to the garage or the mailbox, he kept on going.

He set several clocks. One to tell him when to open the blinds, one when to close them. In conjunction with these alarms, he would turn lights on and off throughout the house. When an occasional child happened by to sell chocolate bars for a school competition or inquire if he would like to subscribe to the *Evening Bulletin,* he was friendly but businesslike, unremarkable.

He kept things to count, and this counting reassured him. They were simple things. A wedding ring, a letter sealed in an envelope, the heel of a shoe, a pair of glasses, an eraser in the shape of a cartoon character, a small bottle of perfume, a plastic bracelet, my Pennsylvania keystone charm, his mother's amber pendant. He would take them out at night long after he was certain that no newsboy or neighbor would knock on his door. He would count them like the beads on a rosary. For some he had forgotten the names. I knew the names. The heel of the shoe was from a girl named Claire, from Nutley, New Jersey, whom he had convinced to walk into the back of a van. She was littler than me. (I like to think I wouldn't have gone into a van. Like to think it was my curiosity about how he could make a hole in the earth that wouldn't collapse.) He had ripped the heel off her shoe before he let Claire go. That was all he did. He got her into the van and took her shoes off. She started crying, and the sound drove into him like screws. He pleaded with her to be quiet and just leave. Step magically out of the van barefoot and uncomplaining while he kept her shoes. But she wouldn't. She cried. He started working on one of the heels of the shoes, prying it loose with his penknife, until someone pounded on the back of the van. He heard men's voices and a woman yelling something about calling the police. He opened the door.

"What the hell are you doing to that kid?" one of the men yelled. This man's buddy caught the little girl as she flew, bawling, out of the back.

"I'm trying to repair her shoe."

The little girl was hysterical. Mr. Harvey was all reason and calm. But Claire had seen what I had—his look bearing down—his wanting something unspoken that to give him would equal our oblivion.

Hurriedly, as the men and woman stood confused, unable to see what Claire and I knew, Mr. Harvey handed the shoes to one of the men and said his goodbyes. He kept the heel. He liked to hold the small leather heel and rub it between his thumb and forefinger—a perfect worry stone.

I knew the darkest place in our house. I had climbed inside of it and stayed there for what I told Clarissa was a whole day but was really about forty-five minutes. It was the crawlspace in the basement. Inside ours there were pipes coming down that I could see with a flashlight and tons and tons of dust. That was it. There were no bugs. My mother, like her own, employed an exterminator for the slightest infestation of ants.

When the alarm had gone off to tell him to shut the blinds and then the next alarm, which told him to shut off most of the lights because the suburbs were asleep after that, Mr. Harvey would go down into the basement, where there were no cracks that light could peek through and people could point to, to say he was strange. By the time he killed me he had tired of visiting the crawlspace, but he still liked to hang out in the basement in an easy chair that faced the dark hole beginning halfway up the wall and reaching to the exposed baseboards of his kitchen floor. He would often drift off to sleep there, and there he was asleep when my father passed the green house at around 4:40 A.M.

Joe Ellis was an ugly little tough. He had pinched Lindsey and me under water in the pool and kept us from going to swim parties because we hated him so much. He had a dog that he dragged around no matter what the dog wanted. It was a small dog and couldn't run very fast, but Ellis didn't care. He would hit it or lift it painfully by the tail. Then one day it was gone, and so was a cat that Ellis had been seen taunting. And then animals from all over the neighborhood began disappearing.

What I discovered, when I followed Mr. Harvey's stare to the crawlspace, were these animals that had gone missing for more than a year. People thought it stopped because the Ellis boy had been sent to military school. When they let their pets loose in the morning, they returned in the evening. This they held as proof. No one could imagine an appetite like the one in the green house. Someone who would spread quicklime on the bodies of cats and dogs, the sooner for him to have nothing left but their bones. By counting the bones and staying away from the sealed letter, the wedding ring, the bottle of perfume, he tried to stay away from what he wanted most — from going upstairs in the dark to sit in the straight chair and look out toward the high school, from imagining the bodies that matched the cheerleaders' voices, which pulsated in waves on fall days during football games, or from watching the buses from the grammar school unload two houses down. Once he had taken a long look at Lindsey, the lone girl on the boys' soccer team out running laps in our neighborhood near dark.

What I think was hardest for me to realize was that he had tried each time to stop himself. He had killed animals, taking lesser lives to keep from killing a child.

By August, Len wanted to establish some boundaries for his sake and for my father's. My father had called the precinct too many times and frustrated the police into irritation, which wouldn't help anyone be found and just might make the whole place turn against him.

The final straw had been a call that came in the first week of July. Jack Salmon had detailed to the operator how, on a morning walk, his dog had stopped in front of Mr. Harvey's house and started howling. No matter what Salmon had done, went the story, the dog wouldn't budge from the spot and wouldn't stop howling. It became a joke at the station: Mr. Fish and his Huckleberry Hound.

Len stood on the stoop of our house to finish his cigarette. It was still early, but the humidity from the day before had intensified. All week rain had been promised, the kind of thunder and lightning rainstorm the area excelled at, but so far the only moisture of which Len was aware was that covering his body in a damp sweat. He had made his last easy visit to my parents' house.

Now he heard humming — a female voice from inside. He stubbed out his cigarette against the cement under the hedge and lifted the heavy brass knocker. The door opened before he let go.

"I smelled your cigarette," Lindsey said.

"Was that you humming?"

"Those things will kill you."

"Is your father home?"

Lindsey stood aside to let him in.

"Dad!" my sister yelled into the house. "It's Len!"

"You were away, weren't you?" Len asked.

"I just got back."

My sister was wearing Samuel's softball shirt and a pair of strange sweatpants. My mother had accused her of returning home without one single item of her own clothing.

"I'm sure your parents missed you."

"Don't bet on it," Lindsey said. "I think they were happy to have me out of their hair."

Len knew she was right. He was certainly sure my mother had seemed less frantic when he had visited the house.

Lindsey said, "Buckley's made you the head of the police squad in the town he built under his bed."

"That's a promotion."

The two of them heard my father's footsteps in the hallway above and then the sounds of Buckley begging. Lindsey could tell that whatever he'd asked for our father had finally granted.

My father and brother descended the stairs, all smiles.

"Len," he said, and he shook Len's hand.

"Good morning, Jack," Len said. "And how are you this morning, Buckley?"

My father took Buckley's hand and stood him in front of Len, who solemnly bent down to my brother.

"I hear you've made me chief of police," Len said.

"Yes sir."

"I don't think I deserve the job."

"You more than anyone," my father said breezily. He loved it when Len Fenerman dropped by. Each time he did, it verified for my father that there was a consensus — a group behind him — that he wasn't alone in all this.

"I need to talk to your father, kids."

Lindsey took Buckley back into the kitchen with the promise of cereal. She herself was thinking of what Samuel had shown her; it was a drink called a jellyfish, which involved a maraschino cherry at the bottom of some sugar and gin. Samuel and Lindsey had sucked the cherries up through the sugar and booze until their heads hurt and their lips were stained red.

"Should I get Abigail? Can I make you some coffee or something?"

"Jack," Len said, "I'm not here with any news — just the opposite. Can we sit?"

I watched my father and Len head into the living room. The living room seemed to be where no living ever actually occurred. Len sat on the edge of a chair and waited for my father to take a seat.

"Listen, Jack," he said. "It's about George Harvey."

My father brightened. "I thought you said you had no news."

"I don't. I have something I need to say on behalf of the station and myself."

"Yes."

"We need you to stop making calls about George Harvey."

"But . . ."

"*I* need you to stop. There is nothing, no matter how much we stretch it, to connect him to Susie's death. Howling dogs and bridal tents are not evidence."

"I know he did it," my father said.

"He's odd, I agree, but as far as we know he isn't a killer."

"How could you possibly know that?"

Len Fenerman talked, but all my father could hear was Ruana Singh saying what she had to him, and of standing outside Mr. Harvey's house and feeling the energy radiating out to him, the coldness at the core of the man. Mr. Harvey was at once unknowable and the only person in the world who could have killed me. As Len denied it, my father grew more certain.

"You are stopping your investigation of him," my father said flatly.

Lindsey was in the doorway, hovering as she'd done on the day Len and the uniformed officer had brought my hat with the jingle bell, the twin of which she owned. That day she had quietly shoved this second hat into a box of old dolls in the back of her closet. She never wanted my mother to hear the sound of those beadlike bells again.

There was our father, the heart we knew held all of us. Held us heavily and desperately, the doors of his heart opening and closing with the rapidity of stops on an instrument, the quiet felt closures, the ghostly fingering, practice and practice and then, incredibly, sound and melody and warmth. Lindsey stepped forward from her place by the door.

"Hello again, Lindsey," Len said.

"Detective Fenerman."

"I was just telling your father . . ."

"That you're giving up."

"If there was any good reason to suspect the man . . ."

"Are you done?" Lindsey asked. She was suddenly the wife to our father, as well as the oldest, most responsible child.

"I just want you all to know that we've investigated every lead."

My father and Lindsey heard her, and I saw her. My mother coming down the stairs. Buckley raced out of the kitchen and charged, propelling his full weight into my father's legs.

"Len," my mother said, pulling her terry-cloth robe tighter when she saw him, "has Jack offered you coffee?"

My father looked at his wife and Len Fenerman.

"The cops are punting," Lindsey said, taking Buckley gently by the shoulders and holding him against her.

"Punting?" Buckley asked. He always rolled a sound around in his mouth like a sourball until he had its taste and feel.

"What?"

"Detective Fenerman is here to tell Dad to stop bugging them."

"Lindsey," Len said, "I wouldn't put it like that."

"Whatever," she said. My sister wanted out, now, into a place where gifted camp continued, where Samuel and she, or even Artie, who at the last minute had won the Perfect Murder competition by entering the icicle-as-murder-weapon idea, ruled her world.

"Come on, Dad," she said. My father was slowly fitting something together. It had nothing to do with George Harvey, nothing to do with me. It was in my mother's eyes.

* * *

That night, as he had more and more often, my father stayed up by himself in his study. He could not believe the world falling down around him — how unexpected it all was after the initial blast of my death. "I feel like I'm standing in the wake of a volcano eruption," he wrote in his notebook. "Abigail thinks Len Fenerman is right about Harvey."

As he wrote, the candle in the window kept flickering, and despite his desk lamp the flickering distracted him. He sat back in the old wooden school chair he'd had since college and heard the reassuring squeak of the wood under him. At the firm he was failing to even register what was needed of him. Daily now he faced column after column of meaningless numbers he was supposed to make square with company claims. He was making mistakes with a frequency that was frightening, and he feared, more than he had in the first days following my disappearance, that he would not be able to support his two remaining children.

He stood up and stretched his arms overhead, trying to concentrate on the few exercises that our family doctor had suggested. I watched his body bend in uneasy and surprising ways I had never seen before. He could have been a dancer rather than a businessman. He could have danced on Broadway with Ruana Singh.

He snapped off the desk light, leaving only the candle.

In his low green easy chair he now felt the most comfortable. It was where I often saw him sleep. The room like a vault, the chair like a womb, and me standing guard over him. He stared at the candle in the window and thought about what to do; how he had tried to touch my mother and she had pulled away over to the edge of the bed. But how in the presence of the police she seemed to bloom.

He had grown used to the ghostly light behind the candle's flame, that quivering reflection in the window. He stared at the two of them — real flame and ghost — and began to work toward a doze, dozing in thought and strain and the events of the day.

As he was about to let go for the night, we both saw the same thing: another light. Outside.

It looked like a penlight from that distance. One white beam slowly moving out across the lawns and toward the junior high. My father watched it. It was after midnight now, and the moon was not full enough, as it often was, to see the outlines of the trees and houses. Mr. Stead, who rode his bike late at night with a flashing light on the front powered by his pedals, would never degrade the lawns of his neighbors that way. It was too late for Mr. Stead anyway.

My father leaned forward in the green chair in his study and watched the flashlight move in the direction of the fallow cornfield.

"Bastard," he whispered. "You murderous bastard."

He dressed quickly from the storage closet in his study, putting on a hunting jacket that he hadn't had on since an ill-fated hunting trip ten years earlier. Downstairs he went into the front hall closet and found the baseball bat he'd bought for Lindsey before she favored soccer.

First he shut off the porch light they kept on all night for me and that, even though it had been eight months since the police said I would not be found alive, they could not bring themselves to stop leaving on. With his hand on the doorknob, he took a deep breath.

He turned the knob and found himself out on the dark front porch. Closed the door and found himself standing in his front yard with a baseball bat and these words: *find a quiet way.*

He walked through his front yard and across the street and then into the O'Dwyers' yard, where he had first seen the light. He passed their darkened swimming pool and the rusted-out swing set. His heart was pumping, but he could not feel anything but the knowledge in his brain. George Harvey had killed his last little girl.

He reached the soccer field. To his right, far into the cornfield but not in the vicinity he knew by heart — the area that had been roped off and cleared and combed and bulldozed — he saw the small light. He clenched his fingers tighter around the bat by his side. For just a second he could not believe what he was about to do, but then, with everything in him, he knew.

The wind helped him. It swept along the soccer field alongside the cornfield and whipped his trousers around the front of his legs; it pushed him forward despite himself. Everything fell away. Once he was among the rows of corn, his focus solely on the light, the wind disguised his presence. The sound of his feet crushing the stalks was swept up in the whistle and bustle of the wind against the broken plants.

Things that made no sense flooded his head — the hard rubber sound of children's roller skates on pavement, the smell of his father's pipe tobacco, Abigail's smile when he met her, like light piercing his confused heart — and then the flashlight shut off and everything went equal and dark.

He took a few more steps, then stopped.

"I know you're here," he said.

I flooded the cornfield, I flashed fires through it to light it up, I sent storms of hail and flowers, but none of it worked to warn him. I was relegated to heaven: I watched.

"I'm here for it," my father said, his voice trembling. That heart bursting in and out, blood gorging the rivers of his chest and then cinching up. Breath and fire and lungs seizing, releasing, adrenaline saving what was left. My mother's smile in his mind gone, mine taking its place.

"Nobody's awake," my father said. "I'm here to finish it."

He heard whimpering. I wanted to cast down a spotlight like they did in the school auditorium, awkwardly, the light not always hitting the right place on the stage. There she would be, crouching and whimpering and now, despite her blue eye shadow and Western-style boots from Bakers', wetting her pants. A child.

She didn't recognize my father's voice infused with hate. "Brian?" Clarissa's quavering voice came out. "Brian?" It was hope like a shield.

My father's hand loosened on the bat, letting it fall.

"Hello? Who's there?"

With wind in his ears, Brian Nelson, the beanstalk scarecrow, parked his older brother's Spyder Corvette in the school lot. Late, always late, sleeping in class and at the dinner table but never when a boy had a *Playboy* or a cute girl walked by, never on a night when he had a girl waiting for him out in the cornfield. Still, he took his time. The wind, glorious blanket and cover for what he had planned, whipped past his ears.

Brian moved toward the cornfield with his giant torch light from his mother's under-the-sink disaster kit. Finally he heard what he would later say were Clarissa's cries for help.

My father's heart was like a stone there, heavy, carried inside his chest as he ran and fumbled toward the sound of the girl's whimpering. His mother was knitting him mittens, Susie was asking for gloves, so cold in the cornfield in winter. Clarissa! Susie's silly friend. Makeup, prissy jam sandwiches, and her tropical tan skin.

He ran blind into her and knocked her down in the darkness. Her screaming filled his ear and poured into the empty spaces, ricocheting inside of him. "Susie!" he screamed back.

Brian ran when he heard my name — full-speed-ahead awake. His light hopped over the cornfield, and, for one bright second, there was Mr. Harvey. No one but me saw him. Brian's light hit his back as he crawled into the high stalks and listened, again, for the sound of whimpering.

And then the light hit target and Brian dragged my father up and off Clarissa to hit him. Hit him on the head and back and face with the survival-kit flashlight. My father shouted and yelped and moaned.

And then Brian saw the bat.

I pushed and pushed against the unyielding borders of my heaven. I wanted to reach out and lift my father up, away, to me.

Clarissa ran and Brian swung. My father's eyes caught Brian's but he could barely breathe.

"You fucker!" Brian was black and white with blame.

I heard mumblings in the dirt. I heard my name. I thought I could taste the blood on my father's face, reach out to draw my fingers across his cut lips, lie down with him in my grave.

But I had to turn my back in heaven. I could do nothing — trapped in my perfect world. The blood I tasted was bitter. Acid. I wanted my father's vigil, his tight love for me. But also I wanted him to go away and leave me be. I was granted one weak grace. Back in the room where the green chair was still warm from his body, I blew that lonely, flickering candle out.

TWELVE

I stood in the room beside him and watched him sleep. During the night the story had come unwound and spun down so that the police understood: Mr. Salmon was crazy with grief and had gone out to the cornfield seeking revenge. It fit what they knew of him, his persistent phone calls, his obsession with the neighbor, and Detective Fenerman having visited that same day to tell my parents that for all intents and purposes my murder investigation had entered a sort of hiatus. No clues were left to pursue. No body had been found.

The surgeon had to operate on his knee to replace the cap with a purselike suture that partially disabled the joint. As I watched the operation I thought of how much like sewing it seemed, and I hoped that my father was in more capable hands than if he had been brought to me. In home ec my hands had been clumsy. Zipper foot or baster, I got them all confused.

But the surgeon had been patient. A nurse had filled him in on the story as he washed and scrubbed his hands. He remembered reading about what had happened to me in the papers. He was my father's age and had children of his own. He shivered as he stretched his gloves out over his hands. How alike he and this man were. How very different.

In the dark hospital room, a fluorescent bar light buzzed just behind my father's bed. As dawn approached it was the only light in the room until my sister walked in.

My mother and sister and brother woke to the sounds of the police sirens and came down into the dark kitchen from their bedrooms.

"Go wake your father," my mother said to Lindsey. "I can't believe he slept through this."

And so my sister had gone up. Everyone now knew where to look for him: in only six months, the green chair had become his true bed.

"Dad's not here!" my sister yelled as soon as she realized. "Dad's gone. Mom! Mom! Dad's gone!" For a rare moment Lindsey was a frightened child.

"Damn!" my mother said.

"Mommy?" Buckley said.

Lindsey rushed into the kitchen. My mother faced the stove. Her back was a riddled mass of nerves as she went about making tea.

"Mom?" Lindsey asked. "We have to do something."

"Don't you see . . . ?" my mother said, stopping for a moment with a box of Earl Grey suspended in the air.

"What?"

She put the tea down, switched on the burner, and turned around. She saw something herself then: Buckley had gone to cling to my sister as he anxiously sucked his thumb.

"He's gone off after that man and gotten himself in trouble."

"We should go out, Mom," Lindsey said. "We should go help him."

"No."

"Mom, we have to help Daddy."

"Buckley, stop milking your thumb!"

My brother burst into hot panicked tears, and my sister reached her arms down to pull him in tighter. She looked at our mother.

"I'm going out to find him," Lindsey said.

"You are doing no such thing," my mother said. "He'll come home in good time. We're staying out of this."

"Mom," Lindsey said, "what if he's hurt?"

Buckley stopped crying long enough to look back and forth from my sister to my mother. He knew what hurt meant and who was missing from the house.

My mother gave Lindsey a meaningful look. "We are not discussing this further. You can go up to your room and wait or wait with me. Your choice."

Lindsey was dumbfounded. She stared at our mother and knew what she wanted most: to flee, to run out into the cornfield where my father was, where I was, where she felt suddenly that the heart of her family had moved. But Buckley stood warm against her.

"Buckley," she said, "let's go back upstairs. You can sleep in my bed."

He was beginning to understand: you were treated special and, later, something horrible would be told to you.

When the call came from the police, my mother went immediately to the front closet. "He's been hit with our own baseball bat!" she said, grabbing her coat and keys and lipstick. My sister felt more alone than she had ever been but also more responsible. Buckley couldn't be left by himself, and Lindsey wasn't even able to drive. Besides, it made the clearest sense in the world. Didn't the wife belong most at the husband's side?

But when my sister was able to get Nate's mother on the line — after all, the commotion in the cornfield had awakened the whole neighborhood — she knew what she would do. She called Samuel next. Within an hour, Nate's mother arrived to take Buckley, and Hal Heckler pulled up to our house on his motorcycle. It should have been exciting — clutching on to Samuel's gorgeous older brother, riding on a motorcycle for the first time — but all she could think of was our father.

My mother was not in his hospital room when Lindsey entered; it was just my father and me. She came up and stood on the other side of his bed and started to cry quietly.

"Daddy?" she said. "Are you okay, Daddy?"

The door opened a crack. It was Hal Heckler, a tall handsome slash of a man.

"Lindsey," he said, "I'll wait for you out in the visitors' area in case you need a ride home."

He saw her tears when she turned around. "Thanks, Hal. If you see my mother . . ."

"I'll tell her you're in here."

Lindsey took my father's hand and watched his face for movement. My sister was growing up before my eyes. I listened as she whispered the words he had sung to the two of us before Buckley was born:

> Stones and bones;
> snow and frost;
> seeds and beans and polliwogs.
> Paths and twigs, assorted kisses,
> We all know who Daddy misses!
> His two little frogs of girls, that's who.
> They know where they are, do you, do you?

I wish a smile had come curling up onto my father's face, but he was deep under, swimming against drug and nightmare and waking dream. For a time leaden weights had been tied by anesthesia to the four corners of his consciousness. Like a firm waxen cover it had locked him away tight into the hard-blessed hours where there was no dead daughter and no gone knee, and where there was also no sweet daughter whispering rhymes.

"When the dead are done with the living," Franny said to me, "the living can go on to other things."

"What about the dead?" I asked. "Where do we go?"

She wouldn't answer me.

Len Fenerman had rushed to the hospital as soon as they put the call through. Abigail Salmon, the dispatcher said, requesting him.

My father was in surgery, and my mother was pacing back and forth near the nurses' station. She had driven to the hospital in her raincoat with only her thin summer nightgown beneath it. She had her beating-around-the-yard ballet flats on her feet. She hadn't bothered to pull her hair back, and there hadn't been any hair elastics in her pockets or purse. In the dark foggy parking lot of the hospital she had stopped to check her face and applied her stock red lipstick with a practiced hand.

When she saw Len approaching from the end of the long white corridor, she relaxed.

"Abigail," he said when he grew closer.

"Oh, Len," she said. Her face puzzled up on what she could say next. His name had been the sigh she needed. Everything that came next was not words.

The nurses at their station turned their heads away as Len and my mother touched hands. They extended this privacy veil habitually, as a matter of course, but even so they could see this man meant something to this woman.

"Let's talk in the visitors' area," Len said and led my mother down the corridor.

As they walked she told him my father was in surgery. He filled her in on what had happened in the cornfield.

"Apparently he said he thought the girl was George Harvey."

"He thought Clarissa was George Harvey?" My mother stopped, incredulous, just outside the visitors' area.

"It was dark out, Abigail. I think he only saw the girl's flashlight. My visit today couldn't have helped much. He's convinced that Harvey is involved."

"Is Clarissa all right?"

"She was treated for scratches and released. She was hysterical. Crying and screaming. It was a horrible coincidence, her being Susie's friend."

Hal was slumped down in a darkened corner of the visitors' area with his feet propped up on the helmet he'd brought for Lindsey. When he heard the voices approaching he stirred.

It was my mother and a cop. He slumped back down and let his shoulder-length hair obscure his face. He was pretty sure my mother wouldn't remember him.

But she recognized the jacket as Samuel's and for a moment thought, *Samuel's here,* but then thought, *His brother.*

"Let's sit," Len said, indicating the connected modular chairs on the far side of the room.

"I'd rather keep walking," my mother said. "The doctor said it will be an hour at least before they have anything to tell us."

"Where to?"

"Do you have cigarettes?"

"You know I do," Len said, smiling guiltily. He had to seek out her eyes. They weren't focusing on him. They seemed to be preoccupied, and he wished he could reach up and grab them and train them on the here and now. On him.

"Let's find an exit, then."

They found a door to a small concrete balcony near my father's room. It was a service balcony for a heating unit, so even though it was cramped and slightly chilly, the noise and the hot exhaust of the humming hydrant beside them shut them into a capsule that felt far away. They smoked cigarettes and looked at each other as if they had suddenly and without preparation moved on to a new page, where the pressing business had already been highlighted for prompt attention.

"How did your wife die?" my mother asked.

"Suicide."

Her hair was covering most of her face, and watching her I was reminded of Clarissa at her most self-conscious. The way she behaved around boys when we went to the mall. She would giggle too much and flash her eyes over at them to see where they were looking. But I was also struck by my mother's red mouth with the cigarette going up and away from it and smoke trailing out. I had seen this mother only once before — in the photograph. This mother had never had us.

"Why did she kill herself?"

"That's the question that preoccupies me most when I'm not preoccupied by things like your daughter's murder."

A strange smile came across my mother's face.

"Say that again," she said.

"What?" Len looked at her smile, wanted to reach out and trace the corners of it with his fingertips.

"My daughter's murder," my mother said.

"Abigail, are you okay?"

"No one says it. No one in the neighborhood talks about it. People call it the 'horrible tragedy' or some variation on that. I just want it to be spoken out loud by somebody. To have it said aloud. I'm ready — I wasn't ready before."

My mother dropped her cigarette onto the concrete and let it burn. She took Len's face in her hands.

"Say it," she said.

"Your daughter's murder."

"Thank you."

And I watched that flat red mouth move across an invisible line that separated her from the rest of the world. She pulled Len in to her and slowly kissed him on the mouth. He seemed to hesitate at first. His body tensed, telling him NO, but that NO became vague and cloudy, became air sucked into the intake fan of the humming hydrant beside them. She reached up and unbuttoned her raincoat. He placed his hand against the thin gauzy material of her summer gown.

My mother was, in her need, irresistible. As a child I had seen her effect on men. When we were in grocery stores, stockers volunteered to find the items on her list and would help us out to the car. Like Ruana Singh, she was known as one of the pretty mothers in the neighborhood; no man who met her could help but smile. When she asked a question, their beating hearts gave in.

But still, it had only ever been my father who stretched her laughter out into the rooms of the house and made it okay, somehow, for her to let go.

By tacking on extra hours here and there and skipping lunches, my father had managed to come home early from work every Thursday when we were little. But whereas the weekends were family time, they called that day "Mommy and Daddy time." Lindsey and I thought of it as good-girl time. It meant no peeps out of us as we stayed quiet on the other side of the house, while we used my father's then sparsely filled den as our playroom.

My mother would start preparing us around two.

"Bath time," she sang, as if she were saying we could go out to play. And in the beginning that was how it felt. All three of us would rush up to our rooms and put on bathrobes. We would meet in the hallway — three girls — and my mother would take us by the hands and lead us into our pink bathroom.

Back then she talked to us about mythology, which she had studied in school. She liked to tell us stories about Persephone and Zeus. She bought us illustrated books on the Norse gods, which gave us nightmares. She had gotten her master's in English — having fought tooth and nail with Grandma Lynn to go so far in school — and still held on to vague ideas of teaching when the two of us were old enough to be left on our own.

Those bath times blur together, as do all the gods and goddesses, but what I remember most is watching things hit my mother while I looked at her, how the life she had wanted and the loss of it reached her in waves. As her firstborn, I thought it was me who took away all those dreams of what she had wanted to be.

My mother would lift Lindsey out of the tub first, dry her, and listen to her chatter about ducks and cuts. Then she would get me out of the tub and though I tried to be quiet the warm water made my sister and me drunk, and we talked to my mother about everything that mattered to us. Boys that teased us or how another family down the block had a puppy and why couldn't we have one too. She would listen seriously as if she were mentally noting the points of our agenda on a steno pad to which she would later refer.

"Well, first things first," she summed up. "Which means a nice nap for the two of you!"

She and I would tuck Lindsey in together. I stood by the bed as she kissed my sister on her forehead and brushed back her hair from her face. I think competition started there for me. Who got the better kiss, the longer time after the bath with Mom.

Luckily, I always won this. When I look back now I see that my mother had become — and very quickly after they moved into that house — lonely. Because I was the oldest, I became her closest friend.

I was too little to know what she was really saying to me, but I loved to be hushed to sleep by the soft lullaby of her words. One of the blessings of my heaven is that I can go back to these moments, live them again, and be with my mother in a way I never could have been. I reach my hand across the Inbetween and take the hand of that young lonely mother in mine.

What she said to a four-year-old about Helen of Troy: "A feisty woman who screwed things up." About Margaret Sanger: "She was judged by her looks, Susie. Because she looked like a mouse, no one expected her to last." Gloria Steinem: "I feel horrible, but I wish she'd trim those nails." Our neighbors: "An idiot in tight pants; oppressed by that prig of a husband; typically provincial and judgmental of everyone."

"Do you know who Persephone is?" she asked me absently one Thursday. But I didn't answer. By then I'd learned to hush when she brought me into my room. My sister's and my time was in the bathroom as we were being toweled off. Lindsey and I could talk about anything then. In my bedroom it was Mommy's time.

She took the towel and draped it over the spindle knob of my four-poster bed. "Imagine our neighbor Mrs. Tarking as Persephone," she said. She opened the drawer of the dresser and handed me my underpants. She always doled out my clothes piecemeal, not wanting to pressure me. She understood my needs early. If I was aware I would have to tie laces I would not have been able to put my feet into socks.

"She's wearing a long white robe, like a sheet draped

over her shoulders, but made out of some nice shiny or light fabric, like silk. And she has sandals made of gold and she's surrounded by torches which are light made out of flames . . ."

She went to the drawer to get my undershirt and absentmindedly put it over my head instead of leaving it to me. Once my mother was launched I could take advantage of it — be the baby again. I never protested and claimed to be grown up or a big girl. Those afternoons were about listening to my mysterious mother.

She pulled back the tough-cord Sears bedspread, and I scooted over to the far side along the wall. She always checked her watch then and afterward she would say, "Just for a little while," and slide off her shoes and slip in between the sheets with me.

For both of us it was about getting lost. She got lost in her story. I got lost in her talk.

She would tell me about Persephone's mother, Demeter, or Cupid and Psyche, and I would listen to her until I fell asleep. Sometimes my parents' laughter in the room beside me or the sounds of their late-afternoon lovemaking would wake me up. I would lie there in half-sleep, listening. I liked to pretend that I was in the warm hold of a ship from one of the stories my father read to us, and that all of us were on the ocean and the waves were rolling gently up against the sides of the ship. The laughter, the small sounds of muffled moaning, would usher me back under into sleep.

But then my mother's escape, her half-measure return to the outside world, had been smashed when I was ten and

Lindsey nine. She'd missed her period and had taken the fateful car trip to the doctor. Underneath her smile and exclamations to my sister and me were fissures that led somewhere deep inside her. But because I didn't want to, because I was a child, I chose not to follow them. I grabbed the smile like a prize and entered the land of wonder of whether I would be the sister to a little boy or to a little girl.

If I had paid attention, I would have noticed signs. Now I see the shifting, how the stack of books on my parents' bedside table changed from catalogs for local colleges, encyclopedias of mythology, novels by James, Eliot, and Dickens, to the works of Dr. Spock. Then came gardening books and cookbooks until for her birthday two months before I died, I thought the perfect gift was *Better Homes and Gardens Guide to Entertaining.* When she realized she was pregnant the third time, she sealed the more mysterious mother off. Bottled up for years behind that wall, that needy part of her had grown, not shrunk, and in Len, the greed to get out, to smash, destroy, rescind, overtook her. Her body led, and in its wake would be the pieces left to her.

It was not easy for me to witness, but I did.

Their first embrace was hurried, fumbled, passionate.

"Abigail," Len said, his two hands now on either side of her waist underneath the coat, the gauzy gown barely a veil between them. "Think of what you're doing."

"I'm tired of thinking," she said. Her hair was floating above her head because of the fan beside them — in an aureole. Len blinked as he looked at her. Marvelous, dangerous, wild.

"Your husband," he said.

"Kiss me," she said. "Please."

I was watching a beg for leniency on my mother's part. My mother was moving physically through time to flee from me. I could not hold her back.

Len kissed her forehead hard and closed his eyes. She took his hand and placed it on her breast. She whispered in his ear. I knew what was happening. Her rage, her loss, her despair. The whole life lost tumbling out in an arc on that roof, clogging up her being. She needed Len to drive the dead daughter out.

He pushed her back into the stucco surface of the wall as they kissed, and my mother held on to him as if on the other side of his kiss there could be a new life.

On my way home from the junior high, I would some-times stop at the edge of our property and watch my mother ride the ride-on mower, looping in and out among the pine trees, and I could remember then how she used to whistle in the mornings as she made her tea and how my father, rushing home on Thursdays, would bring her marigolds and her face would light up yellow in delight. They had been deeply, separately, wholly in love — apart from her children my mother could reclaim this love, but with them she began to drift. It was my father who grew toward us as the years went by; it was my mother who grew away.

Beside his hospital bed, Lindsey had fallen asleep while holding our father's hand. My mother, still mussed, passed by Hal Heckler in the visitors' area, and a moment later so did Len. Hal didn't need more than this. He grabbed his helmet and went off down the hall.

After a brief visit to the ladies' room, my mother was heading in the direction of my father's room when Hal stopped her.

"Your daughter's in there," Hal called out. She turned.

"Hal Heckler," he said, "Samuel's brother. I was at the memorial service."

"Oh, yes, I'm sorry. I didn't recognize you."

"Not your job," he said.

There was an awkward pause.

"So, Lindsey called me and I brought her here an hour ago."

"Oh."

"Buckley's with a neighbor," he said.

"Oh." She was staring at him. In her eyes she was climbing back to the surface. She used his face to climb back to.

"Are you okay?"

"I'm a little upset — that's understandable, right?"

"Perfectly," he said, speaking slowly. "I just wanted to let you know that your daughter is in there with your husband. I'll be in the visitors' area if you need me."

"Thank you," she said. She watched him turn away and paused for a moment to listen to the worn heels of his motorcycle boots reverberate down the linoleum hall.

She caught herself then, shook herself back to where she was, never guessing for a second that that had been Hal's purpose in greeting her.

Inside the room it was dark now, the fluorescent light behind my father flickering so slightly it lit only the most obvious masses in the room. My sister was in a chair pulled up alongside the bed, her head resting on the side of it with her hand extended out to touch my father. My father, deep under, was lying on his back. My mother could not know that I was there with them, that here were the four of us so changed now from the days when she tucked Lindsey and me into bed and went to make love to her husband, our father. Now she saw the pieces. She saw that my sister and father, together, had become a piece. She was glad of it.

I had played a hide-and-seek game of love with my mother as I grew up, courting her attention and approval in a way that I had never had to with my father.

I didn't have to play hide-and-seek anymore. As she stood in the darkened room and watched my sister and father, I knew one of the things that heaven meant. I had a choice, and it was not to divide my family in my heart.

Late at night the air above hospitals and senior citizen homes was often thick and fast with souls. Holly and I watched sometimes on the nights when sleep was lost to us. We came to realize how these deaths seemed choreographed from somewhere far away. Not our heaven. And so we began to suspect that there was a place more all-encompassing than where we were.

Franny came to watch with us in the beginning.

"It's one of my secret pleasures," she admitted. "After all these years I still love to watch the souls that float and spin in masses, all of them clamoring at once inside the air."

"I don't see anything," I said that first time.

"Watch closely," she said, "and hush."

But I felt them before I saw them, small warm sparks along my arms. Then there they were, fireflies lighting up and expanding in howls and swirls as they abandoned human flesh.

"Like snowflakes," Franny said, "none of them the same and yet each one, from where we stand, exactly like the one before."

THIRTEEN

When she returned to junior high in the fall of 1974, Lindsey was not only the sister of the murdered girl but the child of a "crackpot," "nutcase," "looney-tunes," and the latter hurt her more because it wasn't true.

The rumors Lindsey and Samuel heard in the first weeks of the school year wove in and out of the rows of student lockers like the most persistent of snakes. Now the swirl had grown to include Brian Nelson and Clarissa who, thankfully, had both entered the high school that year. At Fairfax Brian and Clarissa clung to each other, exploiting what had happened to them, using my father's debasement as a varnish of cool they could coat themselves with by retelling throughout the school what had happened that night in the cornfield.

Ray and Ruth walked by on the inside of the glass wall that looked out on the outdoor lounge. On the false boulders where the supposed bad kids sat, they would see

Brian holding court. His walk that year went from anxious scarecrow to masculine strut. Clarissa, giggly with both fear and lust, had unlocked her privates and slept with Brian. However haphazardly, everyone I'd known was growing up.

Buckley entered kindergarten that year and immediately arrived home with a crush on his teacher, Miss Koekle. She held his hand so gently whenever she had to lead him to the bathroom or help explain an assignment that her force was irresistible. In one way he profited — she would often sneak him an extra cookie or a softer sit-upon — but in another he was held aloft and apart from his fellow kindergartners. By my death he was made different among the one group — children — in which he might have been anonymous.

Samuel would walk Lindsey home and then go down the main road and thumb his way to Hal's bike shop. He counted on buddies of his brother's to recognize him, and he reached his destination in various pasted-together bikes and trucks that Hal would fine-tune for the driver when they pulled up.

He did not go inside our house for a while. No one but family did. By October my father was just beginning to get up and around. His doctors had told him that his right leg would always be stiff, but if he stretched and stayed limber it wouldn't present too much of an obstacle. "No running bases, but everything else," the surgeon said the morning after his surgery, when my father woke to find

Lindsey beside him and my mother standing by the window staring out at the parking lot.

Buckley went right from basking in the shine of Miss Koekle home to burrow in the empty cave of my father's heart. He asked ceaseless questions about the "fake knee," and my father warmed to him.

"The knee came from outer space," my father would say. "They brought pieces of the moon back and carved them up and now they use them for things like this."

"Wow," Buckley would say, grinning. "When can Nate see?"

"Soon, Buck, soon," my father said. But his smile grew weak.

When Buckley took these conversations and brought them to our mother — "Daddy's knee is made out of moonbone," he would tell her, or "Miss Koekle said my colors were really good" — she would nod her head. She had become aware of what she did. She cut carrots and celery into edible lengths. She washed out thermoses and lunchboxes, and when Lindsey decided she was too old for a lunchbox, my mother caught herself actually happy when she found wax-lined bags that would keep her daughter's lunch from seeping through and staining her clothes. Which she washed. Which she folded. Which she ironed when necessary and which she straightened on hangers. Which she picked up from the floor or retrieved from the car or untangled from the wet towel left on the bed that she made every morning, tucking the corners in, and fluffing the pillows, and propping up stuffed animals, and opening the blinds to let the light in.

In the moments when Buckley sought her out, she often made a barter of it. She would focus on him for a

few minutes, and then she would allow herself to drift
away from her house and home and think of Len.

By November, my father had mastered what he called an
"adroit hobble," and when Buckley egged him on he
would do a contorted skip that, as long as it made his son
laugh, didn't make him think of how odd and desperate
he might look to an outsider or to my mother. Everyone
save Buckley knew what was coming: the first anniversary.

Buckley and my father spent the crisp fall afternoons
out in the fenced-in yard with Holiday. My father would
sit in the old iron lawn chair with his leg stretched out in
front of him and propped up slightly on an ostentatious
boot scraper that Grandma Lynn had found in a curio
shop in Maryland.

Buckley threw the squeaky cow toy while Holiday ran
to get it. My father took pleasure in the agile body of his
five-year-old son and Buckley's peals of delight when
Holiday knocked him over and nudged him with his nose
or licked his face with his long pink tongue. But he
couldn't rid himself of one thought: this too — this perfect boy — could be taken from him.

It had been a combination of things, his injury not the
least among them, that had made him stay inside the
house on an extended sick leave from his firm. His boss
acted differently around him now, and so did his cowork-
ers. They trod gently outside his office and would stop a
few feet from his desk as if, should they be too relaxed in
his presence, what had happened to him would happen to
them — as if having a dead child were contagious. No

one knew how he continued to do what he did, while simultaneously they wanted him to shut all signs of his grief away, place it in a file somewhere and tuck it in a drawer that no one would be asked to open again. He called in regularly, and his boss just as easily agreed that he could take another week, another month if he had to, and he counted this as a blessing of always having been on time or willing to work late. But he stayed away from Mr. Harvey and tried to curb even the thought of him. He would not use his name except in his notebook, which he kept hidden in his study, where it was surprisingly easily agreed with my mother that she would no longer clean. He had apologized to me in his notebook. "I need to rest, honey. I need to understand how to go after this man. I hope you'll understand."

But he had set his return to work for December 2, right after Thanksgiving. He wanted to be back in the office by the anniversary of my disappearance. Functioning and catching up on work — in as public and distracting a place as he could think of. And away from my mother, if he was honest with himself.

How to swim back to her, how to reach her again. She was pulling and pulling away — all her energy was against the house, and all his energy was inside it. He settled on building back his strength and finding a strategy to pursue Mr. Harvey. Placing blame was easier than adding up the mounting figures of what he'd lost.

Grandma Lynn was due for Thanksgiving, and Lindsey had kept to a beautifying regime Grandma had set up for her through letters. She'd felt silly when she first put cucumbers on her eyes (to diminish puffiness), or oatmeal on her face (to cleanse the pores and absorb excess oils), or eggs yolks in her hair (to make it shine). Her use of groceries had even made my mother laugh, then wonder if she too should start to beautify. But that was only for a second, because she was thinking of Len, not because she was in love with him but because being with him was the fastest way she knew to forget.

Two weeks before Grandma Lynn's arrival, Buckley and my father were out in the yard with Holiday. Buckley and Holiday were romping from one large pile of burnished oak leaves to another in an increasingly hyper game of tag. "Watch out, Buck," my father said. "You'll make Holiday nip." And sure enough.

My father said he wanted to try something out.

"We have to see if your old dad can carry you piggyback style again. Soon you'll be too big."

So, awkwardly, in the beautiful isolation of the yard, where if my father fell only a boy and a dog who loved him would see, the two of them worked together to make what they both wanted — this return to father/son normalcy — happen. When Buckley stood on the iron chair — "Now scoot up my back," my father said, stooping forward, "and grab on to my shoulders," not knowing if he'd have the strength to lift him up from there — I crossed my fingers hard in heaven and held my breath. In the cornfield, yes, but, in this moment, repairing the most basic fabric of their previous day-to-day lives, challenging his injury to take a moment like this back, my father became my hero.

"Duck, now duck again," he said as they galumphed through the downstairs doorways and up the stairs, each step a balance my father negotiated, a wincing pain. And with Holiday rushing past them on the stairs, and Buckley joyous on his mount, he knew that in this challenge to his strength he had done the right thing.

When the two of them — with dog — discovered Lindsey in the upstairs bathroom, she whined a loud complaint.

"Daaaaddd!"

My father stood up straight. Buckley reached up and touched the light fixture with his hand.

"What are you doing?" my father said.

"What does it look like I'm doing?"

She sat on the toilet lid wrapped in a large white towel (the towels my mother bleached, the towels my mother hung on the line to dry, the towels she folded, and placed in a basket and brought up to the linen closet . . .). Her left leg was propped up on the edge of the tub, covered with shaving cream. In her hand she held my father's razor.

"Don't be petulant," my father said.

"I'm sorry," my sister said, looking down. "I just want a little privacy is all."

My father lifted Buckley up and over his head. "The counter, the counter, son," he said, and Buckley thrilled at the illegal halfway point of the bathroom counter and how his muddy feet soiled the tile.

"Now hop down." And he did. Holiday tackled him.

"You're too young to shave your legs, sweetie," my father said.

"Grandma Lynn started shaving at eleven."

"Buckley, will you go in your room and take the dog? I'll be in in a while."

"Yes, Daddy."

Buckley was still a little boy who my father could, with patience and a bit of maneuvering, get up on his shoulders so they could be a typical father and son. But he now saw in Lindsey what brought a double pain. I was a little girl in the tub, a toddler being held up to the sink, a girl who had forever stopped just short of sitting as my sister did now.

When Buckley was gone, he turned his attention to my sister. He would care for his two daughters by caring for one: "Are you being careful?" he asked.

"I just started," Lindsey said. "I'd like to be alone, Dad."

"Is that the same blade that was on it when you got it from my shaving kit?"

"Yes."

"Well, my beard stubble dulls the blade. I'll go get you a fresh one."

"Thanks, Dad," my sister said, and again she was his sweet, piggyback-riding Lindsey.

He left the room and went down the hallway to the other side of the house and the master bathroom that he and my mother still shared, though they no longer slept in the same room together. As he reached up into the cabinet for the package of fresh razors, he felt a tear in his chest. He ignored it and focused on the task. There was only a flicker of a thought then: *Abigail should be doing this.*

He brought the razor blades back, showed Lindsey how to change them, and gave her a few pointers on how best to shave. "Watch out for the ankle and the knee," he said. "Your mother always called those the danger spots."

"You can stay if you want," she said, ready now to let him in. "But I might be a bloody mess." She wanted to hit herself. "Sorry, Dad," she said. "Here, I'll move — you sit."

She got up and went to sit on the edge of the tub. She ran the tap, and my father lowered himself onto the toilet lid.

"It's okay, honey," he said. "We haven't talked about your sister in a while."

"Who needs to?" my sister said. "She's everywhere."

"Your brother seems to be all right."

"He's glued to you."

"Yes," he said, and he realized he liked it, this father-courting his son was doing.

"Ouch," Lindsey said, a fine trickle of blood beginning to spread into the white foam of the shaving cream. "This is a total hassle."

"Press down on the nick with your thumb. It stops the bleeding. You could do just to the top of your knee," he offered. "That's what your mother does unless we're going to the beach."

Lindsey paused. "You guys never go to the beach."

"We used to."

My father had met my mother when they were both working at Wanamaker's during the summer break from college. He had just made a nasty comment about how the employee's lounge reeked of cigarettes when she smiled and brought out her then-habitual pack of Pall Malls. "Touché," he said, and he stayed beside her despite the reeking stink of her cigarettes enveloping him from head to toe.

"I've been trying to decide who I look like," Lindsey said, "Grandma Lynn or Mom."

"I've always thought both you and your sister looked like my mother," he said.

"Dad?"

"Yes."

"Are you still convinced that Mr. Harvey had something to do with it?"

It was like a stick finally sparking against another stick — the friction took.

"There is no doubt in my mind, honey. None."

"Then why doesn't Len arrest him?"

She drew the razor sloppily up and finished her first leg. She hesitated there, waiting.

"I wish it was easy to explain," he said, the words coiling out of him. He had never talked at length about his suspicion to anyone. "When I met him that day, in his backyard, and we built that tent — the one he claimed he built for his wife, whose name I thought was Sophie and Len took down as Leah — there was something about his movements that made me sure."

"Everyone thinks he's kind of weird."

"True, I understand that," he said. "But then everyone hasn't had much to do with him either. They don't know whether his weirdness is benign or not."

"Benign?"

"Harmless."

"Holiday doesn't like him," Lindsey offered.

"Exactly. I've never seen that dog bark so hard. The fur on his back stood straight up that morning."

"But the cops think you're nuts."

" 'No evidence' is all they can say. Without evidence and without — excuse me, honey — a body, they have nothing to move on and no basis for an arrest."

"What would be a basis?"

"I guess something to link him to Susie. If someone had seen him in the cornfield or even lurking around the school. Something like that."

"Or if he had something of hers?" Both my father and Lindsey were heatedly talking, her second leg lathered but left unshaved, because what radiated as the two sticks of their interest sparked flame was that I was in that house somewhere. My body — in the basement, first floor, second floor, attic. To keep from acknowledging that horrible — but oh, if it were true, so blatant so perfect so conclusive as evidence — thought, they remembered what I wore that day, remembered what I carried, the Frito Bandito eraser I prized, the David Cassidy button I'd pinned inside my bag, the David Bowie one I had pinned on the outside. They named all the clutter and accessories that surrounded what would be the best, most hideous evidence anyone could find — my corpse cut up, my blank and rotting eyes.

My eyes: the makeup Grandma Lynn had given her helped but did not solve the problem of how much everyone could see my eyes in Lindsey's. When they presented themselves — a compact flashing past her when in use by a girl at a neighboring desk, or an unexpected reflection in the window of a store — she looked away. It was particularly painful with my father. What she realized as they talked was that as long as they were on this subject — Mr. Harvey, my clothes, my book bag, my body, me — the vigilance to my memory made my father see her as Lindsey and not as a tragic combination of his two daughters.

"So you would want to be able to get in his house?" she said.

They stared at each other, a flicker of recognition of a dangerous idea. In his hesitation, before he finally said that that would be illegal, and no, he hadn't thought of that, she knew he was lying. She also knew he needed someone to do it for him.

"You should finish shaving, honey," he said.

She agreed with him and turned away, knowing what she'd been told.

Grandma Lynn arrived on the Monday before Thanksgiving. With the same laser-beam eyes that immediately sought out any unsightly blemish on my sister, she now saw something beneath the surface of her daughter's smile, in her placated, tranquilized movements and in how her body responded whenever Detective Fenerman or the police work came up.

When my mother refused my father's help in cleaning up after dinner that night, the laser eyes were certain. Adamantly, and to the shock of everyone at the table and the relief of my sister — Grandma Lynn made an announcement.

"Abigail, I am going to help you clean up. It will be a mother/daughter thing."

"What?"

My mother had calculated that she could let Lindsey off easily and early and then she would spend the rest of the night over the sink, washing slowly and staring out the window until the darkness brought her own reflection back to her. The sounds of the TV would fade away and she would be alone again.

"I just did my nails yesterday," Grandma Lynn said

after tying on an apron over her camel-colored A-line dress, "so I'll dry."

"Mother, really. This isn't necessary."

"It is necessary, believe me, sweetie," my grandmother said. There was something sober and curt in that *sweetie.*

Buckley led my father by the hand into the adjoining room where the TV sat. They took up their stations and Lindsey, having been given a reprieve, went upstairs to call Samuel.

It was such a strange thing to see. So out of the ordinary. My grandmother in an apron, holding a dish towel up like a matador's red flag in anticipation of the first dish coming her way.

They were quiet as they worked, and the silence — the only sounds being the splash of my mother's hands plunging into the scalding water, the squeak of plates, and the clank of the silver — made a tension fill the room which grew unbearable. The noises of the game from the nearby room were just as odd to me. My father had never watched football; basketball his only sport. Grandma Lynn had never done dishes; frozen meals and takeout menus were her weapons of choice.

"Oh Christ," she finally said. "Take this." She handed the just-washed dish back to my mother. "I want to have a real conversation but I'm afraid I'm going to drop these things. Let's take a walk."

"Mother, I need to . . ."

"You need to take a walk."

"After the dishes."

"Listen," my grandmother said, "I know I'm whatever I am and you're whatever you are, which isn't me, which makes you happy, but I know some things when I see them and I know something is going on that isn't kosher. *Capisce?*"

My mother's face was wavering, soft and malleable — almost as soft and malleable as the image of her that floated on the sullied water in the sink.

"What?"

"I have suspicions and I don't want to talk about them here."

Ten-four, Grandma Lynn, I thought. I'd never seen her nervous before.

It would be easy for the two of them to leave the house alone. My father, with his knee, would never think to join them, and, these days, where my father went or did not go, my brother, Buckley, followed.

My mother was silent. She saw no other option. As an afterthought they removed their aprons in the garage and piled them on the roof of the Mustang. My mother bent down and lifted the garage door.

It was still early enough so the light would hold for the beginning of their walk. "We could take Holiday," my mother tried.

"Just you and your mother," my grandmother said. "The most frightening pairing imaginable."

They had never been close. They both knew it, but it wasn't something they acknowledged very much. They joked around it like two children who didn't particularly like each other but were the only children in a large, barren neighborhood. Now, never having tried to before, having always let her daughter run as fast as she could in whatever direction she wished, my grandmother found that she was suddenly catching up.

They had passed by the O'Dwyers' and were near the Tarkings' before my grandmother said what she had to say.

"My humor buried my acceptance," my grandmother said. "Your father had a long-term affair in New Hampshire. Her first initial was F and I never knew what it stood for. I found a thousand options for it over the years."

"Mother?"

My grandmother kept walking, didn't turn. She found that the crisp fall air helped, filling her lungs until they felt cleaner than they had just minutes before.

"Did you know that?"

"No."

"I guess I never told you," she said. "I didn't think you needed to know. Now you do, don't you think?"

"I'm not sure why you're telling me this."

They had come to the bend in the road that would lead them back around the circle. If they went that way and did not stop, eventually they would find themselves in front of Mr. Harvey's house. My mother froze.

"My poor, poor sweetie," my grandmother said. "Give me your hand."

They were awkward. My mother could count on her fingers how many times her tall father had leaned down and kissed her as a child. The scratchy beard that smelled of a cologne that, after years of searching, she could never identify. My grandmother took her hand and held on as they walked the other way.

They walked into an area of the neighborhood where newer families seemed to be moving in more and more. The anchor houses, I remembered my mother calling them, because they lined the street that led into the whole development—anchored the neighborhood to an original road built before the township was a township. The road that led to Valley Forge, to George Washington and the Revolution.

"Susie's death brought your father's back to me," my grandmother said. "I never let myself mourn him properly."

"I know," my mother said.

"Do you resent me for it?"

My mother paused. "Yes."

My grandmother patted the back of my mother's hand with her free one. "Good, see, that's a nugget."

"A nugget?"

"Something that's coming out of all this. You and me. A nugget of truth between us."

They passed the one-acre lots on which trees had been growing for twenty years. If not exactly towering, they were still twice as tall as the fathers who had first held them and stomped the dirt around them with their weekend work shoes.

"Do you know how alone I've always felt?" my mother asked her mother.

"That's why we're walking, Abigail," Grandma Lynn said.

My mother focused her eyes in front of her but stayed connected to her mother with her hand. She thought of the solitary nature of her childhood. How, when she had watched her two daughters tie string between paper cups and go to separate rooms to whisper secrets to each other, she could not really say she knew how that felt. There had been no one else in the house with her but her mother and father, and then her father had gone.

She stared at the tops of the trees, which, miles from our development, were the tallest things around. They stood on a high hill that had never been cleared for houses and on which a few old farmers still dwelled.

"I can't describe what I'm feeling," she said. "To anyone."

They reached the end of the development just as the sun was going down over the hill in front of them. A moment passed without either of them turning around. My mother watched the last light flicker in a drain-off puddle at the end of the road.

"I don't know what to do," she said. "It's all over now."

My grandmother was not sure what she meant by "it," but she did not press harder.

"Shall we head back?" my grandmother offered.

"How?" my mother said.

"To the house, Abigail. Head back to the house."

They turned and began walking again. The houses one after another, identical in structure. Only what my grandmother thought of as their accessories marked them as different. She had never understood places like this — places where her own child had chosen to live.

"When we get to the turn to the circle," my mother said, "I want to walk past it."

"His house?"

"Yes."

I watched Grandma Lynn turn when my mother turned.

"Would you promise me not to see the man anymore?" my grandmother asked.

"Who?"

"The man you're involved with. That's what I've been talking about."

"I'm not involved with anyone," my mother said. Her mind flew like a bird from one rooftop to the next. "Mother?" she said, and turned.

"Abigail?"

"If I needed to get away for a while, could I use Daddy's cabin?"

"Have you been listening to me?"

They could smell something in the air, and again my mother's anxious, agile mind slipped away. "Someone is smoking," she said.

Grandma Lynn was staring at her child. The pragmatic, prim mistress that my mother had always been was gone. She was flighty and distracted. My grandmother had nothing left to say to her.

"They're foreign cigarettes," my mother said. "Let's go find them!"

And in the fading light my grandmother stared, flabbergasted, as my mother began to follow the scent to its source.

"I'm heading back," my grandmother said.

But my mother kept walking.

She found the source of the smoke soon enough. It was Ruana Singh, standing behind a tall fir tree in her backyard.

"Hello," my mother said.

Ruana did not start as I thought she would. Her calmness had become something practiced. She could make a breath last through the most startling event, whether it was her son being accused of murder by the police or her husband running their dinner party as if it were an academic committee meeting. She had told Ray he could go upstairs, and then she had disappeared out the back door and not been missed.

"Mrs. Salmon," Ruana said, exhaling the heady smell of her cigarettes. In a rush of smoke and warmth my mother met Ruana's extended hand. "I'm so glad to see you."

"Are you having a party?" my mother asked.

"My husband is having a party. I am the hostess."

My mother smiled.

"This is a weird place we both live," Ruana said.

Their eyes met. My mother nodded her head. Back on the road somewhere was her own mother, but for right now she, like Ruana, was on a quiet island off the mainland.

"Do you have another cigarette?"

"Absolutely, Mrs. Salmon, yes." Ruana fished into the pocket of her long black cardigan and held out the pack and her lighter. "Dunhills," she said. "I hope that's all right."

My mother lit her cigarette and handed the blue package with its golden foil back to Ruana. "Abigail," she said as she exhaled. "Please call me Abigail."

Up in his room with his lights off, Ray could smell his mother's cigarettes, which she never accused him of pilfering, just as he never let on that he knew she had them. He heard voices downstairs — the loud sounds of his father and his colleagues speaking six different languages and laughing delightedly over the oh-so-American holiday to come. He did not know that my mother was out on the lawn with his mother or that I was watching him sit in his window and smell their sweet tobacco. Soon he would turn away from the window and switch on the small light by his bed to read. Mrs. McBride had told them to find a sonnet they'd like to write a paper on, but as he read the lines of those available to him in his *Norton Anthology* he kept drifting back to the moment he wished he could take back and do over again. If he had just kissed me on the scaffold, maybe everything would have turned out differently.

Grandma Lynn kept on the course she had set with my mother, and, eventually, there it was — the house they tried to forget while living two houses down. *Jack was right,* my grandmother thought. She could even feel it in the dark. The place radiated something malevolent. She shivered and began to hear the crickets and see the fireflies gathering in a swarm above his front flower beds. She thought suddenly that she would do nothing but sympathize with her daughter. Her child was living inside the middle of a ground zero to which no affair on her own husband's part could offer her insight. She would tell my mother in the morning that the keys to the cabin would always be there for her if she needed them.

That night my mother had what she considered a wonderful dream. She dreamed of the country of India, where she had never been. There were orange traffic cones and beautiful lapis lazuli insects with mandibles of gold. A young girl was being led through the streets. She was taken to a pyre where she was wound in a sheet and placed up on a platform built from sticks. The bright fire that consumed her brought my mother into that deep, light, dreamlike bliss. The girl was being burned alive, but, first, there had been her body, clean and whole.

FOURTEEN

For a week Lindsey cased my killer's house. She was doing exactly what he did to everyone else.

She had agreed to train with the boys' soccer team all year in preparation for the challenge Mr. Dewitt and Samuel encouraged her to take on: qualifying to play in the all-male high school soccer league. And Samuel, to show his support, trained alongside her with no hope of qualifying for anything, he said, other than "fastest guy in shorts."

He could run, even if kicking and fielding and noticing a ball anywhere within his vicinity were all beyond him. And so, while they did laps around the neighborhood, each time Lindsey shot a look toward Mr. Harvey's house, Samuel was out in front, setting the pace for her — unaware of anything else.

Inside the green house, Mr. Harvey was looking out. He saw her watching and he began to itch. It had been almost a year now, but the Salmons remained bent on crowding him.

It had happened before in other towns and states. The family of a girl suspected him but no one else did. He had perfected his patter to the police, a certain obsequious innocence peppered with wonder about their procedures or useless ideas that he presented as if they might help. Bringing up the Ellis boy with Fenerman had been a good stroke, and the lie that he was a widower always helped. He fashioned a wife out of whichever victim he'd recently been taking pleasure in in his memory, and to flesh her out there was always his mother.

He left the house every day for an hour or two in the afternoon. He would pick up any supplies he needed and then drive out to Valley Forge Park and walk the paved roads and the unpaved trails and find himself suddenly surrounded by school tours at George Washington's log cabin or the Washington Memorial Chapel. This would buoy him up — these moments when the children were eager to see history, as if they might actually find a long silver hair from Washington's wig caught on the rough end of a log post.

Occasionally one of the tour guides or teachers would notice him standing there, unfamiliar even if amiable, and he would be met with a questioning stare. He had a thousand lines to give them: "I used to bring my children here." "This is where I met my wife." He knew to ground whatever he said in connection to some imagined family, and then the women would smile at him. Once an attractive, heavy woman tried to engage him in conversation while the park guide told the children about the winter of 1776 and the Battle of the Clouds.

He had used the story of widowhood and talked about a woman named Sophie Cichetti, making her his now-deceased wife and true love. It had been like luscious food to this woman, and, as he listened to her tell him about her cats and her brother, who had three children, whom she loved, he pictured her sitting on the chair in his basement, dead.

After that, when he met a teacher's questioning glare he would shyly back off and go somewhere else inside the park. He watched mothers with their children still in strollers walk briskly along the exposed paths. He saw teenagers who were cutting school necking in the uncut fields or along the interior trails. And at the highest point of the park was a small wood beside which he sometimes parked. He would sit in his Wagoneer and watch lonely men pull up beside him and get out of their cars. Men in suits on their lunch hour or men in flannel and jeans would walk quickly into that wood. Sometimes they would cast a look back in his direction—an inquiry. If they were close enough, these men could see, through his windshield, what his victims saw—his wild and bottomless lust.

On November 26, 1974, Lindsey saw Mr. Harvey leaving the green house, and she began to hang back from the pack of running boys. Later she could claim she had gotten her period and all of them would hush up, even be satisfied that this was proof that Mr. Dewitt's unpopular plan—a girl at regionals!—would never work out.

I watched my sister and marveled. She was becoming everything all at once. A woman. A spy. A jock. The Ostracized: One Man Alone.

She walked, clutching her side in a false cramp, and waved the boys on when they turned to notice her. She kept walking with her hand on her waist until they turned the corner at the far end of the block. At the edge of Mr. Harvey's property was a row of tall, thick pines that had been left untrimmed for years. She sat down by one of them, still feigning exhaustion in case any neighbor was looking out, and then, when she felt the moment was right, she curled up in a ball and rolled in between two pines. She waited. The boys had one more lap. She watched them pass her and followed them with her eyes as they cut up through the vacant lot and back to the high school. She was alone. She calculated she had forty-five minutes before our father would begin to wonder when she'd be home. The agreement had been that if she trained with the boys' soccer team, Samuel would escort her home and have her back by five o'clock.

The clouds had hung heavy in the sky all day, and the late-fall cold raised goose bumps along her legs and arms. The team runs always warmed her, but when she reached the locker room where she shared the showers with the field hockey team, she would begin to shiver until the hot water hit her body. But on the lawn of the green house, her goose bumps were also from fear.

When the boys cut up the path, she scrambled over to the basement window at the side of Mr. Harvey's house. She had already thought of a story if she was caught. She was chasing a kitten that she'd seen dart in between the pine trees. She would say it was gray, that it was fast, that it had run toward Mr. Harvey's house and she'd followed it without thinking.

She could see inside to the basement, where it was

dark. She tried the window, but the latch lock was pushed in. She would have to break the glass. Her mind racing, she worried about the noise, but she was too far along to stop now. She thought of my father at home, ever mindful of the clock near his chair, and took her sweatshirt off and balled it around her feet. Sitting down, she braced her body with her arms and then kicked once, twice, three times with both feet until the window smashed—a muffled cracking.

Carefully, she lowered herself down, searching the wall for a foothold but having to jump the final few feet onto the broken glass and concrete.

The room appeared tidy and swept, different from our own basement, where heaps of holiday-marked boxes—EASTER EGGS AND GREEN GRASS, CHRISTMAS STAR/ORNAMENTS—never made it back on the shelves my father had built.

The cold air from outside came in, and she felt the draft along her neck pushing her out of the shimmering semicircle of shattered glass and into the rest of the room. She saw the easy chair and a little table beside it. She saw the large alarm clock with luminous numbers sitting on the metal shelving. I wanted to guide her eyes to the crawlspace, where she would find the bones of the animals, but I knew, too, that regardless of drawing a fly's eyes on graph paper and excelling that fall in Mr. Botte's biology class, she would imagine the bones were mine. For this, I was glad she went nowhere near them.

Despite my inability to appear or whisper, push or usher, Lindsey, all alone, felt something. Something charged the air in the cold, dank basement and made her cringe. She stood only a few feet from the open window,

knowing that she would, no matter what, be walking farther in and that she had to, no matter what, calm and
focus herself to look for clues; but right then, for one moment, she thought of Samuel running ahead, having
thought he would find her on his last lap, then running
back toward the school, thinking he would find her outside, and then assuming, but with the first trace of a
doubt, that she was showering, and so he too would be
showering now, and then waiting for her before he did
anything else. How long would he wait? As her eyes
mounted the stairs to the first floor before her feet followed, she wished that Samuel were there to climb down
after her and trace her movements, erasing her solitude as
he went, fitting into her limbs. But she had not told him
on purpose — had told no one. What she was doing was
beyond the pale — criminal — and she knew it.

If she thought about it later, she would say that she had
needed air and so that was what had gotten her up the
stairs. Small flecks of white dust collected at the tips of
her shoes as she mounted the stairs, but she didn't notice
them.

She twisted the knob of the basement door and
reached the first floor. Only five minutes had passed.
She had forty left, or so she thought. There was still a
bit of light seeping in through the closed blinds. As she
stood, again, hesitating, in this house identical to our
own, she heard the thwack of the *Evening Bulletin* hit
the stoop and the delivery boy ring the bell on his bike
as he passed.

My sister told herself that she was inside a series of
rooms and spaces that, gone through methodically, might
yield what she needed, provide her the trophy she could

take home to our father, earning her freedom from me that way. Competition always, even between the living and the dead. She saw the flagstones in the hall — the same dark green and gray as ours — and imagined crawling after me when she was a baby and I was just learning to walk. Then she saw my toddler body running delightedly away from her and into the next room, and she remembered her own sense of reaching out, of taking her first steps as I teased her from the living room.

But Mr. Harvey's house was much emptier than ours, and there were no rugs to lend warmth to the decor. Lindsey stepped from the flagstones onto the polished pine floors of what in our house was the living room. She made echoes up the open front hall, the sound of every movement reaching back for her.

She couldn't stop the memories slamming into her. Every one had a brutal report. Buckley riding piggyback on my shoulders down the stairs. Our mother steadying me as Lindsey looked on, jealous that I could reach, with the silver star in my hands, the top of the Christmas tree. Me sliding down the banister and asking her to join. Both of us begging the comics off our father after dinner. All of us running after Holiday as he barked and barked. And the countless exhausted smiles awkwardly dressing our faces for photos at birthdays, and holidays, and after school. Two sisters dressed identically in velvet or plaid or Easter yellows. We held baskets of bunnies and eggs we had sunk in dye. Patent leather shoes with straps and hard buckles. Smiling hard as our mother tried to focus her camera. The photos always fuzzy, our eyes bright red spots. None of them, these artifacts left to my sister, would hold for posterity the moments before and the moments after, when we two girls played in the house or fought over toys. When we were sisters.

Then she saw it. My back darting into the next room. Our dining room, the room that held his finished dollhouses. I was a child running just ahead of her.

She hurried after me.

She chased me through the downstairs rooms and though she was training hard for soccer, when she returned to the front hall she was unable to catch her breath. She grew dizzy.

I thought of what my mother had always said about a boy at our bus stop who was twice as old as us but still in the second grade. "He doesn't know his own strength, so you need to be careful around him." He liked to give bear hugs to anyone who was nice to him, and you could see this dopey love drop into his features and ignite his desire to touch. Before he was removed from regular school and sent somewhere else no one talked about, he had picked up a little girl named Daphne and squeezed her so hard that she fell into the road when he let go. I was pushing so hard on the Inbetween to get to Lindsey that I suddenly felt I might hurt her when I meant to help.

My sister sat down on the wide steps at the bottom of the front hall and closed her eyes, focused on regaining her breath, on why she was in Mr. Harvey's house in the first place. She felt encased in something heavy, a fly trapped in a spider's funnel web, the thick silk binding up around her. She knew that our father had walked into the cornfield possessed by something that was creeping into her now. She had wanted to bring back clues he could use as rungs to climb back to her on, to anchor him with facts, to ballast his sentences to Len. Instead she saw herself falling after him into a bottomless pit.

She had twenty minutes.

Inside that house my sister was the only living being, but she was not alone, and I was not her only company. The architecture of my murderer's life, the bodies of the girls he'd left behind, began to reveal itself to me now that my sister was in that house. I stood in heaven. I called their names:

Jackie Meyer. Delaware, 1967. Thirteen.

A chair knocked over, its underside facing the room. Lying curled toward it, she wore a striped T-shirt and nothing else. Near her head, a small pool of blood.

Flora Hernandez. Delaware, 1963. Eight.

He'd only wanted to touch her, but she screamed. A small girl for her age. Her left sock and shoe were found later. The body, unrecovered. The bones lay in the earthen basement of an old apartment house.

Leah Fox. Delaware, 1969. Twelve.

On a slipcovered couch under a highway on-ramp, he killed her, very quietly. He fell asleep on top of her, lulled by the sound of cars rushing above them. Not until ten hours later, when a vagrant knocked on the small shack Mr. Harvey had built out of discarded doors — did he begin to pack himself and Leah Fox's body up.

Sophie Cichetti, Pennsylvania, 1960. Forty-nine.

A landlady, she had divided her upstairs apartment into two by erecting a Sheetrock wall. He liked the half-circle window this created, and the rent was cheap. But she talked too much about her son and insisted on reading him poems from a book of sonnets. He made love to her on her side of the divided room, smashed her skull in when she started to talk, and brought her body to the bank of a creek nearby.

Leidia Johnson. 1960. Six.

Buck's County, Pennsylvania. He dug an arched cave inside a hill near the quarry and waited. She was the youngest one.

Wendy Richter. Connecticut, 1971. Thirteen.

She was waiting for her father outside a bar. He raped her in the bushes and then strangled her. That time, as he grew conscious, coming up out of the stupor that often clung on, he heard noises. He turned the dead girl's face toward his, and as the voices grew closer he bit down on her ear. "Sorry, man," he heard two drunk men say as they walked into the nearby bushes to take a leak.

I saw now that town of floating graves, cold and whipped by winds, where the victims of murder went in the minds of the living. I could see his other victims as they occupied his house — those trace memories left behind before they fled this earth — but I let them go that day and went to my sister.

Lindsey stood up the moment I focused back on her. Together the two of us walked the stairs. She felt like the zombies in the movies Samuel and Hal loved. One foot in front of the other and staring blankly straight ahead. She reached what was my parents' bedroom in our house and found nothing. She circled the hallway upstairs. Nothing. Then she went into what had been my bedroom in our house, and she found my killer's.

It was the least barren room in the house, and she did her best not to displace anything. To move her hand in between the sweaters stacked on the shelf, prepared to find anything in their warm insides — a knife, a gun, a Bic pen chewed on by Holiday. Nothing. But then, as she heard something but could not identify what it was, she turned toward the bed and saw the bedside table and, lying in the circle of light from a reading lamp left on, his sketchbook. She walked toward it and heard another sound, again, not putting the sounds together. Car pulling up. Car braking with a squeak. Car door slamming shut.

She turned the pages of the sketchbook and looked at the inky drawings of crossbeams and braces or turrets and buttresses, and she saw the measurements and notes, none of which meant anything to her. Then, as she flipped a final page, she thought she heard footsteps outside and very close.

As Mr. Harvey turned the key in the lock of his front door, she saw the light pencil sketch on the page in front of her. It was a small drawing of stalks above a sunken hole, a detail off to the side of a shelf and how a chimney could draw out smoke from a fire, and the thing that sunk into her: in a spidery hand he had written "Stolfuz cornfield." If it were not for the articles in the paper after the discovery of my elbow, she would not have known that the cornfield was owned by a man named Stolfuz. Now she saw what I wanted her to know. I had died inside that hole; I had screamed and fought and lost.

She ripped out the page. Mr. Harvey was in the kitchen making something to eat — the liverwurst he favored, a bowl of sweet green grapes. He heard a board creak. He stiffened. He heard another and his back rose and blossomed with sudden understanding.

The grapes dropped on the floor to be crushed by his left foot, while my sister in the room above sprang to the aluminum blinds and unlocked the stubborn window. Mr.

Harvey mounted the stairs two at a time, and my sister smashed out the screen, scrambling onto the porch roof and rolling down it as he gained the upstairs hall and came barreling toward her. The gutter broke when her body tipped past it. As he reached his bedroom, she fell into the bushes and brambles and muck.

But she was not hurt. Gloriously not hurt. Gloriously young. She stood up as he reached the window to climb out. But he stopped. He saw her running toward the elderberry. The silk-screened number on her back screamed out at him. 5! 5! 5!

Lindsey Salmon in her soccer shirt.

Samuel was sitting with my parents and Grandma Lynn when Lindsey reached the house.

"Oh my God," my mother said, the first to see her through the small square windows that lined either side of our front door.

And by the time my mother opened it Samuel had rushed to fill the space, and she walked, without looking at my mother or even my father hobbling forward, right into Samuel's arms.

"My God, my God, my God," my mother said as she took in the dirt and the cuts.

My grandmother came to stand beside her.

Samuel put his hand on my sister's head and smoothed her hair back.

"Where have you been?"

But Lindsey turned to our father, lessened so now — smaller, weaker, than this child who raged. How alive she was consumed me whole that day.

"Daddy?"

"Yes, sweetheart."

"I did it. I broke into his house." She was shaking slightly and trying not to cry.

My mother balked: "You what?"

But my sister didn't look at her, not once.

"I brought you this. I think it might be important."

She had kept the drawing in her hand, crumpled tightly into a ball. It had made her landing harder, but she had come away anyway.

A phrase my father had read that day appeared in his mind now. He spoke it aloud as he looked into Lindsey's eyes.

"There is no condition one adjusts to so quickly as a state of war."

Lindsey handed him the drawing.

"I'm going to pick up Buckley," my mother said.

"Don't you even want to look at this, Mom?"

"I don't know what to say. Your grandmother is here. I have shopping to do, a bird to cook. No one seems to realize that we have a family. We have a family, a family and a son, and I'm going."

Grandma Lynn walked my mother to the back door but did not try to stop her.

My mother gone, my sister reached her hand out to Samuel. My father saw what Lindsey did in Mr. Harvey's spidery hand: the possible blueprint of my grave. He looked up.

"Do you believe me now?" he asked Lindsey.

"Yes, Daddy."

My father — so grateful — had a call to make.

"Dad," she said.

"Yes."

"I think he saw me."

I could never have imagined a blessing greater to me than the physical safety of my sister that day. As I walked back from the gazebo I shivered with the fear that had held me, the possibility of her loss on Earth not just to my father, my mother, Buckley, and Samuel, but, selfishly, the loss of her on Earth to me.

Franny walked toward me from the cafeteria. I barely raised my head.

"Susie," she said. "I have something to tell you."

She drew me under one of the old-fashioned lampposts and then out of the light. She handed me a piece of paper folded into four.

"When you feel stronger, look at it and go there."

Two days later, Franny's map led me to a field that I had always walked by but which, though beautiful, I'd left unexplored. The drawing had a dotted line to indicate a path. Searching nervously, I looked for an indentation in the rows and rows of wheat. Just ahead I saw it, and as I began to walk between the rows the paper dissolved in my hand.

I could see an old and beautiful olive tree just up ahead.

The sun was high, and in front of the olive tree was a clearing. I waited only a moment until I saw the wheat on the other side begin to pulse with the arrival of someone who did not crest the stalks.

She was small for her age, as she had been on Earth,

and she wore a calico dress that was frayed at the hem and the cuffs.

She paused and we stared at each other.

"I come here almost every day," she said. "I like to listen to the sounds."

All around us, I realized, the wheat was rustling as it moved against itself in the wind.

"Do you know Franny?" I asked.

The little girl nodded solemnly.

"She gave me a map to this place."

"Then you must be ready," she said, but she was in *her* heaven too, and that called for twirling and making her skirt fly out in a circle. I sat on the ground under the tree and watched her.

When she was done she came toward me and breathlessly sat herself down. "I was Flora Hernandez," she said. "What was your name?"

I told her, and then I began to cry with comfort, to know another girl he had killed.

"The others will be here soon," she said.

And as Flora twirled, other girls and women came through the field in all directions. Our heartache poured into one another like water from cup to cup. Each time I told my story, I lost a bit, the smallest drop of pain. It was that day that I knew I wanted to tell the story of my family. Because horror on Earth is real and it is every day. It is like a flower or like the sun; it cannot be contained.

FIFTEEN

A t first no one stopped them, and it was something his mother enjoyed so much, the trill of her laughter when they ducked around the corner from whatever store and she uncovered and presented the pilfered item to him, that George Harvey joined in her laughter and, spying an opportunity, would hug her while she was occupied with her newest prize.

It was a relief for both of them, getting away from his father for the afternoon and driving into the nearby town to get food or other supplies. They were scavengers at best and made their money by collecting scrap metal and old bottles and hauling them into town on the back of the elder Harvey's ancient flatbed truck.

When his mother and he were caught for the first time, the two of them were treated graciously by the woman at the cash register. "If you can pay for it, do. If you can't, leave it on the counter as good as new," she said brightly and winked at the eight-year-old George Harvey. His mother took the small glass bottle of aspirin out of her pocket and placed it sheepishly on the counter. Her face sank. "No better than the child," his father often repri- manded her.

Getting caught became another moment in his life that brought fear — that sick feeling curling into his stomach like eggs being folded into a bowl — and he could tell by the closed faces and hard eyes when the person walking down the aisle toward them was a store employee who had seen a woman stealing.

And she began handing him the stolen items to hide on his body, and he did it because she wanted him to. If they got outside and away in the truck, she would smile and bang the steering wheel with the flat of her hand and call him her little accomplice. The cab would fill with her wild, unpredictable love, and for a little while — until it wore off and they spied something glinting on the side of the road that they would have to investigate for what his mother called its "possibilities" — he did feel free. Free and warm.

He remembered the advice she gave him the first time they drove a stretch of road in Texas and saw a white wooden cross along the road. Around the base of it were clusters of fresh and dead flowers. His scavenger's eye had been drawn immediately by the colors.

"You have to be able to look past the dead," his mother said. "Sometimes there are good trinkets to take away from them."

Even then, he could sense they were doing something

wrong. The two of them got out of the truck and went up to the cross, and his mother's eyes changed into the two black points that he was used to seeing when they were searching. She found a charm in the shape of an eye and one in the shape of a heart and held them out for George Harvey to see.

"Don't know what your father would make of them, but we can keep them, just you and me."

She had a secret stash of things that she never showed his father.

"Do you want the eye or the heart?"

"The eye," he said.

"I think these roses are fresh enough to save, nice for the truck."

That night they slept in the truck, unable to make the drive back to where his father was working a temporary job splitting and riving boards by hand.

The two of them slept curled into each other as they did with some frequency, making the inside of the cab an awkward nest. His mother, like a dog worrying a blanket, moved around in her seat and fidgeted. George Harvey had realized after earlier struggles that it was best to go limp and let her move him as she wished. Until his mother was comfortable, no one slept.

In the middle of the night, as he was dreaming about the soft insides of the palaces in picture books he'd seen in public libraries, someone banged on the roof, and George Harvey and his mother sat bolt upright. It was three men, looking through the windows in a way George Harvey recognized. It was the way his own father looked when he was drunk sometimes. It had a double effect: the whole gaze was leveled at his mother and simultaneously absented his son.

He knew not to cry out.

"Stay quiet. They aren't here for you," she whispered to him. He began to shiver underneath the old army blankets that covered them.

One of the three men was standing in front of the truck. The other two were banging on either side of the truck's roof, laughing and lolling their tongues.

His mother shook her head vehemently, but this only enraged them. The man blocking the truck started rocking his hips back and forth against the front end, which caused the other two men to laugh harder.

"I'm going to move slow," his mother whispered, "and pretend I'm getting out of the truck. I want you to reach forward and turn the keys in the ignition when I say so."

He knew he was being told something very important. That she needed him. Despite her practiced calm, he could hear the metal in her voice, the iron breaking up through fear now.

She smiled at the men, and as they sent up whoops and their bodies relaxed, she used her elbow to knock the gear shift into place. "Now," she said in a flat monotone, and George Harvey reached forward and turned the keys. The truck came to life with its rumbling old engine.

The faces of the men changed, fading from an acquisitive joy and then, as she reversed back to a good degree and they stared after her, uncertainty. She switched into drive and screamed, "On the floor!" to her son. He could feel the bump of the man's body hitting the truck only a few feet from where he lay curled up inside. Then the body was pitched up onto the roof. It lay there for a second until his mother reversed again. He had had a moment of clarity about how life should be lived: not as a child or as a woman. They were the two worst things to be.

His heart had beat wildly as he watched Lindsey make for the elderberry hedge, but then immediately he had calmed. It was a skill his mother, not his father, had taught him — to take action only after calculating the worst possible outcome of each choice available. He saw the notebook disturbed and the missing page in his sketchbook. He checked the bag with the knife. He took the knife with him to the basement and dropped it down the square hole that was drilled through the foundation. From the metal shelving, he retrieved the group of charms that he kept from the women. He took the Pennsylvania keystone charm from my bracelet and held it in his hand. Good luck. The others he spread out on his white handkerchief, and then he brought the four ends together to form a small hobo sack. He put his hand inside the hole under the foundation and got down on the floor on his stomach to push his arm in all the way to the shoulder. He groped, feeling with the free fingers of his hand as the other held the hobo sack, until he found a rusty jut of a metal support over which the workmen had poured the cement. He hung his trophy bag there and then withdrew his arm and stood. The book of sonnets he had buried earlier that summer in the woods of Valley Forge Park, shedding evidence slowly as he always did; now, he had to hope, not too slowly.

Five minutes at the most had gone by. That could be accounted for by shock and anger. By checking what everyone else thought to be valuables — his cuff links, his cash, his tools. But he knew no more time than that could be overlooked. He had to call the police.

He worked himself up. He paced briefly, drew his breath in and out rapidly, and when the operator answered he set his voice on edge.

"My home has been broken into. I need the police," he said, scripting the opening of his version of the story as inside he calculated how quickly he could leave and what he would carry with him.

When my father called the station, he requested Len Fenerman. But Fenerman couldn't be located. My father was informed that two uniforms had already been sent out to investigate. What they found when Mr. Harvey answered his door was a man who was tearfully upset and who in every aspect, save a certain repellent quality that the officers attributed to the sight of a man allowing himself to cry, seemed to be responding rationally to the reported events.

Even though the information about the drawing Lindsey had taken had come in over the radio, the officers were more impressed by Mr. Harvey's readily volunteering to have his home searched. He also seemed sincere in his sympathy for the Salmon family.

The officers grew uncomfortable. They searched the house perfunctorily and found nothing except both the evidence of what they took to be extreme loneliness and a room full of beautiful dollhouses on the second floor, where they switched topics and asked him how long he had been building them.

They noticed, they said later, an immediate and

friendly change in his demeanor. He went into his bedroom and got the sketchbook, not mentioning any stolen drawing. The police took note of his increasing warmth as he showed them the sketches for the dollhouses. They asked their next question delicately.

"Sir," an officer said, "we can take you down to the station for further questioning, and you do have the right to have a lawyer present but —"

Mr. Harvey interrupted him. "I would be happy to answer anything here. I am the wronged party, though I have no wish to press charges against that poor girl."

"The young woman that broke in," the other officer began, "she did take something. It was a drawing of the cornfield and a sort of structure in it . . ."

The way it hit Harvey, the officers would tell Detective Fenerman, was all at once and very convincing. He had an explanation that fit so perfectly, they did not see him as a flight risk — largely because they did not see him first and foremost as a murderer.

"Oh, the poor girl," he said. He placed his fingers to his pursed lips. He turned to his sketchbook and flipped through it until he came to a drawing that was very much like the one Lindsey had taken.

"There, it was a drawing similar to this one, correct?" The officers — now audience — nodded. "I was trying to figure it out," Mr. Harvey confessed. "I admit the horror of it has obsessed me. I think everyone in the neighborhood has tried to think how they could have prevented it. Why they didn't hear something, see something. I mean, surely the girl screamed.

"Now here," he said to the two men, pointing to his drawing with a pen. "Forgive me, but I think in structures, and after hearing about how much blood there was in the cornfield and the churned-up nature of that area where it was found, I decided that perhaps . . ." He looked at them, checking their eyes. Both officers were following him. They wanted to follow him. They had had no leads, no body, no clues. Perhaps this strange man had a workable theory. "Well, that the person who did it had built something underground, a hole, and then I confess I began to worry at it and detail it the way I do the dollhouses, and I gave it a chimney and a shelf, and, well, that's just my habit." He paused. "I have a lot of time to myself."

"So, did it work out?" one of the two officers asked.

"I always did think I had something there."

"Why didn't you call us?"

"I wasn't bringing back their daughter. When Detective Fenerman interviewed me I mentioned how I suspected the Ellis boy, and I turned out to be dead wrong. I didn't want to meddle with any more of my amateur theories."

The officers apologized for the fact that the following day Detective Fenerman would be calling again, most likely wanting to go over the same material. See the sketchbook, hear Mr. Harvey's assertions about the cornfield. All of this Mr. Harvey took as part of being a dutiful civilian, even if it had been he who was victimized. The officers documented my sister's path of break-in from the basement window and then out through the bedroom window. They discussed the damages, which Mr. Harvey said he would take care of out-of-pocket, stressing his awareness of the overwhelming grief the Salmon father had displayed several months ago, and how it now seemed to be infecting the poor girl's sister.

I saw the chances of Mr. Harvey's capture diminish as I watched the end of my family as I had known it ignite.

After picking up Buckley from Nate's house, my mother stopped at a payphone outside the 7-Eleven on Route 30. She told Len to meet her at a loud and raucous store in the mall near the grocery store. He left immediately. As he pulled out of his driveway, the phone in his house was ringing but he didn't hear it. He was inside the capsule of his car, thinking of my mother, of how wrong it all was and then of how he could not say no to her for reasons he couldn't hold on to long enough to analyze or disclaim.

My mother drove the short distance from the grocery store to the mall and led Buckley by the hand through the glass doors to a sunken circle where parents could leave their children to play while they shopped.

Buckley was elated. "The circle! Can I?" he said, as he saw his peers jumping off the jungle gym and turning somersaults on the rubber-covered floor.

"Do you really want to, honey?" she asked him.

"Please," he said.

She phrased it as a motherly concession. "All right," she said. And he went off in the direction of a red metal slide. "Be good," she called after him. She had never allowed him to play there without her.

She left his name with the monitor who watched over the play circle and said that she would be shopping on the lower level near Wanamaker's.

While Mr. Harvey was explaining his theory of my murder, my mother felt a hand brush across the back of her shoulders inside a trashy store called Spencer's. She turned with expectant relief, only to see Len Fenerman's back as he made his way out of the store. Passing glow-in-the-dark masks, black plastic eight balls, fuzzy troll keychains, and a large laughing skull, my mother followed after him.

He did not turn around. She kept following him, at first excited and then annoyed. In between footfalls there was enough time to think, and she did not want to think.

Finally, she saw him unlock a white door that was set flush into the wall, which she had never noticed before.

She could tell by the noises up ahead in the dark corridor that Len had brought her into the inner workings of the mall — the air filtration system or the water pumping plant. She didn't care. In the darkness she imagined herself to be within her own heart, and a vision of the enlarged drawing from her doctor's office entered her head and simultaneously she saw my father, in his paper gown and black socks, perched on the edge of the examining table as the doctor had explained to them the dangers of congestive heart failure. Just as she was about to let go into grief, cry out, and stumble and fall into confusion, she came to the end of the corridor. It opened into a huge room three stories high that throbbed and buzzed and throughout which there were tiny lights mounted higgledy-piggledy on metal tanks and drums. She paused and listened for any sound other than the deafening thrumming of air being sucked out of the mall and reconditioned to be pushed back in. Nothing.

I saw Len before she did. Standing alone in the almost-darkness he watched her for a moment, locating the need in her eyes. He was sorry for my father, for my family, but he fell into those eyes. "I could drown in those eyes, Abigail," he wanted to say to her, but he knew that this he would not be allowed.

My mother began to make out more and more shapes within the bright interconnected jumble of metal, and for a moment I could feel the room begin to be enough for her, the foreign territory enough to soothe her. It was the feeling of being unreachable.

If it had not been for Len's hand stretching out and grazing her fingers with the tips of his own, I might have kept her to myself there. The room could have remained simply a brief vacation from her life as Mrs. Salmon.

But he did touch her, and she did turn. Still, she could not really look at him. He accepted this absence on her part.

I swirled as I watched it and held on to the bench in the gazebo, gulping air. She could never know, I thought, that while she was clutching Len's hair and he was reaching his hand around to the small of her back, bringing her in closer, that the man who had murdered me was escorting two officers out his front door.

I felt the kisses as they came down my mother's neck and onto her chest, like the small, light feet of mice, and like the flower petals falling that they were. Ruinous and marvelous all at once. They were whispers calling her away from me and from her family and from her grief. She followed with her body.

While Len took her hand and brought her away from the wall into the tangle of pipes where the noise overhead added its chorus, Mr. Harvey began to pack his belongings; my brother met a small girl playing Hula-Hoop in the circle; my sister and Samuel lay beside each other on her bed, fully dressed and nervous; my grandmother downed three shots in the empty dining room. My father watched the phone.

My mother grabbed at Len's coat and shirt greedily, and he helped her. He watched as she tugged at her own clothes, pulling her sweater over her head, then her mother-jumper, and her turtleneck, until she was left in her underpants and camisole. He stared at her.

Samuel kissed the back of my sister's neck. She smelled of soap and Bactine, and he wanted, even then, never to leave her.

Len was about to say something; I could see my mother notice his lips just as they parted. She shut her eyes and commanded the world to shut up — screaming the words inside her skull. She opened her eyes again and looked at him. He was silent, his mouth set. She took her cotton camisole over the top of her head and stepped out of her underwear. My mother had my body as it would never become. But she had her own moonlit skin, her ocean eyes. She was hollow and lost and abandoned up.

Mr. Harvey left his house for the final time while my mother was granted her most temporal wish. To find a doorway out of her ruined heart, in merciful adultery.

SIXTEEN

A year to the day after my death, Dr. Singh called to say he would not be home for dinner. But Ruana would do her exercises no matter what. If, as she stretched out on the rug in the one warm spot that the house seemed to hold in the winter, she could not help but turn over and over again her husband's absences in her mind, she would let them consume her until her body pled for her to let him go and to focus — as she leaned forward, her arms outstretched toward her toes now — and move, to shut her brain off and forget everything but the slight and pleasant yearning of muscles stretching and her own body bending.

Reaching almost to the floor, the window in the dining room was interrupted only by the metal baseboard for the heat, which Ruana liked to keep turned off because the noises it made disturbed her. Outside, she could see the cherry tree, its leaves and flowers all gone. The empty bird feeder swung slightly on its branch.

She stretched until she was quite warm and she'd forgotten herself, and the home she stood in fell away from her. Her age. Her son. But still, creeping in on her was the figure of her husband. She had a premonition. She did not believe it was a woman, or even a student who worshiped him, that made him late more and more often. She knew what it was because it was something she too had had and had severed herself from after having been injured long ago. It was ambition.

She heard sounds now. Holiday barking two streets over and the Gilberts' dog answering him and Ray moving around upstairs. Blessedly, in another moment, Jethro Tull erupted again, shutting out all else.

Except for the occasional cigarette, which she smoked as secretly as she could so as not to give Ray license, she had kept herself in good health. Many of the women in the neighborhood commented on how well she kept herself and some had asked her if she would mind showing them how, though she had always taken these entreaties merely as their way of making conversation with their lone foreign-born neighbor. But as she sat in Sukhasana and her breath slowed to a deep rhythm, she could not fully release and let go. The niggling idea of what she would do as Ray grew older and her husband worked increasingly long hours crept up the inside of her foot and along her calf to the back of her knee and began to climb into her lap.

The doorbell rang.

Ruana was happy for the escape, and though she was someone to whom order was also a sort of meditation, she hopped up, wrapped a shawl that was hanging on the back of a chair around her waist, and, with Ray's music barreling down the stairs, walked to the door. She thought only for a moment that it might be a neighbor. A complaining neighbor — the music — and she, dressed in a red leotard and shawl.

Ruth stood on the stoop, holding a grocery sack.

"Hello," Ruana said. "May I help you?"

"I'm here to see Ray."

"Come in."

All of this had to be half-shouted over the noise coming from upstairs. Ruth stepped into the front hall.

"Go on up," Ruana shouted, pointing to the stairs.

I watched Ruana take in Ruth's baggy overalls, her turtleneck, her parka. *I could start with her,* Ruana thought to herself.

Ruth had been standing in the grocery store with her mother when she saw the candles among the paper plates and plastic forks and spoons. At school that day she had been acutely aware of what day it was and even though what she had done so far — lain in bed reading *The Bell Jar,* helped her mother clean out what her father insisted on calling his toolshed and what she thought of as the poetry shed, and tagged along to the grocery store — hadn't consisted of anything that might mark the anniversary of my death, she had been determined to do something.

When she saw the candles she knew immediately that she would find her way over to Ray's house and ask him to come with her. Because of their meetings at the shot-put circle, the kids at school had made them a couple despite all evidence to the contrary. Ruth could draw as many female nudes as she might wish and fashion scarves on her head and write papers on Janis Joplin and loudly protest the oppression of shaving her legs and armpits. In the eyes of her classmates at Fairfax, she remained a weird girl who had been found K-I-S-S-I-N-G a weird boy.

What no one understood — and they could not begin to tell anyone — was that it had been an experiment between them. Ray had kissed only me, and Ruth had never kissed anyone, so, united, they had agreed to kiss each other and see.

"I don't feel anything," Ruth had said afterward, as they lay in the maple leaves under a tree behind the teachers' parking lot.

"I don't either," Ray admitted.

"Did you feel something when you kissed Susie?"

"Yes."

"What?"

"That I wanted more. That night I dreamed of kissing her again and wondered if she was thinking the same thing."

"And sex?"

"I hadn't really gotten that far yet," Ray said. "Now I kiss you and it's not the same."

"We could keep trying," Ruth said. "I'm game if you don't tell anyone."

"I thought you liked girls," Ray said.

"I'll make you a deal," Ruth said. "You can pretend I'm Susie and I will too."

"You are so entirely screwed up," Ray said, smiling.

"Are you saying you don't want to?" Ruth teased.

"Show me your drawings again."

"I may be screwed up," Ruth said, dragging out her

sketchbook from her book bag — it was now full of nudes she'd copied out of *Playboy,* scaling various parts up or down and adding hair and wrinkles where they had been airbrushed out — "but at least I'm not a perv for char-coal."

Ray was dancing around his bedroom when Ruth walked in. He wore his glasses, which at school he tried to do without because they were thick and his father had only sprung for the least expensive, hard-to-break frames. He had on a pair of jeans that were baggy and stained and a T-shirt that Ruth imagined, and I knew, had been slept in.

He stopped dancing as soon as he saw her standing at the doorway holding the grocery bag. His hands went up immediately and collected his glasses, and then, not knowing what to do with them, he waved them at her and said, "Hello."

"Can you turn it down?" Ruth screamed.

"Sure!"

When the noise ceased her ears rang for a second, and in that second she saw something flicker across Ray's eyes.

He now stood on the other side of the room, and in be-tween them was his bed, where sheets were rumpled and balled and over which hung a drawing Ruth had done of me from memory.

"You hung it up," Ruth said.

"I think it's really good."

"You and me and nobody else."

"My mom thinks it's good."

"She's intense, Ray," Ruth said, putting down the bag. "No wonder you're so freak-a-delic."

"What's in the bag?"

"Candles," said Ruth. "I got them at the grocery store. It's December sixth."

"I know."

"I thought we might go to the cornfield and light them. Say goodbye."

"How many times can you say it?"

"It was an idea," Ruth said. "I'll go alone."

"No," Ray said. "I'll go."

Ruth sat down in her jacket and overalls and waited for him to change his shirt. She watched him with his back toward her, how thin he was but also how the muscles seemed to pop on his arms the way they were supposed to and the color of his skin, like his mother's, so much more inviting than her own.

"We can kiss for a while if you want."

And he turned, grinning. He had begun to like the experiments. He was not thinking of me anymore — though he couldn't tell that to Ruth.

He liked the way she cursed and hated school. He liked how smart she was and how she tried to pretend that it didn't matter to her that his father was a doctor (even though not a real doctor, as she pointed out) and her father scavenged old houses, or that the Singhs had rows and rows of books in their house while she was starved for them.

He sat down next to her on the bed.

"Do you want to take your parka off?"

She did.

And so on the anniversary of my death, Ray mashed

himself against Ruth and the two of them kissed and at some point she looked him in the face. "Shit!" she said. "I think I feel something."

When Ray and Ruth arrived at the cornfield, they were silent and he was holding her hand. She didn't know whether he was holding it because they were observing my death together or because he liked her. Her brain was a storm, her usual insight gone.

Then she saw she had not been the only one to think of me. Hal and Samuel Heckler were standing in the cornfield with their hands jammed in their pockets and their backs turned toward her. Ruth saw yellow daffodils on the ground.

"Did you bring those?" Ruth asked Samuel.

"No," Hal said, answering for his brother. "They were already here when we got here."

Mrs. Stead watched from her son's upstairs bedroom. She decided to throw on her coat and walk out to the field. It was not something she even tried to judge, whether or not she belonged there.

Grace Tarking was walking around the block when she saw Mrs. Stead leaving her house with a poinsettia. They talked briefly in the street. Grace said that she was going to stop at home but she would come and join them.

Grace made two phone calls, one to her boyfriend, who lived a short distance away in a slightly richer area, and one to the Gilberts. They had not yet recovered from their strange role in the discovery of my death — their faithful lab having found the first evidence. Grace offered to escort them, since they were older and cutting across neighbors' lawns and over the bumpy earth of the cornfield would be a challenge to them, but yes, Mr. Gilbert had said, he wanted to come. They needed this, he told Grace Tarking, his wife particularly — though I could see how crushed he was. He always covered his pain by being attentive to his wife. Though they had thought briefly of giving their dog away, he was too much comfort to both of them.

Mr. Gilbert wondered if Ray, who ran errands for them and was a sweet boy who had been badly judged, knew, and so he called the Singh household. Ruana said she suspected her son must already be there but that she would be along herself.

Lindsey was looking out the window when she saw Grace Tarking with her arm in Mrs. Gilbert's and Grace's boyfriend steadying Mr. Gilbert as the four of them cut across the O'Dwyers' lawn.

"Something's going on in the cornfield, Mom," she said.

My mother was reading Molière, whom she had studied so intensely in college but hadn't looked at since. Beside her were the books that had marked her as an avant-garde undergraduate: Sartre, Colette, Proust, Flaubert. She had pulled them off the shelves in her bedroom and promised herself she would reread them that year.

"I'm not interested," she said to Lindsey, "but I'm sure your father will be when he gets home. Why don't you go up and play with your brother?"

My sister had dutifully hovered for weeks now, paying court to our mother regardless of the signals she gave. There was something on the other side of the icy surface. Lindsey was sure of it. She stayed by my mother, sitting by her chair and watching our neighbors outside the window.

By the time darkness fell, the candles the latecomers had had the foresight to bring lit the cornfield. It seemed like everyone I'd ever known or sat next to in a classroom from kindergarten to eighth grade was there. Mr. Botte saw that something was happening when he'd come out of the school after preparing his classroom for the next day's annual animal digestion experiment. He'd strolled over, and, when he realized what it was, he let himself back into the school and made some calls. There had been a secretary who had been overcome by my death. She came with her son. There had been some teachers who hadn't come to the official school memorial.

The rumors of Mr. Harvey's suspected guilt had begun to make their way from neighbor to neighbor on Thanksgiving night. By the next afternoon it was the only thing the neighbors could talk about — was it possible? Could that strange man who had lived so quietly among them have killed Susie Salmon? But no one had dared approach my family to find out the details. Cousins of friends or fathers of the boys who cut their lawn were asked if they knew anything. Anyone who might know what the police were doing had been buddied up to in the past week, and so my memorial was both a way to mark my memory and a way for the neighbors to seek comfort from one another. A murderer had lived among them, passed them on the street, bought Girl Scout cookies from their daughters and magazine subscriptions from their sons.

In my heaven I buzzed with heat and energy as more and more people reached the cornfield and lit their candles and began to hum a low, dirgelike song for which Mr. O'Dwyer called back to the distant memory of his Dublin grandfather. My neighbors were awkward at first, but the secretary from the school clung to Mr. O'Dwyer as his voice gave forth, and she added her less melodious one. Ruana Singh stood stiffly in an outer circle away from her son. Dr. Singh had called as she was leaving to say he would be sleeping overnight in his office. But other fathers, coming home from their offices, parked their cars in their driveways only to get out and follow their neighbors. How could they both work to support their families and watch their children to make sure they were safe? As a group they would learn it was impossible, no matter how many rules they laid down. What had happened to me could happen to anyone.

No one had called my house. My family was left undisturbed. The impenetrable barrier that surrounded the shingles, the chimney, the woodpile, the driveway, the fence, was like a layer of clear ice that coated the trees when it rained and then froze. Our house looked the same as every other one on the block, but it was not the same. Murder had a blood red door on the other side of which was everything unimaginable to everyone.

When the sky had turned a dappled rose, Lindsey realized what was happening. My mother never lifted her eyes from her book.

"They're having a ceremony for Susie," Lindsey said.

"Listen." She cracked the window open. In rushed the cold December air and the distant sound of singing.

My mother used all her energy. "We've had the memorial," she said. "That's done for me."

"What's done?"

My mother's elbows were on the armrests of the yellow winged-back chair. She leaned slightly forward and her face moved into shadow, making it harder for Lindsey to see the expression on her face. "I don't believe she's waiting for us out there. I don't think lighting candles and doing all that stuff is honoring her memory. There are other ways to honor it."

"Like what?" Lindsey said. She sat cross-legged on the rug in front of my mother, who sat in her chair with her finger marking her place in Molière.

"I want to be more than a mother."

Lindsey thought she could understand this. She wanted to be more than a girl.

My mother put the Molière book on top of the coffee table and scooted forward on the chair until she lowered herself down onto the rug. I was struck by this. My mother did not sit on the floor, she sat at the bill-paying desk or in the wing chairs or sometimes on the end of the couch with Holiday curled up beside her.

She took my sister's hand in hers.

"Are you going to leave us?" Lindsey asked.

My mother wobbled. How could she say what she already knew? Instead, she told a lie. "I promise I won't leave you."

What she wanted most was to be that free girl again, stacking china at Wanamaker's, hiding from her manager the Wedgwood cup with the handle she broke, dreaming of living in Paris like de Beauvoir and Sartre, and going home that day laughing to herself about the nerdy Jack Salmon, who was pretty cute even if he hated smoke. The cafés in Paris were full of cigarettes, she'd told him, and he'd seemed impressed. At the end of that summer when she invited him in and they had, both for the first time, made love, she'd smoked a cigarette, and for the joke he said he'd have one too. When she handed him the damaged blue china to use as an ashtray, she used all her favorite words to embellish the story of breaking and then hiding, inside her coat, the now homely Wedgwood cup.

"Come here, baby," my mother said, and Lindsey did. She leaned her back into my mother's chest, and my mother rocked her awkwardly on the rug. "You are doing so well, Lindsey; you are keeping your father alive." And they heard his car pull into the drive.

Lindsey let herself be held while my mother thought of Ruana Singh out behind her house, smoking. The sweet scent of Dunhills had drifted out onto the road and taken my mother far away. Her last boyfriend before my father had loved Gauloises. He had been a pretentious little thing, she thought, but he had also been oh-so-serious in a way that let her be oh-so-serious as well.

"Do you see the candles, Mom?" Lindsey asked, as she stared out the window.

"Go get your father," my mother said.

My sister met my father in the mud room, hanging up his keys and coat. Yes, they would go, he said. Of course they would go.

"Daddy!" My brother called from the second floor, where my sister and father went to meet him.

"Your call," my father said as Buckley bodychecked him.

"I'm tired of protecting him," Lindsey said. "It doesn't feel real not to include him. Susie's gone. He knows that."

My brother stared up at her.

"There is a party for Susie," Lindsey said. "And me and Daddy are taking you."

"Is Mommy sick?" Buckley asked.

Lindsey didn't want to lie to him, but she also felt it was an accurate description of what she knew.

"Yes."

Lindsey agreed to meet our father downstairs while she brought Buckley into his room to change his clothes.

"I see her, you know," Buckley said, and Lindsey looked at him.

"She comes and talks to me, and spends time with me when you're at soccer."

Lindsey didn't know what to say, but she reached out and grabbed him and squeezed him to her, the way he often squeezed Holiday.

"You are so special," she said to my brother. "I'll always be here, no matter what."

My father made his slow way down the stairs, his left hand tightening on the wooden banister, until he reached the flagstone landing.

His approach was loud. My mother took her Molière book and crept into the dining room, where he wouldn't see her. She read her book, standing in the corner of the dining room and hiding from her family. She waited for the front door to open and close.

My neighbors and teachers, friends and family, circled an arbitrary spot not far from where I'd been killed. My father, sister, and brother heard the singing again once they were outside. Everything in my father leaned and pitched toward the warmth and light. He wanted so badly to have me remembered in the minds and hearts of everyone. I knew something as I watched: almost everyone was saying goodbye to me. I was becoming one of many little-girl-losts. They would go back to their homes and put me to rest, a letter from the past never reopened or reread. And I could say goodbye to them, wish them well, bless them somehow for their good thoughts. A handshake in the street, a dropped item picked up and retrieved and handed back, or a friendly wave from a distant window, a nod, a smile, a moment when the eyes lock over the antics of a child.

Ruth saw my three family members first, and she tugged on Ray's sleeve. "Go help him," she whispered. And Ray, who had met my father on his first day of what would prove a long journey to try to find my killer, moved forward. Samuel came away too. Like youthful pastors, they brought my father and sister and brother into the group, which made a wide berth for them and grew silent.

My father had not been outside the house except to drive back and forth to work or sit out in the backyard, for months, nor had he seen his neighbors. Now he looked at them, from face to face, until he realized I had been loved by people he didn't even recognize. His heart filled up, warm again as it had not been in what seemed so long to him — save small forgotten moments with Buckley, the accidents of love that happened with his son.

He looked at Mr. O'Dwyer. "Stan," he said, "Susie used to stand at the front window during the summer and listen to you singing in your yard. She loved it. Will you sing for us?"

And in the kind of grace that is granted but rarely, and not when you wish it most — to save a loved one from dying — Mr. O'Dwyer wobbled only a moment on his first note, then sang loud and clear and fine.

Everyone joined in.

I remembered those summer nights my father spoke of. How the darkness would take forever to come and with it I always hoped for it to cool down. Sometimes, standing at the open window in the front hall, I would feel a breeze, and on that breeze was the music coming from the O'Dwyers' house. As I listened to Mr. O'Dwyer run through all the Irish ballads he had ever learned, the breeze would begin to smell of earth and air and a mossy scent that meant only one thing: a thunderstorm.

There was a wonderful temporary hush then, as Lindsey sat in her room on the old couch studying, my father sat in his den reading his books, my mother downstairs doing needlepoint or washing up.

I liked to change into a long cotton nightgown and go out onto the back porch, where, as the rain began falling in heavy drops against the roof, breezes came in the screens from all sides and swept my gown against me. It was warm and wonderful and the lightning would come and, a few moments later, the thunder.

My mother would stand at the open porch door, and, after she said her standard warning, "You're going to catch your death of cold," she grew quiet. We both listened together to the rain pour down and the thunder clap and smelled the earth rising to greet us.

"You look invincible," my mother said one night.

I loved these times, when we seemed to feel the same thing. I turned to her, wrapped in my thin gown, and said:

"I am."

SNAPSHOTS

With the camera my parents gave me, I took dozens of candids of my family. So many that my father forced me to choose which rolls I thought should be developed. As the cost of my obsession mounted, I began keeping two boxes in my closet. "Rolls to be sent out" and "Rolls to hold back." It was, my mother said, the only hint of any organizational skills I possessed.

I loved the way the burned-out flashcubes of the Kodak Instamatic marked a moment that had passed, one that would now be gone forever except for a picture. When they were spent, I took the cubed four-corner flashbulbs and passed them from hand to hand until they cooled. The broken filaments of the flash would turn a molten marble blue or sometimes smoke the thin glass black. I had rescued the moment by using my camera and in that way had found a way to stop time and hold it. No one could take that image away from me because I owned it.

* * *

On a summer evening in 1975, my mother turned to my father and said:

"Have you ever made love in the ocean?"

And he said, "No."

"Neither have I," my mother said. "Let's pretend it is the ocean and that I am going away and we might never see each other again."

The next day she left for her father's cabin in New Hampshire.

That same summer, Lindsey or Buckley or my father would open the front door and find a casserole or a bundt cake on the front stoop. Sometimes an apple pie — my father's favorite. The food was unpredictable. The casseroles Mrs. Stead made were horrible. The bundt cakes Mrs. Gilbert made were overly moist but bearable. The apple pies from Ruana: heaven on Earth.

In his study during the long nights after my mother left, my father would try to lose himself by rereading passages from the Civil War letters of Mary Chestnut to her husband. He tried to let go of any blame, of any hope, but it was impossible. He did manage a small smile once.

"Ruana Singh bakes a mean apple pie," he wrote in his notebook.

In the fall he picked up the phone one afternoon to hear Grandma Lynn.

"Jack," my grandmother announced, "I am thinking of coming to stay."

My father was silent, but the line was riddled with his hesitation.

"I would like to make myself available to you and the children. I've been knocking around in this mausoleum long enough."

"Lynn, we're just beginning to start over again," he stammered. Still, he couldn't depend on Nate's mother to watch Buckley forever. Four months after my mother left, her temporary absence was beginning to take on the feel of permanence.

My grandmother insisted. I watched her resist the remaining slug of vodka in her glass. "I will contain my drinking until"—she thought hard here—"after five o'clock, and," she said, "what the hell, I'll stop altogether if you should find it necessary."

"Do you know what you're saying?"

My grandmother felt a clarity from her phone hand down to her pump-encased feet. "Yes, I do. I think."

It was only after he got off the phone that he let himself wonder, *Where will we PUT her?*

It was obvious to everyone.

By December 1975, a year had passed since Mr. Harvey had packed his bags, but there was still no sign of him. For a while, until the tape dirtied or the paper tore, store owners kept a scratchy sketch of him taped to their windows. Lindsey and Samuel walked in the neighborhood or hung out at Hal's bike shop. She wouldn't go to the diner where the other kids went. The owner of the diner was a law and order man. He had blown up the sketch of George Harvey to twice its size and taped it to the front door. He willingly gave the grisly details to any customer who asked — young girl, cornfield, found only an elbow.

Finally Lindsey asked Hal to give her a ride to the police station. She wanted to know what exactly they were doing.

They bid farewell to Samuel at the bike shop and Hal gave Lindsey a ride through a wet December snow.

From the start, Lindsey's youth and purpose had caught the police off guard. As more and more of them realized who she was, they gave her a wider and wider berth. Here was this girl, focused, mad, fifteen. Her breasts were perfect small cups, her legs gangly but curved, her eyes like flint and flower petals.

While Lindsey and Hal waited outside the captain's office on a wooden bench, she thought she saw something across the room that she recognized. It was on Detective Fenerman's desk and it stood out in the room because of its color. What her mother had always distinguished as Chinese red, a harsher red than rose red, it was the red of classic lipsticks, rarely found in nature. Our mother was proud of her ability to wear Chinese red, noting each time she tied a particular scarf around her neck that it was a color even Grandma Lynn dared not wear.

"Hal," she said, every muscle tense as she stared at the increasingly familiar object on Fenerman's desk.

"Yes."

"Do you see that red cloth?"

"Yes."

"Can you go and get it for me?"

When Hal looked at her, she said: "I think it's my mother's."

As Hal stood to retrieve it, Len entered the squad room

from behind where Lindsey sat. He tapped her on the shoulder just as he realized what Hal was doing. Lindsey and Detective Fenerman stared at each other.

"Why do you have my mother's scarf?"

He stumbled. "She might have left it in my car one day."

Lindsey stood and faced him. She was clear-eyed and driving fast toward the worst news yet. "What was she doing in your car?"

"Hello, Hal," Len said.

Hal held the scarf in his hand. Lindsey grabbed it away, her voice growing angry. "Why do you have my mother's scarf?"

And though Len was the detective, Hal saw it first — it arched over her like a rainbow — Prisma Color understanding. The way it happened in algebra class or English when my sister was the first person to figure out the sum of x or point out the double entendres to her peers. Hal put his hand on Lindsey's shoulder to guide her. "We should go," he said.

And later she cried out her disbelief to Samuel in the back room of the bike shop.

When my brother turned seven, he built a fort for me. It was something the two of us had said we would always do together and something my father could not bring himself to do. It reminded him too much of building the tent with the disappeared Mr. Harvey.

A family with five little girls had moved into Mr. Harvey's house. Laughter traveled over into my father's study from the built-in pool they had poured the spring after George Harvey ran. The sound of little girls — girls to spare.

The cruelty of it became like glass shattering in my father's ears. In the spring of 1976, with my mother gone, he would shut the window of his den on even the hottest evenings to avoid the sound. He watched his solitary little boy in among the three pussy-willow bushes, talking to himself. Buckley had brought empty terra-cotta pots from the garage. He hauled the boot scraper out from where it lay forgotten at the side of the house. Anything to make walls for the fort. With the help of Samuel and Hal and Lindsey, he edged two huge boulders from the front of the driveway into the backyard. This was such an unexpected windfall that it prompted Samuel to ask, "How are you going to make a roof?"

And Buckley looked at him in wonder as Hal mentally scanned the contents of his bike shop and remembered two scrap sheets of corrugated tin he had leaning up against the back wall.

So one hot night my father looked down and didn't see his son anymore. Buckley was nestled inside his fort. On his hands and knees, he would pull the terra-cotta pots in after him and then prop a board against them that reached almost up to the wavy roof. Just enough light came in to read by. Hal had obliged him and painted in big black spray paint letters KEEP OUT on one side of the plywood door.

Mostly he read the Avengers and the X-Men. He dreamed of being Wolverine, who had a skeleton made of the strongest metal in the universe and who could heal from any wound overnight. At the oddest moments he would think about me, miss my voice, wish I would come out from the house and pound on the roof of his fort and demand to be let in. Sometimes he wished Samuel and Lindsey hung out more or that my father would play with him as he once had. Play without that always-worried look underneath the smile, that desperate worry that surrounded everything now like an invisible force field. But my brother would not let himself miss my mother. He tunneled into stories where weak men changed into strong half-animals or used eye beams or magic hammers to power through steel or climb up the sides of skyscrapers. He was the Hulk when angry and Spidey the rest of the time. When he felt his heart hurt he turned into something stronger than a little boy, and he grew up this way. A heart that flashed from heart to stone, heart to stone. As I watched I thought of what Grandma Lynn liked to say when Lindsey and I rolled our eyes or grimaced behind her back. "Watch out what faces you make. You'll freeze that way."

One day, Buckley came home from the second grade with a story he'd written: "Once upon a time there was a kid named Billy. He liked to explore. He saw a hole and went inside but he never came out. The End."

My father was too distracted to see anything in this. Mimicking my mother, he taped it to the fridge in the same place Buckley's long-forgotten drawing of the Inbetween had been. But my brother knew something was wrong with his story. Knew it by how his teacher had reacted, doing a double take like they did in his comic books. He took the story down and brought it to my old room while Grandma Lynn was downstairs. He folded it into a tiny square and put it inside the now-empty insides of my four-poster bed.

* * *

On a hot day in the fall of 1976, Len Fenerman visited the large safety box in the evidence room. The bones of the neighborhood animals he had found in Mr. Harvey's crawlspace were there, along with the lab confirmation of evidence of quicklime. He had supervised the investigation, but no matter how much they dug, or how deep, no other bones or bodies had been found on his property. The blood stain on the floor of his garage was my only calling card. Len had spent weeks, then months, poring over a xerox of the sketch Lindsey had stolen. He had led a team back into the field, and they had dug and then dug again. Finally they found an old Coke bottle at the opposite end of the field. There it was, a solid link: fingerprints matching Mr. Harvey's prints, which were all over his house, and fingerprints matching those on my birth certificate. There was no question in his mind: Jack Salmon had been right from the beginning.

But no matter how hard he looked for the man himself, it was as if George Harvey had evaporated into thin air when he hit the property line. He could find no records with that name attached. Officially, he did not exist.

What he had left behind were his dollhouses. So Len called the man who sold them for him, and who took commissions from select stores, and the wealthy people who ordered replicas of their own homes. Nothing. He had called the makers of the miniature chairs, the tiny doors and windows with beveled glass and brass hardware, and the manufacturer of the cloth shrubs and trees. Nothing.

He sat down among the evidence at a barren communal desk in the basement of the station. He looked through the stack of extra fliers that my father had made up. He had memorized my face, but still he looked at them. He had come to believe that the best hope in my case might be the recent rise in development in the area. With all the land churning and changing, perhaps other clues would be found that would provide the answer he needed.

In the bottom of the box was the bag with my jingle-bell hat. When he'd handed it to my mother, she had collapsed on the rug. He still couldn't pinpoint the moment he'd fallen in love with her. I knew it was the day he'd sat in our family room while my mother drew stick figures on butcher paper and Buckley and Nate slept toe to toe on the couch. I felt sorry for him. He had tried to solve my murder and he had failed. He had tried to love my mother and he had failed.

Len looked at the drawing of the cornfield that Lindsey had stolen and forced himself to acknowledge this: in his cautiousness, he had allowed a murderer to get away. He could not shake his guilt. He knew, if no one else did, that by being with my mother in the mall that day he was the one to blame for George Harvey's freedom.

He took his wallet out of his back pocket and laid down the photos of all the unsolved cases he had ever worked on. Among them was his wife's. He turned them all face-down. "Gone," he wrote on each one of them. He would no longer wait for a date to mark an understanding of who or why or how. He would never understand all the reasons why his wife had killed herself. He would never understand how so many children went missing. He placed these photos in the box with my evidence and turned the lights off in the cold room.

But he did not know this:

In Connecticut on September 10, 1976, a hunter on his way back to his car saw something shiny on the ground. My Pennsylvania keystone charm. Then he saw that the ground nearby had been partially dug up by a bear. Exposed by the bear were the unmistakable bones of a child's foot.

My mother made it through only one winter in New Hampshire before she got the idea of driving all the way to California. It was something she had always thought she would do but had never done. A man she met in New Hampshire had told her about the work to be had in wineries in the valleys above San Francisco. It was easy to get, it was physical, and it could be, if you wanted it to be, very anonymous. All three sounded good to her.

This man had also wanted to sleep with her, but she said no. By then, she knew this wasn't the road out anymore. From the first night with Len in the innards of the mall she had known the two of them weren't building anything. She could not even really feel him.

She packed her bags for California and sent cards to my brother and sister from every town she stopped in. "Hello, I'm in Dayton. Ohio's state bird is the cardinal." "Reached the Mississippi last night at sunset. It certainly is a big river."

In Arizona, when she was eight states beyond the farthest she had ever been, she paid for her room and brought a bucket of ice with her from the machine outside. The next day she would reach California, and to celebrate she had bought herself a bottle of champagne. She thought of what the man in New Hampshire had said, how he had spent one whole year scraping the mold out of the giant casks that held wine. He had lain flat on his back and had to use a knife to peel back the layers of mold. The mold had the color and consistency of liver, and no matter how hard he bathed he would still attract fruit flies for hours afterward.

She sipped champagne from a plastic cup and looked at herself in the mirror. She forced herself to look.

She remembered sitting in our living room then, with me and my sister, my brother and father, on the first New Year's Eve that all five of us had stayed up. She had shaped the day around making sure Buckley got enough sleep.

When he woke up after dark he was sure that someone better than Santa would come that night. In his mind he held a big bang image of the ultimate holiday, when he would be transported to toyland.

Hours later, as he yawned and leaned into my mother's lap and she finger-combed his hair, my father ducked into the kitchen to make cocoa and my sister and I served German chocolate cake. When the clock struck twelve and there was only distant screaming and a few guns shot into the air in our neighborhood, my brother was unbelieving. Disappointment so swiftly and thoroughly overtook him that my mother was at a loss for what to do. She thought of it as sort of an infant Peggy Lee's "Is that all there is?" and then bawling.

She remembered my father had lifted Buckley up into his arms and started singing. The rest of us joined in. "Let ole acquaintance be forgot and never brought to mind, should ole acquaintance be forgot and days of auld lang syne!"

And Buckley had stared at us. He captured the foreign words like bubbles floating above him in the air. "Lang syne?" he said with a look of wonder.

"What does that mean?" I asked my parents.

"The old days," my father said.

"Days long past," my mother said. But then, suddenly, she had started pinching the crumbs of her cake together on her plate.

"Hey, Ocean Eyes," my father said. "Where'd you go on us?"

And she remembered that she had met his question with a closing off, as though her spirit had a tap — twist to the right and she was up on her feet asking me to help her clean up.

In the fall of 1976, when she reached California, she drove directly to the beach and stopped her car. She felt like she had driven through nothing but families for four days — squabbling families, bawling families, screaming families, families under the miraculous strain of the day by day — and she was relieved to see the waves from the windshield of her car. She couldn't help thinking of the books she had read in college. *The Awakening*. And what had happened to one writer, Virginia Woolf. It all seemed so wonderful back then — filmy and romantic — stones in the pocket, walk into the waves.

She climbed down the cliffs after tying her sweater loosely around her waist. Down below she could see nothing but jagged rocks and waves. She was careful, but I watched her feet more than the view she saw — I worried about her slipping.

My mother's desire to reach those waves, touch her feet to another ocean on the other side of the country, was all she was thinking of — the pure baptismal goal of it. Whoosh and you can start over again. Or was life more like the horrible game in gym that has you running from one side of an enclosed space to another, picking up and setting down wooden blocks without end? She was thinking *reach the waves, the waves, the waves,* and I was watching her feet navigate the rocks, and when we heard her we did so together — looking up in shock.

It was a baby on the beach.

In among the rocks was a sandy cove, my mother now saw, and crawling across the sand on a blanket was a baby in knitted pink cap and singlet and boots. She was alone on the blanket with a stuffed white toy — my mother thought a lamb.

With their backs to my mother as she descended were a group of adults — very official and frantic-looking — wearing black and navy with cool slants to their hats and boots. Then my wildlife photographer's eye saw the tripods and silver circles rimmed by wire, which, when a young man moved them left or right, bounced light off or on the baby on her blanket.

My mother started laughing, but only one assistant turned to notice her up among the rocks; everyone else was too busy. This was an ad for something, I imagined, but what? New fresh infant girls to replace your own? As my mother laughed and I watched her face light up, I also saw it fall into strange lines.

She saw the waves behind the girl child and how both beautiful and intoxicating they were — they could sweep up so softly and remove this girl from the beach. All the stylish people could chase after her, but she would drown in a moment — no one, not even a mother who had every nerve attuned to anticipate disaster, could have saved her if the waves leapt up, if life went on as usual and freak accidents peppered a calm shore.

That same week she found work at the Krusoe Winery, in a valley above the bay. She wrote my sister and brother postcards filled with the bright fragments of her life, hoping in a postcard's limited space she would sound cheery.

On her days off, she would walk down the streets of Sausalito or Santa Rosa — tiny upscale towns where everyone was a stranger — and, no matter how hard she tried to focus on the hopeful unfamiliar, when she walked inside a gift shop or café the four walls around her would begin to breathe like a lung. She would feel it then, creeping up the side of her calves and into her gut, the onslaught, the grief coming, the tears like a small relentless army approaching the front lines of her eyes, and she would breathe in, taking a large gulp of air to try to stop herself from crying in a public place. She asked for coffee and toast in a restaurant and buttered it with tears. She went into a flower shop and asked for daffodils, and when there were none she felt robbed. It was such a small wish — a bright yellow flower.

The first impromptu memorial in the cornfield opened in my father the need for more. Yearly now, he organized a memorial, to which fewer and fewer neighbors and friends came. There were the regulars, like Ruth, and the Gilberts, but more and more the group was filled out by kids from the high school who, as time went by, knew only my name and even that only as a large dark rumor invoked as a warning to any student that might prove too much a loner. Especially girls.

Each time my name was said by these strangers it felt like a pinprick. It was not the pleasant sensation that it could be when my father said it or when Ruth wrote it in her journal. It was the sensation of being simultaneously resurrected and buried within the same breath. As if in an economics class I had been ushered over into a column of transmutable commodities: the Murdered. A few teachers, like Mr. Botte, remembered me as a real girl. Sometimes on his lunch hour he would go and sit in his red Fiat and think about the daughter he had lost to leukemia. In the distance, out past his window, the cornfield loomed. Often, he would say a prayer for me.

In just a few short years, Ray Singh grew so handsome that a spell radiated from him when he walked into a crowd. His adult face had still not settled on him, but, now that he was seventeen, it was just around the corner. He exuded a dreamy asexuality that made him attractive to both men and women, with his long lashes and hooded eyelids, his thick black hair, and the same delicate features that were still a boy's.

I would watch Ray with a longing different from that which I had for anyone else. A longing to touch and hold him, to understand the very body that he examined with the coldest of eyes. He would sit at his desk and read his favorite book — *Gray's Anatomy* — and depending on what he was reading about he would use his fingers to palpate his carotid artery or his thumb to press down and follow the longest muscle in his body — the sartorius, which ran from the outside of his hip to the inside of his knee. His thinness was a boon to him then, the bones and muscles clearly distinguished beneath the skin.

By the time he packed his bags for Penn, he had committed so many words and their definitions to memory that I grew worried. With all that, how could his mind contain anything else? Ruth's friendship, his mother's love, my memory would be pushed to the back as he made way for the eye's crystalline lens and its capsule, the semicircular canals of the ear, or my favorite, the qualities of the sympathetic nervous system.

I need not have worried. Ruana cast about the house for something, anything, that her son might bring with him that was equal in heft and weight to *Gray's* and that would, she hoped, keep the flower-gathering side of him alive. Without his knowing, she tucked the book of Indian poetry into his luggage. Inside was the long-forgotten photo of me. When he unpacked inside Hill House dormitory, my picture fell on the floor by his bed. Despite how he could dissect it — the vessels of the globe of my eye, the surgical anatomy of my nasal fossae, the light tincture of my epidermis — he could not avoid them, the lips he had once kissed.

In June 1977, on the day of what would have been my graduation, Ruth and Ray were already gone. The day classes ended at Fairfax, Ruth moved to New York City with her mother's old red suitcase full of new black clothes. Having graduated early, Ray was already at the end of his freshman year at Penn.

In our kitchen that same day, Grandma Lynn gave Buckley a book on gardening. She told him about how plants came from seeds. That radishes, which he hated, grew fastest, but that flowers, which he loved, could grow from seeds as well. And she began to teach him the names: zinnias and marigolds, pansies and lilacs, carnations and petunias, and morning glory vines.

Occasionally my mother called from California. My parents had hurried and difficult conversations. She asked after Buckley and Lindsey and Holiday. She asked how the house was holding up and whether there was anything he needed to tell her.

"We still miss you," he said in December 1977, when the leaves had all fallen and been blown or raked away but even still, with the ground waiting to receive it, there had been no snow.

"I know that," she said.

"What about teaching? I thought that was your plan."

"It was," she conceded. She was on the phone in the office of the winery. Things had slowed up after the lunch crowd, but five limos of old ladies, three sheets to the wind, were soon due in. She was silent and then she said something that no one, least of all my father, could have argued with. "Plans change."

In New York, Ruth was living in an old woman's walk-in closet on the Lower East Side. It was the only thing she could afford, and she had no intention of spending much time there anyway. Daily she rolled her twin-sized futon into the corner so she could have a little floor space in which to dress. She visited the closet only once a day, and she never spent any time there if she could help it. The closet was for sleeping and having an address, a solid if tiny perch in the city.

She worked service bar and walked every inch of Manhattan on her off hours. I watched her pound the cement in her defiant boots, sure that women were being murdered wherever she went. Down in stairwells and up inside beautiful highrises. She would linger at streetlights and scan the facing street. She wrote small prayers in her journal at the cafés and the bars, where she stopped to use the bathroom after ordering the cheapest thing on the menu.

She had become convinced that she had a second sight that no one else had. She didn't know what she would do with it, save taking copious notes for the future, but she had grown unafraid. The world she saw of dead women and children had become as real to her as the world in which she lived.

In the library at Penn, Ray read about the elderly under the boldface heading "The Conditions of Death." It described a study done in nursing homes in which a large percentage of patients reported to the doctors and nurses that they saw someone standing at the end of their bed at night. Often this person tried to talk to them or call their name. Sometimes the patients were in such a high state of agitation during these delusions that they had to be given a sedative or strapped to their beds.

The text went on to explain that these visions were a result of small strokes that often preceded death. "What is commonly thought of by the layman as the Angel of

Death, when discussed at all with the patient's family, should be presented to them as a small series of strokes compounding an already precipitous state of decline."

For a moment, with his finger marking the place in the book, Ray imagined what it would be like if, standing over the bed of an elderly patient, remaining as open as he could to possibility, he might feel something brush past him as Ruth had so many years ago in the parking lot.

Mr. Harvey had been living wild within the Northeast Corridor from the outlying areas of Boston down to the northern tips of the southern states, where he would go to find easier work and fewer questions and make an occasional attempt to reform. He had always liked Pennsylvania and had crisscrossed the long state, camping sometimes behind the 7-Eleven just down the local highway from our development, where a ridge of woods survived between the all-night store and the railroad tracks, and where he found more and more tin cans and cigarette butts each time he passed through. He still liked to drive close to the old neighborhood when he could. He took these risks early in the morning or late at night, when the wild pheasants that had once been plentiful still traversed the road and his headlights would catch the hollow glowing of their eye sockets as they skittered from one side of the road to the other. There were no longer teenagers and young children sent to pick blackberries just up to the edge of our development, because the old farm fence that had hung so heavily with them had been torn down to make room for more houses. He had learned to pick wild mushrooms over time and gorged on them sometimes when staying overnight in the overgrown fields of Valley Forge Park. On a night like this I saw him come upon two novice campers who had died after eating the mushrooms' poisonous look-alikes. He tenderly stripped their bodies of any valuables and then moved on.

Hal and Nate and Holiday were the only ones Buckley had ever allowed into his fort. The grass died underneath the boulders and when it rained, the insides of the fort were a fetid puddle, but it stayed there, though Buckley went there less and less, and it was Hal who finally begged him to make improvements.

"We need to waterproof it, Buck," Hal said one day. "You're ten — that's old enough to work a caulking gun."

And Grandma Lynn couldn't help herself, she loved men. She encouraged Buck to do what Hal said, and when she knew Hal would be coming to visit, she dressed up.

"What are you doing?" my father said one Saturday morning, lured out of his den by the sweet smell of lemons and butter and golden batter rising in pans.

"Making muffins," Grandma Lynn said.

My father did a sanity check, staring at her. He was still in his robe and it was almost ninety degrees at ten in the morning, but she had pantyhose and makeup on. Then he noticed Hal in an undershirt out in the yard.

"My God, Lynn," he said. "That boy is young enough . . ."

"But he's de-lec-ta-ble!"

My father shook his head and sat down at the kitchen table. "When will the love muffins be done, Mata Hari?"

In December 1981, Len did not want to get the call he got from Delaware, where a murder in Wilmington had been connected to a girl's body found in 1976 in Connecticut. A detective, working overtime, had painstakingly traced the keystone charm in the Connecticut case back to a list of lost property from my murder.

"It's a dead file," Len told the man on the other end.

"We'd like to see what you have."

"George Harvey," Len said out loud, and the detectives at neighboring desks turned toward him. "The crime was in December 1973. The murder victim was Susie Salmon, fourteen."

"Any body for the Simon girl?"

"Salmon, like the fish. We found an elbow," Len said.

"She have a family?"

"Yes."

"Connecticut has teeth. Do you have her dentals?"

"Yes."

"That may save the family some grief," the man told Len.

Len trekked back to the evidence box he had hoped never to look at again. He would have to make a phone call to my family. But he would wait as long as possible, until he was certain the detective in Delaware had something.

For almost eight years after Samuel told Hal about the drawing Lindsey had stolen, Hal had quietly worked through his network of biker friends to track George Harvey down. But he, like Len, had vowed not to report anything until he was sure it might be a lead. And he had never been sure. When late one night a Hell's Angel named Ralph Cichetti, who admitted freely he had spent some time in prison, said that he thought his mother had been killed by a man she rented a room to, Hal began asking his usual questions. Questions that held elements of elimination about height and weight and preoccupations. The man hadn't gone by the name George Harvey, though that didn't mean anything. But the murder itself seemed too different. Sophie Cichetti was forty-nine. She was killed in her home with a blunt object and her body had been found intact nearby. Hal had read enough crime books to know that killers had patterns, peculiar and important ways they did things. So as Hal adjusted the timing chain of Cichetti's cranky Harley, they moved on to other topics, then fell silent. It was only when Cichetti mentioned something else that every hair on Hal's neck stood up.

"The guy built dollhouses," Ralph Cichetti said.

Hal placed a call to Len.

Years passed. The trees in our yard grew taller. I watched my family and my friends and neighbors, the teachers whom I'd had or imagined having, the high school I had dreamed about. As I sat in the gazebo I would pretend instead that I was sitting on the topmost branch of the maple under which my brother had swallowed a stick and still played hide-and-seek with Nate, or I would perch on the railing of a stairwell in New York and wait for Ruth to pass near. I would study with Ray. Drive the Pacific Coast

Highway on a warm afternoon of salty air with my mother. But I would end each day with my father in his den.

I would lay these photographs down in my mind, those gathered from my constant watching, and I could trace how one thing — my death — connected these images to a single source. No one could have predicted how my loss would change small moments on Earth. But I held on to those moments, hoarded them. None of them were lost as long as I was there watching.

At Evensong one night, while Holly played her sax and Mrs. Bethel Utemeyer joined in, I saw him: Holiday, racing past a fluffy white Samoyed. He had lived to a ripe old age on Earth and slept at my father's feet after my mother left, never wanting to let him out of his sight. He had stood with Buckley while he built his fort and had been the only one permitted on the porch while Lindsey and Samuel kissed. And in the last few years of his life, every Sunday morning, Grandma Lynn had made him a skillet-sized peanut butter pancake, which she would place flat on the floor, never tiring of watching him try to pick it up with his snout.

I waited for him to sniff me out, anxious to know if here, on the other side, I would still be the little girl he had slept beside. I did not have to wait long: he was so happy to see me, he knocked me down.

SEVENTEEN

A t twenty-one Lindsey was many things I would never become, but I barely grieved this list anymore. Still, I roved where she roved. I collected my college diploma and rode on the back of Samuel's bike, clinging on to him with my arms wrapped around his waist, pressing into his back for warmth . . .

Okay, it was Lindsey. I realized that. But in watching her I found I could get lost more than with anyone else.

On the night of their graduation from Temple University, she and Samuel rode his bike back to my parents' house, having promised my father and Grandma Lynn repeatedly that they would not touch the champagne tucked inside the bike's pannard until they reached the house. "After all, we're college graduates!" Samuel had said. My father was soft in his trust with Samuel — years had gone by when the boy had done nothing but right by his surviving daughter.

But on the ride back from Philadelphia down Route 30, it began to rain. Lightly at first, small pinpricks flashing into my sister and Samuel at fifty miles per hour. The cool rain hit the hot dry tar of the road and lifted up smells that had been baked in all day under the hot June sun. Lindsey liked to rest her head between Samuel's shoulder blades and take in the scent of the road and the scrappy shrubs and bushes on either side. She had been remembering how the breeze in the hours before the storm had filled all the white gowns of the graduating seniors as they stood outside Macy Hall. Everyone looked poised, for just a moment, to float away.

Finally, eight miles away from the turnoff that led to our house, the rain grew heavy enough to hurt, and Samuel shouted back to Lindsey that he was going to pull off.

They passed into a slightly more overgrown stretch of road, the kind that existed between two commercial areas and that gradually, by accretion, would be eliminated by another strip mall or auto parts store. The bike wobbled but did not fall on the wet gravel of the shoulder. Samuel used his feet to help brake the bike, then waited, as Hal had taught him, for my sister to get off and step a few feet away before he got off himself.

He opened the visor of his helmet to yell to her. "This is no good," he said, "I'm going to roll her under those trees."

Lindsey followed behind him, the sound of rain hushed inside her padded helmet. They picked their way through the gravel and mud, stepping over branches and litter that had gathered at the side of the road. The rain seemed to be getting heavier still, and my sister was glad she had changed out of the dress she'd worn to commencement and into the leather pants and jacket that Hal had insisted on getting her despite her protests that she looked like a pervert.

Samuel wheeled the bike into the stand of oaks close to the road, and Lindsey followed. They had gone the week before to get haircuts at the same barber shop on Market Street, and though Lindsey's hair was lighter and finer than Samuel's, the barber had given them identical short, spiky cuts. Within a moment of removing their helmets their hair caught the large drops that filtered through the trees, and Lindsey's mascara began to bleed. I watched as Samuel used his thumb to wipe the traces from Lindsey's cheek. "Happy graduation," he said in the darkness, and stooped to kiss her.

Since their first kiss in our kitchen two weeks after my death, I had known that he was — as my sister and I had giggled with our Barbies or while watching Bobby Sherman on TV — her one and only. Samuel had pressed himself into her need, and the cement between the two of them had begun to set immediately. They had gone to Temple together, side by side. He had hated it and she had pushed him through. She had loved it and this had allowed him to survive.

"Let's try and find the densest part of this underbrush," he said.

"What about the bike?"

"Hal will probably have to rescue us when the rain stops."

"Shit!" Lindsey said.

Samuel laughed and grabbed her hand to start walking. The moment they did, they heard the first thunderclap and Lindsey jumped. He tightened his hold on her. The lightning was in the distance still, and the thunder would grow louder on its heels. She had never felt about it the way I did. It made her jumpy and nervous. She imagined trees split down the middle and houses on fire and dogs cowering in basements throughout the suburbs.

They walked through the underbrush, which was getting soaked despite the trees. Even though it was the middle of the afternoon, it was dark except for Samuel's safety light. Still they felt the evidence of people. Their boots crunched down on top of tin cans and pushed up against empty bottles. And then, through the thick weeds and darkness both of them saw the broken window panes that ran along the top of an old Victorian house. Samuel shut off the safety light immediately.

"Do you think there's someone inside?" Lindsey asked.

"It's dark."

"It's spooky."

They looked at each other, and my sister said what they both were thinking. "It's dry!"

They held hands in the heavy rain and ran toward the house as fast as they could, trying not to trip or slide in the increasing mud.

As they drew closer, Samuel could make out the steep pitch of the roof and the small wooden cross work that hung down from the gables. Most of the windows on the bottom floor had been covered over with wood, but the front door swung back and forth on its hinges, banging against the plaster wall on the inside. Though part of him wanted to stand outside in the rain and stare up at the eaves and cornices, he rushed into the house with Lindsey. They stood a few feet inside the doorway, shivering and staring out into the presuburban forest that surrounded them. Quickly I scanned the rooms of the old house. They were alone. No scary monsters lurked in corners, no wandering men had taken root.

More and more of these undeveloped patches were disappearing, but they, more than anything, had marked my childhood. We lived in one of the first developments to be built on the converted farmland in the area—a development that became the model and inspiration for what now seemed a limitless number—but my imagination had always rested on the stretch of road that had not been filled in with the bright colors of shingles and drainpipes, paved driveways and super-size mailboxes. So too had Samuel's.

"Wow!" Lindsey said. "How old do you think this is?"

Lindsey's voice echoed off the walls as if they stood alone in a church.

"Let's explore," said Samuel.

The boarded-up windows on the first floor made it hard to see anything, but with the help of Samuel's safety light they could pick out both a fireplace and the chair rail along the walls.

"Look at the floor," Samuel said. He knelt down, taking her with him. "Do you see the tongue and groove work? These people had more money than their neighbors."

Lindsey smiled. Just as Hal cared only for the inner workings of motorcycles, Samuel had become obsessed with carpentry.

He ran his fingers over the floor and had Lindsey do it too. "This is a gorgeous old wreck," he said.

"Victorian?" Lindsey asked, making her best guess.

"It blows my mind to say this," Samuel said, "but I think it's gothic revival. I noticed cross-bracing on the gable trim, so that means it was after 1860."

"Look," said Lindsey.

In the center of the floor someone had once, long ago, set a fire.

"And *that* is a tragedy," Samuel said.

"Why didn't they use the fireplace? There's one in every room."

But Samuel was busy looking up through the hole the fire had burned into the ceiling, trying to make out the patterns of the woodwork along the window frames.

"Let's go upstairs," he said.

"I feel like I'm in a cave," said Lindsey as they climbed the stairs. "It's so quiet in here you can barely hear the rain."

Samuel bounced the soft side of his fist off the plaster as he went. "You could wall someone into this place."

And suddenly it was one of those awkward moments that they had learned to let pass and I lived to anticipate. It begged a central question. Where was I? Would I be mentioned? Brought up and discussed? Usually now the answer was a disappointing no. It was no longer a Susie-fest on Earth.

But something about the house and the night—markers like graduations and birthdays always meant that I was more alive, higher up in the register of thoughts—made Lindsey dwell on me more in that moment than she normally might. Still, she didn't mention it. She remembered the heady feeling she had had in Mr. Harvey's house and that she had often felt since—that I was with her somehow, in her thoughts and limbs—moving with her like a twin.

At the top of the stairs they found the entrance to the room they had stared up at.

"I want this house," Samuel said.

"What?"

"This house needs me, I can feel it."

"Maybe you should wait until the sun comes out to decide," she said.

"It's the most beautiful thing I've ever seen," he said.

"Samuel Heckler," my sister said, "fixer of broken things."

"One to talk," he said.

They stood for a moment in silence and smelled the damp air coming through the chimney and flooding the room. Even with the sound of rain, Lindsey still felt hidden away, tucked safely in an outside corner of the world with the one person she loved more than anyone else.

She took his hand, and I traveled with them up to the doorway of a small room at the very front. It jutted out over what would be the entrance hall of the floor below and was octagonal in shape.

"Oriels," Samuel said. "The windows"—he turned to Lindsey—"when they're built out like that, like a tiny room, that's called an oriel."

"Do they turn you on?" Lindsey asked, smiling.

I left them in the rain and darkness. I wondered if Lindsey noticed that when she and Samuel began to unzip their leathers the lightning stopped and the rumble in the throat of God—that scary thunder—ceased.

In his den, my father reached out to hold the snow globe in his hand. The cold glass against his fingers comforted him, and he shook it to watch the penguin disappear and then slowly be uncovered by the gently falling snow.

Hal had made it back from the graduation ceremonies

on his motorcycle but instead of calming my father — providing some assurance that if one motorcycle could maneuver the storm and deliver its rider safe to his door, another one could too — it seemed to stack the probabilities in the reverse in his mind.

He had taken what could be called a painful delight in Lindsey's graduation ceremony. Buckley had sat beside him, dutifully prompting him when to smile and react. He often *knew* when, but his synapses were never as quick now as normal people's — or at least that was how he explained it to himself. It was like reaction time in the insurance claims he reviewed. There was an average number of seconds for most people between when they saw something coming — another car, a rock rolling down an embankment — and when they reacted. My father's response times were slower than most, as if he moved in a world where a crushing inevitability had robbed him of any hope of accurate perception.

Buckley tapped on the half-open door of my father's den.

"Come in," he said.

"They'll be okay, Dad." At twelve, my brother had become serious and considerate. Even if he didn't pay for the food or cook the meals, he managed the house.

"You looked good in your suit, son," my father said.

"Thanks." This mattered to my brother. He had wanted to make my father proud and had taken time with his appearance, even asking Grandma Lynn that morning to help trim the bangs that fell in his eyes. My brother was in the most awkward stage of adolescence — not boy, not man. Most days he hid his body in big T-shirts and sloppy jeans, but he had liked wearing the suit that day. "Hal and Grandma are waiting for us downstairs," he said.

"I'll be down in a minute."

Buckley closed the door all the way this time, letting the latch snap into place.

That fall my father had developed the last roll of film that I'd kept in my closet in my "rolls to hold back" box, and now, as he often did when he begged just a minute before dinner or saw something on TV or read an article in the paper that made his heart ache, he drew back his desk drawer and gingerly lifted the photos in his hand.

He had lectured me repeatedly that what I called my "artistic shots" were foolhardy, but the best portrait he ever had was one I took of him at an angle so his face filled the three-by-three square when you held it so it was a diamond.

I must have been listening to his hints on camera angles and composition when I took the pictures he held now. He had had no idea what order the rolls were in or what they were of when he had them developed. There were an inordinate number of photos of Holiday, and many a shot of my feet or the grass. Gray balls of blurs in the air which were birds, and a grainy attempt at a sunset over the pussy-willow tree. But at some point I had decided to take portraits of my mother. When he'd picked the roll up at the photo lab my father sat in the car staring at photos of a woman he felt he barely knew anymore.

Since then he had taken these photos out too many times to count, but each time he looked into the face of this woman he had felt something growing inside him. It took him a long time to realize what it was. Only recently had his wounded synapses allowed him to name it. He had been falling in love all over again.

He didn't understand how two people who were married, who saw each other every day, could forget what each other looked like, but if he had had to name what had happened—this was it. And the last two photos in the roll provided the key. He had come home from work—I remember trying to keep my mother's attention as Holiday barked when he heard the car pull into the garage.

"He'll come out," I said. "Stay still." And she did. Part of what I loved about photography was the power it gave me over the people on the other side of the camera, even my own parents.

Out of the corner of my eye I saw my father walk through the side door into the yard. He carried his slim briefcase, which, years before, Lindsey and I had heatedly investigated only to find very little of interest to us. As he set it down I snapped the last solitary photo of my mother. Already her eyes had begun to seem distracted and anxious, diving under and up into a mask somehow. In the next photo, the mask was almost, but not quite, in place and the final photo, where my father was leaning slightly down to give her a kiss on the cheek—there it was.

"Did I do that to you?" he asked her image as he stared at the pictures of my mother, lined up in a row. "How did that happen?"

"The lightning stopped," my sister said. The moisture of the rain on her skin had been replaced by sweat.

"I love you," Samuel said.

"I know."

"No, I mean I love you, and I want to marry you, and I want to live in this house!"

"What?"

"That hideous, hideous college shit is over!" Samuel screamed. The small room absorbed his voice, barely bouncing back an echo from its thick walls.

"Not for me, it isn't," my sister said.

Samuel got up off the floor, where he had been lying beside my sister, and came to his knees in front of her. "Marry me."

"Samuel?"

"I'm tired of doing all the right things. Marry me and I'll make this house gorgeous."

"Who will support us?"

"We will," he said, "somehow."

She sat up and then joined him kneeling. They were both half-dressed and growing colder as their heat began to dissipate.

"Okay."

"Okay?"

"I think I can," my sister said. "I mean, yes!"

Some clichés I understood only when they came into my heaven full speed. I had never seen a chicken with its head cut off. It had never meant much to me except something else that had been treated much the same as me. But that moment I ran around my heaven like . . . a chicken with its head cut off! I was so happy I screamed over and over and over again. My sister! My Samuel! My dream!

She was crying, and he held her in his arms, rocking her against him.

"Are you happy, sweetheart?" he asked.

She nodded against his bare chest. "Yes," she said,

then froze. "My dad." She raised her head and looked at Samuel. "I know he's worried."

"Yes," he said, trying to switch gears with her.

"How many miles is it to the house from here?"

"Ten maybe," Samuel said. "Maybe eight."

"We could do that," she said.

"You're nuts."

"We have sneakers in the other pannard."

They could not run in leather, so they wore their underwear and T-shirts, as close to streakers as anyone in my family would ever be. Samuel, as he had for years, set a pace just ahead of my sister to keep her going. There were hardly any cars on the road, but when one passed by a wall of water would come up from the puddles near the side of the road and make the two of them gasp to get air back in their lungs. Both of them had run in rain before but never rain this heavy. They made a game of who could gain the most shelter as they ran the miles, waltzing in and out to gain cover under any overhanging trees, even as the dirt and grime of the road covered their legs. But by mile three they were silent, pushing their feet forward in a natural rhythm they had both known for years, focusing on the sound of their own breath and the sound of their wet shoes hitting the pavement.

At some point as she splashed through a large puddle, no longer trying to avoid them, she thought of the local pool of which we had been members until my death brought the comfortably public existence of my family to a close. It had been somewhere along this road, but she did not lift her head to find the familiar chain-link fence. Instead, she had a memory. She and I were under water in our bathing suits with their small ruffled skirts. Both of our eyes were open under water, a new skill — newer for her — and we were looking at each other, our separate bodies suspended under water. Hair floating, small skirts floating, our cheeks bulging with captured air. Then, together, we would grab on to each other and shoot up out of the water, breaking the surface. We sucked air into our lungs — ears popping — and laughed together.

I watched my beautiful sister running, her lungs and legs pumping, and the skill from the pool still there — fighting to see through the rain, fighting to keep her legs lifting at the pace set by Samuel, and I knew she was not running away from me or toward me. Like someone who has survived a gut-shot, the wound had been closing, closing — braiding into a scar for eight long years.

By the time the two of them were within a mile of my house, the rain had lightened and people were beginning to look out their windows toward the street.

Samuel slowed his pace and she joined him. Their T-shirts were locked onto their bodies like paste.

Lindsey had fought off a cramp in her side, but as the cramp lifted she ran with Samuel full-out. Suddenly she was covered in goose bumps and smiling ear to ear.

"We're getting married!" she said, and he stopped short, grabbed her up in his arms, and they were still kissing when a car passed them on the road, the driver honking his horn.

When the doorbell rang at our house it was four o'clock and Hal was in the kitchen wearing one of my mother's old white chef's aprons and cutting brownies for Grandma Lynn. He liked being put to work, feeling useful, and my grandmother liked to use him. They were a simpatico team. While Buckley, the boy-guard, loved to eat.

"I'll get it," my father said. He had been propping himself up during the rain with highballs, mixed, not measured, by Grandma Lynn.

He was spry now with a thin sort of grace, like a retired ballet dancer who favored one leg over the other after long years of one-footed leaps.

"I was so worried," he said when he opened the door.

Lindsey was holding her arms over her chest, and even my father had to laugh while he looked away and hurriedly got the extra blankets kept in the front closet. Samuel draped one around Lindsey first, as my father covered Samuel's shoulders as best he could and puddles collected on the flagstone floor. Just as Lindsey had covered herself up, Buckley and Hal and Grandma Lynn came forward into the hallway.

"Buckley," Grandma Lynn said, "go get some towels."

"Did you manage the bike in this?" Hal asked, incredulous.

"No, we ran," Samuel said.

"You what?"

"Get into the family room," my father said. "We'll set a fire going."

While the two of them sat with their backs to the fire, shivering at first and drinking the brandy shots Grandma Lynn had Buckley serve them on a silver tray, everyone heard the story of the bike and the house and the octagonal room with windows that had made Samuel euphoric.

"And the bike's okay?" Hal asked.

"We did the best we could," Samuel said, "but we'll need a tow."

"I'm just happy that the two of you are safe," my father said.

"We ran home for you, Mr. Salmon."

My grandmother and brother had taken seats at the far end of the room, away from the fire.

"We didn't want anyone to worry," Lindsey said.

"Lindsey didn't want you to worry, specifically."

The room was silent for a moment. What Samuel had said was true, of course, but it also pointed too clearly to a certain fact — that Lindsey and Buckley had come to live their lives in direct proportion to what effect it would have on a fragile father.

Grandma Lynn caught my sister's eye and winked. "Hal and Buckley and I made brownies," she said. "And I have some frozen lasagna I can break out if you'd like." She stood and so did my brother — ready to help.

"I'd love some brownies, Lynn," Samuel said.

"Lynn? I like that," she said. "Are you going to start calling Jack 'Jack'?"

"Maybe."

Once Buckley and Grandma Lynn had left the room, Hal felt a new nervousness in the air. "I think I'll pitch in," he said.

Lindsey, Samuel, and my father listened to the busy noises of the kitchen. They could all hear the clock ticking in the corner, the one my mother had called our "rustic colonial clock."

"I know I worry too much," my father said.

"That's not what Samuel meant," Lindsey said.

Samuel was quiet and I was watching him.

"Mr. Salmon," he finally said—he was not quite ready to try "Jack." "I've asked Lindsey to marry me."

Lindsey's heart was in her throat, but she wasn't looking at Samuel. She was looking at my father.

Buckley came in with a plate of brownies, and Hal followed him with champagne glasses hanging from his fingers and a bottle of 1978 Dom Perignon. "From your grandmother, on your graduation day," Hal said.

Grandma Lynn came through next, empty-handed except for her highball. It caught the light and glittered like a jar of icy diamonds.

For Lindsey, it was as if no one but herself and my father were there. "What do you say, Dad?" she asked.

"I'd say," he managed, standing up to shake Samuel's hand, "that I couldn't wish for a better son-in-law."

Grandma Lynn exploded on the final word. "My God, oh, honey! Congratulations!"

Even Buckley let loose, slipping out of the knot that usually held him and into a rare joy. But I saw the fine, wavering line that still tied my sister to my father. The invisible cord that can kill.

The champagne cork popped.

"Like a master!" my grandmother said to Hal, who was pouring.

It was Buckley, as my father and sister joined the group and listened to Grandma Lynn's countless toasts, who saw me. He saw me standing under the rustic colonial clock and stared. He was drinking champagne. There were strings coming out from all around me, reaching out, waving in the air. Someone passed him a brownie. He held it in his hands but did not eat. He saw my shape and face, which had not changed—the hair still parted down the middle, the chest still flat and hips undeveloped — and wanted to call out my name. It was only a moment, and then I was gone.

Over the years, when I grew tired of watching, I often sat in the back of the trains that went in and out of Suburban Station in Philadelphia. Passengers would get on and off as I listened to their conversations mix with the sounds of the train doors opening and closing, the conductors yelling their stops, and the shuffle and staccato of shoe soles and high heels going from pavement to metal to the soft *thump thump* on the carpeted train aisles. It was what Lindsey, in her workouts, called an active rest; my muscles were still engaged but my focus relaxed. I listened to the sounds and felt the train's movement and sometimes, by doing this, I could hear the voices of those who no longer lived on Earth. Voices of others like me, the watchers.

Almost everyone in heaven has someone on Earth they watch, a loved one, a friend, or even a stranger who was once kind, who offered warm food or a bright smile when one of us had needed it. And when I wasn't watching I could hear the others talking to those they loved on Earth: just as fruitlessly as me, I'm afraid. A one-sided cajoling and coaching of the young, a one-way loving and desiring of their mates, a single-sided card that could never be signed.

The train would be still or stop-starting from 30th Street to near Overbrook, and I could hear them say names and sentences: "Now be careful with that glass." "Mind your father." "Oh, look how big she looks in that dress." "I'm with you, Mother," ". . . Esmeralda, Sally, Lupe, Keesha, Frank . . ." So many names. And then the train would gain speed, and as it did the volume of all these unheard phrases coming from heaven would grow louder and louder; at its height between stations, the noise of our longing became so deafening that I had to open my eyes.

I saw women hanging or collecting wash as I peered from the windows of the suddenly silent trains. They stooped over baskets and then spread white or yellow or pink sheets along the line. I counted men's underwear and boys' underwear and the familiar lollipop cotton of little girls' drawers. And the sound of it that I craved and missed — the sound of life — replaced the endless calling of names.

Wet laundry: the snap, the yank, the wet heaviness of double- and queen-sized sheets. The real sounds bringing back the remembered sounds of the past when I had lain under the dripping clothes to catch water on my tongue or run in between them as if they were traffic cones through which I chased Lindsey or was chased by Lindsey back and forth. And this would be joined by the memory of our mother attempting to lecture us about the peanut butter from our hands getting on the good sheets, or the sticky lemon-candy patches she had found on our father's shirts. In this way the sight and smell of the real, of the imagined, and of the remembered all came together for me.

After I turned away from Earth that day, I rode the trains until I could think of only one thing:

"Hold still," my father would say, while I held the ship in the bottle and he burned away the strings he'd raised the mast with and set the clipper ship free on its blue putty sea. And I would wait for him, recognizing the tension of that moment when the world in the bottle depended, solely, on me.

EIGHTEEN

When her father mentioned the sinkhole on the phone, Ruth was in the walk-in closet that she rented on First Avenue. She twirled the phone's long black cord around her wrist and arm and gave short, clipped answers of acknowledgment. The old woman that rented her the closet liked to listen in, so Ruth tried not to talk much on the phone. Later, from the street, she would call home collect and plan a visit.

She had known she would make a pilgrimage to see it before the developers closed it up. Her fascination with places like the sinkhole was a secret she kept, as was my murder and our meeting in the faculty parking lot. They were all things she would not give away in New York, where she watched others tell their drunken bar stories, prostituting their families and their traumas for popularity and booze. These things, she felt, were not to be passed around like disingenuous party favors. She kept an honor code with her journals and her poems. "Inside, inside," she would whisper quietly to herself when she felt the urge to tell, and she would end up taking long walks through the city, seeing instead the Stolfuz cornfield or an image of her father staring at his pieces of rescued antique molding. New York provided a perfect background for her thoughts. Despite her willed stomping and pitching in its streets and byways, the city itself had very little to do with her interior life.

She no longer looked haunted, as she had in high school, but still, if you looked closely at her eyes you could see the skittery rabbit energy that often made people nervous. She had an expression of someone who was constantly on the lookout for something or someone that hadn't yet arrived. Her whole body seemed to slant forward in inquiry, and though she had been told at the bar where she worked that she had beautiful hair or beautiful hands or, on the rare occasions when any of her patrons saw her come out from behind the bar, beautiful legs, people never said anything about her eyes.

She dressed hurriedly in black tights, a short black skirt, black boots, and a black T-shirt, all of them stained from serving double-duty as work clothes and real clothes. The stains could be seen only in the sunlight, so Ruth was never really aware of them until later, when she would stop at an outdoor café for a cup of coffee and look down at her skirt and see the dark traces of spilled vodka or whiskey. The alcohol had the effect of making the black cloth blacker. This amused her; she had noted in her journal: "booze affects material as it does people."

Once outside the apartment, on her way for a cup of coffee on First Avenue, she made up secret conversations with the bloated lap dogs — Chihuahuas and Pomeranians — that the Ukrainian women held on their laps as they sat on their stoops. Ruth liked the antagonistic little dogs, who barked ardently as she passed.

Then she walked, walked flat out, walked with an ache coming up through the earth and into the heel of her striking foot. No one said hello to her except creeps, and she made a game of how many streets she could navigate without having to stop for traffic. She would not slow down for another person and would vivisect crowds of NYU students or old women with their laundry carts, creating a wind on either side of her. She liked to imagine that when she passed the world looked after her, but she also knew how anonymous she was. Except when she was at work, no one knew where she was at any time of day and no one waited for her. It was an immaculate anonymity.

She would not know that Samuel had proposed to my sister and, unless it trickled down to her through Ray, the sole person she had kept in touch with from school, she would never find out. While still at Fairfax she had heard my mother had left. A fresh ripple of whispers had gone through the high school, and Ruth had watched my sister cope with them as best she could. Occasionally the two of them would meet up in the hallway. Ruth would say a few words of support if she could manage them without doing what she thought of as harming Lindsey by talking to her. Ruth knew her status as a freak at school and knew that their one night at the gifted symposium had been exactly what it felt like — a dream, where elements let loose came together unbidden outside the damning rules of school.

But Ray was different. Their kisses and early pushing and rubbings were objects under glass to her — memories that she kept preserved. She saw him every time she visited her parents and had known immediately that it would be Ray she took when she went back to see the sinkhole. He would be happy for the vacation from his constant studying grind, and, if she was lucky, he would describe, as he often did, a medical procedure that he had observed. Ray's way of describing such things made her feel as if she knew exactly what it felt like — not just what it looked like. He could evoke everything for her, with small verbal pulse points of which he was completely unaware.

Heading north on First, she could tick off all the places she'd formerly stopped and stood, certain that she had found a spot where a woman or girl had been killed. She tried to list them in her journal at the end of each day, but often she was so consumed with what she thought might have happened in this or that dark overhang or tight alleyway that she neglected the simpler, more obvious ones, where she had read about a death in the paper and visited what had been a woman's grave.

She was unaware that she was somewhat of a celebrity up in heaven. I had told people about her, what she did, how she observed moments of silence up and down the city and wrote small individual prayers in her journal, and the story had traveled so quickly that women lined up to know if she had found where they'd been killed. She had fans in heaven, even though she would have been disappointed to know that often these fans, when they gathered, resembled more a bunch of teenagers poring over an issue of *TeenBeat* than Ruth's image of low dirge-like whisperings set to a celestial timpani.

I was the one who got to follow and watch, and, as opposed to the giddy choir, I often found these moments as painful as they were amazing. Ruth would get an image and it would burn into her memory. Sometimes they were only bright flashes — a fall down the stairs, a scream, a shove, the tightening of hands around a neck — and at other times it was as if an entire scenario spun out in her head in just the amount of time that it took the girl or woman to die.

No one on the street thought anything of the downtown girl dressed in black who had paused in the middle of midtown foot traffic. In her art student camouflage she could walk the entire length of Manhattan and, if not blend in, be classified and therefore ignored. Meanwhile, for us, she was doing important work, work that most people on Earth were too frightened even to contemplate.

The day after Lindsey and Samuel's graduation I joined her on her walk. By the time she got up to Central Park it was well past lunchtime, but the park was still busy. Couples sat on the clipped grass of the Sheep Meadow. Ruth peered at them. Her ardentness was offputting on a sunny afternoon, and when the open faces of young men caught sight of her they closed down or looked away.

She zigzagged up and across the park. There were obvious places where she could go, like the Rambles, to document the history of violence there without even leaving the trees, but she preferred those places people considered safe. The cool shimmering surface of the duck pond tucked into the busy southeast corner of the park, or the placid man-made lake, where old men sailed beautiful hand-carved boats.

She sat on a bench on a path leading to the Central Park Zoo and looked out across the gravel at children with their nannies and lone adults reading books in various patches of shade or sun. She was tired from the walk uptown, but still she took her journal out from her bag. She placed it open on her lap, holding the pen as her thinking prop. It was better to look like you were doing something when you stared into the distance, Ruth had learned. Otherwise it was likely that strange men would come over and try to talk to you. Her journal was her closest and most important relationship. It held everything.

Across from her a little girl had strayed from the blanket where her nanny slept. She was making her way for the bushes that lined a small rise before giving way to a fence separating the park from Fifth Avenue. Just as Ruth was about to enter the world of human beings whose lives impinged on one another by calling out to the nanny, a thin cord, which Ruth had not seen, warned the nanny to wake. She immediately sat bolt upright and barked an order at the little girl to return.

In moments like this she thought of all the little girls who grew into adulthood and old age as a sort of cipher alphabet for all of those who didn't. Their lives would somehow be inextricably attached to all the girls who had been killed. It was then, as the nanny packed up her bag and rolled up the blanket, preparing for whatever came next in their day, that Ruth saw her — a little girl who had strayed for the bushes one day and disappeared.

She could tell by the clothes that it had happened some time ago, but that was all. There was nothing else — no nanny or mother, no idea of night or day, only a little girl gone.

I stayed with Ruth. Her journal open, she wrote it down. "Time? Little girl in C.P. strays toward bushes. White lace collar, fancy." She closed the journal and tucked it into her bag. Close at hand was a place that soothed her. The penguin house at the zoo.

We spent the afternoon together there, Ruth sitting on the carpeted seat that ran the length of the exhibit, her black clothes making only her face and hands visible in the room. The penguins tottered and clucked and dived, slipping off the habitat rocks like amiable hams but living under water like tuxedoed muscles. Children shouted and screamed and pressed their faces against the glass. Ruth counted the living just as much as she counted the dead, and in the close confines of the penguin house the joyous screams of the children echoed off the walls with such vibrancy that, for a little while, she could drown out the other kinds of screams.

That weekend my brother woke early, as he always did. He was in the seventh grade and bought his lunch at school and was on the debate team and, like Ruth had been, was always picked either last or second to last in gym. He had not taken to athletics as Lindsey had. He practiced instead what Grandma Lynn called his "air of dignification." His favorite teacher was not really a teacher at all but the school librarian, a tall, frail woman with wiry hair who drank tea from her thermos and talked about having lived in England when she was young. After this he had affected an English accent for a few months and shown a heightened interest when my sister watched *Masterpiece Theatre.*

When he had asked my father that year if he could re-claim the garden my mother had once kept, my father had said, "Sure, Buck, go crazy."

And he had. He had gone extraordinarily, insanely crazy, reading old Burpee catalogs at night when he was unable to sleep and scanning the few books on gardening that the school library kept. Where my grandmother had suggested respectful rows of parsley and basil and Hal had suggested "some plants that really matter" — eggplants, cantaloupes, cucumbers, carrots, and beans — my brother had thought they were both right.

He didn't like what he read in books. He saw no reason to keep flowers separated from tomatoes and herbs segregated in a corner. He had slowly planted the whole garden with a spade, daily begging my father to bring him seeds and taking trips to the grocery with Grandma Lynn, where the price of his extreme helpfulness in fetching things would be a quick stop at the greenhouse for a small flowering plant. He was now awaiting his toma-toes, his blue daisies, his petunias, and pansies and salvias of all kinds. He had made his fort a sort of work shed for the garden, where he kept his tools and supplies.

But my grandmother was preparing for the moment when he realized that they couldn't grow all together and that some seeds would not come up at certain times, that the fine downy tendrils of cucumber might be abruptly stopped by the thickening underground bosses of carrot and potato, that the parsley might be camouflaged by the more recalci-trant weeds, and bugs that hopped about could blight the tender flowers. But she was waiting patiently. She no longer believed in talk. It never rescued anything. At seventy she had come to believe in time alone.

Buckley was hauling up a box of clothes from the basement and into the kitchen when my father came down for his coffee.

"What ya got there, Farmer Buck?" my father said. He had always been at his best in the morning.

"I'm making stakes for my tomato plants," my brother said.

"Are they even above ground yet?"

My father stood in the kitchen in his blue terry-cloth robe and bare feet. He poured his coffee from the coffee maker that Grandma Lynn set up each morning, and sipped at it as he looked at his son.

"I just saw them this morning," my brother said, beaming. "They curl up like a hand unfolding."

It wasn't until my father was repeating this description to Grandma Lynn as he stood at the counter that he saw, through the back window, what Buckley had taken from the box. They were my clothes. My clothes, which Lindsey had picked through for anything she might save. My clothes, which my grandmother, when she had moved into my room, had quietly boxed while my father was at work. She had put them down in the basement with a small label that said, simply, SAVE.

My father put down his coffee. He walked out through the screened-in porch and strode forward, calling Buckley's name.

"What is it, Dad?" He was alert to my father's tone.

"Those clothes are Susie's," my father said calmly when he reached him.

Buckley looked down at my blackwatch dress that he held in his hand.

My father stepped closer, took the dress from my

brother, and then, without speaking, he gathered the rest of my clothes, which Buckley had piled on the lawn. As he turned in silence toward the house, hardly breathing, clutching my clothes to him, it sparked.

I was the only one to see the colors. Just near Buckley's ears and on the tips of his cheeks and chin he was a little orange somehow, a little red.

"Why can't I use them?" he asked.

It landed in my father's back like a fist.

"Why can't I use those clothes to stake my tomatoes?"

My father turned around. He saw his son standing there, behind him the perfect plot of muddy, churned-up earth spotted with tiny seedlings. "How can you ask me that question?"

"You have to choose. It's not fair," my brother said.

"Buck?" My father held my clothes against his chest.

I watched Buckley flare and light. Behind him was the sun of the goldenrod hedge, twice as tall as it had been at my death.

"I'm tired of it!" Buckley blared. "Keesha's dad died and she's okay!"

"Is Keesha a girl at school?"

"Yes!"

My father was frozen. He could feel the dew that had gathered on his bare ankles and feet, could feel the ground underneath him, cold and moist and stirring with possibility.

"I'm sorry. When did this happen?"

"That's not the point, Dad! You don't get it." Buckley turned around on his heel and started stomping the tender tomato shoots with his foot.

"Buck, stop!" my father cried.

My brother turned.

"You don't get it, Dad," he said.

"I'm sorry," my father said. "These are Susie's clothes and I just . . . It may not make sense, but they're hers — something she wore."

"You took the shoe, didn't you?" my brother said. He had stopped crying now.

"What?"

"You took the shoe. You took it from my room."

"Buckley, I don't know what you're talking about."

"I saved the Monopoly shoe and then it was gone. You took it! You act like she was yours only!"

"Tell me what you want to say. What's this about your friend Keesha's dad?"

"Put the clothes down."

My father laid them gently on the ground.

"It isn't about Keesha's dad."

"Tell me what it is about." My father was now all immediacy. He went back to the place he had been after his knee surgery, coming up out of the druggie sleep of painkillers to see his then-five-year-old son sitting near him, waiting for his eyes to flicker open so he could say, "Peek-a-boo, Daddy."

"She's dead."

It never ceased to hurt. "I know that."

"But you don't act that way. Keesha's dad died when she was six. Keesha said she barely even thinks of him."

"She will," my father said.

"But what about us?"

"Who?"

"Us, Dad. Me and Lindsey. Mom left because she couldn't take it."

"Calm down, Buck," my father said. He was being as generous as he could as the air from his lungs evaporated out into his chest. Then a little voice in him said, *Let go, let go, let go.* "What?" my father said.

"I didn't say anything."

Let go. Let go. Let go.

"I'm sorry," my father said. "I'm not feeling very well." His feet had grown unbelievably cold in the damp grass. His chest felt hollow, bugs flying around an excavated cavity. There was an echo in there, and it drummed up into his ears. *Let go.*

My father dropped down to his knees. His arm began to tingle on and off as if it had fallen asleep. Pins and needles up and down. My brother rushed to him.

"Dad?"

"Son." There was a quaver in his voice and a grasping outward toward my brother.

"I'll get Grandma." And Buckley ran.

My father whispered faintly as he lay on his side with his face twisted in the direction of my old clothes: "You can never choose. I've loved all three of you."

That night my father lay in a hospital bed, attached to monitors that beeped and hummed. Time to circle around my father's feet and along his spine. Time to hush and usher him. But where?

Above his bed the clock ticked off the minutes and I thought of the game Lindsey and I had played in the yard together: "he loves me/he loves me not" picked out on a daisy's petals. I could hear the clock casting my own two greatest wishes back to me in this same rhythm: "Die for me/don't die for me, die for me/don't die for me." I could not help myself, it seemed, as I tore at his weakening heart. If he died, I would have him forever. Was this so wrong to want?

At home, Buckley lay in bed in the dark and pulled the sheet up to his chin. He had not been allowed past the emergency room where Lindsey had driven them, following the shrieking ambulance inside which lay our father. My brother had felt a huge burden of guilt descend in the silences from Lindsey. In her two repeated questions: "What were you talking about? Why was he so upset?"

My little brother's greatest fear was that the one person who meant so much to him would go away. He loved Lindsey and Grandma Lynn and Samuel and Hal, but my father kept him stepping lightly, son gingerly monitoring father every morning and every evening as if, without such vigilance, he would lose him.

We stood — the dead child and the living — on either side of my father, both wanting the same thing. To have him to ourselves forever. To please us both was an impossibility.

My father had only missed nighttimes twice in Buckley's life. Once after he had gone into the cornfield at night looking for Mr. Harvey and now as he lay in the hospital and they monitored him in case of a second heart attack.

Buckley knew he should be too old for it to matter, but I sympathized with him. The good-night kiss was something at which my father excelled. As my father stood at the end of the bed after closing the venetian blinds and running his hands down them to make sure they were all down at the same slant — no rebel venetian stuck to let the sunlight in on his son before he came to wake him — my brother would often get goose bumps on his arms and legs. The anticipation was so sweet.

"Ready, Buck?" my father would say, and sometimes Buckley said "Roger," or sometimes he said "Takeoff," but when he was most frightened and giddy and waiting for peace he just said "Yes!" And my father would take the thin cotton top sheet and bunch it up in his hands while being careful to keep the two corners between his thumb and forefinger. Then he would snap it out so the pale blue (if they were using Buckley's) or lavender (if they were using mine) sheet would spread out like a parachute above him and gently, what felt wonderfully slowly, it would waft down and touch along his exposed skin — his knees, his forearms, his cheeks and chin. Both air and cover somehow there in the same space at the same time — it felt like the ultimate freedom and protection. It was lovely, left him vulnerable and quivering on some edge and all he could hope was that if he begged him, my father would oblige and do it again. Air and cover, air and cover — sustaining the unspoken connection between them: little boy, wounded man.

That night his head lay on the pillow while his body was curled in the fetal position. He had not thought to close the blinds himself, and the lights from the nearby houses spotted the hill. He stared across his room at the louvered doors of his closet, out of which he had once imagined evil witches would escape to join the dragons beneath his bed. He no longer feared these things.

"Please don't let Daddy die, Susie," he whispered. "I need him."

* * *

When I left my brother, I walked out past the gazebo and under the lights hanging down like berries, and I saw the brick paths branching out as I advanced.

I walked until the bricks turned to flat stones and then to small, sharp rocks and then to nothing but churned earth for miles and miles around me. I stood there. I had been in heaven long enough to know that something would be revealed. And as the light began to fade and the sky turn a dark, sweet blue as it had on the night of my death, I saw someone walking into view, so far away I could not at first make out if it was man or woman, child or adult. But as moonlight reached this figure I could make out a man and, frightened now, my breathing shallow, I raced just far enough to see. Was it my father? Was it what I had wanted all this time so desperately?

"Susie," the man said as I approached and then stopped a few feet from where he stood. He raised his arms up toward me.

"Remember?" he said.

I found myself small again, age six and in a living room in Illinois. Now, as I had done then, I placed my feet on top of his feet.

"Grandaddy," I said.

And because we were all alone and both in heaven, I was light enough to move as I had moved when I was six and he was fifty-six and my father had taken us to visit. We danced so slowly to a song that on Earth had always made my grandfather cry.

"Do you remember?" he asked.

"Barber!"

"Adagio for Strings," he said.

But as we danced and spun — none of the herky-jerky

awkwardness of Earth — what I remembered was how I'd found him crying to this music and asked him why.

"Sometimes you cry, Susie, even when someone you love has been gone a long time." He had held me against him then, just briefly, and then I had run outside to play again with Lindsey in what seemed like my grandfather's huge backyard.

We didn't speak any more that night, but we danced for hours in that timeless blue light. I knew as we danced that something was happening on Earth and in heaven. A shifting. The sort of slow-to-sudden movement that we'd read about in science class one year. Seismic, impossible, a rending and tearing of time and space. I pressed myself into my grandfather's chest and smelled the old-man smell of him, the mothball version of my own father, the blood on Earth, the sky in heaven. The kumquat, skunk, grade-A tobacco.

When the music stopped, it could have been forever since we'd begun. My grandfather took a step back, and the light grew yellow at his back.

"I'm going," he said.

"Where?" I asked.

"Don't worry, sweetheart. You're so close."

He turned and walked away, disappearing rapidly into spots and dust. Infinity.

NINETEEN

When she reached Krusoe Winery that morning, my mother found a message waiting for her, scrawled in the imperfect English of the caretaker. The word *emergency* was clear enough, and my mother bypassed her morning ritual of an early coffee drunk while staring out at the grapevines grafted on row upon row of sturdy white crosses. She opened up the part of the winery reserved for public tastings. Without turning on the overhead, she located the phone behind the wooden bar and dialed the number in Pennsylvania. No answer.

Then she dialed the operator in Pennsylvania and asked for the number of Dr. Akhil Singh.

"Yes," Ruana said, "Ray and I saw an ambulance pull up a few hours ago. I imagine they're all at the hospital."

"Who was it?"

"Your mother, perhaps?"

But she knew from the note that her mother had been

the one who *called*. It was one of the children or it was Jack. She thanked Ruana and hung up. She grabbed the heavy red phone and lifted it up from underneath the bar. A ream of color sheets that they passed out to customers — "Lemon Yellow = Young Chardonnay, Straw-colored = Sauvignon Blanc . . ." — fell down and around her feet from where they had been kept weighted by the phone. She had habitually arrived early ever since taking the job, and now she gave a quick thanks that this was so. After that, all she could think of were the names of the local hospitals, so she called the ones to which she had rushed her young children with unexplained fevers or possible broken bones from falls. At the same hospital where I had once rushed Buckley: "A Jack Salmon was seen in emergency and is still here."

"Can you tell me what happened?"

"What is your relationship to Mr. Salmon?"

She said the words she had not said in years: "I'm his wife."

"He had a heart attack."

She hung up the phone and sat down on the rubber-and-cork mats that covered the floor on the employee side. She sat there until the shift manager arrived and she repeated the strange words: *husband, heart attack.*

When she looked up later she was in the caretaker's truck, and he, this quiet man who barely ever left the premises, was barreling toward San Francisco International Airport.

She paid for her ticket and boarded a flight that would connect to another in Chicago and finally land her in Philadelphia. As the plane gained height and they were buried in the clouds, my mother listened distantly to the signature bells of the plane which told the crew what to do or what to prepare for, and she heard the cocktail cart jiggling past, but instead of her fellow passengers she saw the cool stone archway at the winery, behind which the empty oak barrels were stored, and instead of the men who often sat inside there to get out of the sun she imagined my father sitting there, holding the broken Wedgwood cup out toward her.

By the time she landed in Chicago with a two-hour wait, she had steadied herself enough to buy a toothbrush and a pack of cigarettes and place a call to the hospital, this time asking to speak to Grandma Lynn.

"Mother," my mother said. "I'm in Chicago and on my way."

"Abigail, thank God," my grandmother said. "I called Krusoe again and they said you were headed for the airport."

"How is he?"

"He's asking for you."

"Are the kids there?"

"Yes, and Samuel. I was going to call you today and tell you. Samuel has asked Lindsey to marry him."

"That's wonderful," my mother said.

"Abigail?"

"Yes." She could hear her mother's hesitation, which was always rare.

"Jack's asking for Susie, too."

She lit a cigarette as soon as she walked outside the terminal at O'Hare, a school tour flooding past her with small overnight bags and band instruments, each of which had a bright yellow nametag on the side of the case. HOME OF THE PATRIOTS, they read.

It was muggy and humid in Chicago, and the smoky exhaust of double-parked cars made the heavy air noxious.

She burned through the cigarette in record time and lit another, keeping one arm tucked hard across her chest and the other one extended on each exhale. She was wearing her winery outfit: a pair of faded but clean jeans and a pale orange T-shirt with KRUSOE WINERY embroidered over the pocket. Her skin was darker now, which made her pale blue eyes seem even bluer in contrast, and she had taken to wearing her hair in a loose ponytail at the base of her neck. I could see small wisps of salt and pepper hair near her ears and at her temples.

She held on to two sides of an hourglass and wondered how this could be possible. The time she'd had alone had been gravitationally circumscribed by when her attachments would pull her back. And they had pulled now — double-fisted. A marriage. A heart attack.

Standing outside the terminal, she reached into the back pocket of her jeans, where she kept the man's wallet she had started carrying when she got the job at Krusoe because it was easier not to worry about stowing a purse beneath the bar. She flicked her cigarette into the cab lane and turned to find a seat on the edge of a concrete planter, inside of which grew weeds and one sad sapling choked by fumes.

In her wallet were pictures, pictures she looked at every day. But there was one that she kept turned upside down in a fold of leather meant for a credit card. It was the same one that rested in the evidence box at the police station, the same one Ray had put in his mother's book of Indian poetry. My class photo that had made the papers and been put on police fliers and in mailboxes.

After eight years it was, even for my mother, like the ubiquitous photo of a celebrity. She had encountered it so many times that I had been neatly buried inside of it. My cheeks never redder, my eyes never bluer than they were in the photograph.

She took the photo out and held it face-up and slightly cupped in her hand. She had always missed my teeth— their small rounded serrations had fascinated her as she watched me grow. I had promised my mother a wide-open smile for that year's picture, but I was so self-conscious in front of the photographer that I had barely managed a close-lipped grin.

She heard the announcement for the connecting flight over the outdoor speaker. She stood. Turning around she saw the tiny, struggling tree. She left my class portrait propped up against its trunk and hurried inside the auto-matic doors.

On the flight to Philadelphia, she sat alone in the middle of a row of three seats. She could not help but think of how, if she were a mother traveling, there would be two seats filled beside her. One for Lindsey. One for Buckley. But though she was, by definition, a mother, she had at some point ceased to be one too. She couldn't claim that right and privilege after missing more than half a decade of their lives. She now knew that being a mother was a calling, something plenty of young girls dreamed of being. But my mother had never had that dream, and she had been punished in the most horrible and unimaginable way for never having wanted me.

I watched her on the plane, and I sent a wish into the clouds for her release. Her body grew heavy with the dread of what would come but in this heaviness was at least relief. The stewardess handed her a small blue pillow and for a little while she fell asleep.

When they reached Philadelphia, the airplane taxied down the runway and she reminded herself both where she was and what year it was. She hurriedly clicked through all the things she might say when she saw her children, her mother, Jack. And then, when they finally shivered to a halt, she gave up and focused only on getting off the plane.

She barely recognized her own child waiting at the end of the long ramp. In the years that had passed, Lindsey had become angular, thin, every trace of body fat gone. And standing beside my sister was what looked like her male twin. A bit taller, a little more meat. Samuel. She was staring so hard at the two of them, and they were staring back, that at first she didn't even see the chubby boy sitting off to the side on the arm of a row of waiting-area seats.

And then, just before she began walking toward them — for they all seemed suspended and immobile for the first few moments, as if they had been trapped in a viscous gelatin from which only her movement might free them — she saw him.

She began walking down the carpeted ramp. She heard announcements being made in the airport and saw passengers, with their more normal greetings, rushing past her. But it was as if she were entering a time warp as she took him in. 1944 at Camp Winnekukka. She was twelve, with chubby cheeks and heavy legs — all the things she'd felt grateful her daughters had escaped had been her son's to endure. So many years she had been away, so much time she could never recover.

If she had counted, as I did, she would have known that in seventy-three steps she had accomplished what she had been too afraid to do for almost seven years.

It was my sister who spoke first:

"Mom," she said.

My mother looked at my sister and flashed forward thirty-eight years from the lonely girl she'd been at Camp Winnekukka.

"Lindsey," my mother said.

Lindsey stared at her. Buckley was standing now, but he looked first down at his shoes and then over his shoulder, out past the window to where the planes were parked, disgorging their passengers into accordioned tubes.

"How is your father?" my mother asked.

My sister had spoken the word *Mom* and then frozen. It tasted soapy and foreign in her mouth.

"He's not in the greatest shape, I'm afraid," Samuel said. It was the longest sentence anyone had said, and my mother found herself disproportionately grateful for it.

"Buckley?" my mother said, preparing no face for him. Being who she was — whoever that was.

He turned his head toward her like a racheted gun. "Buck," he said.

"Buck," she repeated softly and looked down at her hands.

Lindsey wanted to ask, *Where are your rings?*

"Shall we go?" Samuel asked.

The four of them entered the long carpeted tunnel that would bring them from her gate into the main terminal. They were headed toward the cavernous baggage claim when my mother said, "I didn't bring any bags."

They stood in an awkward cluster, Samuel looking for the right signs to redirect them back to the parking garage.

"Mom," my sister tried again.

"I lied to you," my mother said before Lindsey could say anything further. Their eyes met, and in that hot wire that went from one to the other I swore I saw it, like a rat bulging, undigested, inside a snake: the secret of Len.

"We go back up the escalator," Samuel said, "and then we can take the overhead walkway into the parking lot."

Samuel called for Buckley, who had drifted off in the direction of a cadre of airport security officers. Uniforms had never lost the draw they held for him.

They were on the highway when Lindsey spoke next. "They won't let Buckley in to see Dad because of his age."

My mother turned around in her seat. "I'll try and do something about that," she said, looking at Buckley and attempting her first smile.

"Fuck you," my brother whispered without looking up.

My mother froze. The car opened up. Full of hate and tension—a riptide of blood to swim through.

"Buck," she said, remembering the shortened name just in time, "will you look at me?"

He glared over the front seat, boring his fury into her.

Eventually my mother turned back around and Samuel, Lindsey, and my brother could hear the sounds from the passenger seat that she was trying hard not to make. Little peeps and a choked sob. But no amount of tears would sway Buckley. He had been keeping, daily, weekly, yearly, an underground storage room of hate. Deep inside this, the four-year-old sat, his heart flashing. Heart to stone, heart to stone.

"We'll all feel better after seeing Mr. Salmon," Samuel said, and then, because even he could not bear it, he leaned forward toward the dash and turned on the radio.

It was the same hospital that she had come to eight years ago in the middle of the night. A different floor painted a different color, but she could feel it encasing her as she walked down the hall — what she'd done there. The push of Len's body, her back pressed into the sharp stucco wall. Everything in her wanted to run — fly back to California, back to her quiet existence working among strangers. Hiding out in the folds of tree trunks and tropical petals, tucked away safely among so many foreign plants and people.

Her mother's ankles and oxford pumps, which she saw from the hallway, brought her back. One of the many simple things she'd lost by moving so far away, just the commonplace of her mother's feet — their solidity and humor — seventy-year-old feet in ridiculously uncomfortable shoes.

But as she walked forward into the room, everyone else — her son, her daughter, her mother — fell away.

My father's eyes were weak but fluttered open when he heard her enter. He had tubes and wires coming out of his wrist and shoulder. His head seemed so fragile on the small square pillow.

She held his hand and cried silently, letting the tears come freely.

"Hello, Ocean Eyes," he said.

She nodded her head. This broken, beaten man — her husband.

"My girl," he breathed out heavily.

"Jack."

"Look what it took to get you home."

"Was it worth it?" she said, smiling bleakly.

"We'll have to see," he said.

To see them together was like a tenuous belief made real.

My father could see glimmers, like the colored flecks inside my mother's eyes — things to hold on to. These he counted among the broken planks and boards of a long-ago ship that had struck something greater than itself and sunk. There were only remnants and artifacts left to him now. He tried to reach up and touch her cheek, but his arm felt too weak. She moved closer and laid her cheek in his palm.

My grandmother knew how to move silently in heels. She tiptoed out of the room. As she resumed her normal stride and approached the waiting area, she intercepted a nurse with a message for Jack Salmon in Room 582. She had never met the man but knew his name. "Len Fenerman, will visit soon. Wishes you well." She folded the note neatly. Just before she came upon Lindsey and Buckley, who had gone to join Samuel in the waiting room, she popped open the metal lip of her purse and placed it between her powder and comb.

TWENTY

By the time Mr. Harvey reached the tin-roofed shack in Connecticut that night, it promised rain. He had killed a young waitress inside the shack several years before and then bought some new slacks with the tips he'd found in the front pocket of her apron. By now the rot would have been eclipsed, and it was true, as he approached the area, that no rank smell greeted him. But the shack was open and inside he could see the earth had been dug up. He breathed in and approached the shack warily.

He fell asleep beside her empty grave.

At some point, to counter the list of the dead, I had begun keeping my own list of the living. It was something I noticed Len Fenerman did too. When he was off duty he would note the young girls and elderly women and every other female in the rainbow in between and count them among the things that sustained him. That young girl in the mall whose pale legs had grown too long for her now-too-young dress and who had an aching vulnerability that went straight to both Len's and my own heart. Elderly women, wobbling with walkers, who insisted on dyeing their hair unnatural versions of the colors they had in youth. Middle-aged single mothers racing around in grocery stores while their children pulled bags of candy off the shelves. When I saw them, I took count. Living, breathing women. Sometimes I saw the wounded — those who had been beaten by husbands or raped by strangers, children raped by their fathers — and I would wish to intervene somehow.

Len saw these wounded women all the time. They were regulars at the station, but even when he went somewhere outside his jurisdiction he could sense them when they came near. The wife in the bait-'n'-tackle shop had no bruises on her face but cowered like a dog and spoke in apologetic whispers. The girl he saw walk the road each time he went upstate to visit his sisters. As the years passed she'd grown leaner, the fat from her cheeks had drained, and sorrow had loaded her eyes in a way that made them hang heavy and hopeless inside her mallowed skin. When she was not there it worried him. When she was there it both depressed and revived him.

He had not had much to write in my file for a long time, but a few items had joined the log of old evidence in the last few months: the name of another potential victim, Sophie Cichetti, the name of her son, and an alias of George Harvey's. There was also what he held in his hands: my Pennsylvania keystone charm. He moved it around inside the evidence bag, using his fingers, and found, again, my initials. The charm had been checked for any clues it could provide, and, besides its presence at the scene of another girl's murder, it had come up clean under the microscope.

He had wanted to give the charm back to my father from the first moment he was able to confirm it was mine. Doing so was breaking the rules, but he had never had a body for them, just a sodden schoolbook and the pages from my biology book mixed in with a boy's love note. A Coke bottle. My jingle-bell hat. These he had cataloged and kept. But the charm was different, and he meant to give it back.

A nurse he'd dated in the years after my mother left had called him when she noticed the name Jack Salmon on a list of patients admitted. Len had determined that he would visit my father in the hospital and bring my charm along with him. In Len's mind he saw the charm as a talisman that might speed my father's recovery.

I couldn't help but think, as I watched him, of the barrels of toxic fluids that had accrued behind Hal's bike shop where the scrub lining the railroad tracks had offered local companies enough cover to dump a stray container or two. Everything had been sealed up, but things were beginning to leak out. I had come to both pity and respect Len in the years since my mother left. He followed the physical to try to understand things that were impossible to comprehend. In that, I could see, he was like me.

Outside the hospital, a young girl was selling small bouquets of daffodils, their green stems tied with lavender ribbons. I watched as my mother bought out the girl's whole stock.

Nurse Eliot, who remembered my mother from eight

years ago, volunteered to help her when she saw her coming down the hall, her arms full of flowers. She rounded up extra water pitchers from a supply closet and together she and my mother filled them with water and placed the flowers around my father's room while he slept. Nurse Eliot thought that if loss could be used as a measure of beauty in a woman, my mother had grown even more beautiful.

Lindsey, Samuel, and Grandma Lynn had taken Buckley home earlier in the evening. My mother was not ready to see the house yet. She focused solely on my father. Everything else would have to wait, from the house and its silent reproach to her son and daughter. She needed something to eat and time to think. Instead of going to the hospital cafeteria, where the bright lights made her think only of all the futile efforts that hospitals contained to keep people awake for more bad news — the weak coffee, the hard chairs, the elevators that stopped on every floor — she left the building and walked down the sloped sidewalk leading away from the entrance.

It was dark out now, and the parking lot where she had once driven in the middle of the night in her nightgown was spotted with only a few cars. She hugged the cardigan her mother had left behind tightly to her.

She crossed the parking lot, looking into the dark cars for signs of who the people inside the hospital were. There were cassette tapes spread out on the passenger seat of one car, the bulky shape of a baby's carseat in another. It became a game to her then, seeing what she could in each car. A way not to feel so alone and alien, as if she were a child playing a spy game in the house of her parents' friends. Agent Abigail to Mission Control. I see a fuzzy dog toy, I see a soccer ball, I see a woman! There she was, a stranger sitting in the driver's side behind the wheel. The woman did not see my mother looking at her, and as soon as she saw her face my mother turned her attention away, focusing on the bright lights of the old diner she had as her goal. She did not have to look back to know what the woman was doing. She was girding herself up to go inside. She knew the face. It was the face of someone who wanted more than anything to be anywhere but where she was.

She stood on the landscaped strip between the hospital and the emergency room entrance and wished for a cigarette. She had not questioned anything that morning. Jack had had a heart attack; she would go home. But now here, she didn't know what she was supposed to do anymore. How long would she have to wait, what would have to happen, before she could leave again? Behind her in the parking lot, she heard the sound of a car door opening and closing—the woman going in.

The diner was a blur to her. She sat in a booth alone and ordered the kind of food—chicken-fried steak— that didn't seem to exist in California.

She was thinking about this when a man directly across from her gave her the eye. She registered every detail of his appearance. It was automatic and something she didn't do out west. While living in Pennsylvania after my murder, when she saw a strange man whom she didn't trust, she did an immediate breakdown in her mind. It was quicker— honoring the pragmatics of fear—than pretending she shouldn't think this way. Her dinner arrived, the chicken-fried steak and tea, and she focused on her food, on the gritty breading around the rubbery meat, on the metallic taste of old tea. She did not think she could handle being home more than a few days. Everywhere she looked she saw me, and at the booth across from her she saw the man who could have murdered me.

She finished the food, paid for it, and walked out of the diner without raising her eyes above waist level. A bell mounted on the door jingled above her, and she started, her heart jumping up in her chest.

She made it back across the highway in one piece, but she was breathing shallowly as she passed back across the parking lot. The car of the apprehensive visitor was still there.

In the main lobby, where people rarely sat, she decided to sit down and wait for her breathing to come back again.

She would spend a few hours with him and when he woke, she would say goodbye. As soon as her decision was made, a welcome coolness flew through her. The sudden relief of responsibility. Her ticket to a far-away land.

It was late now, after ten, and she took an empty elevator to the fifth floor, where the hall lights had been dimmed. She passed the nurses' station, behind which two nurses were quietly gossiping. She could hear the lilt and glee of nuanced rumors being exchanged between them, the sound of easy intimacy in the air. Then, just as one nurse was unable to suppress a high-pitched laugh, my mother opened my father's door and let it swing shut again.

Alone.

It was as if there was a vacuum hush when the door closed. I felt I did not belong, that I should go too. But I was glued.

Seeing him sleeping in the dark, with only the low-wattage fluorescent light on at the back of the bed, she remembered standing in this same hospital and taking steps to sever herself from him.

As I saw her take my father's hand, I thought of my sister and me sitting underneath the grave rubbing in the upstairs hallway. I was the dead knight gone to heaven with my faithful dog and she was the live wire of a wife. "How can I be expected to be trapped for the rest of my life by a man frozen in time?" Lindsey's favorite line.

My mother sat with my father's hand in hers for a long while. She thought how wonderful it would be to climb up on the fresh hospital sheets and lie beside him. And how impossible.

She leaned close. Even under the smells of antiseptics and alcohol, she could smell the grassy smell of his skin. When she'd left, she had packed her favorite shirt of my father's and would sometimes wrap it around her just to have something of his on. She never wore it outside, so it kept his scent longer than it might have. She remembered one night, when she missed him most, buttoning it over a pillow and hugging it to her as if she were still a high school girl.

In the distance beyond the closed window she could hear the hum of far-off traffic on the highway, but the hospital was shutting down for the night. Only the rubber soles of the night nurses' shoes made sounds as they passed in the hallway.

Just that winter she had found herself saying to a young woman who worked with her at the tasting bar on Saturdays that between a man and a woman there was always one person who was stronger than the other one. "That doesn't mean the weaker one doesn't love the stronger," she'd pleaded. The girl looked at her blankly.

But for my mother what mattered was that as she spoke, she had suddenly identified herself as the weaker one. This revelation sent her reeling. What had she thought all those years but the opposite?

She pulled her chair as close to his head as she could and laid her face on the edge of his pillow to watch him breathing, to see the flutter of his eye beneath his eyelid when he dreamed. How could it be that you could love someone so much and keep it secret from yourself as you woke daily so far from home? She had put bill-boards and roads in between them, throwing roadblocks behind her and ripping off the rearview mirror, and thought that that would make him disappear? erase their life and children?

It was so simple, as she watched him, as his regular breathing calmed her, that she did not even see it hap-pening at first. She began to think of the rooms in our house and the hours that she had worked so hard to for-get spent inside of them. Like fruit put up in jars and for-gotten about, the sweetness seemed even more distilled as she returned. There on that shelf were all the dates and silliness of their early love, the braid that began to form of their dreams, the solid root of a burgeoning family. The first solid evidence of it all. Me.

She traced a new line on my father's face. She liked the silvering of his temples.

Shortly after midnight, she fell asleep after trying as hard as she could to keep her eyes open. To hold on to everything all at once while she looked at that face, so that when he woke she could say goodbye.

When her eyes were closed and they both slept silently together, I whispered to them:

Stones and bones;
snow and frost;
seeds and beans and polliwogs.
Paths and twigs, assorted kisses,
We all know who Susie misses . . .

Around two A.M. it began to rain, and it rained down
on the hospital and on my old home and in my heaven.
On the tin-roofed shack where Mr. Harvey slept, it was
raining too. As the rain beat its tiny hammers above his
head, he dreamed. He did not dream of the girl whose remains had been removed and were now being analyzed
but of Lindsey Salmon, of the 5! 5! 5! hitting the border
of elderberry. He had this dream whenever he felt threat-
ened. It had been in the flash of her soccer shirt that his
life had begun to spin out of control.

It was near four when I saw my father's eyes open and saw
him feel the warmth of my mother's breath on his cheek
even before he knew she was asleep. We wished together
that he could hold her, but he was too weak. There was another way and he took it. He would tell her the things he had
felt after my death—the things that came into his mind so
frequently but that no one knew but me.

But he did not want to wake her. The hospital was
silent except for the sound of rain. Rain was following
him, he felt, darkness and damp—he thought of Lindsey
and Samuel at the doorway, soaked and smiling, having
run all that way to relieve him. He often found himself repeatedly commanding himself back to center. Lindsey.
Lindsey. Lindsey. Buckley. Buckley. Buckley.

The way the rain looked outside the windows, lit up in circular patches by the lights in the hospital parking lot, reminded him of the movies he had gone to see as a boy — Hollywood rain. He closed his eyes with the breath of my mother reassuringly exhaling against his cheek and listened to it, the slight patter on the slim metal window sills, and then he heard the sound of birds — small birds chirping, but he could not see them. And the idea of this, that there might be a nest right outside his window where baby birds had woken in the rain and found their mother gone, made him want to rescue them. He felt my mother's limp fingers, which had loosened their hold on his hand in sleep. She was here, and this time, despite all, he was going to let her be who she was.

It was then that I slipped inside the room with my mother and father. I was present somehow, as a person, in a way I had never been. I had always hovered but had never stood beside them.

I made myself small in the darkness, unable to know if I could be seen. I had left him for hours every day for eight and a half years as I had left my mother or Ruth and Ray, my brother and sister, and certainly Mr. Harvey, but he, I now saw, had never left me. His devotion to me had made me know again and again that I had been beloved. In the warm light of my father's love I had remained Susie Salmon — a girl with my whole life in front of me.

"I thought if I was very quiet I would hear you," he whispered. "If I was still enough you might come back."

"Jack?" my mother said, waking. "I must have fallen asleep."

"It's wonderful to have you back," he said.

And my mother looked at him. Everything stripped away. "How do you do it?" she asked.

"There's no choice, Abbie," he said. "What else can I do?"

"Go away, start over again," she said.

"Did it work?"

They were silent. I reached out my hand and faded away.

"Why don't you come lie down up here?" my father said. "We have a little time before the enforcers come on duty and kick you out."

She didn't move.

"They've been nice to me," she said. "Nurse Eliot helped me put all the flowers in water while you slept."

He looked around him and made out their shapes. "Daffodils," he said.

"It's Susie's flower."

My father smiled beautifully. "See," he said, "that's how. You live in the face of it, by giving her a flower."

"That's so sad," my mother said.

"Yes," he said, "it is."

My mother had to balance somewhat precariously on one hip near the edge of his hospital bed, but they managed. They managed to stretch out together beside each other so they could stare into each other's eyes.

"How was it seeing Buckley and Lindsey?"

"Incredibly hard," she said.

They were silent for a moment and he squeezed her hand.

"You look so different," he said.

"You mean older."

I watched him reach up and take a strand of my

mother's hair and loop it around her ear. "I fell in love with you again while you were away," he said.

I realized how much I wished I could be where my mother was. His love for my mother wasn't about looking back and loving something that would never change. It was about loving my mother for everything — for her brokenness and her fleeing, for her being there right then in that moment before the sun rose and the hospital staff came in. It was about touching that hair with the side of his fingertip, and knowing yet plumbing fearlessly the depths of her ocean eyes.

My mother could not bring herself to say "I love you."

"Will you stay?" he asked.

"For a while."

This was something.

"Good," he said. "So what did you say when people asked you about family in California?"

"Out loud I said I had two children. Silently I said three. I always felt like apologizing to her for that."

"Did you mention a husband?" he asked.

And she looked at him. "No."

"Man," he said.

"I didn't come back to pretend, Jack," she said.

"Why did you come back?"

"My mother called me. She said it was a heart attack and I thought about your father."

"Because I might die?"

"Yes."

"You were sleeping," he said. "You didn't see her."

"Who?"

"Someone came in the room and then left. I think it was Susie."

"Jack?" my mother asked, but her alarm was only at half-mast.

"Don't tell me you don't see her."

She let go.

"I see her everywhere," she said, breathing out her relief. "Even in California she was everywhere. Boarding buses or on the streets outside schools when I drove by. I'd see her hair but it didn't match the face or I'd see her body or the way she moved. I'd see older sisters and their little brothers, or two girls that looked like sisters and I imagined what Lindsey wouldn't have in her life — the whole relationship gone for her and for Buckley, and then that would just hit me, because I had left too. It would just spin onto you and even to my mother."

"She's been great," he said, "a rock. A spongelike rock, but a rock."

"So I gather."

"So if I tell you that Susie was in the room ten minutes ago, what would you say?"

"I'd say you were insane and you were probably right."

My father reached up and traced the line of my mother's nose and brought his finger over her two lips. As he did, the lips parted ever so slightly.

"You have to lean down," he said, "I'm still a sick man."

And I watched as my parents kissed. They kept their eyes open as they did, and my mother was the one to cry first, the tears dropping down onto my father's cheeks until he wept too.

TWENTY-ONE

After I left my parents in the hospital, I went to watch Ray Singh. We had been fourteen together, he and I. Now I saw his head on his pillow, dark hair on yellow sheets, dark skin on yellow sheets. I had always been in love with him. I counted the lashes of each closed eye. He had been my almost, my might-have-been, and I did not want to leave him any more than I did my family.

On the listing scaffold behind the stage, with Ruth below us, Ray Singh had gotten close enough to me so that his breath was near mine. I could smell the mixture of cloves and cinnamon that I imagined he topped his cereal with each morning, and a dark smell too, the human smell of the body coming at me where deep inside there were organs suspended by a chemistry separate from mine.

From the time I knew it would happen until the time it did, I had made sure not to be alone with Ray Singh inside or outside school. I was afraid of what I wanted most — his kiss. That it would not be good enough to match the stories everyone told or those I read in *Seventeen* and *Glamour* and *Vogue*. I feared that I would not be good enough — that my first kiss would equal rejection, not love. Still, I collected kiss stories.

"Your first kiss is destiny knocking," Grandma Lynn said over the phone one day. I was holding the phone while my father went to get my mother. I heard him in the kitchen say "three sheets to the wind."

"If I had it to do over again I would have worn something stupendous — like Fire and Ice, but Revlon didn't make that lipstick back then. I would have left my mark on the man."

"Mother?" my mother said into the bedroom extension.

"We're talking kiss business, Abigail."

"How much have you had?"

"See, Susie," Grandma Lynn said, "if you kiss like a lemon, you make lemonade."

"What was it like?"

"Ah, the kiss question," my mother said. "I'll leave you to it." I had been making my father and her tell it over and over again to hear their different takes. What I came away with was an image of my parents behind a cloud of cigarette smoke — the lips only vaguely touching inside the cloud.

A moment later Grandma Lynn whispered, "Susie, are you still there?"

"Yes, Grandma."

She was quiet for a while longer. "I was your age, and my first kiss came from a grown man. A father of a friend."

"Grandma!" I said, honestly shocked.

"You're not going to tell on me, are you?"

"No."

"It was wonderful," Grandma Lynn said. "He knew how to kiss. The boys who kissed me I couldn't even tolerate. I'd put my hand flat against their chests and push them away. Mr. McGahern knew how to use his lips."

"So what happened?"

"Bliss," she said. "I knew it wasn't right, but it was wonderful — at least for me. I never asked him how he felt about it, but then I never saw him alone after that."

"But did you want to do it again?"

"Yes, I was always searching for that first kiss."

"How about Grandaddy?"

"Not much of a kisser," she said. I could hear the clink of ice cubes on the other end of the phone. "I've never forgotten Mr. McGahern, even though it was just for a moment. Is there a boy who wants to kiss you?"

Neither of my parents had asked me this. I now know that they knew this already, could tell, smiled at each other when they compared notes.

I swallowed hard on my end. "Yes."

"What's his name?"

"Ray Singh."

"Do you like him?"

"Yes."

"Then what's the holdup?"

"I'm afraid I won't be good at it."

"Susie?"

"Yes?"

"Just have fun, kid."

* * *

But when I stood by my locker that afternoon and I heard Ray's voice say my name — this time behind me and not above me — it felt like anything but fun. It didn't feel not fun either. The easy states of black and white that I had known before did not apply. I felt, if I were to say any word, churned. Not as a verb but as an adjective. Happy + Frightened = Churned.

"Ray," I said, but before the name had left my mouth, he leaned into me and caught my open mouth in his. It was so unexpected, even though I had waited weeks for it, that I wanted more. I wanted so badly to kiss Ray Singh again.

The following morning Mr. Connors cut out an article from the paper and saved it for Ruth. It was a detailed drawing of the Flanagan sinkhole and how it was going to be filled in. While Ruth dressed, he penned a note to her. "This is a crock of shit," it said. "Someday some poor sap's car is going to fall into it all over again."

"Dad says this is the death knell for him," Ruth said to Ray, waving the clipping at him as she got into Ray's ice blue Chevy at the end of her driveway. "Our place is going to be swallowed up in subdivision land. Get this. In this article they have four blocks like the cubes you draw in beginning art class, and it's supposed to show how they're going to patch the sinkhole up."

"Nice to see you too, Ruth," Ray said, reversing out of the driveway while making eyes at Ruth's unbuckled seat belt.

"Sorry," Ruth said. "Hello."

"What does the article say?" Ray asked.

"Nice day today, beautiful weather."

"Okay, okay. Tell me about the article."

Every time he saw Ruth after a few months had passed, he was reminded of her impatience and her curiosity—two traits that had both made and kept them friends.

"The first three are the same drawing only with different arrows pointing to different places and saying 'topsoil,' 'cracked limestone,' and 'dissolving rock.' The last one has a big headline that says, 'Patching it' and underneath it says, 'Concrete fills the throat and grout fills the cracks.'"

"Throat?" Ray said.

"I know," said Ruth. "Then there's this other arrow on the other side as if this was such a huge project that they had to pause a second so readers could understand the concept, and this one says, 'Then the hole is filled with dirt.'"

Ray started laughing.

"Like a medical procedure," Ruth said. "Intricate surgery is needed to patch up the planet."

"I think holes in the earth draw on some pretty primal fears."

"I'll say," Ruth said. "They have throats, for God's sake! Hey, let's check this out."

A mile or so down the road there were signs of new construction. Ray took a left and drove into the circles of freshly paved roads where the trees had been cleared and small red and yellow flags waved at intervals from the tops of waist-high wire markers.

Just as they had lulled themselves into thinking that they were alone, exploring the roads laid out for a territory as yet uninhabited, they saw Joe Ellis walking up ahead.

Ruth didn't wave and neither did Ray, nor did Joe make a move to acknowledge them.

"My mom says he still lives at home and can't get a job."

"What does he do all day?" Ray asked.

"Look creepy, I guess."

"He never got over it," Ray said, and Ruth stared out into the rows and rows of vacant lots until Ray connected with the main road again and they crossed back over the railroad tracks moving toward Route 30, which would take them in the direction of the sinkhole.

Ruth floated her arm out the window to feel the moist air of the morning after rain. Although Ray had been accused of being involved in my disappearance, he had understood why, knew that the police were doing their job. But Joe Ellis had never recovered from being accused of killing the cats and dogs Mr. Harvey had killed. He wandered around, keeping a good distance from his neighbors and wanting so much to take solace in the love of cats and dogs. For me the saddest thing was that these animals smelled the brokenness in him — the human defect — and kept away.

Down Route 30 near Eels Rod Pike, at a spot that Ray and Ruth were about to pass, I saw Len coming out of an apartment over Joe's barbershop. He carried a lightly stuffed student knapsack out to his car. The knapsack had been the gift of the young woman who owned the apartment. She had asked him out for coffee one day after they met down at the station as part of a criminology course at West Chester College. Inside the knapsack he had a combination of things — some of which he would show my father and some that no child's parent needed to see. The latter included the photos of the graves of the recovered bodies — both elbows there in each case.

When he had called the hospital, the nurse had told him Mr. Salmon was with his wife and family. Now his guilt thickened as he pulled his car into the hospital parking lot and sat for a moment with the hot sun coming through the windshield, baking in the heat.

I could see Len working on how to state what he had to say. He could work with only one assumption in his head — after almost seven years of ever more dwindling contact since late 1975, what my parents would hope for most was a body or the news that Mr. Harvey had been found. What he had to give them was a charm.

He grabbed his knapsack and locked up the car, passing by the girl outside with her replenished buckets of daffodils. He knew the number of my father's room, so he did not bother announcing himself to the fifth-floor nurses' station but merely tapped lightly on my father's open door before walking in.

My mother was standing with her back toward him. When she turned, I could see the force of her presence hit him. She was holding my father's hand. I suddenly felt terribly lonely.

My mother wobbled a bit when she met Len's eyes, and then she led with what came easiest.

"Is it *ever* wonderful to see you?" she tried to joke.

"Len," my father managed. "Abbie, will you tilt me up?"

"How are you feeling, Mr. Salmon?" Len asked as my mother pressed the up arrow button on the bed.

"Jack, please," my father insisted.

"Before you get your hopes up," Len said, "we haven't caught him."

My father visibly deflated.

My mother readjusted the foam pillows behind my father's back and neck. "Then why are you here?" she asked.

"We found an item of Susie's," Len said.

He had used almost the same sentence when he'd come to the house with the jingle-bell hat. It was a distant echo in her head.

The night before, as first my mother watched my father sleeping and then my father woke to see her head beside his on his pillow, they had both been staving off the memory of that first night of snow and hail and rain and how they had clung to each other, neither of them voicing aloud their greatest hope. Last night it had been my father who'd finally said it: "She's never coming home." A clear and easy piece of truth that everyone who had ever known me had accepted. But he needed to say it, and she needed to hear him say it.

"It's a charm off her bracelet," Len said. "A Pennsylvania keystone with her initials on it."

"I bought that for her," my father said. "At Thirtieth Street Station when I went into the city one day. They had a booth, and a man wearing safety glasses etched in initials for free. I brought Lindsey one too. Remember, Abigail?"

"I remember," my mother said.

"We found it near a grave in Connecticut."

My parents were suddenly still for a moment—like animals trapped in ice—their eyes frozen open and beseeching whoever walked above them to release them now, please.

"It wasn't Susie," Len said, rushing to fill the space. "What it means is that Harvey has been linked to other murders in Delaware and Connecticut. It was at the grave site outside Hartford where we found Susie's charm."

My father and mother watched as Len fumbled to open the slightly jammed zipper of his knapsack. My mother smoothed my father's hair back and tried to catch his eye. But my father was focused on the prospect Len presented—my murder case reopening. And my mother, just when she was beginning to feel on more solid ground, had to hide the fact that she'd never wanted it to begin again. The name George Harvey silenced her. She had never known what to say about him. For my mother, connecting her life to his capture and punishment spoke more about choosing to live with the enemy than about having to learn to live in the world without me.

Len pulled out a large Ziploc bag. At the bottom corner of the bag my parents could see the glint of gold. Len handed it to my mother, and she held it in front of her, slightly away from her body.

"Don't you need this, Len?" my father asked.

"We did all the tests on it," he said. "We've documented where it was found and taken the required photographs. The time may come when I would have to ask for it back, but until then, it's yours to keep."

"Open it, Abbie," my father said.

I watched my mother hold open the bag and lean over

the bed. "It's for you, Jack," she said. "It was a gift from you."

As my father reached in, his hand shook, and it took him a second to feel the small, sharp edges of the keystone against the flesh of his fingers. The way he drew it out of the bag reminded me of playing the game Operation with Lindsey when we were little. If he touched the sides of the Ziploc bag an alarm would go off and he would have to forfeit.

"How can you be sure he killed these other girls?" my mother asked. She stared at the tiny ember of gold in my father's palm.

"Nothing is ever certain," Len said.

And the echo rang in her ears again. Len had a fixed set of phrases. It was this same phrase that my father had borrowed to soothe his family. It was a cruel phrase that preyed on hope.

"I think I want you to leave now," she said.

"Abigail?" my father queried.

"I can't hear any more."

"I'm very glad to have the charm, Len," my father said.

Len doffed an imaginary cap to my father before turning to go. He had made a certain kind of love to my mother before she went away. Sex as an act of willful forgetting. It was the kind he made more and more in the rooms above the barbershop.

I headed south toward Ruth and Ray, but I saw Mr. Harvey instead. He was driving an orange patchwork car that had been pieced together from so many different versions of the same make and model that it looked like Frankenstein's monster on wheels. A bungee cord held the front hood, which fluttered up and down as it caught the oncoming air.

The engine had resisted anything but a shimmer above the speed limit no matter how hard he pressed the gas pedal. He had slept next to an empty grave, and while he'd been sleeping he had dreamed of the 5! 5! 5!, waking near dawn to make the drive to Pennsylvania.

The edges of Mr. Harvey seemed oddly blurred. For years he had kept at bay the memories of the women he killed, but now, one by one, they were coming back.

The first girl he'd hurt was by accident. He got mad and couldn't stop himself, or that was how he began to weave it into sense. She stopped going to the high school that they were both enrolled in, but this didn't seem strange to him. By that time he had moved so many times that he assumed that was what the girl had done. He had regretted it, this quiet, muffled rape of a school friend, but he didn't see it as something that would stay with either one of them. It was as if something outside him had resulted in the collision of their two bodies one afternoon. For a second afterward, she'd stared. It was bottomless. Then she put on her torn underpants, tucking them into her skirt's waistband to keep them in place. They didn't speak, and she left. He cut himself with his penknife along the back of his hand. When his father asked about the blood, there would be a plausible explanation. "See," he could say, and point to the place on his hand. "It was an accident."

But his father didn't ask, and no one came around looking for him. No father or brother or policeman.

Then what I saw was what Mr. Harvey felt beside him. This girl, who had died only a few years later when her brother fell asleep smoking a cigarette. She was sitting in the front seat. I wondered how long it would take before he began to remember me.

The only signs of change since the day Mr. Harvey had delivered me up to the Flanagans' were the orange pylons set around the lot. That and the evidence that the sinkhole had expanded. The house's southeast corner sloped downward, and the front porch was quietly sinking into the earth.

As a precaution, Ray parked on the other side of Flat Road, under a section of overgrown shrubbery. Even so, the passenger side skimmed the edge of the pavement. "What happened to the Flanagans?" Ray asked as they got out of his car.

"My father said the corporation that bought the property gave them a settlement and they took off."

"It's spooky around here, Ruth," Ray said.

They crossed the empty road. Above them the sky was a light blue, a few smoky clouds dotting the air. From where they stood they could just make out the back of Hal's bike shop on the other side of the railroad tracks.

"I wonder if Hal Heckler still owns that?" Ruth said. "I had a crush on him when we were growing up."

Then she turned toward the lot. They were quiet. Ruth moved in ever-diminishing circles, with the hole and its vague edge as their goal. Ray trailed just behind Ruth as she led the way. If you saw it from a distance, the sinkhole seemed innocuous — like an overgrown mud puddle just starting to dry out. There were spots of grass and weeds surrounding it and then, if you looked close enough, it was as if the earth stopped and a light cocoa-colored flesh began. It was soft and convex, and it drew in items placed on top of it.

"How do you know it won't swallow us?" Ray asked.

"We're not heavy enough," Ruth said.

"Stop if you feel yourself sinking."

Watching them I remembered holding on to Buckley's hand the day we went to bury the refrigerator. While my father was talking to Mr. Flanagan, Buckley and I walked up to the point where the earth sloped down and softened, and I swore I felt it give ever so slightly beneath my feet. It had been the same sensation as walking in the graveyard of our church and suddenly sinking into the hollow tunnels that the moles had dug among the headstones.

Ultimately it was the memory of those very moles — and the pictures of their blind, nosy, toothsome selves that I sought out in books — that had made me accept more readily being sunk inside the earth in a heavy metal safe. I was mole-proof, anyway.

Ruth tiptoed up to what she took to be the edge, while I thought of the sound of my father's laughter on that long-ago day. I made up a story for my brother on the way home. How underneath the sinkhole there was a whole village inside the earth that no one knew about and the people who lived there greeted these appliances like gifts from an Earthly heaven. "When our refrigerator reaches them," I said, "they will praise us, because they are a race of tiny repairmen who love to put things back together again." My father's laughter filled the car.

"Ruthie," Ray said, "that's close enough."

Ruth's toes were on the soft part, her heels were on the hard, and there was a sense as I watched her that she might point her fingers and raise her arms and dive right in to be beside me. But Ray came up behind her.

"Apparently," he said, "the earth's throat burps."

All three of us watched the corner of something metal as it rose.

"The great Maytag of 'sixty-nine," Ray said.

But it was not a washer or a safe. It was an old red gas stove, moving slow.

"Do you ever think about where Susie Salmon's body ended up?" asked Ruth.

I wanted to walk out from underneath the overgrown shrubs that half-hid their ice blue car and cross the road and walk down into the hole and back up and tap her gently on the shoulder and say, "It's me! You've done it! Bingo! Score!"

"No," Ray said. "I leave that to you."

"Everything is changing here now. Every time I come back something is gone that made it not just every other place in the country," she said.

"Do you want to go inside the house?" Ray asked, but he was thinking of me. How his crush had come when he was thirteen. He had seen me walking home from school ahead of him, and it was a series of simple things: my awkward plaid skirt, my peacoat covered in Holiday's fur, the way what I thought of as my mousy brown hair caught the afternoon sun so that the light moved fluidly from spot to spot as we walked home, one behind the other. And then, a few days later, when he had stood in social science class and accidentally read from his paper on *Jane Eyre* instead of the War of 1812 — I had looked at him in a way he thought was nice.

Ray walked toward the house that would soon be demolished, and that had already been stripped of any valuable doorknobs and faucets late one night by Mr. Connors, but Ruth stayed by the sinkhole. Ray was already inside the house when it happened. As clear as day, she saw me standing there beside her, looking at the spot Mr. Harvey had dumped me.

"Susie," Ruth said, feeling my presence even more solidly when she said my name.

But I said nothing.

"I've written poems for you," Ruth said, trying to get me to stay with her. What she had wished for her whole life happening, finally. "Don't you want anything, Susie?" she asked.

Then I vanished.

Ruth stood there reeling, waiting in the gray light of the Pennsylvania sun. And her question rang in my ears: "Don't you want anything?"

On the other side of the railroad tracks, Hal's shop was deserted. He had taken the day off and brought Samuel and Buckley to a bike show in Radnor. I could see Buckley's hands move over the curved front-wheel casing of a red minibike. It would be his birthday soon, and Hal and Samuel watched him. Hal had wanted to give Samuel's old alto sax to my brother, but my Grandma Lynn had intervened. "He needs to bang on things, honey," she said. "Save the subtle stuff." So Hal and Samuel had chipped in together and bought my brother a secondhand set of drums.

Grandma Lynn was at the mall trying to find simple yet elegant clothes that she might convince my mother to wear. With fingers made dexterous from years of practice, she pulled a near-navy dress from a rack of black. I could see the woman near her alight on the dress in greenish envy.

At the hospital, my mother was reading aloud to my father from a day-old *Evening Bulletin,* and he was watching her lips move and not really listening. Wanting to kiss her instead.

And Lindsey.

I could see Mr. Harvey take the turn into my old neighborhood in broad daylight, past caring who spotted him, even depending on his standard invisibility — here, in the neighborhood where so many had said they would never forget him, had always thought of him as strange, had come easily to suspect that the dead wife he spoke of by alternate names had been one of his victims.

Lindsey was at home alone.

Mr. Harvey drove by Nate's house inside the anchor area of the development. Nate's mother was picking the wilted blossoms from her front kidney-shaped flower bed. She looked up when the car passed. She saw the unfamiliar, patched-together car and imagined it was a college friend of one of the older children home for the summer. She had not seen Mr. Harvey in the driver's seat. He turned left onto the lower road, which circled around to his old street. Holiday whined at my feet, the same kind of sick, low moan he would let out when we drove him to the vet.

Ruana Singh had her back to him. I saw her through the dining room window, alphabetizing stacks of new books and placing them in carefully kept bookshelves. There were children out in their yards on swings and pogo sticks and chasing one another with water pistols. A neighborhood full of potential victims.

He rounded the curve at the bottom of our road and passed the small municipal park across from where the Gilberts lived. They were both inside, Mr. Gilbert now infirm. Then he saw his old house, no longer green, though to my family and me it would always be "the green house." The new owners had painted it a lavendery mauve and installed a pool and, just off to the side, near the basement window, a gazebo made out of redwood, which overflowed with hanging ivy and children's toys. The front flower beds had been paved over when they expanded their front walk, and they had screened in the front porch with frost-resistant glass, behind which he saw an office of some sort. He heard the sound of girls laughing out in the backyard, and a woman came out of the front door carrying a pair of pruning shears and wearing a sun hat. She stared at the man sitting in his orange car and felt something kick inside her—the queasy kick of an empty womb. She turned abruptly and went back inside, peering at him from behind her window. Waiting.

He drove down the road a few houses further.

There she was, my precious sister. He could see her in the upstairs window of our house. She had cut all her hair off and grown thinner in the intervening years, but it was her, sitting at the drafting board she used as a desk and reading a psychology book.

It was then that I began to see them coming down the road.

While he scanned the windows of my old house and

wondered where the other members of my family were — whether my father's leg still made him hobble — I saw the final vestiges of the animals and the women taking leave of Mr. Harvey's house. They straggled forward together. He watched my sister and thought of the sheets he had draped on the poles of the bridal tent. He had stared right in my father's eyes that day as he said my name. And the dog — the one that barked outside his house — the dog was surely dead by now.

Lindsey moved in the window, and I watched him watching her. She stood up and turned around, going farther into the room to a floor-to-ceiling bookshelf. She reached up and brought another book down. As she came back to the desk and he lingered on her face, his rearview mirror suddenly filled with a black-and-white cruising slowly up the street behind him.

He knew he could not outrace them. He sat in his car and prepared the last vestiges of the face he had been giving authorities for decades — the face of a bland man they might pity or despise but never blame. As the officer pulled alongside him, the women slipped in the windows and the cats curled around his ankles.

"Are you lost?" the young policeman asked when he was flush with the orange car.

"I used to live here," Mr. Harvey said. I shook with it. He had chosen to tell the truth.

"We got a call, suspicious vehicle."

"I see they're building something in the old cornfield," Mr. Harvey said. And I knew that part of me could join the others then, swoop down in pieces, each body part he had claimed raining down inside his car.

"They're expanding the school."

"I thought the neighborhood looked more prosperous," he said wistfully.

"Perhaps you should move along," the officer said. He was embarrassed for Mr. Harvey in his patched-up car, but I saw him jot the license plate down.

"I didn't mean to scare anyone."

Mr. Harvey was a pro, but in that moment I didn't care. With each section of road he covered, I focused on Lindsey inside reading her textbooks, on the facts jumping up from the pages and into her brain, on how smart she was and how whole. At Temple she had decided to be a therapist. And I thought of the mix of air that was our front yard, which was daylight, a queasy mother and a cop — it was a convergence of luck that had kept my sister safe so far. Every day a question mark.

Ruth did not tell Ray what had happened. She promised herself she would write it in her journal first. When they crossed the road back to the car, Ray saw something violet in the scrub halfway up a high dirt berm that had been dumped there by a construction crew.

"That's periwinkle," he said to Ruth. "I'm going to clip some for my mom."

"Cool, take your time," Ruth said.

Ray ducked into the underbrush by the driver's side and climbed up to the periwinkle while Ruth stood by the car. Ray wasn't thinking of me anymore. He was thinking of his mother's smiles. The surest way to get them was to find her wildflowers like this, to bring them home to her and watch her as she pressed them, first opening their petals flat against the black and white of dictionaries or reference books. Ray walked to the top of the berm and disappeared over the side in hopes of finding more.

It was only then that I felt a prickle along my spine, when I saw his body suddenly vanish on the other side. I heard Holiday, his fear lodged low and deep in his throat, and realized it could not have been Lindsey for whom he had whined. Mr. Harvey crested the top of Eels Rod Pike and saw the sinkhole and the orange pylons that matched his car. He had dumped a body there. He remembered his mother's amber pendant, and how when she had handed it to him it was still warm.

Ruth saw the women stuffed in the car in blood-colored gowns. She began walking toward them. On that same road where I had been buried, Mr. Harvey passed by Ruth. All she could see were the women. Then: blackout.

That was the moment I fell to Earth.

TWENTY-TWO

Ruth collapsing into the road. Of this I was aware. Mr. Harvey sailing away unwatched, unloved, unbidden—this I lost.

Helplessly I tipped, my balance gone. I fell through the open doorway of the gazebo, across the lawn and out past the farthest boundary of the heaven I had lived in all these years.

I heard Ray screaming in the air above me, his voice shouting in an arc of sound. "Ruth, are you okay?" And then he reached her and grabbed on.

"Ruth, Ruth," he yelled. "What happened?"

And I was in Ruth's eyes and I was looking up. I could feel the arch of her back against the pavement, and scrapes inside her clothes where flesh had been torn away by the gravel's sharp edges. I felt every sensation—the warmth of the sun, the smell of the asphalt—but I could not see Ruth.

I heard Ruth's lungs bubbling, a giddiness there in her stomach, but air still filling her lungs. Then tension stretching out the body. Her body. Ray above, his eyes— gray, pulsing, looking up and down the road hopelessly for help that was not coming. He had not seen the car but had come through the scrub delighted, carrying a bouquet of wildflowers for his mother, and there was Ruth, lying in the road.

Ruth pushed up against her skin, wanting out. She was fighting to leave and I was inside now, struggling with her. I willed her back, willed that divine impossible, but she wanted out. There was nothing and no one that could keep her down. Flying. I watched as I had so many times from heaven, but this time it was a blur beside me. It was lust and rage yearning upward.

"Ruth," Ray said. "Can you hear me, Ruth?"

Right before she closed her eyes and all the lights went out and the world was frantic, I looked into Ray Singh's gray eyes, at his dark skin, at his lips I had once kissed. Then, like a hand unclasping from a tight lock, Ruth passed by him.

Ray's eyes bid me forward while the watching streamed out of me and gave way to a pitiful desire. To be alive again on this Earth. Not to watch from above but to be—the sweetest thing—beside.

Somewhere in the blue blue Inbetween I had seen her—Ruth streaking by me as I fell to Earth. But she was no shadow of a human form, no ghost. She was a smart girl breaking all the rules.

And I was in her body.

I heard a voice calling me from heaven. It was Franny's. She ran toward the gazebo, calling my name.

Holiday was barking so loud that his voice would catch and round in the base of his throat with no break. Then, suddenly, Franny and Holiday were gone and all was silent. I felt something holding me down, and I felt a hand in mine. My ears were like oceans in which what I had known, voices, faces, facts, began to drown. I opened my eyes for the first time since I had died and saw gray eyes looking back at me. I was still as I came to realize that the marvelous weight weighing me down was the weight of the human body.

I tried to speak.

"Don't," Ray said. "What happened?"

I died, I wanted to tell him. How do you say, "I died and now I'm back among the living"?

Ray had kneeled down. Scattered around him and on top of me were the flowers he'd been gathering for Ruana. I could pick out their bright elliptical shapes against Ruth's dark clothes. And then Ray leaned his ear to my chest to listen to me breathing. He placed a finger on the inside of my wrist to check my pulse.

"Did you faint?" he asked when these checked out.

I nodded. I knew I would not be granted this grace on Earth forever, that Ruth's wish was only temporary.

"I think I'm fine," I tried, but my voice was too faint, too far away, and Ray did not hear me. My eyes locked on to his then, opening as wide as I could make them. Something urged me to lift up. I thought I was floating back to heaven, returning, but I was trying to stand up.

"Ruth," Ray said. "Don't move if you feel weak. I can carry you to the car."

I smiled at him, one-thousand-watted. "I'm okay," I said.

Tentatively, watching me carefully, he released my arm but continued to hold on to my other hand. He went with me as I stood, and the wildflowers fell to the pavement. In heaven, women were throwing rose petals as they saw Ruth Connors.

I watched his beautiful face break into a stunned smile. "So you're all right," he said. Cautious, he came close enough to kiss me, but he told me he was checking my pupils to see if they were equal in size.

I was feeling the weight of Ruth's body, both the luscious bounce of breasts and thighs but also an awesome responsibility. I was a soul back on Earth. AWOL a little while from heaven, I had been given a gift. By force of will I stood as straight as I could.

"Ruth?"

I tried to get used to the name. "Yes," I said.

"You've changed," he said. "Something's changed."

We stood near the center of the road, but this was my moment. I wanted so much to tell him, but what could I say then? "I'm Susie, I have only a little time." I was too afraid.

"Kiss me," I said instead.

"What?"

"Don't you want to?" I reached my hands up to his face and felt the light stubble of a beard that had not been there eight years ago.

"What's happened to you?" he said, bewildered.

"Sometimes cats fall ten flights out of the windows of highrises and land on their feet. You only believe it because you've seen it in print."

Ray stared at me, mystified. He leaned his head down and our lips touched, tender. At the roots I felt his cool lips deep down inside me. Another kiss, precious package, stolen gift. His eyes were so close to me I saw the green flecks in the gray.

I took his hand, and we walked back to the car in silence. I was aware that he dragged behind, stretching my arm out behind me as we held hands and scanning Ruth's body to make sure she was walking fine.

He opened the door of the passenger side, and I slid into the seat and placed my feet on the carpeted floor. When he came around to his side and ducked inside he looked hard at me once more.

"What's wrong?" I asked.

He kissed me lightly again, on the lips. What I had wanted for so long. The moment slowed down, and I drank it in. The brush of his lips, the slight stubble of his beard as it grazed me, and the sound of the kiss — the small smack of suction as our lips parted after the pushing together and then the more brutal breaking away. It reverberated, this sound, down the long tunnel of loneliness and making do with watching the touch and caress of others on Earth. I had never been touched like this. I had only been hurt by hands past all tenderness. But spreading out into my heaven after death had been a moonbeam that swirled and blinked on and off — Ray Singh's kiss. Somehow Ruth knew this.

My head throbbed then, with the thought of it, with me hiding inside Ruth in every way but this — that when Ray kissed me or as our hands met it was my desire, not Ruth's, it was *me* pushing out at the edges of her skin. I could see Holly. She was laughing, her head tilted back, and then I heard Holiday howling plaintively, for I was back where we had both once lived.

"Where do you want to go?" Ray asked.

And it was such a wide question, the answer so vast. I knew I did not want to chase after Mr. Harvey. I looked at Ray and knew why I was there. To take back a piece of heaven I had never known.

"Hal Heckler's bike shop," I stated firmly.

"What?"

"You asked," I said.

"Ruth?"

"Yes?"

"Can I kiss you again?"

"Yes," I said, my face flushing.

He leaned over as the engine warmed and our lips met once more and there she was, Ruth, lecturing a group of old men in berets and black turtlenecks while they held glowing lighters in the air and called her name in a rhythmic chant.

Ray sat back and looked at me. "What is it?" he asked.

"When you kiss me I see heaven," I said.

"What does it look like?"

"It's different for everyone."

"I want details," he said, smiling. "Facts."

"Make love to me," I said, "and I'll tell you."

"Who are you?" he asked, but I could tell he didn't know what he was asking yet.

"The car is warmed up," I said.

His hand grabbed the shiny chrome stick on the side of the steering wheel and then we drove — normal as day — a boy and a girl together. The sun caught the broken mica in the old patched pavement as he made the U-turn.

We drove down to the bottom of Flat Road, and I pointed to the dirt path on the other side of Eels Rod Pike, which led up to a place where we could cross the railroad tracks.

"They'll have to change this soon," Ray said as he shot across the gravel and up onto the dirt path. The railroad stretched to Harrisburg in one direction and Philadelphia in the other, and all along it buildings were being razed and old families were moving out and industrial tenants in.

"Will you stay here," I asked, "after you're done with school?"

"No one does," Ray said. "You know that."

I was almost blinded by it, this choice; the idea that if I'd remained on Earth I could have left this place to claim another, that I could go anywhere I wanted to. And I wondered then, was it the same in heaven as on Earth? What I'd been missing was a wanderlust that came from letting go?

We drove onto the slim patch of cleared earth that ran along either side of Hal's bike shop. Ray stopped and braked the car.

"Why here?" Ray asked.

"Remember," I said, "we're exploring."

I led him around to the back of the shop and reached up over the doorjamb until I felt the hidden key.

"How do you know about that?"

"I've watched hundreds of people hide keys," I said. "It doesn't take a genius to guess."

Inside it was as I remembered it, the smell of bike grease heavy in the air.

I said, "I think I need to shower. Why not make yourself at home?"

I walked past the bed and turned on the light switch on

the cord — all the tiny white lights above Hal's bed glittered then, the only light save the dusty light coming from the small back window.

"Where are you going?" Ray asked. "How do you know about this place?" His voice had a frantic sound it hadn't just a moment before.

"Give me just a little time, Ray," I said. "Then I'll explain."

I walked into the small bathroom but kept the door slightly ajar. As I took Ruth's clothes off and waited for the hot water to heat up, I hoped that Ruth could see me, could see her body as I saw it, its perfect living beauty.

It was damp and musty in the bathroom, and the tub was stained from years of having anything but water poured down its drain. I stepped up into the old claw-foot tub and stood under the water. Even at the hottest I could make it, I still felt cold. I called Ray's name. I begged him to step inside the room.

"I can see you through the curtain," he said, averting his eyes.

"It's okay," I said. "I like it. Take your clothes off and join me."

"Susie," he said, "you know I'm not like that."

My heart seized up. "What did you say?" I asked. I focused my eyes on his through the white translucent liner Hal kept for a curtain — he was a dark shape with a hundred small pinpoints of light surrounding him.

"I said I'm not that kind."

"You called me Susie."

There was silence, and then a moment later he drew back the curtain, being careful to look only at my face.

"Susie?"

"Join me," I said, my eyes welling up. "Please, join me."

I closed my eyes and waited. I put my head under the water and felt the heat of it prickling my cheeks and neck, my breasts and stomach and groin. Then I heard him fumbling, heard his belt buckle hit the cold cement floor and his pockets lose their change.

I had the same sense of anticipation then as I sometimes had as a child when I lay down in the back seat and closed my eyes while my parents drove, sure we would be home when the car stopped, that they would lift me up and carry me inside. It was an anticipation born of trust.

Ray drew back the curtain. I turned to face him and opened my eyes. I felt a marvelous draft on the inside of my thighs.

"It's okay," I said.

He stepped slowly into the tub. At first he did not touch me, but then, tentatively, he traced a small scar along my side. We watched together as his finger moved down the ribbony wound.

"Ruth's volleyball incident, nineteen seventy-five," I said. I shivered again.

"You're not Ruth," he said, his face full of wonder.

I took the hand that had reached the end of the cut and placed it under my left breast.

"I've watched you both for years," I said. "I want you to make love to me."

His lips parted to speak, but what was on his lips now was too strange to say out loud. He brushed my nipple with his thumb, and I pulled his head toward me. We kissed. The water came down between our bodies and wet the sparse hair along his chest and stomach. I kissed him because I wanted to see Ruth and I wanted to see Holly and I wanted to know if they could see me. In the shower I could cry and Ray could kiss my tears, never knowing exactly why I shed them.

I touched every part of him and held it in my hands. I cupped his elbow in my palm. I dragged his pubic hair out straight between my fingers. I held that part of him that Mr. Harvey had forced inside me. Inside my head I said the word *gentle,* and then I said the word *man.*

"Ray?"

"I don't know what to call you."

"Susie."

I put my fingers up to his lips to stop his questioning. "Remember the note you wrote me? Remember how you called yourself the Moor?"

For a moment we both stood there, and I watched the water bead along his shoulders, then slip and fall.

Without saying anything further, he lifted me up and I wrapped my legs around him. He turned out of the path of the water to use the edge of the tub for support. When he was inside of me, I grabbed his face in my hands and kissed him as hard as I could.

After a full minute, he pulled away. "Tell me what it looks like."

"Sometimes it looks like the high school did," I said, breathless. "I never got to go there, but in my heaven I can make a bonfire in the classrooms or run up and down the halls yelling as loud as I want. But it doesn't always look like that. It can look like Nova Scotia, or Tangiers, or Tibet. It looks like anything you've ever dreamed."

"Is Ruth there?"

"Ruth is doing spoken word, but she'll come back."

"Can you see yourself there?"

"I'm here right now," I said.

"But you'll be gone soon."

I would not lie. I bowed my head. "I think so, Ray. Yes."

We made love then. We made love in the shower and in the bedroom and under the lights and fake glow-in-the-dark stars. While he rested, I kissed him across the line of his backbone and blessed each knot of muscle, each mole and blemish.

"Don't go," he said, and his eyes, those shining gems, shut and I could feel the shallow breath of sleep from him.

"My name is Susie," I whispered, "last name Salmon, like the fish." I leaned my head down to rest on his chest and sleep beside him.

When I opened my eyes, the window across from us was dark red and I could feel that there was not much time left. Outside, the world I had watched for so long was living and breathing on the same earth I now was. But I knew I would not go out. I had taken this time to fall in love instead — in love with the sort of helplessness I had not felt in death — the helplessness of being alive, the dark bright pity of being human — feeling as you went, groping in corners and opening your arms to light — all of it part of navigating the unknown.

Ruth's body was weakening. I leaned on one arm and watched Ray sleeping. I knew that I was going soon.

When his eyes opened a short while later, I looked at him and traced the edge of his face with my fingers.

"Do you ever think about the dead, Ray?"

He blinked his eyes and looked at me.

"I'm in med school."

"I don't mean cadavers, or diseases, or collapsed organs, I mean what Ruth talks about. I mean us."

"Sometimes I do," he said. "I've always wondered."

"We're here, you know," I said. "All the time. You can talk to us and think about us. It doesn't have to be sad or scary."

"Can I touch you again?" He shook the sheets from his legs to sit up.

It was then that I saw something at the end of Hal's bed. It was cloudy and still. I tried to convince myself that it was an odd trick of light, a mass of dust motes trapped in the setting sun. But when Ray reached out to touch me, I didn't feel anything.

Ray leaned close to me and kissed me lightly on the shoulder. I didn't feel it. I pinched myself under the blanket. Nothing.

The cloudy mass at the end of the bed began to take shape now. As Ray slipped out of the bed and stood, I saw men and women filling the room.

"Ray," I said, just before he reached the bathroom. I wanted to say "I'll miss you," or "don't go," or "thank you."

"Yes."

"You have to read Ruth's journals."

"You couldn't pay me not to," he said.

I looked through the shadowy figures of the spirits forming a mass at the end of the bed and saw him smile at me. Saw his lovely fragile body turn and walk through the doorway. A tenuous and sudden memory.

As the steam began to billow out from the bathroom, I made my way, slowly, to the small child's desk where Hal stacked bills and records. I began to think of Ruth again, how I hadn't seen any of it coming — the marvelous possibility that Ruth had dreamed of since our meeting in the parking lot. Instead, I saw how hope was what I had traded on in heaven and on Earth. Dreams of being a wildlife photographer, dreams of winning an Oscar in junior year, dreams of kissing Ray Singh once more. Look what happens when you dream.

In front of me I saw a phone and picked it up. Without thinking, I punched in the number to my house, like a lock whose combination you know only when you spin the dial in your hand.

On the third ring, someone picked up.

"Hello?"

"Hello, Buckley," I said.

"Who is this?"

"It's me, Susie."

"Who's there?"

"Susie, honey, your big sister."

"I can't hear you," he said.

I stared at the phone for a minute, and then I felt them. The room was full now of these silent spirits. Among them were children as well as adults. "Who are you? Where did you all come from?" I asked, but what had been my voice made no noise in the room. It was then that I noticed it. I was sitting up and watching the others, but Ruth was lying sprawled across the desk.

"Can you throw me a towel?" Ray yelled after shutting off the water. When I did not answer he pulled back the curtain. I heard him get out of the tub and come to the doorway. He saw Ruth and ran toward her. He touched her shoulder and, sleepily, she roused. They looked at each other. She did not have to say anything. He knew that I was gone.

I remembered once, with my parents and Lindsey and Buckley, riding backward on a train into a dark tunnel. That was how it felt to leave Earth the second time. The destination somehow inevitable, the sights seen in passing so many times. But this time I was accompanied, not ripped away, and I knew we were taking a long trip to a place very far away.

Leaving Earth again was easier than coming back had been. I got to see two old friends silently holding each other in the back of Hal's bike shop, neither of them ready to say aloud what had happened to them. Ruth was both more tired and more happy than she had ever been. For Ray, what he had been through and the possibilities this opened up for him were just starting to sink in.

TWENTY-THREE

The next morning the smell of his mother's baking had sneaked up the stairs and into Ray's room where he and Ruth lay together. Overnight, their world had changed. It was that simple.

After leaving Hal's bike shop, being careful to cover any trace that they had ever been there, Ray and Ruth drove in silence back to Ray's house. Later that night, when Ruana found the two of them curled up together asleep and fully clothed, she was glad that Ray had at least this one weird friend.

Around three A.M., Ray had stirred. He sat up and looked at Ruth, at her long gangly limbs, at the beautiful body to which he had made love, and felt a sudden warmth infuse him. He reached out to touch her, and just then a bit of moonlight fell across the floor from the window where I had watched him sit and study for so many years. He followed it. There on the floor was Ruth's bag.

Careful not to wake her, he slid off the bed and walked over to it. Inside was her journal. He lifted it out and began to read:

"At the tips of feathers there is air and at their base: blood. I hold up bones; I wish like broken glass they could court light . . . still I try to place these pieces back together, to set them firm, to make murdered girls live again."

He skipped ahead:

"Penn Station, bathroom stall, struggle which led to the sink. Older woman.
"Domestic. Ave. C. Husband and wife.
"Roof on Mott Street, a teenage girl, gunshot.
"Time? Little girl in C.P. strays toward bushes. White lace collar, fancy."

He grew incredibly cold in the room but kept reading, looking up only when he heard Ruth stir.
"I have so much to tell you," she said.

Nurse Eliot helped my father lower himself into the wheelchair while my mother and sister fussed about the room, collecting the daffodils to take home.
"Nurse Eliot," he said, "I'll remember your kindness but I hope it will be a long time before I see you again."
"I hope so too," she said. She looked at my family gathered in the room, standing awkwardly about.

"Buckley, your mother's and sister's hands are full. It's up to you."

"Steer her easy, Buck," my father said.

I watched the four of them begin to trail down the hall to the elevator, Buckley and my father first while Lindsey and my mother followed behind, their arms full of dripping daffodils.

In the elevator going down, Lindsey stared into the throats of the bright yellow flowers. She remembered that Samuel and Hal had found yellow daffodils lying in the cornfield on the afternoon of the first memorial. They had never known who placed them there. My sister looked at the flowers and then my mother. She could feel my brother's body touching hers, and our father, sitting in the shiny hospital chair, looking tired but happy to be going home. When they reached the lobby and the doors opened I knew they were meant to be there, the four of them together, alone.

While Ruana's hands grew wet and swollen paring apple after apple, she began to say the word in her mind, the one she had avoided for years: *divorce.* It had been something about the crumpled, clinging postures of her son and Ruth that finally freed her. She could not remember the last time she had gone to bed at the same time as her husband. He walked in the room like a ghost and like a ghost slipped in between the sheets, barely creasing them. He was not unkind in the ways that the television and newspapers were full of. His cruelty was in his absence. Even when he came and sat at her dinner table and ate her food, he was not there.

She heard the sound of water running in the bathroom above her and waited what she thought was a considerate interval before calling up to them. My mother had called that morning to thank her for having talked to her when she called from California, and Ruana had decided to drop off a pie.

After handing a mug of coffee each to Ruth and Ray, Ruana announced that it was already late and she wanted Ray to accompany her to the Salmons', where she intended to run quietly to the door and place a pie on their doorstep.

"Whoa, pony," Ruth managed.

Ruana stared at her.

"Sorry, Mom," Ray said. "We had a pretty intense day yesterday." But he wondered, might his mother ever believe him?

Ruana turned toward the counter and brought one of two pies she had baked to the table, where the scent of it rose in a steamy mist from the holes cut into the crust. "Breakfast?" she said.

"You're a goddess!" said Ruth.

Ruana smiled.

"Eat your fill and then get dressed and both of you can come with me."

Ruth looked at Ray while she said, "Actually, I have somewhere to go, but I'll drop by later."

Hal brought the drum set over for my brother. Hal and my grandmother had agreed. Though it was still weeks before Buckley turned thirteen, he needed them. Samuel had let Lindsey and Buckley meet my parents at the hospital without him. It would be a double homecoming for them. My mother had stayed with my father for forty-eight hours straight, during which the world had changed for them and for others and would, I saw now, change again and again and again. There was no way to stop it.

"I know we shouldn't start too early," Grandma Lynn said, "but what's your poison, boys?"

"I thought we were set up for champagne," Samuel said.

"We are later," she said. "I'm offering an apéritif."

"I think I'm passing," Samuel said. "I'll have something when Lindsey does."

"Hal?"

"I'm teaching Buck the drums."

Grandma Lynn held her tongue about the questionable sobriety of known jazz greats. "Well, how about three scintillating tumblers of water?"

My grandmother stepped back into the kitchen to get their drinks. I had come to love her more after death than I ever had on Earth. I wish I could say that in that moment in the kitchen she decided to quit drinking, but I now saw that drinking was part of what made her who she was. If the worst of what she left on Earth was a legacy of inebriated support, it was a good legacy in my book.

She brought the ice over to the sink from the freezer and splurged on cubes. Seven in each tall glass. She ran the tap to make the water as cold as it would come. Her Abigail was coming home again. Her strange Abigail, whom she loved.

But when she looked up and through the window, she swore she saw a young girl wearing the clothes of her youth sitting outside Buckley's garden-shed fort and staring back at her. The next moment the girl was gone. She shook it off. The day was busy. She would not tell anyone.

When my father's car pulled into the drive, I was beginning to wonder if this had been what I'd been waiting for, for my family to come home, not to me anymore but to one another with me gone.

In the afternoon light my father looked smaller somehow, thinner, but his eyes looked grateful in a way they had not in years.

My mother, for her part, was thinking moment by moment that she might be able to survive being home again.

All four of them got out at once. Buckley came forward from the rear passenger seat to assist my father perhaps more than he needed assistance, perhaps protecting him from my mother. Lindsey looked over the hood of the car at our brother — her habitual check-in mode still operating. She felt responsible, just as my brother did, just as my father did. And then she turned back and saw my mother looking at her, her face lit by the yellow light of the daffodils.

"What?"

"You are the spitting image of your father's mother," my mother said.

"Help me with the bags," my sister said.

They walked to the trunk together as Buckley led my father up the front path.

Lindsey stared into the dark space of the trunk. She wanted to know only one thing.

"Are you going to hurt him again?"

"I'm going to do everything I can not to," my mother said, "but no promises this time." She waited until Lindsey glanced up and looked at her, her eyes a challenge now as much as the eyes of a child who had grown up fast, run fast since the day the police had said too much blood in the earth, your daughter/sister/child is dead.

"I know what you did."

"I stand warned."

My sister hefted the bag.

They heard shouting. Buckley ran out onto the front porch. "Lindsey!" he said, forgetting his serious self, his heavy body buoyant. "Come see what Hal got me!"

He banged. And he banged and he banged and he banged. And Hal was the only one still smiling after five minutes of it. Everyone else had glimpsed the future and it was loud.

"I think now would be a good time to introduce him to the brush," Grandma Lynn said. Hal obliged.

My mother had handed the daffodils to Grandma Lynn and gone upstairs almost immediately, using the bathroom as an excuse. Everyone knew where she was going: my old room.

She stood at the edge of it, alone, as if she were standing at the edge of the Pacific. It was still lavender. The furniture, save for a reclining chair of my grandmother's, was unchanged.

"I love you, Susie," she said.

I had heard these words so many times from my father that it shocked me now; I had been waiting, unknowingly, to hear it from my mother. She had needed the time to know that this love would not destroy her, and I had, I now knew, given her that time, could give it, for it was what I had in great supply.

She noticed a photograph on my old dresser, which Grandma Lynn had put in a gold frame. It was the very first photograph I'd ever taken of her — my secret portrait of Abigail before her family woke and she put on her lipstick. Susie Salmon, wildlife photographer, had captured a woman staring out across her misty suburban lawn.

She used the bathroom, running the tap noisily and disturbing the towels. She knew immediately that her mother had bought these towels — cream, a ridiculous color for towels — and monogrammed — also ridiculous, my mother thought. But then, just as quickly, she laughed at herself. She was beginning to wonder how useful her scorched-earth policy had been to her all these years. Her mother was loving if she was drunk, solid if she was vain. When was it all right to let go not only of the dead but of the living — to learn to accept?

I was not in the bathroom, in the tub, or in the spigot; I did not hold court in the mirror above her head or stand in miniature at the tip of every bristle on Lindsey's or Buckley's toothbrush. In some way I could not account for — had they reached a state of bliss? were my parents back together forever? had Buckley begun to tell someone his troubles? would my father's heart truly heal? — I was done yearning for them, needing them to yearn for me. Though I still would. Though they still would. Always.

Downstairs Hal was holding Buckley's wrist as it held the brush stick. "Just pass it over the snare lightly." And

Buckley did and looked up at Lindsey sitting across from him on the couch.

"Pretty cool, Buck," my sister said.

"Like a rattlesnake."

Hal liked that. "Exactly," he said, visions of his ultimate jazz combo dancing in his head.

My mother arrived back downstairs. When she entered the room she saw my father first. Silently she tried to let him know she was okay, that she was still breathing the air in, coping with the altitude.

"Okay, everyone!" my grandmother shouted from the kitchen, "Samuel has an announcement to make, so sit down!"

Everyone laughed and before they realigned into their more closed selves — this being together so hard for them even if it was what they all had wanted — Samuel came into the room along with Grandma Lynn. She held a tray of champagne flutes ready to be filled. He glanced at Lindsey briefly.

"Lynn is going to assist me by pouring," he said.

"Something she's quite good at," my mother said.

"Abigail?" Grandma Lynn said.

"Yes?"

"It's nice to see you too."

"Go ahead, Samuel," my father said.

"I wanted to say that I'm happy to be here with you all."

But Hal knew his brother. "You're not done, wordsmith. Buck, give him some brush." This time Hal let Buckley do it without assistance, and my brother backed Samuel up.

"I wanted to say that I'm glad that Mrs. Salmon is

home, and that Mr. Salmon is home too, and that I'm honored to be marrying their beautiful daughter."

"Hear! Hear!" my father said.

My mother stood to hold the tray for Grandma Lynn, and together they distributed the glasses across the room.

As I watched my family sip champagne, I thought about how their lives trailed backward and forward from my death and then, I saw, as Samuel took the daring step of kissing Lindsey in a room full of family, became borne aloft away from it.

These were the lovely bones that had grown around my absence: the connections — sometimes tenuous, sometimes made at great cost, but often magnificent — that happened after I was gone. And I began to see things in a way that let me hold the world without me in it. The events that my death wrought were merely the bones of a body that would become whole at some unpredictable time in the future. The price of what I came to see as this miraculous body had been my life.

My father looked at the daughter who was standing there in front of him. The shadow daughter was gone.

With the promise that Hal would teach him to do drum rolls after dinner, Buckley put up his brush and drumsticks, and the seven of them began to trail through the kitchen into the dining room, where Samuel and Grandma Lynn had used the good plates to serve her trademark Stouffer's frozen ziti and Sara Lee frozen cheesecake.

"Someone's outside," Hal said, spotting a man through the window. "It's Ray Singh!"

"Let him in," my mother said.

"He's leaving."

All of them save my father and grandmother, who stayed together in the dining room, began to go after him.

"Hey, Ray!" Hal said, opening the door and nearly stepping directly in the pie. "Wait up!"

Ray turned. His mother was in the car with the engine running.

"We didn't mean to interrupt," Ray said now to Hal. Lindsey and Samuel and Buckley and a woman he recognized as Mrs. Salmon were all crowded together on the porch.

"Is that Ruana?" my mother called. "Please ask her in."

"Really, that's fine," Ray said and made no move to come closer. He wondered, *Is Susie watching this?*

Lindsey and Samuel broke away from the group and came toward him.

By that time my mother had walked down the front path to the driveway and was leaning in the car window talking to Ruana.

Ray glanced at his mother as she opened the car door to go inside the house. "Anything but pie for the two of us," she said to my mother as they walked up the path.

"Is Dr. Singh working?" my mother asked.

"As usual," Ruana said. She watched to see Ray walking, with Lindsey and Samuel, through the door of the house. "Will you come smoke stinky cigarettes with me again?"

"It's a date," my mother said.

"Ray, welcome, sit," my father said when he saw him coming through the living room. He had a special place in his heart for the boy who had loved his daughter, but

Buckley swooped into the chair next to my father before anyone else could get to him.

Lindsey and Samuel found two straight chairs from the living room and brought them in to sit by the sideboard. Ruana sat between Grandma Lynn and my mother and Hal sat alone on one end.

I realized then that they would not know when I was gone, just as they could not know sometimes how heavily I had hovered in a particular room. Buckley had talked to me and I had talked back. Even if I hadn't thought I'd been talking to him, I had. I became manifest in whatever way they wanted me to be.

And there she was again, alone and walking out in the cornfield while everyone else I cared for sat together in one room. She would always feel me and think of me. I could see that, but there was no longer anything I could do. Ruth had been a girl haunted and now she would be a woman haunted. First by accident and now by choice. All of it, the story of my life and death, was hers if she chose to tell it, even to one person at a time.

It was late in Ruana and Ray's visit when Samuel started talking about the gothic revival house that Lindsey and he had found along an overgrown section of Route 30. As he told Abigail about it in detail, describing how he had realized he wanted to propose to Lindsey and live there with her, Ray found himself asking, "Does it have a big hole in the ceiling of the back room and cool windows above the front door?"

"Yes," Samuel said, as my father grew alarmed. "But it can be fixed, Mr. Salmon. I'm sure of it."

"Ruth's dad owns that," Ray said.

Everyone was quiet for a moment and then Ray continued.

"He took out a loan on his business to buy up old places that aren't already slated for destruction. He wants to restore them," Ray said.

"My God," Samuel said.

And I was gone.

BONES

You don't notice the dead leaving when they really choose to leave you. You're not meant to. At most you feel them as a whisper or the wave of a whisper undulating down. I would compare it to a woman in the back of a lecture hall or theater whom no one notices until she slips out. Then only those near the door themselves, like Grandma Lynn, notice; to the rest it is like an unexplained breeze in a closed room.

Grandma Lynn died several years later, but I have yet to see her here. I imagine her tying it on in her heaven, drinking mint juleps with Tennessee Williams and Dean Martin. She'll be here in her own sweet time, I'm sure.

If I'm to be honest with you, I still sneak away to watch my family sometimes. I can't help it, and sometimes they still think of me. They can't help it.

After Lindsey and Samuel got married they sat in the empty house on Route 30 and drank champagne. The

branches of the overgrown trees had grown into the upstairs windows, and they huddled beneath them, knowing
the branches would have to be cut. Ruth's father had
promised he would sell the house to them only if Samuel
paid him in labor as his first employee in a restoration
business. By the end of that summer, Mr. Connors had
cleared the lot with the help of Samuel and Buckley and
set up a trailer, which during the day would be his work
quarters and at night could be Lindsey's study room.

In the beginning it was uncomfortable, the lack of
plumbing and electricity, and having to go home to either
one of their parents' houses to take showers, but Lindsey
buried herself in school work and Samuel buried himself
in tracking down the right era doorknobs and light pulls.
It was a surprise to everyone when Lindsey found out she
was pregnant.

"I thought you looked fatter," Buck said, smiling.

"You're one to talk," Lindsey said.

My father dreamed that one day he might teach another child to love ships in bottles. He knew there would
be both sadness and joy in it; that it would always hold an
echo of me.

I would like to tell you that it is beautiful here, that I am,
and you will one day be, forever safe. But this heaven is
not about safety just as, in its graciousness, it isn't about
gritty reality. We have fun.

We do things that leave humans stumped and grateful,
like Buckley's garden coming up one year, all of its crazy
jumble of plants blooming all at once. I did that for my
mother who, having stayed, found herself facing the yard

again. Marvel was what she did at all the flowers and herbs and budding weeds. Marveling was what she mostly did after she came back — at the twists life took.

And my parents gave my leftover possessions to the Goodwill, along with Grandma Lynn's things.

They kept sharing when they felt me. Being together, thinking and talking about the dead, became a perfectly normal part of their life. And I listened to my brother, Buckley, as he beat the drums.

Ray became Dr. Singh, "the real doctor in the family," as Ruana liked to say. And he had more and more moments that he chose not to disbelieve. Even if surrounding him were the serious surgeons and scientists who ruled over a world of black and white, he maintained this possibility: that the ushering strangers that sometimes appeared to the dying were not the results of strokes, that he had called Ruth by my name, and that he had, indeed, made love to me.

If he ever doubted, he called Ruth. Ruth, who had graduated from a closet to a closet-sized studio on the Lower East Side. Ruth, who was still trying to find a way to write down whom she saw and what she had experienced. Ruth, who wanted everyone to believe what she knew: that the dead truly talk to us, that in the air between the living, spirits bob and weave and laugh with us. They are the oxygen we breathe.

Now I am in the place I call this wide wide Heaven because it includes all my simplest desires but also the most humble and grand. The word my grandfather uses is *comfort*.

So there are cakes and pillows and colors galore, but underneath this more obvious patchwork quilt are places like a quiet room where you can go and hold someone's hand and not have to say anything. Give no story. Make no claim. Where you can live at the edge of your skin for as long as you wish. This wide wide Heaven is about flathead nails and the soft down of new leaves, wild roller coaster rides and escaped marbles that fall then hang then take you somewhere you could never have imagined in your small-heaven dreams.

One afternoon I was scanning Earth with my grandfather. We were watching birds skip from top to top of the very tallest pines in Maine and feeling the bird's sensations as they landed then took flight then landed again. We ended up in Manchester, visiting a diner my grandfather remembered from his days traveling up and down the East Coast on business. It had gotten seedier in the fifty intervening years and after taking stock we left. But in the instant I turned away, I saw him: Mr. Harvey coming out of the doors of a Greyhound bus.

He went into the diner and ordered a cup of coffee at the counter. To the uninitiated, he still looked every bit as ordinary as he could, except around the eyes, but he no longer wore his contacts and no one took the time to look past his thick lenses anymore.

As an older waitress passed him a Styrofoam cup full of boiling coffee, he heard a bell over the door behind him tinkle and felt a cold blast of air.

It was a teenage girl who had sat a few rows ahead of him for the last few hours, playing her Walkman and humming along with the songs. He sat at the counter until she was done using the bathroom, and then he followed her out.

I watched him trail her in the dirty snow along the side of the diner and out to the back of the bus station, where she would be out of the wind for a smoke. While she stood there, he joined her. She wasn't even startled. He was another boring old man in bad clothes.

He calculated his business in his mind. The snow and cold. The pitched ravine that dropped off immediately in front of them. The blind woods on the other side. And he engaged her in conversation.

"Long ride," he said.

She looked at him at first as if she couldn't believe he was talking to her.

"Um hmmm," she said.

"Are you traveling alone?"

It was then that I noticed them, hanging above their heads in a long and plentiful row. Icicles.

The girl put out her cigarette on the heel of her shoe and turned to go.

"Creep," she said, and walked fast.

A moment later, the icicle fell. The heavy coldness of it threw him off balance just enough for him to stumble and pitch forward. It would be weeks before the snow in the ravine melted enough to uncover him.

But now let me tell you about someone special:

Out in her yard, Lindsey made a garden. I watched her weed the long thick flower bed. Her fingers twisted inside the gloves as she thought about the clients she saw in her practice each day — how to help them make sense of the cards life had dealt them, how to ease their pain. I remembered that the simplest things were the ones that often eluded what I thought of as her big brain. It took her forever to figure out that I always volunteered to clip the grass inside the fence so I could play with Holiday while we did yard work. She remembered Holiday then, and I followed her thoughts. How in a few years it would be time to get her child a dog, once the house was settled and fenced-in. Then she thought about how there were now machines with whipcords that could trim a fence post to post in minutes — what it had taken us hours of grumbling to achieve.

Samuel walked out to Lindsey then, and there she was in his arms, my sweet butterball babe, born ten years after my fourteen years on Earth: Abigail Suzanne. Little Susie to me. Samuel placed Susie on a blanket near the flowers. And my sister, my Lindsey, left me in her memories, where I was meant to be.

And in a small house five miles away was a man who held my mud-encrusted charm bracelet out to his wife.

"Look what I found at the old industrial park," he said. "A construction guy said they were bulldozing the whole lot. They're afraid of more sinkholes like that one that swallowed the cars."

His wife poured him some water from the sink as he fingered the tiny bike and the ballet shoe, the flower basket and the thimble. He held out the muddy bracelet as she set down his glass.

"This little girl's grown up by now," she said.

Almost.

Not quite.

I wish you all a long and happy life.

ACKNOWLEDGMENTS

I owe a debt to my passionate early readers: Judith Grossman, Wilton Barnhardt, Geoffrey Wolff, Margot Livesey, Phil Hay, and Michelle Latiolais. As well as the workshop at the University of California, Irvine.

To those who joined the party late but brought the most awesome refreshments: Teal Minton, Joy Johannessen, and Karen Joy Fowler.

To the pros: Henry Dunow, Jennifer Carlson, Bill Contardi, Ursula Doyle, Michael Pietsch, Asya Muchnick, Ryan Harbage, Laura Quinn, and Heather Fain.

Abiding thanks to: Sarah Burnes, Sarah Crichton, and the glorious MacDowell Colony.

A smarty-pants badge of honor to my informants: Dee Williams, Orren Perlman, Dr. Carl Brighton, and the essential facts-on-file team of Bud and Jane.

And to my continuing troika, whose sustaining friendship and rigorous reading and rereading are, next to tapioca and coffee, what keep me going on a day-to-day basis: Aimee Bender, Kathryn Chetkovich, Glen David Gold.

And a *woof!* to Lilly.

ABOUT THE AUTHOR

Alice Sebold is the author of *Lucky*, a memoir, and the novels *The Lovely Bones* and *The Almost Moon*. She lives in California with her husband, the novelist Glen David Gold.

...AND HER MOST RECENT BOOK

Following is an excerpt from the opening pages of *The Almost Moon*, which is available in paperback from Back Bay Books.

ONE

———

When all is said and done, killing my mother came easily. Dementia, as it descends, has a way of revealing the core of the person affected by it. My mother's core was rotten like the brackish water at the bottom of a weeks-old vase of flowers. She had been beautiful when my father met her and still capable of love when I became their late-in-life child, but by the time she gazed up at me that day, none of this mattered.

If I hadn't picked up my ringing phone, Mrs. Castle, my mother's unlucky neighbor, would have continued down the list of emergency numbers posted on my mother's almond-colored fridge. But within the hour, I found myself rushing over to the house where I was born.

It was a cool October morning. When I arrived, my mother was sitting upright in her wing chair, wrapped in a mohair shawl, and mumbling to herself. Mrs. Castle said my mother hadn't recognized her that morning when she'd brought the paper to the door.

"She tried to slam the door on me," Mrs. Castle said. "She screamed like I was scalding her. It was the most pitiful thing imaginable."

My mother sat, a totemic presence, in the flocked red-and-white wing chair in which she'd spent the more than two decades since my father's death. She'd aged slowly in that chair, retiring first to read books and work her needlepoint, and then, when her eyes began to fail, to watch public television from dawn until she fell asleep in front of it after her evening meal. In the last year or two, she would sit in the chair and not even bother to turn on the television. Often she placed the twisted skeins of yarn that my older daughter, Emily, still sent each Christmas, in the center of her lap. She petted them the way some old women might pet cats.

I thanked Mrs. Castle and assured her I would handle everything.

"You know it's time," she said, turning toward me on the front stoop. "She's been in the house alone an awfully long while."

"I know," I said, and shut the door.

Mrs. Castle walked down the steps of my mother's front porch with three empty dishes of various sizes she had found in the kitchen and that she claimed to be hers. I didn't doubt it. My mother's neighbors were a godsend. When I was young, my mother had railed against the Greek Orthodox church down the road, calling its parishioners, for no reason that made sense, "those stupid Holy-Rolling Poles." But it was this congregation that had often called upon its ranks to make sure the cranky old woman who had lived forever in the run-down house got fed and clothed. If occasionally she got robbed, well, it was precarious to be a woman living alone.

"People are living in my walls," she had said to me more than once, but it was only when I found a condom lying beside my childhood bed that I'd put two and two together. Manny, a boy who occasionally repaired things for my mother, was bringing girls into her upstairs rooms. I had talked to Mrs. Castle and hired a locksmith. It was not my fault my mother refused to move.

"Mother," I said, calling the name only I, as her sole child, had the right to call her. She looked up at me and smiled.

"Bitch," she said.

The thing about dementia is that sometimes you feel like the afflicted person has a trip wire to the truth, as if they can see beneath the skin you hide in.

"Mother, it's Helen," I said.

"I know who you are!" she barked at me.

Her hands clasped the curved ends of the armrests, and I could see how hard she pressed, her anger flaring up and out at me like involuntary claws.

"That's good," I said.

I stood there a moment longer, until it felt like an established fact. She was my mother and I was her daughter. I thought we could go forward from this into our usual unpleasant encounter.

I walked over to the windows and began to draw up the metal blinds by the increasingly threadbare cloth tape that bound them. Outside, the yard of my childhood was so overgrown it was difficult to make out the original shapes of the bushes and trees, those places I had played with other children until my mother's behavior began to garner a reputation outside our house.

"She steals," my mother said.

My back was to her. I was looking at a vine that had

crawled into the huge fir tree in the corner of the yard and consumed the shed where my father had once done carpentry. He had always been happiest inside that space. On my darkest days, I had come to imagine him there, laboriously sanding the round wooden globes that had replaced all his other projects.

"Who steals?"

"That bitch."

I knew she was talking about Mrs. Castle. The woman who daily made sure my mother had woken up. Who brought her the *Philadelphia Inquirer* and not infrequently cut flowers from her own yard and placed them in plastic iced-tea pitchers that wouldn't shatter if my mother knocked them over.

"That's not true," I told her. "Mrs. Castle is a lovely woman who takes good care of you."

"What happened to my blue Pigeon Forge bowl?"

I knew the bowl and realized I had not seen it for weeks. In my youth it had always held what I thought of as imprisoned food—walnuts and Brazil nuts and filberts that my father would crack and dig out with a tiny fork.

"I gave it to her, Mother," I lied.

"You what?"

"She's been so wonderful and I knew she liked it, and so I just gave it to her one day when you were napping."

Help doesn't come free, I felt like telling her. *These people owe you nothing.*

My mother looked at me. It was a horrible bottomless look. She pouted first, her lower lip jutting out and then quivering. She was going to cry. I left the room and walked to the kitchen. Whenever I came, I found good reason to spend many of the hours I was supposed to be with my mother in every room of the house but the one in which she sat. I heard the low moan begin that I'd been hearing all my life. It was a moan the notes of which were orchestrated to elicit pity. My father had always been the one to run to her. After his death, it fell to me. For more than twenty years, with greater or lesser diligence, I had been attending to her, rushing over when she called saying her heart would burst, or taking her on increasing rounds of doctors' visits as she?aged.

Late in the afternoon of that day, I was in the screened-in back porch, sweeping out the straw mat. I had left the door open a crack so that I could hear her. Then into the cloud of dust that surrounded me came the unmistakable odor of shit. My mother had needed to go to the bathroom but couldn't get up.

I dropped the broom and ran to my mother. She had not, as I may have momentarily hoped, died and suffered the resultant loosening of bowels. Dead in her own home as she might have wished. Instead, she sat in her chair, having soiled herself.

"Number two!" she said. This time, the smile was different than the smile of Bitch. Bitch had had life to it. This smile was alien to me. It held neither fear nor malice.

Often, when I recounted to my youngest, Sarah, the events of a given day, she told me that no matter how much she loved me, she wasn't going to strip and diaper me when I grew old. "I'll hire someone," she said. "I've never heard a better incentive for hitting the big time than avoiding that."

The smell had filled the room within seconds. I walked back to the porch twice to take in huge drafts of dusty air and could think of nothing else but presenting my mother in the way she would have wanted to be seen. I knew I was going to have to call the ambulance. I knew, as I had for some time, that my mother was heading out of this life, but I did not want her arriving at the hospital caked in shit. I should say I knew *she* would not want that, and so what had mattered most to her throughout her life—appearances—became what mattered most to me.

I took a final breath out on the porch and walked back to her. No longer smiling, she was agitated in the extreme.

"Mom," I said, certain as I said it that she did not recognize the name or the daughter who said it, "I'm going to help you clean up, and then we're going to make some calls." *You'll never make a call again,* I thought, and I didn't mean it cruelly. Why is it that pragmatics are so often interpreted this way? Shit is shit and truth is truth. Done.

I knelt down in front of her and looked up into her face. I hated her more than I'd ever hated anyone. Still, I reached up, as if I were finally allowed to touch a precious thing, and ran my fingers down her long silver braid. "Mom," I whispered. I said it because I knew it would be still in the air. No reverberations, no response.

But the wetness was making her unhappy. Like a snail trapped in sunlight, say—anxious to get away from an element that caused pain. I went from kneeling to half bending over. I placed my shoulders against her shoulders, careful not to put any weight on her. I leaned in like a football player on a tackle and then lifted up. She was both lighter and heavier than I'd expected.

I got her to standing with ease, but once she was upright, she collapsed in my arms. It was all I could do not to drop her, bringing both of us to the ground. As I adapted to the balance of holding her full weight, I could not help but think of my father, how year after year he carried the burden of her, apologized to the neighbors, dried her copious tears, and how this body had folded into his over and over again like so much batter until the two of them became one.

I felt like weeping myself then. We were near the end of us and of the secrets of the house. I was forty-nine and my mother was eighty-eight. My father had been dead for almost the entire lifetime of my younger child—a few months after she'd turned four. Sarah could never know the full measure of his sweetness, or play in the workshop among his thrice-glued carpentry. I thought of the mutant rocking horses rotting in the shed, and my arms, with my mother in them, weakened dangerously. How the house and my life had changed after his death.

I dragged my mother, with her trying, I could feel, to help, over to the staircase leading up to her bath. I questioned my sanity. How, I wondered, did I think this feat was possible? She had to weigh at least a hundred pounds, and despite my midlife fitness regime, I had never lifted more than sixty. It was not going to work. I collapsed onto the stairs, with my mother soiled and damp on top of me.

I panted on the carpeted steps but did not give up. I was determined to clean my mother and to dress her in fresh clothes before I called the ambulance. As we lay there and her weight grew familiar, like the strange feeling of being pinned by a dozing lover, I thought of the alternatives. I could bring her to the bathroom in the back and try to wash her from the sink. There was also the kitchen. But where would I prop her up? How to hold her and wash her at the same time, not to mention the mess of water all over the floor and the potential for slipping and cracking both our skulls.

My mother began to snore. Her head tilted back over my shoulder so that I could see her ancient mottled face and neck. I looked at her cheekbones, as sharp as they had always been—almost painful now in her cadaverous flesh. *Who will love me?* I thought, and then banished this question by looking out at the birch leaves in the fading sunlight. I had been there all day. I hadn't even called to cancel at Westmore. I saw the empty space on the platform in Life Drawing 101 and the students, at their easels, staring at my absence, the useless charcoal in their hands.

I knew that if I did not move, my mother might sleep for hours, and darkness would come. I pictured my friend Natalie looking for me in the halls of the art building, vainly querying the students in class. Natalie would call my house—perhaps drive over alone or with Hamish, her son. The doorbell would ring in the empty house, and then Natalie would imagine that something must have happened to me or to Sarah or to Emily.

I lifted my arms up under my mother's arms and raised them slightly off the carpeted stairs. First one and then the other, like manipulating a life-size doll. To have controlled her as easily as that, impossible. I had to get through this without calling my daughters. This was something to be done on my own. I twisted out from under her, and she moaned like a collapsing bag of air. I sat by her body on the stairs. The house had a weight and a force that I knew could crush me. I had to get out of there, and I thought, suddenly, of the bathtub among the rocking horses in the shed.

I left my mother dozing and turned and ran up the stairs, darting into her cluttered bedroom for blankets, and the pink powder room for towels. In the mirror over the sink, I checked myself. My eyes seemed smaller and even bluer than they had been, as if the intensity of the situation affected color and its perception. For years now I'd kept my hair so short that I could almost see my scalp. When I'd walked into my mother's house, she'd taken one glance and said, "Don't tell me you have cancer too. Everyone has cancer these days." I explained that my haircut made life easier, from exercise to gardening to work. It was the ambiguity that got to me—would she have cared if I had had cancer or would it have just been competition for her? Her intonation pointed toward the latter, but it was hard to believe this of one's own mother.

I stood at the top of the stairs with the blankets and towels. I kept at bay my realization that she would never see these rooms again and that now they would become, for me, empty shells littered with possessions. I noticed the hush in the upstairs hallway and looked at the pictures on the walls, pictures that would soon be gone. I imagined the dark squares they would leave behind them where no sun had reached for years, and the echoes that would resound from the curtainless storm windows and the thick plaster-and-brick walls. I began to sing. I sang nonsense. Cat-food commercials and childhood songs, the latter a habit that had been handed down from my mother, a way to stave off the onset of nerves. The need for noise overwhelmed me, but as I headed down the stairs, I grew quiet again. I saw that my mother had slumped down and lay on the floor, her body on the old wine-red Persian rug.

"No, Mother, no," I said, realizing as I did so that it was more useless than talking to a dog. A dog cocked her head. A dog gave you a soulful look. My mother was a passed-out bag of bones who reeked of shit.

"Why like this?" I asked. I stood over her body with my arms full of blankets and towels, and I began to weep. I whispered a prayer that no one would knock on the door, that Mrs. Castle would not think to check on us, though right about now Manny the handyboy might help me tote and haul.

I placed the towels on the bottom stair and took my grand?father's red-and-black Hudson Bay blanket, spreading it out on the floor beside her. It extended into the dining room. Then, so the wool would not scratch, I put a white Mexican wedding blanket down on top of that. I was not thinking sanely; I was wrapping fish or making spring rolls; I was thinking, *Super Giant Mother Burrito.*

I bent down, taking air in and neutralizing my spine—thank you, Stella, at World Gym—and put my arms up under my mother's armpits.

Her eyes snapped open.

"What on earth are you doing?"

I blinked. With our faces reversed to each other, I felt she could suck my eyes into her mouth. The rest of me, like the tail of a lizard or the end of a flat noodle, would swoop in and be gone in mere seconds. I kept my arms tense. Would she ever be powerless?

"Daniel!" she brayed. "Daniel!"

"Dad's not here, Mom," I said.

She looked up at me, her face dimmed and then reignited again, like a match flaring in the dark.

"I want that bowl," she said. "Now!"

To be that close to her. To be holding on to her and to see her brain open up like that, its scrambled insides, it was all I could do to keep to my task. As she spoke about things—Emily, the "pretty baby" (Emily had just turned thirty and had babies of her own); the kudzu near her father's cabin that had to be cut back with a scythe (the cabin was on land that was at the base of the Smokies and long out of our lives); and the stealing, conniving, not-to-be-trusted neighbors—I placed her body in the blankets and made an open-ended package with her talking head sticking out. Then I rested the towels on top of her chest and breathed slowly, counting to ten before I spoke.

"We are going on a sleigh ride," I said to her. And in my fists, I balled up the two free ends of the blanket, partially lifting her body off the floor. I heaved her over the carpet of the dining room, in through the kitchen, and out the side door.

"Toot! Toot!" she said. "Toot! Toot!" And then she grew silent and stared at the outside like a child in front of flickering Christmas lights. I wanted to ask her, *When was the last time you went into your backyard? When was the last time you smelled a flower or trimmed a shrub or just sat in the rusted white iron lawn chair?*

Grief was coming heavily now. Something about being outside, being in the fresh air, away from the acrid scent of her and the mothball smell of the closed-up house. My mother lay in her blanketed cocoon on the small raised side porch, which thankfully was at least partially shielded from the next-door neighbors by vine-covered latticework.

I went down the three stairs to the cinder-block path and walked around to the back of the porch, where as a child I had sat and kicked my legs over the edge and where now my mother lay as if on a shipping-and-receiving shelf. I was sweating, but I knew by the slant of the sun at my back that it would be less than an hour before light slipped below the houses that surrounded my mother's and left us alone in the last long night we would spend together.

I touched her treasured braid again. Some years ago her hair had passed out of its wiry stage and become soft. It had always been her crowning glory. Her brief life as a lingerie model before she met my father was one I'd envied growing up. Whatever else she was, she had been the most beautiful mother in the neighborhood, and watching her had taught me everything I knew about physical beauty. It was a bitter truth—my discovery— that daughters were not made in cookie-cutter patterns from the genes of their mothers alone. Random accidents of ancestry could blunt a nose or tip a forehead until beauty's delicate tracery gave way to an ordinary Jane.

Outside, with the air rushing over her, the fecal scent dissipated and I could think realistically again. I would not make it to the shed. What had I thought? The damage of dragging her down the three steps, of trying to heave her off the porch. And what would I fill the ancient bathtub with? Cold water from the backyard hose? The bathtub would be dirty and full of old lumber and broken bits of refuse that I would have to clean out. The last time I'd been in the shed, I'd noticed that my father's tool board, with all the ghost shapes of tools, had fallen off the wall and pitched forward against the tub. What had I been thinking?

"This is it, Mom," I said. "This is as far as we go."

She did not smile or say "bitch" or wail some final lament. I like to think, when I think about it, that by that time she was busy taking in the scent of her garden, feeling the late-afternoon sun on her face, and that somehow in the moments that had elapsed since she'd last spoken, she'd forgotten she'd ever had a child and that, for so many years now, she'd had to pretend she loved it.

I wish I could say that as my mother lay on the side porch and the wind began to pick up more and more so that the crows clinging on to the tops of the trees took flight, that she made it easy on me. That she pointedly listed all the sins she had committed during her long life.

She was eighty-eight. The lines on her face were now the cross-hatchings of fine old porcelain. Her eyes were closed. Her breathing ragged. I looked at the tops of the empty trees. There is no excuse to give, I know, so here is what I did: I took the towels with which I had meant to bathe her, and not thinking that near the latticework or by the back fence there might stand a witness, I smashed these downy towels into my mother's face. Once begun, I did not stop. She struggled, her blue-veined hands, with the rings she feared would be stolen if she ever took them off, grabbed at my arms. First her diamonds and then her rubies briefly flickered in the light. I pushed down harder. The towels shifted, and I saw her eyes. I held the towels for a long time, staring right at her, until I felt the tip of her nose snap and saw the muscles of her body go suddenly slack and knew that she had died.